Snake Skin

Snake Skin

CJ Lyons

CANELO

First published in United States in 2011 by Legacy Books

This edition published in the United Kingdom in 2018 by

Canelo Digital Publishing Limited
57 Shepherds Lane
Beaconsfield, Bucks HP9 2DU
United Kingdom

A CIP catalogue record for this book is available from the British Library.

Print ISBN 978 1 78863 151 8
Ebook ISBN 978 1 910859 41 4

This book is a work of fiction. Names, characters, businesses, organizations, places and events are either the product of the author's imagination or are used fictitiously. Any resemblance to actual persons, living or dead, events or locales is entirely coincidental.

'CJ Lyons' and 'Thrillers with Heart' are registered trademarks of CJ Lyons, LLC

Look for more great books at www.canelo.co

Printed and bound in Great Britain by Clays Ltd, Elcograf S.p.A.

Chapter 1

She stroked the tip of her thumbnail against her tongue, testing. Not sharp enough. Yet.

Nibbling the edge, enjoying the crunch of keratin against enamel, Ashley propped both elbows on the table and hunched forward. Other than the old guy behind the counter giving her an oogly-woogly pervert stare, the Tastee Treet was empty.

It was your typical hotdog shack. Cracked vinyl booths crowded the dining area, waiting to be filled by squealing cheerleaders and boasting football players after Friday night football games. A fifties-style melamine radio behind the counter warbled some tune older than even Ashley's parents, something about fast cars and fast boys and the dangers of loving them, punctuated by the sizzle and pop of the fryer.

No sign of Bobby. She couldn't help but glance behind her, out to the gravel parking lot, even though she knew she'd hear his car easily through the Plexiglas windows and plywood walls. Her stomach knotted with anticipation—he was so handsome, and God, those eyes, they saw right into her soul—would he like her once they finally met in person?

Would he be disappointed? Think she was too young? Too immature? Worry gnawed at her as she raised a finger to her mouth. *No.* She'd outgrown that nasty habit. There wasn't room in her life for any of that. Not once she and Bobby made their escape.

She glanced at her watch before removing it, then slid it over the top of the chrome and glass peppershaker. The last vestige of her past, it had served her well. Despite taking three buses and walking half a mile, she was still ten minutes early.

Each leg of the journey had left her feeling buoyant, discarding bits and pieces of herself the way her father's beloved creepy snakes shed their skin. As if her old life was made up of fourteen years' worth of flaky, parchment-thin memories that she'd out-grown and left behind to crumble into dust and blow away.

"Did you want to order anything, miss?" the counter guy asked, startling her. His face was shadowed by a Steelers ball cap pulled low. She'd felt his stare ever since she entered.

The grease-laden aroma of French fries and burgers perfumed the air, making her stomach growl. She ignored it. It was important to stay in control. "No. I'm just waiting for someone."

Control. She adjusted the watch, centering it exactly, brushing stray pepper grains away, trying to deny her flutter of anxiety. And failing.

Abandoning the watch, she spread her palms flat on the table top, her breath coming in fast, sharp gasps. What if Bobby thought she was ugly? What if he didn't like her? What if…

She turned her left hand palm up, slashing her thumbnail against the bare skin of her wrist.

Ahhh… Relief sighed through her at the sight of the red welt, the tiny beads of crimson, the oh-so straight and precise line.

Staring at her blood, she was able to breathe again.

Her tongue slid between her teeth and lips as the urge to taste the blood became overwhelming. Just this once. She would quit after she and Bobby were together. Promise.

Flexing her wrist, she forced another small dot of crimson to the surface. So shiny, so wet.

She held her wrist perfectly steady, denying the tremors vibrating beneath her skin, a current of palpable electricity. Her stomach tensed with anticipation as each beat of her heart made the red blossoms shudder.

Not yet… not yet. She was in control.

Ashley raised her eyes. The geezer at the counter still stared at her. Fuckwad. He had to be as old as her father. Double fuckwad. She sharpened her gaze into a deadly glare. He flinched, looked away. Lech.

Bobby should be here any moment. Escape was almost at hand. She'd been such a good girl, waiting, controlling her impulse to cut and run.

She carefully rolled her sleeve back, exposing the other trophies her control had won. Each scar a triumph. Each scar a time she hadn't run screaming out into the night or thrown herself in front of a bus or jumped from a bridge.

Each scar reminding her that she could win, that she mattered, that somewhere inside this cold, numb husk, she was alive.

Raising her wrist, she slowly, with gentle flicks, not wasting a drop, licked the blood. Still warm, so salty as it slipped across her tongue, down her throat.

Sometimes, she felt like she was floating outside her body, searching for another life. Cutting helped her reconnect, grounding her, even if she did always find herself right back where she started. Same old body, same old life.

Same nowhere future.

This was her last time. Promise. As soon as Bobby came to rescue her, she'd never do it again. Never need to. As soon as Bobby got here, everything would be fine.

He'd promised.

"Excuse me, miss?" It was the scuzzy counter guy, leaning over her, bending much too close as he reached for the napkin dispenser.

Ashley tried to pull away but he had her pinned against the side of the booth. His arm brushed the back of her neck, caressing her hair. Pervert.

"Hey, back off!" Something sharp jabbed her neck. "What the—"

Disappointment trumped her fear for one impossibly long instant. She'd never get to see Bobby... then the ramifications of that fleeting thought flash-froze her with terror.

"Don't be afraid," he said, sliding down to sit beside her, his arm wrapping her in an embrace impossible to escape. Not with her entire body turning to melted jello, soft and mushy, and swimming away from her.

It took a few seconds for his words to penetrate as she tried to speak and failed, the only thing emerging a trail of drool. She slumped against him, her head lolling to one side, the taste of blood lingering, fresh on her tongue. *Bobby, where was Bobby?*

"Don't worry, Ashley," he said as her vision danced with kaleidoscope colors. "I'm here to save you."

Chapter 2

Lucy Guardino hated this part. The right before it started part. The waiting part.

Killing time, she rummaged through her frayed denim bag as she sat in the Blazer's passenger seat. Fletcher had done a good job. Little girl's barrette, a hair scrunchie, crumbled Giant Eagle receipt, and two key chains: one with a set of house keys, the other with a single Dodge van key. She closed her fist around the van key, its sharp edges biting into her skin. The pain helped her to focus, chased away silent stirrings of panic.

All part of the waiting. She'd be fine once it came time for doing. She always was.

The bank's parking lot was quiet at this early hour, heat already steaming the blacktop. The air smelled of fertilizer, mowed hay, and burnt oil. Frogs trilled a duet with cicadas in the field across the parking lot, punctuated by the squeal of airbrakes from the highway beyond it. September in Pennsylvania.

Steadying her breathing, she pictured Katie, only four years old. Pictured what the men wanted to do with her.

No, that was no good—all she saw was her own daughter, all she felt was rage that animals like them were allowed to roam free.

Tossing her head to crack her neck, she took another deep breath. Shoved the image of her daughter aside and thought instead about what the men wanted: power, devotion, adoration... control.

She knew these men, knew how they thought, what they desired. The passions that woke them at three in the morning, sweaty and sick

5

with need. The visions they held in their mind as they jacked off. The longing, sweet anticipation, clawing its way through their veins until they were as powerless to resist as a junkie offered a free hit …

Oh yes, Lucy knew these men.

Calm settled over her, hypnotic as the burble of childhood streams, cool water, warm mud between her toes. She and her father had loved to go fishing. He always said fishing was all about the art of dangling bait. Showing them what they wanted but not ever letting them have it. That's all this was, a different kind of fishing.

She closed her eyes for a moment, smiling at the memory. Dad was right. And Lucy was a good fisherman. She lived for that instant when the line snapped taut, ready to break, adrenalin stretching the moment, time holding its breath until she took control and finessed the fish into shore—right where she wanted it.

Her phone rang, shattering the calm.

"Now, don't worry," Nick said, which of course sent her pulse racing into overdrive. He always said that when there was something to worry about. "Megan just called. Her fever's back. And her throat is sore again. I got a hold of the doctor. He can see her if we can get her there by nine, but my first client is already on their way—"

Lucy glanced at the dashboard clock. The meet should be a quick in and out, just to confirm all the details and make sure there weren't any new players to add to their roster. With Nick's practice so new, he couldn't risk angering clients by canceling. "I can do it."

"You sure?"

She didn't take offense—he had reason to doubt, she'd been held up before by work.

But it was a Saturday. And he'd taken Megan to the doctor two weeks ago—if the strep had come back, Lucy wanted to be there to get some answers.

"No problem. I'm sure."

"Call me, let me know what the doctor says."

"I will. She's okay until I get there?" Megan had been miserable with the strep; she hoped it wasn't back again. Guilt washed over her. Work had been busy, too busy, and she couldn't remember the last time she'd been home in time to do more than tuck Megan in. Although, of course Megan refused to be tucked in by her mom anymore. Twelve going on twenty.

"She's fine. Worried about missing soccer."

"It's time," Fletcher called to her from outside the window.

"I've got to go. Love ya. Bye." Lucy hung up, pushing all thoughts of her family aside, locking them away safe and sound.

She searched for that calm again. No luck. All she found was an electric current of adrenalin sparking her skin.

One last check in the mirror that she looked the part: large dangling earrings, clunky ugly choker, too-small Lycra tank top, tight fitting black stretch jeans, way too much makeup, big hair teased and sprayed to an inch of its life, and three-inch high heeled boots.

Typical trailer trash mom doing whatever it took to make ends meet, that was her. Except for one small detail.

She slid her wedding band free and completed her final ritual. A quick kiss for luck, smearing the ring with her too-bright lipstick, she carefully placed the ring in the change section of her real wallet inside her real bag.

She climbed out of Fletcher's Blazer and slowly spun around for him.

"Wow. You look good," he said as he approached from the side of the SUV. Fletcher wasn't a tall man, was reedy thin as if he forgot to eat sometimes, with the permanent squint of someone who spent most of his waking hours staring at computer monitors. Lucy shot him a glare and he stammered, "I mean, you look, er—"

"Everything ready?" she asked him.

"Yeah, sure, I think."

She folded her arms across her chest, interrupting his appraisal, and he looked up, flushing. "I mean, yes, I'm ready."

It was time. Lucy crossed the parking lot to where the battered Caravan with tinted windows waited. The macadam, soft with heat, grabbed onto her boot heels, giving her one last chance to change her mind.

She wasn't changing her mind. She peered into the back seat, scrutinizing the still form buckled into a booster seat. She circled the van. Checked from every angle. A girl, sleeping, dressed in her Sunday best, slumped in the seat, streams of golden curls tangled and askew, concealing her features.

Lucy got into the van and turned on the ignition, cranking the AC. It was even hotter than yesterday, already eighty-three degrees according to the bank thermometer. Pittsburgh's idea of Indian summer. "Okay, Katie Mae, it's just you and me, kid."

The men had changed the meeting place at the last minute. She hadn't liked that, but it happened. Not too surprising given what they were meeting for. Now it was an old water pumping station off of Route 60. Her team had already done their recon, said the building had been bought by Walter, their main target after standing empty for a decade.

By the time Lucy arrived, the AC had only begun to cool the inside of the van, leaving her clammy with half-dried sweat. Two other cars waited in the gravel parking lot—a beat up Pontiac sedan and a Ford 350 pickup. The whitewashed concrete building was on a wooded lot with a stream running along the east side, rusting pipes tunneling through the building's side wall down to the water. She knew her team's positions but couldn't spot them in the woods surrounding the lot. Good.

A crudely forged steel cross perched on the roof's peak—a call to worship or a lightning rod? Then she noticed the hand carved wooden sign hanging over the front door, one end a little lower than the other—Lucy itched to straighten it—reading: Church of the Holy Redeemer.

A church?

She worked her jaw from side to side, ligaments crackling with tension. A church.

These guys were full of surprises. Nothing much she could do about it except hope this was the last one.

She left the van running and locked the door behind her. The only obvious luxury the Caravan had was the keypad door lock. In her line of work, it wasn't a luxury, it was a necessity. She touched the window, her fingers tracing Katie's sleeping form. Anxiety resurfaced, splashing through her gut, a trout caught in a net. Another deep breath reined it in.

She wasn't expecting trouble. She'd had meetings like this before—so many, she'd lost count—and had never had any trouble.

That didn't mean she wasn't prepared. A short-barreled Smith and Wesson .32 concealed in her denim jacket. Single working mom type of gun.

Tugging her jacket into place, shifting her shoulders until she felt her thirty-two nestle against her ribcage, she walked towards the building. The cornerstone read 1923, the windows were arched and mullioned with carved keystones over the top of each. Back then even a lowly pumping station received an artisan's attention.

The door, an arched slab of wood, popped open while she was still ten feet away. A bearded man, thin, with wire-rim glasses, wearing black slacks and a starched white shirt buttoned all the way to the top collar button, emerged. "Sister Ruby?"

"Yes." She stopped a few feet shy of the entrance. He stood directly beneath the crooked sign. "Are you Walter?"

"I am."

"I'm not sure about this—I mean, a church?"

"Would you like to see our facilities?" He spread an arm open in invitation. Despite his formal tone, his accent was strictly country, rolling in cadence just like the hills surrounding them. He was working hard to play a role.

Lucy's jaw spasmed, sending a shock wave of pain down her neck and spine. On the phone Walter and Henry had been very explicit in what they wanted. But now Walter was acting like she was here for a prayer meeting.

"Where's Henry?"

"Pastor Henry is waiting for us downstairs. Getting everything ready for Katie's visit." His voice snagged on Katie's name, a tiny thrill there. She relaxed a tiny bit, reassured by the slip in his facade. "Where is the child?"

9

"Sleeping in the van. I left the engine on. It's too hot to leave her in there without the AC running."

He nodded his approval. "Mind if I take a quick peek?"

"Of course not. That's what we're here for. Just don't wake her— I want her fresh when you and Henry are ready."

His tongue darted free, kissing his top lip for an instant before disappearing again. He walked past her, his gait stiff with anticipation, and peered inside the van window at Katie. "My, she's even lovelier in person. You must be mighty proud of her."

He returned to Lucy's side and opened the church door. The middle finger of his right hand was missing, a mass of scar tissue contorted his palm. Playing with fireworks? Or something more deadly?

"Shall we go inside and finish our preparations?"

She crossed the threshold, fingering her choker as she looked around. The room was maybe twenty by thirty, whitewashed walls, white linoleum floor, white ceiling. The only color came from a stack of grey folding chairs standing against one wall and a dark wood cross hanging from the ceiling at the far end of the room. To the right was a set of concrete stairs going down. Walter crossed over to the stairs.

Lucy stalled. "What kind of church is this?"

He stopped on the top step and turned back to her. "We're a Pentecostal denomination. Small but actively recruiting." He followed her gaze as she glanced around the empty space. "We don't do a lot of sitting during our services. Not once the good Lord starts moving in us."

She had to fight to hide her cringe. Two men arranging for a private visit from a four-year-old little girl in a house of worship, and Walter acted like this was perfectly acceptable. Lucy had dealt with some major weirdos in her time, but the creep factor here was at an all-time high. She swept the thought aside along with the emotions that ran with it. The business at hand required all of her focus.

She followed Walter down the stairs. Each footfall vibrated through her, jarring her to her core, unleashing her fear.

Her father once told her there were only two true emotions: fear and love. His words haunted her at times like this. She loved her family, was constantly in fear that she might not be able to keep them safe.

But that fear wouldn't stop her from getting what she came for. She hoped that, God forbid, if her own child ever needed help, someone would do the same for Megan.

The chill scent of earth, mildew, and metal long exposed to water filled her nostrils. Sharp, nasty, the stench of dirty, wet socks shoved into a hamper for too long.

At the bottom of the steps was a heavy wooden door with hinges as thick as her fist. Pipes lined the wall beside the door, traveling towards the outside wall and the stream beyond. Walter heaved the door open and gestured for her to precede him.

She paused just inside the door, looking around. It was an antechamber, half the size of the room above them, poorly lit by a few smudgy glass block windows high up in the wall across from her. Pipes of various sizes, bristling with valves, covered the wall beside her, converging into a rectangular pool dug into the floor, maybe eight feet by ten. The air smelled worse here. Small things crawling away in dark, dank corners to die.

She couldn't tell how deep the pool was—some kind of retaining area? Maybe for testing the water? Surely they didn't use it for baptisms—the wall that she could see was slimy with algae but enough water lined the bottom to paint the walls with reflected light.

A man emerging from a doorway leading to another room on the far side of the pool grabbed her attention. He was dressed like Walter and carried a black leather Bible, using both hands. Pastor Henry.

"Did you see the girl?" he asked Walter, his gaze flicking off Lucy as if she were a scrap of trash the wind had blown past.

"Yes. She's safe in the van. A little angel." Walter still stood at the door. Lucy had no choice but to move further into the room so that he could swing it shut behind them. His voice had gained a singsong quality, his anticipation revving up.

"Before we go any farther," Lucy said, taking control of the situation, "I want to get everything clear. First, I need the rest of the money. We agreed on two thousand dollars up front, another thousand when I got here."

"You'll get your reward, never fear," Henry said. "All we want is the girl."

"Where's your camera?" Lucy looked around. This was feeling wrong on so many levels. Were they planning to double cross her? She curled her arms around her chest as if she were cold, slipping her hand inside her jacket, grabbing the thirty-two. "You said all you wanted was to take pictures. That's what we agreed on. No touching."

"That's what we said," Walter confirmed. He was still behind her, blocking her exit.

She stepped backwards, closer to the pool, so that she could keep them both in sight. As she did, she felt more than heard a strange vibration. Rattling in the pipes? Whatever it was, she didn't like it, it made it hard to concentrate. And she needed to concentrate.

The men stood on opposite sides of the pool. She had no idea who or what was behind the second door, the one that Henry had emerged from, and tried to angle herself to keep it in her periphery. "Do you want more? We can arrange it—if you have enough cash."

Henry's smirk made it clear that he wanted much more than photos. He stepped into the room, skirting the edge of the pool, to stand shoulder to shoulder with Walter. Between her and the door she came in through.

The water in the pool shimmered, bouncing light over the white walls. There was something wrong about that; there was no breeze in the room, what was making the water ripple? A circulating pump? Was that the source of the strange buzzing noise?

"What exactly do you want?" she asked, refusing to be distracted by the sparks of jade colored light dancing across the walls or the eerie hum that made the hair on her neck stand at attention. Both men kept their hands in plain sight, but their faces now shared identical expressions of lust.

"We want to save Katie's soul, Sister Ruby," Walter said.

The door beside her opened. Lucy whirled to keep it in sight as well as the two men. It meant putting her back to the pool. The movement released a fresh cascade of adrenalin and anxiety. Something about that pool wasn't right. It felt more dangerous than the two men.

A woman emerged from the rear room, shutting the door behind her before Lucy could see what lay beyond. She wore a simple gray dress—homemade? Her hands were empty, clasped before her as if in prayer. "Is she here yet? My baby, has she come home?"

"What the hell is going on here?" Lucy demanded, her voice booming against the concrete walls.

"Pastor Henry and Sister Norma lost their daughter recently." Walter spoke as if he were teaching catechism to a particularly dim student.

The rear door opened again, this time releasing another man and two more women. They stood, watching in silence. Waiting.

Norma kept walking towards Lucy, her face upturned, seeking the sun, the truth, something. Whatever it was, she seemed to think Lucy had it. She stretched her arms out in front of her. "Please, where is my baby?"

"Lady, I don't know what you're talking about." Lucy made a judgment call. "The deal's off. There won't be any play date." The last words emerged loud, adrenalin giving them extra emphasis.

The thudding noise of the church door being shoved open answered her use of the code word. Lucy allowed herself to relax. Her team was on top of things.

"No!" Norma screeched across the space between them, her body moving faster than her words. "You can't take her from me!"

Lucy drew the thirty-two. "FBI. Stop right there."

Too late. Norma plowed into Lucy with the force of a linebacker. Lucy and Norma flew backwards. Into the pool.

Lucy smacked into the concrete bottom, landing on her left side and skidding across a scant inch or two of water and algae. She brought her gun hand up, barely managing to hang onto the thirty-two. Not that it was doing her any good. Norma landed on top of her, knocking Lucy's breath away, clawing at her face.

The pool was only four feet deep and the algae-choked water barely came to Lucy's ankles. She pushed off the slimy bottom and rolled her weight on top of Norma who now was writhing like she was possessed, drool streaming from her mouth as she spoke in some weird, keening language that made Lucy's ears wince.

"Cast out this devil, oh Lord!" Henry cried out, holding his Bible aloft as he knelt at the edge of the pool, eyes closed, body rocking, lurching, arching to and fro, his face filled with rapture. The others followed suit, kneeling above Lucy at the rim of the pool, rocking and rolling and praying.

Lucy tried to get her feet under her and control of Norma. The floor was slimy, the water murky, and, worse, there was definitely something moving in it. Fish?

Henry opened his Bible and intoned, "In my name shall they cast out devils; they shall speak with new tongues; they shall take up serpents…"

Lucy sat up. Not fish.

The sound buzzing through her bones, setting her teeth on edge, wasn't solely the product of Norma's keening or Henry's prayers or even the thudding of boots as her team ran down the stairs.

Clumps of snakes huddled on a foot-high ledge that ran around the bottom of the pool. A timber rattler as thick as her wrist lazily raised his head and regarded her as if she were lunch. The smaller diamondback beside him wasn't so sanguine, his fangs showing as he shook his rattles.

A dark streak darted through the murky water, followed by two more.

Norma's eyes flew open and she shouted, "Amen!" just as the first of the snakes launched itself at Lucy.

Chapter 3

Lucy scrambled to her feet and hauled Norma aside. The water moccasin charged, a black blur, churning through the water, slamming itself into the retaining wall then ricocheting into the air. With blinding speed it changed direction in mid-flight, using its powerful body to hurl itself at them once more.

Norma plopped down into the water, her gray dress billowing, algae clinging to the folds, laughing. She splashed the water as if she wanted the snakes to attack her. "Hallelujah!"

She grabbed Lucy's ankle, trying to pull Lucy back down into the water. Lucy lunged to one side, a snake's fangs whispering against her jeans. Missing.

Adrenalin jolted through Lucy, almost drowning out the sound of armed men swarming into the room, shouting, "FBI, hands, hands! Down, now!"

In her periphery she saw her team taking the other five adults into custody. The women put up a fight, the men continued intoning prayers, not resisting. Least of her worries. The ledge the snakes called home completely encircled the bottom of the pool. Coiled, hissing, writhing mounds of rattlesnakes and copperheads greeted her as soon as she made a move in any direction.

Norma wasn't helping. The woman scrambled for the snakes, Lucy had to haul her in with an arm around her waist.

With her free hand, Lucy aimed her weapon at one writhing mass after another, despite the futility of trying to shoot the snakes. An instinct she couldn't suppress. Shit, shit, shit. How the hell had this happened? She reined in her internal monologue, fighting for control.

Another water moccasin churned its way through the water, aiming at her, a deadly torpedo, but two more of its own kind intercepted it, the water frothing as the enraged snakes battled each other.

A copperhead that had tumbled into the shallow water slithered across Lucy's boots. She forced herself to hold still, not agitate it. Even as her flesh crawled and her finger tightened on her trigger guard. Denying every primal instinct carved into her DNA, she holstered her weapon.

"Throw me some cuffs," she called to her team. A Statie pinned his suspect, Walter, to the wall with one hand and threw her a pair of Flex-cuffs with his other.

Lucy caught the cuffs and quickly restrained Norma. The woman still struggled, not attacking Lucy, just writhing and throwing her weight in one direction, then another, screaming incoherent words punctuated by the occasional "Amen!"

"Everyone stay calm," she ordered, trying to take her own advice, despite the adrenalin skipping stones across her nerve endings.

The other snake handlers continued their praying, now droning Psalm 23. Lucy tuned them out. She really did not want to think about the valley of death.

"What about using a Taser?" Fletcher called from the edge of the pool. The ICE surveillance tech wasn't a field agent, but he was the only one volunteering any ideas on how to handle the snakes. "Stun them long enough for us to pull you out."

"Won't work, the water will dissipate the energy."

Norma suddenly dropped her weight, almost taking Lucy with her. Lucy hauled her to her feet once more.

"You can't fight God's will," Walter called to Lucy as two Staties propelled him to the door. His words barely carried over the feverish buzzing the rattlers produced.

"You must have some way to tranquilize the snakes." Lucy did not make any sudden movements—not with the space between her and safety carpeted with snakes. She held Norma in a bear hug, finally stilling the woman. That didn't stop a baby rattler from arching up, its body twanging like a wire sparking, fangs dripping venom as it quivered, debating.

Lucy stared it down. Its hissing sang along her nerves, until her own body hummed to the same tune.

"Go away. Scat," she told it in her best mommy voice, placing herself between it and Norma.

"Snakes don't have ears," Fletcher told her, not-so-helpfully.

Lucy didn't break her staring match with the reptile. Finally it shook itself one last time and slid over its companions to another part of the ledge.

"We prove ourselves to God by facing evil in its natural form." Walter's voice boomed through the small space. "We expect to be bitten—God will decide if we live or die. That's how we lost Norma's daughter. Through God's will. And God's will brought you and little Katie to us."

"Hate to tell you this, but little Katie is a mannequin. And if you don't help us out of here, you'll be charged with assault with a deadly weapon and attempted murder of a federal agent."

Lucy was bluffing. She had no idea what charges the Assistant US attorney might file—if any. Federal prosecutors were notorious for wimping out on cases that weren't clear-cut. Lord knew this one qualified. What a cluster fuck. Her boss was going to laugh his ass off. He loved crazy bat shit stories of ops gone wrong. Right after he ripped her a new one for not bringing home the bacon, his term for an airtight case that even a newbie AUSA couldn't fuck up.

Greally had no right to laugh. She'd only been here in Pittsburgh leading the new squad for three months and in that time she'd brought home enough bacon for him to hold a BBQ. But Nick—how the hell was she going to explain this to him?

Her leg shook. Just nerves—and a need to pee. Norma's weight, now slack in Lucy's arms, was getting heavy.

"We'll be judged by God's laws, not man's," Walter continued triumphantly, smirking at her predicament.

Great. Big help that was. Lucy surveyed the situation. Trying to clear her mind, focus. Her gaze skittered from the pipes on the walls, to the mounds of reptiles surrounding her, to the light reflected from the water.

Water. Could they open the valves on the pipes, flood the snakes?

A water moccasin swam towards her, not as aggressive as the first she'd encountered, but too close for comfort. She discarded her idea—it would take too long and probably just piss off the snakes.

Fire. Too bad the FBI didn't issue flamethrowers as standard weapons.

No. Not fire. Ice.

"Hand me that fire extinguisher," she ordered one of her agents, pointing to the industrial-sized silver container hanging in the corner behind the door.

He pulled it from its brackets. "Looks pretty old, boss." He shook it. "Feels like there's something left in it, though."

"Have someone gather the ones from the trucks in case we need more." He nodded and heaved the extinguisher across the empty air separating their outstretched arms. Lucy caught it awkwardly with one hand; it was heavier than it looked.

The area around them appeared fairly safe, most of the snakes fighting with each other. Norma was now quiet, muttering to herself. Lucy would have to risk that the woman wouldn't do something suicidal and agitate the snakes. She sat Norma down, straddling her to confine her movements as much as possible.

"Careful with that, Lucy," Fletcher called. "You might just make them angry."

"Not as angry as I am." She shook the extinguisher and peered at the faded instructions. Hefted it and aimed the nozzle. Pulled the trigger.

Nothing.

"Damn." She shook it more vigorously, wiped the nozzle against her jeans to clear any clogs. Aimed.

This time she was rewarded with a spurt of liquid. The snakes recoiled, angrily. The ones who took a direct hit convulsed and fell away from her, frost glittering their scales.

The swoosh of the fire extinguisher mixed with the hiss and rattle of furious snakes. She splashed through the water, jostling the extinguisher from one side to the other, her fingers clutching the nozzle burning with the cold. A cloud of white powder and smoke filled the air before her.

Blinded snakes flung themselves at her, at each other, at the wall. Some sank their fangs into their own flesh; others launched themselves at Lucy. The water churned with frenzied movement as she fought to clear a path.

Fletcher waited at the edge of the pool, watching anxiously. Two burly men joined him, one FBI and one State trooper, reaching their arms to her.

The spray sputtered and died.

She threw the extinguisher onto the concrete ledge. Turning back, she dragged Norma through the path, to the ledge. The men hoisted her out of the water and onto dry land.

Then they reached for Lucy. Just as the stunned snakes began to stir. Lucy grabbed onto the men's arms and leapt.

A snake tried to follow, landing on her boot with a heavy thud that rocked through her. She kicked it free and rolled onto the pool's edge. Out of reach of the snakes.

She sagged there for a moment, just long enough to cast her own quick prayer into the heavens. Hoping *He* really wasn't a big fan of snakes since she'd just freeze-dried a couple dozen of them.

"You okay, Lucy?" Fletcher asked. "Did they bite you?"

"Someone check Norma and get EMS." Lucy checked herself for injuries. Just a bruised left shoulder where she'd landed in the pool. No bites that she could find. Relief washed over her. "Did someone call animal control?"

She flexed her fingers, numb from the CO_2. Probably got frost-bite. Better than snake bite.

The bad joke was the product of fear and adrenalin. She stalled for time, scraping her boot heels clean along the ledge, regaining control.

"Hey, boss," one of the ICE agents called from the rear room. "You're gonna want to see this."

Glad to have an excuse to move and work off her residual adrenalin, Lucy rushed past the pool to the room. It was decorated with everything a kid could want—bean bag chairs, a Wii console, toys, stuffed animals, footballs, a mini-basketball hoop... more swag than a Toys"R"Us.

Huddled together on a twin sized racecar bed were two identical blond boys. Maybe six years old. They were scared and crying, terrified by the men with guns.

Lucy scattered her people with a jerk of her chin. They backed away from the boys and watched from outside the open door.

She smoothed a hand across her slime and hair spray shellacked hair, hoping she didn't look too scary, and knelt before the boys, her eyes level with theirs.

"Hi guys. I'm Lucy. What's your name?"

One of them, the smaller by a hair, swallowed hard then spoke up. "I'm Hank and this is Teddy. Can we go home now?"

"Sure you can. That's why we're here." She sat back on her heels, giving them space. "Do you know your last name? Can you tell me where home is?"

"My dad is David Jankowsky and my mom is Nancy and we live at 712 Pennsacola Drive, Monroeville, Pennsylvania," he said, intoning the information in a singsong.

"Jankowsky, that's the pediatric dentist on trial for fondling his patients," Fletcher told her from the doorway. "His kids were kidnapped four months ago—taken from the wife while she was grocery shopping."

Even though it was before her arrival in Pittsburgh, Lucy knew the case—her second in command, Isaac Walden, had been working with the Monroeville PD and Allegheny County Sheriff on it. So far they'd had no leads, just frustration and a media frenzy.

She smiled at the boys. "We're going to call your mommy right away. I think she'll be very happy to see you."

Hank nodded, sniffing hard, being a big boy and not crying. Teddy did the same but his tears escaped.

—

"Walter said their church was actively recruiting," Lucy told Fletcher as they walked out to the parking lot, leaving the evidence recovery techs to their business. Child services was on the way to pick up the twins who were being treated by the state troopers to law enforcement's universal antidote: orange juice and Snickers bars.

"You sure you're okay?" Fletcher asked. The ICE surveillance tech looked like he'd been the one almost killed, his glasses were askew, shirt half untucked, face flushed and sweaty. "Where the heck do you think they got all those snakes from?"

Setting up the boutique online child-modeling agency as part of Operation Honeypot had been Fletcher's idea. So far they'd nabbed several US nationals trafficking for sex with minors as well as drawing Canadians across the border—hence the need for Immigration and Customs Enforcement on the taskforce.

As a lowly GS06 civilian tech, not even a full-fledged ICE agent, Fletcher was flushed with pride at the operation's success. Lucy already had to turn down his request to play a more active field role when their next group of sex tourists arrived tomorrow. Worse than telling a kid he wasn't allowed to go trick-or-treating.

He trailed after her as Lucy walked to his SUV, now double-parked ten feet away from the van where "Katie" slept. She opened the rear of the Blazer and sat down on the running board, her legs wobbly, adrenalin finally abandoning her.

With trembling fingers she retrieved her wedding ring. She brushed it against her lips. Her pulse finally calmed as she slid it back where it belonged. She reached for her bag, grabbed a water bottle and took a deep gulp, spilling water down her shirt and not caring.

Then she emptied the muck from her boots and checked her arms and legs again for bite marks. She'd seen guys shot and not know it because of the masking effects of adrenalin. Nothing. She wiggled her bare toes in the sun, soaking up the heat.

The thought of trying to explain a rattlesnake bite to her husband, Nick, made her wince. Although it might finally get her back on Megan's "cool" list—a welcome change from the cold shoulder her twelve-year-old had been giving her lately.

"I can't wait to get my hands on their computer. See what else they've been up to," Fletcher prattled as he packed up his surveillance equipment. "Oh, by the way, your cell phone has been going nuts."

He handed her the cell and she glanced at the missed calls. All from Megan. Along with texts asking if they were going to be late for the doctor's appointment.

Damn it, she hated leaving, but really all that needed done here was paperwork and documentation. Nothing Lucy needed to stay for. In fact, if she wasn't the only woman on her squad rated for UC work, she wouldn't be here on a Saturday at all—she'd be home and looking forward to getting back to work on Monday to shuffle paperwork and review reports.

Still hadn't gotten used to that part of being promoted. She wasn't sure she ever would—she loved being in the field. Used to be she always told fellow agents that supervisory special agents never made arrests, just supervised and took all the credit. Now that she held the rank and had her own team, she was trying to find a way to lead from the front lines and still get all the administrative work done.

As always, she wanted it all. Usually she figured out a way to get it.

Fletcher handed her a key ring. "The van needs to go back. Why don't you take it?"

Still, she hesitated. Men and women carrying guns and displaying a variety of law enforcement insignia bustled around the parking lot in an efficiently choreographed mob. The FBI's Sexual Assault Felony Enforcement squad was multi-jurisdictional: ICE agents mingled with her own FBI team, there were several Staties as well.

Back at the office, they shared space with the High Tech Computer Crime Taskforce, Operation Predator, the Innocent Images Initiative, and even had a few postal inspectors and IRS agents working with them.

To some it might seem like a motley crew, seasoned street operators working side by side with computer geeks like Fletcher. But it was her crew and she hated to leave them with the job unfinished.

Of course, with this job, there was never any finishing. Something Nick was constantly reminding her of. But she'd only been here three months, charged with setting up and running the FBI's newest SAFE unit, and she hadn't yet figured out where to draw the line.

Nick had. That was for sure. After a month of not seeing her unless she woke him as she climbed into bed at night, he'd insisted that she establish some kind of routine so that she could spend time with him and Megan.

Which sounded great... unless you were the parent who was constantly delinquent.

She glanced at the state trooper's vehicle where the twins beamed as they tried on Smokey Bear hats eighteen sizes too big for them. The breeze carried their burble of laughter. She smiled.

"Let the Staties take credit on this one," she told Fletcher. "I'll make it up to Walden, clear it with Greally."

Fletcher's frown let her know he didn't appreciate her generosity. Or more likely, he didn't think his boss would.

Tough. This morning she was enjoying being one of the good guys. Her phone rang. She glanced at the caller ID. Megan. Sigh. Even if her pre-teen didn't always see her that way.

"Call me if you need me," she told Fletcher, heading towards the van with the mannequin in the back seat. She flipped her phone open. "Hey sweetie, I hear you're not feeling well."

"If you're too busy, I can call Dad. Again," Megan said. Somehow the twelve-year-old's tone managed to carry more disapproval than a Taliban watching a striptease.

"No, it's fine. I'll be there in twenty minutes." Thank God the operation was on the right side of the Fort Pitt tunnel. And there'd be no traffic on a Saturday morning.

"The doctor said he has to leave for the hospital by nine-thirty."

"I know, Megan. I'll get you there. I promise." Silence. "Did you take some ibuprofen? That will help you feel better."

"Yeah, Dad told me to take some. And to drink lots of fluids."

"Good." Lucy started the van and pulled away from her team, resisting the urge to go back and remind them that they had another meet set for tomorrow. This one was in a motel, so no room for snakes. At least she hoped not. She shuddered, told herself it was the AC. "I'll be there soon."

"When we lived in Virginia, I never got sick."

Lucy tightened her grip on the wheel. Bad enough she had the powers-that-be in the Bureau judging her every move, she really didn't need it coming from her twelve-year-old daughter. "Think of it as building up your immune system."

Megan grunted in reply.

"Well, if you're really sick, I can call your gram to come watch you." One of the few perks of moving to Pittsburgh was that Lucy's mother was only forty minutes away in Latrobe.

Megan used to love spending time with her gram. But not since adolescence had gotten a stranglehold on her. Now family was soooo boring.

"Whatever," Megan said and hung up.

Lucy tossed the phone aside and hit the gas pedal. Maybe the stress of moving and starting a new school, making the soccer team, was too much for Megan. One more thing to feel guilty about. As if trying to juggle a career and her family weren't enough already.

Way she figured it, every kid she rescued here at work put another penny in the karma bank, saving up to protect Megan. That was some consolation for time spent away from her family. Not that she could ever explain that to Nick or Megan.

She glanced in the rearview, caught the mannequin's eye and winked. "Let's not tell her about the snakes, okay, Katie Mae?"

Chapter 4

Lucy twirled her wedding band around her ring finger, rubbing it clean of the smudge of Ruby's lipstick. Megan swung her legs from her perch on the exam table, her gown flapping open, revealing tanned legs and the bruises she wore with pride ever since making the soccer team.

There were so many things Lucy should be doing: double-checking on the snake handlers' processing and paperwork, prepping for tomorrow's op, reviewing the latest NCMEC bulletins, cleaning her guns...

Megan rustled through a tattered copy of *National Geographic*, looking up over the top of the pages, glaring at Lucy.

"You know you look like a slut," she finally observed in a bored, world-weary tone. As if her mother always dressed like a trailer-trash single-mom ready to sell her kid to strangers. "And what's that smell?"

Lucy remained silent, staring at the duckling wallpaper above Megan's head. Lately, since they'd—no, *she'd*—uprooted Megan and moved to Pittsburgh, everything Lucy said only made things worse.

"You could wait outside," Megan continued. "Really, it's fine. I go in alone for my checkups now, you know."

Lucy wasn't sure she liked that idea either. Hard to believe her baby was twelve, almost a teenager. The thought was laced with strychnine. Lucy knew all too well what dangers waited for Megan as she grew older. Hated that no matter how good she and Nick were as parents, Megan would still eventually face them alone.

"Don't forget soccer next week," Megan said, adding one more thing to Lucy's to-do list. "You promised brownies. And not those lame store-bought ones with the gooey icing."

"Only if the doctor says it's all right for you to play."

"Mom..." With the single syllable Megan assigned Lucy responsibility for the fall of civilization and the fate of the future of all mankind. "I can't miss anything. I'm the new kid, remember?"

"We've been here three months. Think maybe it's time you let up on the guilt trip?"

Instead of appearing chastised, Megan merely grinned as if she had plenty more tricks up her sleeve and was just waiting to use them on her mom. Or more likely, her much more gullible and malleable father.

Megan was a pro at getting what she wanted—took after Lucy in that respect. Just as her features reflected Lucy's Italian heritage more than Nick's Irish. Thick, almost black hair, high cheekbones, dark eyes. The only thing Megan inherited from Nick was her creamy complexion with its propensity to freckle easily.

"I want to be certain the doctor has all the facts," Lucy said. She used her work voice, although she knew Megan saw right through her mask of control. "We need to get to the bottom of this."

Megan shot her a look that said, "whatever", but stopped short of actually rolling her eyes. "You always assume the worst."

When it came to imagining "the worst," Megan did not have a clue. Lucy fully intended to keep things that way for as long as possible.

"And you worry too much," Megan continued her analysis of everything wrong with her mother. "That's because of what you see at work. It's just strep throat. I already feel better after the Advil. But you think everyone's always in danger."

That's because everyone *was* always in danger. In Lucy's world, at least. But she forced a smile and said, "Glad to hear it. And no, you're not getting a Facebook page."

Megan's eyes widened at her mother's omniscience. Then her lips curled into a wheedling smile. "You could use it too, you know—like a stake-out or something."

Despite the stuffy heat of the exam room, Lucy shivered at the thought of inviting the creeps she hunted into her home. Letting them anywhere near Nick or Megan. "That's not funny. Keep this up and you won't be going online again until you're old enough to vote."

The door swung open, interrupting Megan's protest. The doctor breezed in, wearing jeans and a polo shirt. He did a double take at Lucy's worse-for-wear appearance. "Hi, sorry to keep you waiting. This beeper won't shut up. Now, what brings you guys here on such a beautiful Saturday morning?"

Megan opened her mouth, but Lucy jumped in before she could say anything, earning her another glare. This time complete with eye-roll. "Megan saw Dr. Collins two weeks ago and he said she had strep. She took ten days of the medicine but her glands are still swollen and the fever came back."

"Hmm…" He flipped through her chart. "Strep test was positive, but there's no guarantee it can't come back again. We call it the boomerang effect. Anyone else at home sick?"

"No." Lucy hesitated, knowing she sounded over-protective. "She's been looking pale to me even before the strep, and she has no energy. She's not herself."

"I'm fine." Megan threw Lucy a Magnum caliber stare before she could say more. "It's only that we just moved here and with a new school and new friends and soccer and teachers giving out so much homework—"

"I'll bet that wasn't easy, leaving your old friends behind." The pediatrician stood in front of Megan, focused on her, warming his stethoscope with one hand, skillfully shutting Lucy out of the conversation. She straightened, irritated at first, but then took a breath and relaxed when she saw how he put Megan at ease.

As he examined Megan, he kept talking. "Mono is pretty common in kids your age and a lot of kids will get it and strep at

27

the same time. Open up." He glanced at Megan's tonsils. "Actually those look pretty normal. Let's feel those neck glands."

Lucy watched as he danced his fingers up and down Megan's neck. Then he had her lift her arms up and felt her armpits. Finally, after examining her belly and groin, he sat back down. "She definitely does have a few nice-sized nodes. I'd like to do some more testing."

Megan straightened at that, her hands clenching the edge of the table, casting off her world-weary facade. "What kind of tests?"

"I'll get another strep test here in the office today. But if that's negative, then I want you to go to the hospital for some blood work."

"Blood work? With a needle?" Megan squeaked. "No way. Mom, I feel fine—really, I don't need any tests."

Before Lucy could answer, her cell phone rang. She turned the sound off without looking at the display and stood, taking control of the situation. "Megan, you'll do what the doctor says. What are these tests for?"

"Just a blood count and a mono test. If the strep test is negative."

"That's all? Mono, that's not too bad." The tension that had locked her jaws eased. Mono she could handle. Her phone began to vibrate and her pager went off as well. Damn. "I'm sorry." She yanked the pager from her belt and glanced at the message: 911. "I really need to get this. I apologize."

"No problem. I'm just glad it wasn't mine. Why don't you go ahead and make your call while I start the strep test?"

"You okay with that?" she asked Megan, her cell phone already in her hand.

The new Megan, the stranger who gleefully channeled Bette Davis at will, resurfaced. "Mom. I'm not a baby. Go."

Summarily dismissed as superfluous, Lucy stepped out into the hall and punched the speed dial for her office at the Federal Building. "Guardino here."

"I like that doctor," Megan said as Lucy drove them home through the twists and curves of Pittsburgh's South Side. "He was kind of cute."

Lucy resisted the urge to steer the car to the nearest cloistered convent. Over the past year her daughter had gone from thinking that boys had cooties to comparing their "pecs" and "six packs." And now Megan was noticing *men*.

She was *so* not ready for this.

She'd always told Nick that she'd be the go-to person for anything from dirty diapers to broken arms—right up to puberty. Then it was time for him to take over.

After all, he was the psychologist, able to unravel the mysteries of the adolescent mind far better than she could. He'd agreed, saying it wasn't politically correct to deal with horny teenaged boys by threatening them with a loaded forty caliber Glock.

"At least I don't have to get the blood work," Megan continued, legs crossed on the front seat as she swung her foot in time with Led Zeppelin's Black Dog.

"He said you didn't have to get the blood work *today*."

Good thing because Lucy was already losing precious time taking Megan home. Plus she needed to change clothes—couldn't go out on a high-risk missing child case looking like, as Megan so bluntly put it, a slut. She wished she'd have time for a shower, she stank of sweat and algae and adrenalin. And snakes.

"If your throat culture is negative Monday, then we'll take you in for the tests."

"But Mom—"

"No buts."

Megan's lips blanched, pressed together in a thin line. Lucy pressed her hand on Megan's shoulder, stroked her upper arm. "It's okay. Either Dad or I will be there with you."

Megan shrugged her hand away. Lucy swallowed her sigh. She couldn't remember the last time Megan had welcomed her touch. Since before they left Virginia.

"If I feel better on Monday, can I at least play soccer?"

"We'll see, no promises."

Megan blew her breath out in a sigh more sorrowful than a funeral dirge. As if Lucy had just condemned her to a fate worse than death. Lucy was glad Megan had no idea how lucky she was that skipping a soccer game was the worst catastrophe life could offer.

After she dropped Megan off, she had to face a parent's greatest nightmare. A fourteen-year-old missing since sometime yesterday afternoon—at least eighteen hours gone already. Multi-jurisdiction nightmare, divorced parents, evidence the kid may have covered her tracks, no witnesses, delay in reporting—all conspiring against their chances of finding the girl alive.

Apparently the parents wielded some political clout and were waving it like a club, unhappy with the local response. So it had been dropped into Lucy's lap. Probably with some relief.

Exactly the kind of case the SAFE squad and Crimes Against Children initiative were designed to handle. The kind of case that rarely had a happily-ever-after ending.

Statistically, if Ashley Yeager had been taken against her will, then she was already dead. If she'd been coerced away from home, then there was a good chance she was either dead or being prepared to enter the trade as a sex worker.

Best-case scenario, she ran away and right this moment was hiding out at a friend's house, laughing at all the commotion she'd caused… Unfortunately, by the time local law enforcement called in Lucy and her people, things were usually way beyond best-case scenario.

When Lucy and her team were called in, it usually meant worst-case nightmares.

She pulled the Subaru into the driveway of their new home—a remodeled Victorian in a gentrified area of West Homestead. Pittsburgh's entire South Side was undergoing a renaissance, its flats and slopes bristling with new construction and renovations. They had been lucky to find this house so close to her work and Nick's office and in their price range.

Lucy herded Megan into the foyer and reset the alarm. "Your dad has clients until one. Will you be all right until then?"

"Mom, I'm not a baby." She gave an irritated shake of her head and started to flounce away, implying Lucy had gone senile.

Lucy was running late, a kid's life ticking away with the seconds, but she couldn't restrain her need. She caught Megan from behind, giving her a bear hug and a noisy smooch on the top of the head, inhaling the almond-vanilla scent of Megan's shampoo. She'd liked the No More Tears scent better—it felt safer with its memories of Megan splashing in her baby tub, Lucy's hands supporting her; nights spent with her and Nick bleary eyed with exhaustion, rocking Megan, watching over her...

"Mom!" Megan protested, breaking free. "You smell awful. Gross." She stomped into the living room where she threw herself onto the sofa and reached for the TV remote.

Lucy reluctantly started up the steps. Ten minutes later, face scrubbed, hair combed, a fresh swipe of deodorant, and a change of clothes, she was racing back down them again. "Remember, drink lots of fluid and tell your dad you had ibuprofen at eight, so you're not due again—"

"Mom, would you just go already? I can handle it. Go on, they're waiting."

"Okay, okay. I'm out of here. Love ya!"

Apparently the last was too soporific for the Queen of Apathy, who gave Lucy a shrug and a wave, muttering, "Yeah, right."

–

"I can't stay long, Mom." Jimmy gently combed no-rinse shampoo through his mother's silver-white locks. Her hair was heavy, thick. Once upon a time it had been dark as ebony, her crowning glory. The nurses here at Golden Years did a good enough job, but Alicia always insisted that Jimmy was the only one who could take care of her hair.

Alicia patted her hand against his thigh and shifted in her chair so that he could reach better. "Tell me all about your new girl, Jimmy. I want to hear everything."

He grasped her hair above the comb so that when he tugged against snarls it wouldn't hurt. Just the way she had taught him. "I think she might be the one. She's smart, really brave, and so beautiful."

"How old is she? Not too old, I hope. I keep telling you, Jimmy, a man like you, he needs a young woman to keep up with him. Just like your father had me."

He closed his eyes, swaying in time with her words. Her voice was whisper soft, his one constant companion until her health had forced her to leave his side three years ago. Even so, he visited every day.

"Your father was only a few years younger than you are now when he came and stole me away. Climbed up on the porch roof, slipped into my window like Errol Flynn, so handsome he was. Rescued me, carried me away before my father even knew it. Good thing too. He would have shot us both." She shuddered. "Or worse."

Jimmy wrapped his arms around her from behind. She was so petite that it was no effort at all to reach around her wasted body. Years of unchecked diabetes had stolen her vision, aged her beyond her seventy-eight years and now threatened to finish her off if the doctors couldn't fix her kidneys. Her hand fluttered up, landing on his arm.

"How old were you?" he asked, following their familiar litany.

"I was fourteen. But I knew enough of the world, that's for sure. Enough to know that anything was better than staying in my father's house. If not for your father, big, brave, bold, beautiful man that he was, I would have died. He saved me."

Jimmy set the comb aside, rested his head against hers, inhaling the lemony scent of the shampoo. So much better than the sickly-sweet-dead-flesh smell that shimmered from the other denizens of the Golden Years Home. "Tell me about my father."

"Ah, how I wish you knew him. Even for one day. Being near him was like being near the sun. He was so brilliant you had to sometimes shut your eyes or be blinded by the beauty of him." Her

32

hand tightened on his arm. "I would have done anything for the man."

"Why didn't he stay after I was born?"

She straightened, dropping his arm and pulling away, leaving him cold and alone. That question was *not* part of the ritual. He'd never dared to ask it before, but he needed to know.

"I don't know what you're talking about." She snapped each word between clicks of her dentures. "If you're going to talk like that about your father, then maybe you should just go, be with your girl and forget all about me." She rocked the chair to one side, away from him.

"No, Mom. I'm sorry. Please don't send me away." He knelt at her side, reaching for her, but she blindly batted his hands away.

"Why not? When I'm dead, you'll be all alone."

Ice seared Jimmy's belly. "Don't say that. You can't leave me."

"A man is nothing without his family. Your father taught me that."

"Tell me more. Please. About my father, how he saved you."

"Ahh… your father." A stray shaft of sunlight spun past her, leaving her face in shadows, giving her the illusion of youth. "You'll never be half the man he was. Never."

Jimmy had no answer to that other than to lay his head in her lap as he knelt on the hard, cold floor. Finally she relented, feathered her fingers through his hair. "Poor, poor boy. You'll never find a woman as good for you as I am. Maybe now that I'm dying, you'd be better off dead too."

Chapter 5

Damn, she'd seen riots less chaotic than this. Lucy hit her horn, attracting the attention of the patrolman manning the barricades. He held a hand up, ignoring her as he argued with several civilians. A TV crew set up their equipment not ten feet away from him. This was what happened when a case was getting older and colder by the second and an investigation went from being a case file to a political agenda to a full-blown media storm.

All with one girl's life hanging in the balance—and now very much in the spotlight.

The neighborhood was an upper-middle class development in Plum Borough, a suburb northeast of Pittsburgh. Large stone and brick homes shoehorned to fit on small lots lining streets named Deer Run and Pheasant Way. The development was surrounded by farmland and forested acres holding their breath, waiting to be bulldozed in the next round of suburban sprawl.

Lucy counted squad cars from Plum Borough, the Allegheny County Sheriff, neighboring Monroeville, and the State Police. Parked haphazardly between the various squad cars blocking the cul-de-sac were several unmarked cars: brown Fords courtesy of the Staties, white Impalas from the Pittsburgh Bureau of Police.

The mother lode was the large black RV, bright yellow letters, large enough to be read a block away, proclaiming it the Incident Command Center. It held the spotlight, straddling the driveway of a beige brick two-story house with no porch and rigid, unwelcoming landscaping.

Worse were the two news vans at the end of the street. She wondered who called them, who was thirsting for the limelight. It wasn't like they could do more than offer a description of the missing girl—with no vehicle involved they couldn't even issue an AMBER alert.

Tapping her wedding ring against the steering wheel, Lucy blew out her breath in a string of expletives, knowing it would be her last chance to indulge herself. Part of her job was to play nice with all the other boys in blue.

She exited the car and strode up to the patrolman. His cheeks were flushed, sweat rolling from below his hatband as he whirled on her. "Lady, get back in the car!"

Given the noise and crowd and chaos—including, she now saw, a few enterprising kids who had set up a lemonade stand on the curb—she might have forgiven him. If not for the fact that his hand went to rest on the butt of his gun, leveraging it a fraction of an inch from his holster.

Bad instinct if you're directing traffic at a media event crowded with civilians and the press.

The guy was obviously not only out of his element, he looked exhausted—she'd bet his shift had ended hours ago but he'd been stuck out here and forgotten.

"Officer Nowicki," she read his name tag, "I'm Supervisory Special Agent Lucia Theresa Guardino." She smiled and held her credentials up where he could see them.

He squinted at her, comparing her likeness to the photo on her credentials. "FBI?"

"Yes sir. I know my vehicle is in the way here, but I need to get up to the scene as soon as possible. Do you know who the responding officer is? I'll need to speak with him as well."

"That would be me, ma'am."

"Wonderful. Tell you what. Why don't you call your commanding officer and tell him I'm interviewing you and to send someone to relieve you while you escort me to the scene and we chat. Oh and, if someone could possibly move my vehicle to a more

35

convenient location?" She dangled her keys and he took them. "I don't want it in your way."

Nowicki nodded and spoke into his radio. When he'd finished, she asked, "So what's the story?"

"Mom got an anonymous call at three eighteen a.m. Found the girl missing and called us. Apparently the girl told mom she'd be babysitting, but when mom called the family they said they'd never asked her to babysit. So when we got here, we thought it was a runaway. No signs of forced entry, no signs of anything except the kid and her stuff was gone."

"Kid have a history? Anything in NCIC?"

"Nope. But then after dad arrives—they're divorced—mom insists the phone call was a ransom demand."

Nowicki's replacement arrived and they began up the street to the end of the cul-de-sac and the beige brick house.

"Really? So we've got a ransom kidnapping?" Lucy wondered why she wasn't called sooner. Ransom kidnappings were not only rare; they were the kind of case a small town department immediately booted to folks with more resources.

"See, there's the problem. Looks like the kid went voluntarily, even covered her tracks, last time she was seen was yesterday at school."

"But the phone call?"

"Mom says it was a man's voice. He said 'we got what you want,' laughed, then hung up."

"Sounds like a prank call. Could just be a coincidence." Lucy walked faster, trying to process all the pieces of the puzzle. What a mess.

"And then you've got dad. Who's apparently a friend of Pittsburgh's mayor, who's a friend of the Sheriff—"

Ah, that explained a lot as well. They reached the scene at the end of the street where there were less civilians but if anything, more chaos.

"Thanks, Officer Nowicki."

36

"Good luck." He scrambled back towards the safe haven of perimeter duty.

Ashley Yeager's home was a brick two-story house, too large for the lot it sat on. It was the kind of house kids avoided on Halloween because they knew they'd either get no answer or a scrawny box of raisins. But the kind they'd also never TP or egg—the house was too grim, too empty-hearted to make the tricks any fun.

A blonde stood in the middle of the barren lawn, beating her fists against a man's chest as he tried in vain to restrain her. Her silver satin robe had come unbelted, its hem trailing on the ground. Her feet were bare and muddy. The man wore crisply pressed navy slacks and a matching silk polo.

He grabbed the woman's arms and held her in place. The expression on his face was as blank as the brick wall behind them.

"It's all your fault!" the woman screamed.

A group of men surrounded the couple, none of them attempting to intervene, all watching and listening closely. No one seemed to notice the news crews at the end of the block, their telephoto lenses aimed at the gathering.

Lucy pushed past several uniformed officers, noting representatives from several jurisdictions: Plum, Monroeville, Allegheny County. The Staties and PBP reps were in plainclothes, wearing various shades of brown suits—a good color for crime scenes, it hid most of everything you might come in contact with.

Lucy had exchanged her jeans and too-tight tank top for khakis and a pair of white Reeboks. Had hoped to make amends with Megan by wearing the twin-set she'd gotten Lucy for her birthday, even though the light blue knit would make her look washed out and sallow if the TV crews caught her in it. Which was only one of many reasons why she had no intention of allowing that to happen.

Although the Allegheny County Sheriff had called the FBI in for assistance, Lucy had no intention of strutting onto center stage and taking over their case. Her greatest value lay behind the scenes, far from the spotlight.

The mother's hysterics continued unabated. From the exasperated looks on the cops' faces, Lucy guessed this had gone on for quite some time. She pushed through to the inner sanctum, a cluster of three men, two in suits, one in a brass-riddled uniform.

"Who's Incident Commander?" she asked.

"I am," all three said at once, confirming her suspicions. Cluster-fuck with a capital fuck.

The three men stared at her. Since she arrived in Pittsburgh, she'd begun a whirlwind tour of local cop shops, introducing herself to law enforcement brass of the one hundred and twenty-three Pennsylvania agencies the SAFE/CAC unit would be working with. She recognized one of the men: Dunmar of the Allegheny County Sheriff's department. Ahh... the man with the fancy toys.

He and his boss were the only cops involved who were elected officials. She'd bet a dozen Krispy Kremes he was the one with the hotline to the local media.

"Nice to see you again, Chief Deputy," she said, extending her hand and plastering a smile on her face. From his scowl it was obvious her invitation to join the game hadn't been his idea.

"I'm so glad you were able to bring your new incident command van out here to help us today." She bolstered her lie by widening her smile until she feared her face would crack. Tact, diplomacy, team building—she needed these men as much as they needed her.

Not to mention a missing fourteen-year-old girl who should be home right now listening to bubble-gum pop rock and painting her toenails. Or whatever Ashley Yeager did to amuse herself in the large, looming house that reminded Lucy of San Quentin.

"Would you mind introducing me to your colleagues?"

"Uh, sure." Dunmar jerked a thumb at the brown-haired man in the tan suit to his right. "Don Burroughs from the Pittsburgh Bureau of Police's Major Crimes Squad, and this," the thumb waggled to indicate a tan-haired man in a brown suit on his left, "is Adam Lowery from the State Police."

Dunmar didn't introduce her, as if he thought that would make her disappear. "Nice to meet you, gentlemen. I'm Supervisory

Special Agent Lucy Guardino from the FBI's Sexual Assault Felony Enforcement Squad."

"Sexual assault? We don't need—"

She interrupted Lowery. "I'm sure you're all aware that crimes against children fall under the SAFE unit's purview. That includes abductions as well as high-risk juvenile runaways. Do we know which we're dealing with here?"

"Runaway," the Statie said.

"Snatched," Dunmar said.

Burroughs, the PBP detective remained silent. He was too busy checking her out, his body posture realigning itself into a wide-based stance, hands on his hips, pushing his suit coat back, revealing his very big gun.

Ahh, one of those. She'd bet he didn't walk, not like other mere mortals, instead he swaggered.

Ignoring his smile so wide that she could count all his teeth if she was inclined to take the time, she continued, "All right then. My job is to coordinate, to help in any way possible."

All three men bristled immediately. Lucy kept her voice calm, non-confrontational. "To start with, which of you is going to be our media liaison? Chief Deputy, I expect that would be you?"

Dunmar puffed his chest out with self-importance.

"Great. We're definitely having some crowd control issues down the street. Maybe you could get some of your people to deal with it and escort the media to a secure location?" She eyed the obnoxious Incident Command van. She'd love to get it out of sight, but the news crews and the family had already seen it. Too late now.

"Who is conducting the search of the house and the location where Ashley was last seen?" They appeared startled at her use of the victim's name.

Cops usually tried to depersonalize victims, especially when it involved kids. But right now, this early in the case, she wanted these guys focused on Ashley—not on jurisdiction or who would look best on the ten o'clock news. "Has someone secured Ashley's room?"

"My guys cleared the house after the Plum police did an initial sweep," Lowery, the Statie, said. "No sign of her. Missus said a school bag and jacket were missing. Couldn't get much more out of her than that."

He nodded in the direction of Ashley's mother; now quiet, slumped against the rigid chest of the man she'd been screaming at earlier. Still no tears, Lucy noticed. Right, she'd get to the family in a minute. "Have you started a canvass?"

"The last place she was sighted was yesterday at school. In Monroeville," Burroughs said. "They called us in as mutual aid—they're not equipped to deal with this kind of thing."

"Sounds good. We'll need all the resources we can get. Why don't you coordinate a search of her school, canvass her teachers and as many classmates as you can track down? We'll also need a walk and talk centering on the school, see if we can nail down her movements. Can you and the Monroeville PD handle that?"

Burroughs straightened his shoulders, taking obvious umbrage at her implication. "We're good. I've already got them working on photos and flyers."

"Has anyone contacted NCMEC yet?"

They looked at each other. "Er, we were just getting to that."

"Lowery, why don't you take care of that since we'll want statewide coordination. I guess that leaves me to deal with the family."

She frowned and darted a doubtful glance at the couple standing a few feet away from them. The men seemed more than relieved to relinquish that particular duty. Fine with her. If they were going to get anywhere with this, it was going to come from the family and what they did—or did not—know.

Even with stranger abductions, it was always about the family. The ones left behind. Waiting.

"I'll get them inside." She gave the other officers her card with her contact numbers and steeled herself to handle the grieving family. The two detectives and Dunmar closed ranks behind her, watching, judging the new kid on the block.

She didn't mind that—hell, she'd been weighing their measure ever since she arrived on scene. It was juggling the emotional napalm of the mother and father that was going to be tricky.

"Hey, LT!" A familiar voice called. At last, the cavalry had arrived.

Two very disparate men approached Lucy. Special Agent Zach Taylor was SAFE's forensic computer technician, fresh enough from his graduation from the Academy that he still dressed in Hollywood inspired G-man fashion: narrow-lapelled black suit, white shirt, dark tie, and Oakley sunglasses. His enthusiasm and frequent repetition of the phrase, "back at Quantico they told us..." made Lucy's teeth ache, but when it came to tech-stuff he knew how to get the job done.

With him was an older, bald black man. Her second in command, Isaac Walden, had the longest tenure of anyone at SAFE: almost four years, first in Atlanta, now here with the new unit in Pittsburgh. He was six years older than Lucy and no one had been able to explain to her why he hadn't moved on. By all rights he should have been promoted long ago to Supervisory Special Agent in charge of his own team. In a unit where the stress level was so high that mandatory psych evals occurred every six months, it was unheard of for an agent to remain as long as Walden.

Taylor she had pegged as the class clown—she'd already had to quash some of his rambunctious limit testing. No problem for a mother who'd survived one toddler.

Walden, she wasn't as certain about. He could be a serious head-case, burnt out, biding his time until mandatory retirement. She hoped not, but for now she was withholding judgment.

"Thanks for inviting us to the party," Taylor said as he reached her side. "Where do you want us?"

"You take the girl's room and any electronics she may have access to. Walden, let's divide and conquer the folks." She glanced beyond them to the ever-present fourth estate whose ranks were swollen now from two news trucks to three. "Inside."

Taylor bounded into the house like a lost puppy scenting dinner. Walden remained at her side, letting her take the lead.

"Hear you found my boys," Walden said as they approached the distraught mother and the stone-faced father.

"Safe and sound. It was a team effort—hope you don't mind, I let the Staties take the credit."

He merely shrugged. Angry or agreeing with her, she wasn't certain. She didn't have time to think about it.

"Mr. and Mrs. Yeager? I'm Special Agent Guardino from the FBI. Could we talk inside?" Both were silent. Mrs. Yeager had her eyes squeezed shut and fists raised as she leaned against the man. Lucy pried her away, the woman almost collapsed in her arms, and led her to the house.

"My baby, where's my baby?" the mother sobbed.

Chapter 6

Lucy settled Melissa Yeager into a kitchen chair. Without the red blotches covering her cheeks and the runny nose, she would have been a beautiful woman. She had long blonde hair, pulled back into a ponytail that emphasized high, cavernous cheekbones, perfect teeth, a wide mouth, and a slender patrician neck.

"Would it be all right if I made tea?" Lucy asked. A panacea for grieving mothers.

"The cupboard beside the oven," the mother stirred herself to answer. "What's your name again?"

She seemed calmer, more focused now that it was just the two of them. Had the drama queen act been a performance put on for the men outside? For the husband—rather, ex-husband? The press? Or the cops?

Maybe all of the above. In Lucy's experience, shock and fear brought out the worst in people—including the need some people had to center the drama on themselves rather than the true victims. She busied herself microwaving two cups of herbal tea while examining the kitchen for clues to its occupants.

Even though Lucy and her family had moved here only three months ago, still had boxes to unpack, their kitchen had already become the center of their universe. A large calendar filled with everyone's schedule hung on the wall, Megan's soccer cleats and shin pads lay on the floor beside the back door sharing space with Lucy's running shoes, Nick's bike helmet hung on the door knob, lopsided pottery coffee mugs proclaiming "greatest Mom in the world" and "world's best Dad" were displayed with pride on the windowsill above the sink along with a plaster cast of Megan's pre-school handprint.

Here, in the Yeager kitchen, there existed none of that detritus of everyday life.

Instead, it was cold, sterile. All chrome and black, relieved only by white semi-gloss trim and sandstone tile on the floors. No photos except a framed black and white print of the Eiffel tower. There was a desk, but instead of overflowing with bills and coupons and school notices like Lucy's, it contained only a memo pad—blank—a black enameled pen in a holder, and the phone.

"Were there any messages?" Lucy asked as she delivered the tea to the lacquered black pub-height table perfectly aligned in the center of the room. Two chairs only.

Melissa shook her head. A few wisps had escaped her ponytail holder and were plastered against her cheeks. "The police took the answering machine, but there was nothing on it. If anyone wants me, they call my cell."

The tea's cinnamon laden aroma filled the room, the only sign of life except for the two women. A plant would help, Lucy thought. Even a dead plant—a sign that someone human, fallible, lived here.

"We'll need the cell phone. And access to your computer, Black-berry, iPad, anything like that."

"That's what the State police said. They took everything. Have someone monitoring the phones." She stared down into her mug. "I hate him for this. This is all his fault."

"Who?"

"Him. Gerald. Everything was fine until he decided we weren't good enough anymore, until he left."

"How long ago was that?"

"Ten months. Bastard packed his bags and walked out and that was that."

"That must have been tough on Ashley. How'd she take it?"

Melissa frowned as if she'd forgotten about her daughter. "She was fine until this summer. This summer it was like she was having her own mid-life crisis."

"When did you first notice something was wrong?"

"Just before school ended. I took her shopping for a bathing suit—God, that was a fiasco." She looked past Lucy, rolling her eyes and making a clicking sound with her tongue that reminded Lucy of Megan and her twelve-year-old friends.

"Ashley developed early. She's had her period for two years now and she's already got twice the figure I do. Not to mention all that baby fat." Melissa glanced down at her own perfect size two and straightened her posture, pulling her robe around her, re-knotting the ties with elegant grace. "Good thing she never wanted to follow in my footsteps, she never would have made it."

"Your footsteps?"

"I was a model. Put Gerald through veterinarian school, earned enough to buy this," she gestured to the house, "and to start my own agency after we moved here. I know, Pittsburgh is nothing compared to New York, but Gerald had a once in a lifetime job offer from the Pittsburgh Zoo."

"He works at the Zoo?"

"He's in charge of their herpetology department. Reptiles," she added when Lucy gave her a questioning look. "He was responsible for the new snake house. It won some kind of big prize. Way he acted you'd think it was the Oscar or something."

Great. More snakes. Lucy changed the subject. "You had no idea Ashley was missing until the phone call?"

Melissa's frown barely made a dent in her forehead. Botox? Or did nothing penetrate her polished facade?

"I fell asleep reading. She told me she'd be home by midnight, it's not a school night, so—" She shrugged one shoulder. "The phone woke me. At first there was silence, just a man breathing. I almost hung up. But then he said he had Ashley and I ran to her room and her bed hadn't been slept in." Melissa's face was still blank, but her words sped up, in danger of derailing.

"He used Ashley's name?"

"No. No, he just said, 'we have what you want'—but Ashley was gone. He had to be talking about her. He hung up before I could say anything."

"No instructions, no demands for money?"

"Nothing. Just laughed and hung up. I searched the house. Ashley was gone. I called the Martins—she was supposed to be babysitting for them, put it on the calendar a week ago. But they said they'd never asked her." She swiveled in her chair, staring at the backdoor as if she expected Ashley to walk in. "Someone took my baby. Why? Why would anyone do that to me?"

Still no tears.

Melissa turned back to Lucy as if she expected Lucy to have the answers she needed.

Lucy had no answers. Just more questions—things weren't adding up. "Maybe you can show me Ashley's room and tell me more about her. I'd like to get to know her better."

Melissa tugged her belt even tighter and stood. "Not much to tell. She's like any kid. Goes to school, comes home, goes to her room, and goes to bed. A little spacey at times, but you know how girls her age are."

Lucy followed her from the kitchen to the stairs leading to the second floor. Melissa's description didn't sound like any "normal" fourteen-year-old girl she knew. It sounded like a kid headed for trouble. With parents too caught up in their own concerns to care.

Ashley's room confirmed her suspicions. It was a dull room, painted eggshell white with a beige rug. No individuality expressed here. Instead, there were coordinating sheets, comforter, pillow shams and drapes.

The only artwork was a framed reproduction of Monet's water lilies that matched the bedspread. No stuffed animals. No *Cosmos* poking out from under the mattress, no earrings and underwear littering the dresser top. No rock stars taped to the wall, wearing lipstick kisses.

Sterile, like a hotel room. A room where no one was ever coming home.

"Any luck?" Lucy asked Taylor who was packaging Ashley's computer. He'd sealed the tower in a plastic evidence bag, labeled it, and was photographing it from all angles to document the chain of custody.

"I won't know until I get it back to the lab," he said. "But there was something funky."

"What?"

"When I got here the computer was on—but the monitor was blank except for a prompt."

"You lost me."

"It's the kind of screen you'd see if the hard drive has been erased."

"How long would that take, a computer this size?"

He shrugged. "Depends on how thorough you were. Reformatting the hard drive, minutes. Scrubbing it clean, several hours."

Anticipation tickled Lucy's nerve endings, an itch she couldn't scratch.

This wasn't a typical teenage angst runaway—this was someone who had meticulously covered her tracks. Lucy glanced around the room again. It hadn't just been stripped of personality, it had been stripped of anything that could help her find Ashley.

And it hadn't happened overnight.

"Did Ashley erase the hard drive herself?" Because Melissa Yeager stood in the doorway, listening, Lucy didn't add the question foremost in her mind: or had someone else deleted the information for Ashley?

"I won't know until I analyze it."

"How long?"

"Dunno." Taylor exhaled the word, his initial optimism evaporating faster than helium from a balloon. It was clear the admission cost him. "It depends if I can extract anything—if there's anything left to extract."

"What about her cell and other electronics?"

47

"Her cell phone is gone but I'm working with the provider to get a list of calls and text messages. If anyone turns it on, we'll have GPS tracking. The Staties have got mom's cell and laptop. Dad gave us consent for his, but I'm working on search warrants anyway."

"Focus on Ashley's. Did she have anything else?" Lucy asked Melissa Yeager. The mom hovered still outside the room as if some invisible barrier blocked her entrance. "An iPad, another computer, laptop?"

Melissa's shook her head. "No, just the damn phone. Like it was surgically implanted. Texted on it day and night. Sometimes I'd come in to check on her at night and she'd be typing away."

Exactly why Lucy refused to give Megan texting privileges to anyone but her and Nick. Technology was great until predators learned how to manipulate it for their own purposes.

That familiar itch curled her fingers again. Was that what she was dealing with here? A predator? A man like Pastor Walter, only slicker, sleeker and able to convince his prey to cover her tracks? Or smart enough to cover them for her...

She returned to stand in the doorway with the mom, mirroring her anxious posture. "Do you have anyone to stay with you? Someone you'd feel safe with?"

Melissa shook her head.

"So, you're not seeing anyone?" Lucy tried again.

"No. Not—" Melissa broke off, stared at Lucy. "What are you asking?"

Lucy stared back, unabashed. "I need to know about the people in Ashley's life. Where does your boyfriend live?"

Melissa made an exacerbated noise without parting her lips. "He's not—I don't even know what you'd call him. An old friend. We had a thing, once, ages ago. It was only natural, after Gerald betrayed me—"

"What's his name?" Lucy asked.

"Jon. Jon Tardiff. The photographer. He lives in Manhattan."

"Did Ashley know Jon?" A nod from Melissa. But she also broke eye contact, looked down at the floor, her fingers picking at the knot on her robe. "Did she like him?"

Melissa gave a shrug and slouched—totally out of character for the perfect-postured fashion model image she'd portrayed earlier. "No. Ashley didn't like Jon. He came to visit when she was at Gerald's, or we'd see each other when I was in the city."

Lucy stood aside as Taylor gathered up Ashley's computer and his equipment and left. There was more going on here, something she couldn't quantify. "Why didn't Ashley like Jon Tardiff?"

Gerald Yeager and Isaac Walden joined them. Gerald stiffened at the mention of Tardiff but his expression remained as blank as ever. "Ashley hated him," he spat the words. "The pervert used to take naked pictures of her when she was young."

"He's an artist," Melissa protested. "I was naked in them as well, that never bothered you."

"Tardiff has a history of molesting young girls?"

"No. Of course not." Melissa stood up straight again, challenging her ex.

"Not that I could ever prove," Gerald said.

Isaac and Lucy exchanged a glance. Isaac jotted a few words in his notebook and Lucy knew he'd run down the truth.

If it was true, if Tardiff had a thing for girls, then Melissa was living every mother's worst nightmare. The thing you never, ever thought about—for fear that if you did, even for a second, you might be inviting the monster into your home.

Maybe that's what Melissa was hiding. She'd let the monster waltz right in and steal her only child.

"What's missing?" Lucy asked the parents, deciding to table further discussion of Tardiff until she had more facts. "What could Ashley have taken with her?"

Melissa's eyes darted around the room. Lucy followed her glance and spotted something shiny on one wall. A torn triangle of transparent tape. "Did something used to hang here?"

Melissa nodded, one hand covering her mouth as if to keep from screaming.

Gerald answered for her. "What happened to her drawings? Ashley was a fantastic artist, loved to sketch and paint." He pushed past Melissa and stalked around the room. "Where are they?"

She kept shaking her head, small little shakes, watching her made Lucy dizzy. "I don't know." The words sounded frayed, torn. "After she got back from your place that one time, the next day they were all gone. I thought she had grown tired of them, threw them out."

"Threw them out? Ashley would never do that. Did you take them from her, was that your way of punishing her for coming to me when she ran away? You bitch, you had no right!"

"Hold on, hold on." Lucy stepped between the two, restraining her impulse to bash their heads together and send them both into time-out. "Ashley ran away? When?"

"Last month. We had a fight and I woke the next morning and she was missing."

"She wasn't missing, she came to my place," Gerald interjected. "And she left you a note, don't over-dramatize."

"Dramatize? My daughter is missing, gone lord only knows where, she could be dead, and you accuse me of—"

"Calm down, everyone. No one's found a note this time, right? No messages?" Both parents shook their heads. "Okay. Walk me through what's missing."

Lucy opened the closet door. It was like falling into a fashion model's travel trunk. Lining the shelf stood boxes upon boxes of designer shoes and purses, each labeled with color and style. The hangers were brimming over with colorful gowns, lovingly protected in clear plastic garment bags with attached photos of Melissa strutting her stuff on the runway. On the back of the door hung a silk cloth with small pockets sewn into it, each bulging with a different piece of jewelry.

"Those aren't Ashley's," Melissa said. "I ran out of room in my closet and since Ashley refused to hang up her clothes anyway, I started using hers."

Lucy blinked. Fourteen-year-old girl, already angsting over her looks, being forced to live with fashion Barbie-mom's runway successes. Sounded like cruel and unusual punishment.

Then she looked again. Several of the outfits were out of place, not in the bags labeled with their photos. "Did Ashley ever wear these?"

"She could maybe put them on, but they wouldn't fit her properly. Not with her figure." The mother made it sound as if Ashley were a candidate for stomach stapling.

"How about the shoes?" A thin layer of dust covered the shoeboxes. But several of the jewelry pockets were empty.

"Never. I'm a six, Ashley wears an eight already."

Lucy pushed hard against the closet door to latch it shut, taking the opportunity to master her annoyance before turning around to face the parents once more. "Where are Ashley's clothes?"

"All summer she's insisted on wearing the same clothes over and over. Black jeans two sizes too large, a baggy black sweatshirt and a tank top under it. And those ugly clunky shoes you bought her."

"Dansko, they're called Dansko," Gerald put in.

"Whatever. She did her own laundry, so I told her as long as her clothes were clean I didn't care what she wore. You have to pick your battles, right?"

"Those are gone? Didn't she have anything else?" Lucy began to open the dresser drawers. Except for the ones on top, which were filled with underwear and socks—mixed together and not folded, she was relieved to see, so Ashley wasn't a space-mutant-neat-freak after all—the rest were empty.

"She took some things over to Goodwill a few weeks ago. Said they didn't fit her anymore." Melissa peered into the empty drawers, a wrinkle daring to dig itself into her Botoxed forehead. "Surely she didn't give them all away…"

"Oh my God—you have no idea what was going on with your own daughter's life!" Gerald thundered.

"Shut up! It's not like you had a clue either."

Lucy stepped between the two parents. "What was the fight about? The one that made her run away."

"She wanted an advance on her allowance—five hundred dollars. I told her no, but that I'd happily give her the money if she told me what it was for. She wouldn't. We exchanged words and the next morning she was gone."

"Is that what she told you?" Lucy asked Gerald.

"She wouldn't tell me what the fight was about. I fed her breakfast, took her shopping but she wasn't interested in anything except those ugly damned shoes. Then I drove her home to her mother's."

Why did Lucy have the sudden feeling that Ashley was the most mature member of the Yeager family? "Did she seem depressed, moody lately?"

"No," said Gerald.

"Yes." Melissa blanched. "Giving away her clothes, do you think she could be thinking of killing herself? No, never, she wouldn't do that to me." She sank onto the bed and began massaging her temples as if she had a headache.

"We don't have enough information to decide anything yet, Mrs. Yeager. Has Ashley's weight changed? Any new friends? Arguments or falling out with old friends?"

Both parents looked blank.

"Can you give us a list of any of her friends? In particular any close friends or boyfriends."

"I have her class list from school. She was very popular. But we didn't allow boyfriends."

Lucy didn't comment on the mom's use of the past tense. "I know these questions might be hard, but they're important. Is she taking any prescription medication? Are her periods regular? Any signs of drinking or drug use?"

Gerald looked away, shoulders hunched, hands thrust deep into his pockets, marring the perfect lines of his trousers. Melissa stared at the floor, entranced by the beige rug, shaking her head again, her ponytail whacking the bare skin of her neck like a scourge.

"No, no drugs or medicines. But it's been awhile since she had her period—girls her age are always irregular, though. That doesn't mean anything." She looked up. No one would meet her gaze except Lucy. "Does it?"

"You self-centered bitch!" Gerald's attack was sudden, cutting through the silence in the room. "Why do you think she wore baggy clothing all summer? Why do you think she wanted money? You turned our little girl into a whore just like her mother and now she's run off to get an abortion!"

"How dare you call me a whore! You were the one who couldn't keep his dick in his pants." Melissa launched to her feet, hands held high, claws aimed at his face.

Walden, bless his heart, sidled to one side, effortlessly catching her around the waist and pivoting her back down onto the bed where she landed in a flutter of floral chintz.

The Pittsburgh guy, Burroughs, came into the room at a run, stopped when he saw things were under control.

"Agent Walden, why don't you take Mrs. Yeager back downstairs and document her statement. Mr. Yeager, if you wouldn't mind finishing yours with Detective Burroughs?" Lucy made little soothing sounds, guiding the parents out. "We really appreciate your help. Remember, nothing is too insignificant, so take your time."

She shut the door behind them, savoring the quiet. Christ, the room even smelled sterile. But somewhere in this empty space existed the ghost of a teenaged girl. A girl who was either taken or ran... And if she ran, did she run alone? Or did she have help?

The itchy-crawly feeling tingling beneath her skin told Lucy that whatever happened, Ashley hadn't been alone. But she had no proof. Yet.

"All right Miz Ashley, come out, come out wherever you are."

Chapter 7

Ashley woke for the second time. The first time she'd been bouncing along in the dark, like on some kind of weird roller coaster ride. She'd convinced herself it was only a dream. A bad dream, but just a dream.

Wrong, dummy. It was a nightmare. Her worst nightmare come true.

Her tongue stuck to the back of her teeth, her lips were cracked, her head throbbed, pins and needles raced up and down her arms and legs, she was ready to hurl at any moment, and she had to pee. Her eyes were wide-open, but she saw nothing but impenetrable black.

Had he blinded her? She blinked hard. Still nothing. Then she realized there were no noises. God, what had he done to her?

She tried to scream but all that emerged was a tiny squeak. But she heard it, she could hear it. That small triumph gave her the energy to take a deep breath, try to clear her fuzzy brain. She choked on the rank smell—good God, what was that?

Whatever the cause of the sickly sweet odor, it was too much for her stomach to handle. She rolled over, onto all fours, retching. Nothing came except the sour taste of acid and a mouthful of saliva. That didn't stop her guts from trying their best to kick their way from the inside out.

Finally the cramps and nausea passed. She rested her head on the cool floor. It was smooth. Cement? No, not cold enough. Her fingers traced over it, felt embossing. Small squares or diamonds. Linoleum.

Thinking seemed to help the buzzing in her brain, so she cautiously crawled forward, hands sweeping out before her, exploring her new universe. Trying hard not to panic.

How had she gotten here? Bobby—she had gone to meet Bobby. Oh God, had something happened to him?

"Bobby?" Her voice was a hoarse croak. She swallowed and tried again. "Bobby? Anyone, is there anyone there?"

Now she was screaming, which only made her head pound more and burned her throat. She had the feeling she'd tried screaming the first time she woke, her throat felt shredded.

She flailed forward only to be yanked hard by one ankle. Flopping over, she stretched, patting her clothing, reassured that other than her jacket missing and her pockets emptied, nothing seemed disturbed. Wait, that was weird—her shoes were gone as well. Above her sock on her left ankle was a thick wire cable, the kind used when you tied a dog to a stake.

She wanted to scream again but instead forced herself to examine the wire. It was cinched tight around her leg, not even a fingertip could fit below it. A metal clasp held it in place, fastened by a small padlock. Reversing her orientation, she followed the cable back to its origin. A round pole, smooth, metal, rose up from the floor.

Hauling herself up the length of the pole, she stood. A wave of nausea and dizziness hit her. She grabbed onto the pole, liking its cold against her forehead and cheek. It helped to ease the headache.

Her clothing was soaked in sweat but her teeth were chattering. Like she had a fever or something. Once the vertigo passed, she stood on tiptoe, tried to follow the pole up. And hit nothing. She tried to follow the wire, but couldn't walk. The darkness was so complete and disorienting that without the pole to hang on to, she fell. She couldn't even see her hand when she waved it in front of her face.

Blind, she was blind—no, no, it was just dark. A basement—but basements had windows, basements had sounds: water pipes and furnaces and outside noises. All right, not a basement. A soundproofed room with no windows. Like a vault.

She shuddered, hugging her pole. Or like a coffin.

What if there was no air either? Maybe she was using up all her oxygen, wasting it by screaming and crawling around when she should be saving it?

Who cared? A distant voice echoed through her brain. If she was dead, she was dead. But since it hadn't happened yet, no sense giving up. What if Bobby was lying just beyond her, what if she was his only hope?

Emboldened by the thought, she dropped back to her hands and knees and followed the wire out to its end, measuring the dimensions of her prison. It stretched eight feet in all directions, the pole at the center.

Maybe she was trapped in a storage unit? Or she could be underground in an old mine shaft or abandoned swimming pool that had been built over or a secret government lab like in that horror film... Quashing the leading edge of her hysteria, she continued forward. No signs of Bobby or any other living person. Her hand brushed something plastic. A bucket of water that she almost up-dumped. No cup or ladle. She dunked her face into it, slurping the lukewarm, stale water as fast as she could. She couldn't remember ever being this thirsty.

Next to the bucket she found a bedside commode, like the ones at the nursing home where she'd gone to sing Christmas carols last year. Better than wetting her pants. With her bladder empty and her thirst slacked, she returned to sit with her back against her pole, the new center of her universe, knees drawn up to her chest, arms hugging herself.

She'd almost gotten used to the stench—as long as she remembered to breathe through her mouth. But now that she had time to think, she remembered where she'd recognized the odor from.

It smelled like road kill.

-

Burroughs led Gerald Yeager downstairs and outside to the patio. Figured it was best to get the mister as far away from his blushing ex-bride as possible. He gave Yeager the seat in the shade, all the better to watch his eyes without the sunlight making the man squint.

Not that he was a suspect in his daughter's disappearance. No, of course not. This was just a polite exchange of information. Two guys shooting the breeze. While one of their daughters could be a rotting corpse putrefying in a shallow grave.

God, he hoped not. Last DB he'd caught was past ripe and well into the creepy crawly stage, maggots squirming all over.

He wasn't in the mood to be looking at no dead kid's body today. In fact, he was seriously regretting switching weekends with Jimmy Dolan, but Dolan had a family reunion and Burroughs' kids, well, right now he wasn't exactly in the running for father of the year.

He'd barely seen the boys all summer, had claimed overwork, falling into a pattern of letting his ex keep them even on his weekends. He loved his boys, he really, really did—he just didn't have what it took to be a full-time father. Or, according to his ex, a full-time husband.

Thing of it was, Kim was right. On both counts.

What the hell was wrong with him? Same question he'd been asking the better part of two years. He just never seemed to find the energy to answer it.

When he'd seen Ashley Yeager's room it looked perfectly normal to Burroughs. The barren walls, beige decor, mass produced furniture and linens could have been his own apartment.

Maybe that's why he'd stuck around. He felt a kinship with the Yeager girl. Like she was sleepwalking through days and nights filled with apathy, just like Burroughs. Until finally she couldn't take it anymore.

Pretty sad. The person he'd felt most connected with in ages was a girl most likely dead.

"You need a drink or anything?" he asked Yeager after giving the man a few minutes to stew. "Glass of water or something?"

"No." Yeager's gaze kept darting back to the house like he expected someone to interrupt them.

Who? Burroughs wondered. Ashley? That would mean he was innocent. Or maybe the guy was guilty and simply couldn't look him square in the eye.

"I'm just gonna take notes so I don't forget anything, okay?" Burroughs pulled his digital recorder from his pocket and clicked it on. Yeager didn't even seem to notice. "So tell me about this photographer, Tardiff."

Yeager bristled, his body practically vibrating out of the chaise lounge even though his face showed little expression. But little was more than Burroughs had seen from the man so far today. And what little seeped through the chink in Yeager's mask was enough to tell him Yeager hated Tardiff. A lot.

Good. A little bit of hate was good for baring the soul.

"He's tried to wreck my marriage before," Yeager said, his lip twisted in a sneer. "Wanted to destroy my family, take it away from me."

It? Didn't he mean *them*? Burroughs merely nodded sympathetically. Yeager kept talking.

"He's a big deal fashion photographer, wanted to become known as an artist. Melissa was trying to make a comeback after having Ashley, so they started working together. Only he also wanted more artistic," Yeager slashed finger-quotes through the air with the last word, "intimate photos. Not just of her but of Ashley as well. Melissa never asked me, never said nothing. Not until I saw them. Displayed in New York galleries, made a splash. He slept with Melissa, too."

The last was an afterthought. Yeager wasn't upset by the sex, but rather the fact that he'd lost control of what was his. Family as possession.

Burroughs scratched a few notes, nothing to imply the father was a suspect—no need to give the defense any fuel—but just to show he was actively listening to Yeager's rant.

But the other man said nothing more. Only sat there, rigid, his back not touching the seat cushions.

"Did you call child services? Launch an investigation?"

Yeager looked offended. "Of course not. I wasn't about to have strangers invade my privacy. Bad enough those photos were out there, being bought and sold. Melissa made no secret that they were of her—they relaunched her career. For a few years at least."

"Did you confront Tardiff? Ask him if anything more than taking photos happened?"

"What good would that do? The damage was done."

Burroughs scratched his cheek with his pen, closed his notebook. It was clear Yeager had nothing concrete, only a long-held grudge that was more about his pride and less about any possible abuse of his daughter.

"Thank you very much, Mr. Yeager." He left the father hiding in the shade while he went to see what Guardino was up to. She was infinitely more interesting than the cold-blooded father.

He found her still in the girl's bedroom. She was sitting on the floor Indian-style, a collection of items spread out around her on the beige carpet. An archeologist trying to reconstruct a vanished tribe from discarded artifacts.

"Anything good?" Burroughs asked from the doorway.

She beckoned for him to join her. He crouched down beside her, poking at her cache with his ballpoint pen. She'd found several pieces of good quality costume jewelry that corresponded to the missing items from the closet. A very expensive digital SLR camera. A few artists' pens.

And one item that changed everything.

"This kid is different from any teenaged girl I've ever worked with." Guardino played a drum tattoo with two marking pens, the small sounds drowned out by the room's emptiness.

"Isn't that the whole point of being a teenage girl—standing out from the crowd, being an individual?" he asked, checking the camera for a memory card and finding it missing.

"Not this girl. Instead, it's like she's trying to erase herself."

Burroughs turned over the item that had most caught his eye. A metal letter opener with an intricate gold and silver-etched handle. "Where'd you find this?"

"Taped to the back of the commode. In its own little cardboard sheath. I'd bet money she stole it from mom."

"For what? It's no good as a defensive weapon. Too flimsy."

She balanced the opener on end so he could see the bloodstained tip. "Our Ashley is a cutter."

"Great. Self-destructive tendencies and a high rate of suicide."

"Not to mention these kids often feel disconnected from reality, seek out fantasy worlds where they can control their environment, escape to."

"Aren't cutters usually abused? Maybe we should look at this Tardiff guy more closely. See if he's been in recent contact with Ashley." He filled her in with the little information Yeager had given him on Tardiff.

She tapped her wedding ring against the letter opener, gold against silver, considering their options. He sympathized. Some cases you had no leads at all, some you had too many—all leading nowhere. This case was starting to feel like that.

"Any evidence she was knocked up?" he asked.

"I can't rule anything out at this point. But I think an eating disorder is more likely than pregnancy."

"Fits with the mom."

"And her attitude about Ashley's developing figure." She scooped a handful of Austrian crystal necklaces and let them trickle through her fingers. "We need to know what was on her computer. And where she got this camera from—looks like at least a five hundred dollar camera to me. Or possibly something a professional photographer like Tardiff might give a kid."

"To bribe her or groom her?"

Guardino held the beads up before her face like a veil she was trying to see through.

"You think she was doing some modeling of her own?" Burroughs asked. "For Tardiff or a friend out in cyber land?"

"Someone who told her she was as beautiful as her perfect mother, who gave her what she needed: validation, attention."

"Love," he said with disdain. "Or maybe she was doing it for money to finance her escape. Lord knows, I can understand why a kid might want to bug out from this life."

She stood without using her hands, her grace distracting Burroughs. Guardino was quite a looker—and what made her even more attractive was that she didn't even seem to realize it. He extended a hand to her and she leveraged him up to stand beside her.

He held on a moment too long, smiling his thanks. Then his phone rang. He listened for a short minute. "Maybe we've finally caught a break. Monroeville PD thinks they've found a witness. Thought you might want to head on over with me. It could very well be the last person to see Ashley alive."

Chapter 8

Lucy told Walden where she was going and followed Burroughs to his unmarked white Impala. "This isn't exactly your jurisdiction, you could get out before things get nasty," she said as he steered them through the street littered with cop cars and looky-lou's. "Or do you have nothing better to do on a Saturday afternoon?"

He caught her staring at the pale ring of skin on his left hand. "Not for a while," he admitted. "I usually get the kids on weekends, but not when I'm on call."

"How old are they?"

She liked the way his smile made it all the way up to his eyes when he thought about his kids—Nick did that too, every time Megan came into sight. Burroughs' smile looked a little droopy around the edges. Weighed down with sadness.

"Boys. Nine and six. Still young enough to think their dad's a hero." He nodded at the gold wedding band on her own ring finger. "You?"

"One girl, twelve. She still thinks her dad's a hero, not so sure about me right now."

"You moved because of your job."

"That and there's the whole puberty thing. Hormones." She rolled her eyes in a good approximation of Megan.

"Girls are tough. I'm glad I have boys." He pulled out of the development onto a two-lane road leading them into the woods and down the mountain. "I mean, look at this case. She could have run away. With a boy. To have an abortion. To get away from Mr. Freeze

62

and Miss America back there. She could have been taken—coerced or forcibly. She could have planned an elaborate scheme to get her parents back together again or to get some attention or whatever.

"If it was a guy—I mean, bad things happen to boys, too. But it's just more straightforward, you know where to look, what you're getting into. Know what I mean?"

"Right now I'd settle for any forward motion. I hate that we're spinning our wheels like this."

"Hey, you've only been on the case for what, two hours? You accomplished more than everyone else in the hours before they called you."

"It's not enough. Not when she's already been gone twenty-one hours."

He darted a glance at her. "You getting that feeling too, eh?"

"I *always* have that feeling on cases like this."

The road leading away from the development twisted and curved down the side of a mountain ridge. He drove with confidence, one wrist draped over the steering wheel, eyes darting from the road to her and back again.

"Did you invite company?" she asked after watching in the side mirror and seeing a red BMW 6 series following them.

Burroughs glanced in his mirror and made a snorting sound. "That's no company, that's Pittsburgh's ace girl reporter, Cindy Ames."

"Sounds like you two know each other."

"She sicced a camera crew on my kids, following them to school when I wouldn't give her an exclusive on a big time murder case last year. My kids, especially my oldest, went through hell after. Guess you could say Cindy was the straw that broke my marriage." He scowled into the mirror. "She's ruthless, vindictive, and as cold blooded as any serial killer. You want me to lose her?"

"No, pull over. Let's have a chat and lay down some ground rules." She was surprised to see his expression change to one of concern.

"You're new around here. Much as I'd love to rattle Cindy's cage, you don't want to get caught in the crossfire. She'll go after you, your family, whatever it takes to create a headline."

"It's all right. I can take care of myself. Just pull over." Lucy had dealt with reporters before, veterans of the bloodthirsty Metro DC's Capital beat. She doubted Ames would be much of a problem in comparison.

"Ma'am, yes ma'am." He grinned as he stopped the car, angling it across the road to block any escape.

"Grab your recorder and follow my lead." Lucy got out, leaning against the side of the car, arms crossed nonchalantly. The BMW hit its brakes and squealed to a stop less than a yard away from her. The driver, a brunette built for TV news, emerged, slamming the door.

"What the hell! I almost hit you—"

"Good afternoon, Ms. Ames. I don't believe we've met." Lucy borrowed some of the Southern charm Nick and his relatives always showered her with and laid it on thick. "I'm Supervisory Special Agent Guardino. I understand you have an interest in the Ashley Yeager case."

Avarice glittered in Ames' eyes. She reached into the car and brought out a small digital recorder.

"Nice to meet you, Agent Guardino," she said, her heels clicking on the macadam as she crossed to Lucy. She darted a look at Burroughs who leaned with his arms on the Impala's roof, watching, his face impassive except for one skeptical eyebrow arched in Ames' direction. Ames scowled, then returned her attention to Lucy. "Tell me about Ashley's tragic disappearance. Is she dead? Is the father a suspect?"

Lucy ignored Ames' outthrust hand holding the recorder inches away from her face. Instead she stared straight into the reporter's heavily eye-lined and camera-ready eyes. "We are investigating every possibility. Why would you assume the father is a suspect or that Ashley is dead?"

Ames blinked as if not used to having anyone answer her questions, much less turn her interrogation into a dialogue. "Well, so much time has passed, the odds are Ashley is dead. The family is always suspected in cases like this, especially the opposite-sex parent. And sexual abuse isn't uncommon."

"Go on. Cases like what?"

"Kids missing, especially kids from broken homes like Ashley's. That father, he's hiding something. Molestation or worse."

"So you have reason to believe Ashley is dead?"

"Um—well, it's obvious—" Too late Ames saw the trap.

Lucy smiled. Not a genuine smile, it was what Nick called her saber-tooth-tiger smile. "Did you get all that, Detective Burroughs?"

"Yes ma'am." He held up his own recorder for Ames to see.

"Now, Ms. Ames, you obviously have insight into this case above and beyond the general public. I think that makes you a person of interest. Don't you, Detective Burroughs?"

"Should I call for a squad to take her in for questioning?"

"What? You can't! You have no right—"

"Yes ma'am, I'm afraid we do. But, you'd miss the press conference Chief Deputy Dunmar will be holding shortly. And lose your chance to get your face on the six o'clock news."

Ames regrouped quickly. "So what? I'd make headlines: journalist terrorized by police, upholds first amendment rights. I'd be a hero."

Lucy nodded as if she hadn't considered this. "Maybe, maybe. But we'd be obliged to release your statements. Your network may not appreciate a civil action brought against you by the Yeagers."

The reporter was silent for a long moment, a shrewd expression etched into her face. "You wouldn't be wasting your time talking with me if you didn't want something."

"True. We want your cooperation in our efforts to locate Ashley Yeager. That means no interference with our investigation, no end runs to focus the public's attention on us—or our families," Lucy added with a glance over her shoulder at Burroughs.

"The public has a right—"

"Ashley Yeager is part of the public and she has a right to have her safety protected."

"She's dead already and you know it."

Lucy pushed off the car and stepped forward into the reporter's space. She was shorter than Ames but that didn't stop Ames from backing away until the BMW stopped her.

"I do not know that, nor do I believe that. But you can believe me, Ms. Ames, I will do whatever it takes to bring Ashley Yeager home safely. If you interfere in any way whatsoever, I will take you into custody. Is that understood?"

Ames opened her mouth for another protest then clamped it shut. She nodded. Lucy wasn't satisfied and stepped even farther into Ames' space, forcing her to lean back. "I asked if you understood my position in this matter, Ms. Ames."

"Yes." The single syllable was clipped. Ames' lips compressed into a single line and appeared chalky beneath their wine-colored stain of lipstick.

Lucy backed away. "Right. Very good. Thanks for your cooperation. I'm sure you won't want to miss the press conference, so we'll let you be on your way."

Ames took a moment to glower at her, a sneer twisting her lips. "Good thing I didn't have my camera man with me. A woman with your coloring should *never* wear pastels."

With that, Ames flounced into her car, adjusted her hair in the mirror, then turned the BMW around, and sped back up the road.

"Nice work," Burroughs said as he returned them onto their previous course. "You know it's going to come back to haunt you."

"As long as it gets Ames off our backs until we find Ashley."

"Don't count on it. And, for the record, I think you look just fine in that top."

Lucy glanced down at the baby-blue sweater set Megan had given her for her birthday two days ago. Ames was right, it was the wrong color for her. Sometimes she worried Megan had inherited her father's color blindness. The knit was comfortable in the heat but maybe a little too clingy. Burroughs' gaze darted down to rest on her bust line. Not for the first time.

She grabbed her cell phone. "My daughter's home sick, I'd better check in."

The annoying beep of the busy signal greeted her. "Great. Busy. That means she's on both lines at once." She dialed Nick's work number.

"Dr. Callahan, please," she asked the operator. "It's his wife. Thank you." She waited to be connected. "Hey, just wanted to let you know this thing is going to probably go long. I already pissed off some reporter, so be careful. Did you get my voice mail about Megan?"

"Hello to you as well. I got the voice mail and sent her a text. She says she's fine and wants to know if she can make mac and cheese for lunch."

Lucy laughed—she never used the IM or text functions her daughter and husband found so useful. She seldom e-mailed either. In her line of work the miracles of modern communication represented danger more than convenience.

"Her throat must be feeling better. I called and both lines were busy."

"So, did you catch your bad guys?"

"Yeah, but then I got called in on something else. Listen, this case is pretty complicated, I'm not sure how long I'll be tied up."

"One step ahead of you. I already called your mom. She has a date tonight but will come tomorrow if we need her."

"Thanks, should have known you'd—hey, did you say she has a date? With who? We are talking my mother, Coletta Guardino, the last of the Italian martyred widows, right?"

His chuckle reverberated through the tiny handset. "Said she met him on the Internet, a group for Catholics who have lost their spouses."

Lucy lost her focus for a moment, still reeling with the concept of her mother shrugging off her widow's weeds. Going out with someone she met online? What was the woman thinking? Didn't she know what kind of predators were out there?

"Did she give you the," she caught herself before she said "subject", "guy's name?"

"No, she did not. I think she was afraid you'd run a background check on him and send surveillance. She said she'd tell you all about it tomorrow and not to worry."

Not to worry? Her fifty-nine year-old mother, alone for a quarter of a century, was venturing back into the dating scene with a stranger she met in some dark alley of a chat room. "I can't believe this is happening."

Nick's voice was calm, reassuring. One of the few things she hated about her husband. She could project calm, take control over chaos no matter the crisis, but dammit, he really *was* calm. Like some kind of Southern-Irish-Zen Master.

"Everything's going to be fine, Lulu," he said, using his private name for her. "Are you going to have time for lunch?"

A Zen master with twice the maternal instincts she had. "Dunno. We might stop at Mickey D's on the way." She glanced over to Burroughs and he nodded his agreement. Yeah, cops loved donuts, but it was beef and grease that you needed to get through a long day with no end in sight.

"If you get stuck, I left you a present."

She took a look inside her purse. And found an evidence bag marked: For Emergency Use Only. It contained two Power Bars, a package of Aleve, breath mints, and a Hershey's Special Dark. Lucy didn't try to hide her smile. "Have I told you lately exactly how wonderful you are?"

"No. But you can show me later when you get home."

"Hey, what can you tell me about kids who cut themselves?"

The abrupt change of topic didn't knock him off his stride. Nick was well accustomed to Lucy's hyper-kinetic thought patterns. "Girl or boy?"

"Girl. Fourteen. Parents divorced about ten months ago and it looks like she's been having some self-image problems. Wearing baggy clothing, locking herself in her room."

"You'll probably find that she has peer problems, especially in school. Often times the self-mutilation decreases during the vacations and escalates when back in school. These girls are usually shy, low self-esteem, unable to make their needs known, so they disassociate from their lives, from their reality. The pain of cutting is an attempt to regain control, to feel something."

"Sounds like our girl. Thanks, sweetie."

"No problem. I know you'll probably miss dinner tonight, but will you make a point of coming to Mass tomorrow? Megan's CCD class is ushering."

Lucy grimaced. Damn, how had she forgotten that? "We've got the Canadians tomorrow."

Nick made no sound at all. He didn't need to.

Her sigh echoed through the phone. "But our meet's not until afternoon. I should be able to make it. If she feels good enough to go, that is."

She hated using Megan's sore throat as a hedge. Of course, Nick saw right through her.

"Should I tell her that?" Nick never made a promise he couldn't keep. One of the ways he kept his halo shiny and polished bright.

Lucy wished her own parental halo wasn't so tarnished. She tried to put a positive spin on things. "No. Let's make it a surprise."

She disconnected and returned the cell phone to her belt. Burroughs was watching her, a gleam in his eyes.

"Just so you know," he said, returning his attention to the traffic in front of them. "I wasn't going to hit on you or anything."

He was an average-sized man with above average looks, not too handsome, not too plain, but his body language screamed alpha male on the prowl. The way he held his stare a little too long, stood a little too close.

Alpha male or not, Burroughs wasn't her type. Her type of guy, the one and only guy she was interested in, pampered her with neck massages and doing the laundry and Hershey's Special Dark. Her guy didn't have to flash a toothy grin to make her knees wobble. All he

69

had to do was walk into the room, say her name or brush her with his gaze.

Not that Nick didn't have plenty of flaws—after fourteen years of marriage she still hadn't been able to train him to put the toilet seat down or to share the remote. And he had an irritating habit of taking the high road when she'd rather slug it out, down and dirty, in the mud, baring her soul.

Seemed like lately neither of them had the energy to fight—God, how she missed their fights. Passionate, fierce, just like the sex that always followed.

Another sigh escaped her. "Sorry, I usually don't make personal calls at work."

"No need to explain. It was kind of nice to hear a man and wife talking instead of shouting at each other. Your kid gonna be all right?"

"The doctor thinks it might be mono."

"Mono? That sucks, I had that when I was a kid. Felt crappy as hell."

"Fingers crossed it's just strep or a virus."

"Your husband's a doctor?"

"Psychologist. He specializes in post-traumatic stress and anxiety. When we lived in Virginia, he worked at the VA with guys coming back from Iraq and their families."

"High-powered stuff. You two don't take the easy way out on anything, do you?"

She had to laugh at that. "Guess we're both compulsive over-achievers."

"A match made in heaven. Unlike the two back there. What's with them? The mister, I swore he never even blinked the whole time I was talking with him. Eyes like a dead fish."

"Maybe that's from studying snakes and reptiles all day long. He's not used to us warm-blooded creatures."

"Guess that's why he picked her. She's not exactly warm and fuzzy, is she?"

"More like lost in her own little universe. I think maybe they both are—which left no place for Ashley."

"Poor kid. As bad as it sounds, I kind of hope she ran away, maybe with a boyfriend who really cares about her."

"Too bad that usually translates to: pedophile who seduces young girls. You know as well as I, most of these guys know exactly how to manipulate kids, give them all the love, attention and affection they need."

Burroughs' expression went to cop-neutral but his knuckles tightened on the steering wheel. "Yeah. Just what every kid needs and wants. Until the pervs start asking for more." He cut her a look. "I don't know how you deal with these bastards every day, seeing what you see, knowing what you know."

"Someone has to."

"Better you than me."

Lucy shrugged and stared out the window. She hadn't perfected a way to "deal" yet—other than insulating Nick and Megan from her world as much as possible. And she was beginning to worry that insulation was fraying—or maybe working too well. Sometimes she felt disconnected, working to get back inside the bonds Megan and Nick forged when work pulled her away from them.

A stranger to her own family. Probably a lot like how Ashley felt.

They pulled up in front of a small strip mall directly across from Gateway High. "Cashier at the Stop N Go says she saw a girl fitting Ashley's description yesterday afternoon."

Lucy got out of the car and looked around. There was a bus stop on the curb, a chiropractor's office, the Stop N Go, and a nail salon. "Let's hope she saw more than that. We need to get a bead on Ashley. Soon."

-

This was the hardest part, Jimmy told himself, swiveling his chair to decrease the glare on the computer screen. Another day—a minimum forty-eight hours, that's what all the experts said. He had to do it right this time, couldn't fail.

Not again. He scrubbed his hand over his face, trying to block out the images. Sweet, sweet Connie with her heart-shaped face and lilting voice. And Vera—God, that had been awful, whoever would have guessed that such a tiny thing could be so strong?

Enough. They were the past. Ashley was his future.

He had to stay in control, follow the plan. He had to save her. He needed her as much as she needed him. What else could you expect from family?

He focused on the ghostly green images the night vision camera projected. He'd heard her screams. His palms still held the imprint of screws from gripping the edge of his seat. He wasn't ashamed to say that her terror and despair had driven him to tears. True love had its price.

Step one. Establish control.

Ashley crawled across the screen, jerked short by her leash. Step one, complete.

Step two. Foster dependence for survival.

The sounds of Ashley gulping the water he'd left her carried through the speakers. He turned his head, gave her privacy as she used the commode. Step two, finished.

Step three. Complete disorientation. Break old reality.

He'd soundproofed the barn, blacked out every speck of light. Forty-eight hours, they said. Of course there were ways to hasten the process. Drugs. Sleep deprivation. Dehydration. He'd use those if need be, but he knew how frail she was, knew her weaknesses.

She'd already told him all her secret shames, her fears. He'd already prepared her; a long, long time he'd spent. She was ready, malleable.

Part of him wanted to rush, eagerly anticipating Ashley's liberation. Finally, he'd have someone by his side once more. It'd been almost three years since Alicia left for the nursing home. With each passing day alone he felt the thin edge of control slipping from him.

So much so, that some days—especially after his first two failures—he wondered if his mother wasn't right.

If he wouldn't be better off dead.

But not now. Now he had Ashley and she would save him. As he would save her.

Because that's what family did.

He rubbed his eyebrow, watching her hug herself as if she were cold, even though it had to be over ninety degrees in the barn. Wished he could make things easier for the both of them.

Knowing the worst was yet to come.

Chapter 9

Burroughs showed the cashier at the Stop N Go Ashley's picture. She was a gum-cracking, twenty-something named Jalonna. "Sure, I seen her," she said. "Same as I told the other cops."

Knowing Guardino was watching, judging, Burroughs toned down his usual style, instead adopting a soft, polite tone and thanking the less-than-helpful numb-nuts for her time.

"She came in here, bought a diet Dr. Pepper, went out and waited for the bus," she continued, her eyes and fingers busy sorting lottery tickets. "It was about one o'clock or so. She got on the East Liberty bus." She paused, still looking down, a hitch in her sorting. "That was it."

Burroughs looked at Guardino, shrugging as he put his notebook away. "One o'clock yesterday, East Liberty bus. Okay, thanks a lot."

He started for the door but Guardino stepped forward. The clerk didn't notice her at first, not until Guardino slammed her palm down over the stack of tickets. "Tell me what else you saw."

Was Guardino trying to show off for him? To let him know who was boss or to impress him? The move was pretty darn aggressive to use on a cooperating witness.

The clerk jerked away, backed up a step, rattling the cigarette display. "Nuthin. I didn't see nuthin' else."

Guardino let her go, but not without a knowing look. "You sure as hell didn't see the bus number from in here. You went outside, followed Ashley. Why?"

Whoa. How'd he miss that? The clerk looked to him for sympathy, but he gave her nothing.

Then she cocked her head to one side, trying to challenge Guardino with a tight-lidded gaze and failing. Her eyes slunk away in defeat, coming to rest on an iPod sitting beside the stack of lottery tickets. A mandatory accessory for any well-dressed suburban kid.

"The place was empty so I went out to have a smoke. That's how I saw the bus number."

"And?" Guardino prodded.

Jalonna's chest heaved with a sigh that made her double-E's bounce like basketballs. "And she left this on the bench." She handed Guardino the iPod. "If she's saying I stole it or something, the bitch is a liar. I kept it safe right back here in the," she hesitated then brightened, "in our lost and found."

Guardino took the iPod. Most of the kids Burroughs knew, including his own, lived with the thing plugged into their ears, wore it like jewelry. "Kind of a hard thing to lose."

"Yeah, it was weird. Kid saw the bus coming, took the earbuds out and set it down on the bench. Like she planned to leave it behind. So y'all can't blame me for picking it up."

"No problem, Jalonna. Thanks for your help." Guardino shoved the iPod into her bag and followed Burroughs outside.

"Why on earth would a kid leave their music behind?" Burroughs asked, pausing in the shade of the awning. He couldn't believe he'd almost let that clerk off the hook—that's what he got for trying to play Mr. Niceguy. "Her age, music is a kid's life."

The theme song from the Mickey Mouse Club sang out from Guardino's purse. Burroughs watched as she grabbed two phones from the bag. One was labeled in pink: Katie, the other in bright blue: Joey. She flipped open the pink one and shoved the second phone back. Edging away from him, her face blanked for a moment before she spoke.

"This is Ruby." She listened for a moment. "You want to change the time to tomorrow morning? Oh no, I don't think so, me and Katie have church. She has the cutest little outfit to wear: all pink with white ribbons, oh and these adorable panties with lace ruffles. What?"

His fist closed around the car keys as he realized what he was witnessing. Guardino honestly looked as open and friendly as her tone of voice. Burroughs doubted he could ever be that good of an actor.

"No, no I don't think that's a good idea. How about if I just send you some more pictures if you want. Why not? Because this is happening real fast, ya know what I mean? I mean, how do I know you're not some cop or something. All this wanting to meet, I'm just not sure about that. Anyway, I wouldn't have any time free until after church tomorrow."

He marveled as she dangled the bait. No fear of entrapment here, the perv on the other end of the line was obviously working hard to convince her. She tapped her fingers on the Impala's roof, caught his stare and rolled her eyes.

"Well... maybe I could bring Katie to meet you all. But I'd have to be there the whole time, watching out for her. Yeah, I guess that's okay. No, no, I'm not promising any more until we check you out. And we're not going out our front door until the money's there. You said two thousand? Yeah, that will be all right, but you'll need to buy us breakfast too. Some place nice, no drive-thru garbage. Okay then, see you tomorrow."

She flipped the phone shut and her face lost its animation once more. For a fleeting moment she looked disoriented, as if trying to find her balance. Then she took a deep breath. "Sorry about that. While we're here, might as well check out Ashley's locker."

He drove them over to Gateway. "That was some show you put on back there. Does that happen a lot?"

"More than you want to know. We've been working overtime these past two weeks, did a sting this morning, in fact."

"You can't be sending them porn, that would be entrapment." Not to mention against the law.

"No, we set up a child actor website. The kids are fictional and fully dressed. When someone nibbles, requesting more info on the kids' availability, we check them out and then pose as a parent, and usually it's way too easy to go from there."

"So that guy," he nodded to the phone in her purse, "and his buddies think you're going to just hand your daughter over to them? How stupid are they?"

"They're not stupid. Just thinking with the wrong set of brains. They want—no, they *need*—to believe me when I offer them a dream come true. Of course I make them work for it."

"Yeah, so I saw. And their dream come true is?"

"A four year-old girl dressed up for Sunday school." She shook her head. "Hey, we don't have time for this. Especially since these bozos are gonna take up some of my time tomorrow."

They exited the car and walked toward the yellow brick single-story school. The football team was hard at work on the practice field as were the cheerleaders. The marching band drilled in the parking lot, a tinny rendition of "Ghostbusters" mixing in with the whistles of coaches. A typical September weekend in western Pennsylvania.

"Gateway Gators, they have a chance this year?" she surprised him by asking as they entered the school.

"If they can beat Latrobe. Man, those guys looked great last season."

A smiled crossed her lips. "The Wildcats."

"You talk like you're from around here."

"Grew up in Latrobe. My mom worked at the Rolling Rock plant until they moved it to New Jersey."

"And your dad?"

"Died when I was a kid." She pushed open the door to the principal's office.

"So coming back here is like homecoming? Local girl makes good, that kind of thing?"

A brief frown clouded her face. "Yeah, people love hearing about the FBI part. Just not the rest of my job."

She shivered in the air conditioning. Damn, he did admire the way that top fit her. She had to be at least in her late thirties, but with her long dark hair and smooth, unwrinkled face, she could pass for a decade younger.

Guardino leaned over the receptionist's desk. "Hello? Anyone home?"

A harried looking black man with wire-rim glasses emerged from one of the offices. "I'm sorry, we're in the middle of a crisis here—" He stopped when he saw Guardino's credentials. "Oh. Well. Now. I've just got off the phone with our attorney and he said to let you see Ashley's locker and belongings. Right this way."

Burroughs trailed after Guardino. The view from the rear was a nice distraction, made him forget where he was for a moment. He hated schools—the budding sociopaths, the cliques, the hierarchy that forced a kid to accept whichever hole his peers pigeoned him into.

The vice-principal was prattling on about the disruption the police had made in the school's routine, removing his glasses to wipe them three times during the twenty-foot march down the hall to Ashley's locker.

"Well, now here you are." He fumbled with the master key. Guardino didn't rush him, didn't get in his space or take the key away like Burroughs itched to. Instead, she used the opportunity to pump the guy for info.

Not that the guy had anything helpful to offer, but it was pretty slick to see her milk him dry in seconds flat. She seemed to have a gift of finding her subject's weak spot and using it to get them to spill everything. Handy talent for a cop, especially one with her job.

Finally, the door sprang open. The vice-principal jumped back as if he were about to bolt, but Guardino restrained him with a gracious hand on his arm as Burroughs plunged into the teenager's treasure trove.

No help here—just textbooks and a binder. Other than her gym clothes, Ashley had left nothing personal behind. Still, Guardino acted like it was the mother lode, flipping through every page in the loose-leaf binder, examining the bored doodling of a seventh grader.

"Think we could see any of her artwork?" she asked the vice-principal who hovered as if uncertain that they weren't there to arrest him.

"According to her schedule, she's in Mrs. Dunkin's art class. She's also Ashley's faculty advisor. I saw her here a while ago—something about firing some pots the students made."

Guardino smiled at the man and gestured. "Let's go meet Mrs. Dunkin."

Burroughs felt exceedingly small walking the tile-walled corridors. Trapped. Back to being thirteen again. The rows upon rows of steel lockers, the shiny linoleum, the noise bouncing from one wall to the next, the teachers making you feel stupid just 'cause you didn't talk so hot. Not to mention the humiliation of leaving class for speech therapy, constantly being labeled a dummy or retard.

A sheen of sweat broke out over him as their footsteps echoed down the empty hallway. He caught Guardino looking at him and shoved his hands into his pockets before she could see his clenched fists. As long as he didn't open his mouth, make a fool of himself, it would be all right.

They turned the corner and entered a brightly lit room festooned with colorful paintings, textiles and papier-mâché sculptures. A petite woman knelt before a kiln, adjusting something.

"Mrs. Dunkin? These are the police. They're trying to find Ashley Yeager and have some questions for you." With that the assistant principal left them.

"I was so sorry to hear about Ashley," Mrs. Dunkin said, turning to face them. She wore frayed jeans and a Pitt T-shirt smeared with paint. If more of his teachers looked like her when he was a kid, school might not have been so bad. "She's a promising artist. Transferred here from Plum to take advantage of our art program."

"We'd love to see her work," Guardino said when Burroughs didn't respond. She gave him a look like he was acting like a fool, tongue-tied and gawking. He balanced Ashley's binder under his arm, took out his notebook and pretended to be busy taking notes.

Dunkin brushed clay dust from her hands on the back of her jeans. She laid out several cardboard canvases of Ashley's work. Seeing it, Burroughs had the feeling he wasn't the only one with bad feelings when it came to school.

"Her work is quite advanced from a stylistic view point," Dunkin said. "But very primal in its energy."

Primal. That was a tame word for it.

Terrified, a child trying to claw her way out of a dungeon, desperate and despairing would be a better description. Each canvas revealed an amorphously feminine shadow dwarfed by one nightmare image after another.

In one, the girl—for all its womanly curves, the figure felt immature, very young—was about to be stamped on by a giant boot. It was impossible to tell if the black Doc Marten was a man's or woman's.

In the next, she ran, looking over her shoulder at dark shadows, not realizing that she was trapped in a labyrinth formed by the coils of a monstrous serpent. It waited ahead of her, mouth open in anticipation.

And so on. Darkness, shadows, fear, helplessness, bleak despair. No hope, no light, no escape.

"Were her grades dropping?" Guardino asked.

"Yes, last year she went from a B student to C's and D's," Dunkin said. "I tried to arrange a meeting with the parents, but," she shrugged, "they were too busy."

"Did Ashley talk with you at all, give you any idea what was going on?"

"I tried to get her to open up, but she only spoke through her art. These were from the end of last year. This year, I hoped things were looking up." Dunkin reached into a vertical cabinet and pulled out a heavy sheet of watercolor paper. "She left the acrylics and her dark palette behind. Started this two weeks ago."

Burroughs wouldn't have recognized the watercolor as being the work of the same artist. Here there were two forms, drawn proportionately, one male, one female. They were silhouetted by either a sunset or sunrise, features hidden, but their posture was one of purpose. Most telling of all, they held hands. Partners. Traveling into an unknown, unseen future. But together.

"It's a bit precious, but I encourage experimentation."

Guardino turned the paper so he could read the scrawled words at the bottom corner. Ashley had titled her painting: The Escape.

–

The art teacher hadn't been able to give them any more helpful information, but she did let Lucy take Ashley's most recent work. They had just gotten back on Route 22, were planning to stop for lunch, when Lucy's cell rang. "Guardino here."

"Hey, LT. I got something. That camera you found in the vic's room—"

"The victim has a name, Taylor."

"Yeah, right. The camera you found in *Ashley's* room belongs to her father, not Tardiff."

"Is he still at the house?"

"Hang on, I'll check." She filled in Burroughs while she waited. Taylor returned. "No. The dad's back at his home." He rattled off an address and Burroughs nodded, making an illegal U-turn and ignoring the honking of disgruntled drivers.

"Do we have a warrant for his place?"

"Yep. I can meet you there, go over his electronics." Taylor was eager, ready to take credit for cracking the case.

She hated to remind him that no one would care about the credit unless they found Ashley alive. If the father was involved with her disappearance, the odds of that just took a drastic plunge.

"Sounds like a plan." She hung up and stared at Burroughs as he finessed the car through the weekend traffic on the Parkway. "What's your beef with schools?"

He yanked the wheel, cutting off a semi as he changed lanes. "Huh?"

His pretense of being preoccupied with traffic didn't fool her. "You didn't say a word the entire time we were in there. And don't blame it on the pretty art teacher with the cute ass you couldn't take your eyes off."

"Hey, I can look, c-can't I?"

Ahh, when he was angry she caught the slight stutter. Okay, just so it wasn't something bigger, something that might interfere with her search for Ashley. She was silent for a moment. "You're right, my mistake."

He turned to look at her, a scowl crossing his features. "You thought—Jesus lady, g-get your mind out of the g-gutter, why don't you!"

"Sorry." She meant it; she should have used more tact. "But this case is technically out of your jurisdiction and last thing I need is some zealot fucking up my case."

"Just for the record, I was never molested by anyone when I was a kid. Laughed at and picked on 'cause I happened to stutter, yes. But I fought my own battles and no one ever messed with me. Okay?"

She raised her hands in surrender. "Look, I said I was sorry. It's happened too many times for me to ignore the warning signs is all."

"Well, I'd say your radar is due for recalibration."

"I can't take any chances. Not with a girl's life at stake."

He relaxed back in his seat and was silent for a moment as they exited the parkway at Regent Square.

"You're right. If it'd been my case, I'd be suspicious too, I guess." He glanced at her, a smile crossing his features. "You're a pretty smart lady, Guardino." They stopped at a light. A horde of kids were squealing and chasing each other in Frick Park. "So how'd you get into this line of work anyway? If you don't mind me getting personal."

She chuckled. "*Quid pro quo*, you mean. No, I was never a victim myself. And none of my family are cops, so can't blame it on that. Guess I'm just a control freak. I have this need to make sense of this crazy world and this seems like the best way to do it."

"Hanging out with perverts and child molesters helps you make sense of the world?"

"No. Catching them does."

Chapter 10

Gerald Yeager's home was a three-bedroom apartment in a glass and steel high-rise complex in Highland Park. It looked out of place among the two story row houses, shops, and single-family homes, yet the anonymous, cold-blooded building fit Yeager to a T. They arrived before Taylor but Lucy elected not to wait. She called Walden for an update from the building's lobby.

Nothing yet on Tardiff, except he wasn't a registered sex offender. Mrs. Yeager had agreed to a polygraph but the Mister hadn't. Yeager had also refused to allow a policeman to accompany him home, a phone tap, or a search of his premises. Which, right now, made him suspect *numero uno* in Lucy's mind.

Cold, calculating, clever… Yeager was all that.

Only downside to Yeager being their man was that there was no good reason for him to take the time, risk, and energy to spirit Ashley away unless he wanted her silenced. Permanently.

Lucy sighed, only half listening as Walden finished his report. She held the phone to her ear while she and Burroughs waited for the elevator. She really didn't want to find another dead kid. Her job was to save the children. At least the best part of her job.

"I followed up with the Staties about the NCIC report and list of registered sex offenders. Pretty clean neighborhood," Walden continued. "Nearest registry offender is two miles away. I'm letting the troopers handle those."

Lucy decided his instincts were probably on target. This didn't feel like a stranger-danger quick grab. Just the opposite. Someone

83

had taken the time and energy to devote himself to Ashley's needs—
and to have his own gratified as well. "Anything from the hospitals
or morgue?"

"Nope. Dunmar didn't do so bad with the press conference.
Their emergency response center is manning the hotline but so far
nothing promising other than the cashier."

"No bus drivers reported anything?" The elevator dinged its
arrival. Burroughs held it for her while she finished.

"No, but you knew that was a long shot." Walden's tone was
slightly chiding. She agreed; there would be no easy way out on this
case. "Nothing's popped on background checks or financials. Still
waiting to hear back from New York on the photographer, Tardiff.
You want me to stay here, babysit some more or can I turn the duty
over to the locals?"

She wondered if the Sheriff was prepared for the overtime hit their
budget was going to take, manning the control center and keeping
people at the house with the mom. Not her concern, officially, she
was just there to advise and make the locals look good.

"Hang out there a while longer. I'm taking another crack at the
dad, then I'll be back. Call me if anything comes up." She hung up
and entered the elevator. Her ears popped as they were hurtled up
to the fourteenth floor.

"Convenient place for dad," Burroughs told her. "The zoo is
right down the street, he can walk to work."

"What kind of man devotes his life to working with snakes and
lizards?"

He arched his eyebrow, a smile quirking at his mouth as if he were
about to question her own career choice again. The doors slid open
before he could say anything.

Gerald Yeager did not appear happy to see them. He stood at his
door, blocking their view of his personal space, keeping them in the
hallway. "Did you find Ashley?"

"Not yet, Mr. Yeager." Lucy stood so that she was the focus
of his attention, leaving Burroughs to observe from the periphery.

Observe and watch her back. Something hinky was going on with Yeager, something she couldn't quite put her finger on. Yet.

"Then why are you here? You should be out looking for her."

She noticed he didn't use Ashley's name. Didn't or couldn't? "We need to speak with you. May we come in?"

"Is this about the lie detector test? I already told you people, I'm her father. I love her. I shouldn't have to prove it." His voice came out flat, allowing no argument.

His body betrayed him. A band of sweat on his upper lip, the way his gaze dropped to focus on the floor, a shift in his weight as he shrank away from Lucy.

She decided to take a gamble. "Actually, Gerald, I'm here about the camera. Your camera. The one I found in Ashley's room."

Bingo. The transformation from outraged parent to cowering liar took only two heartbeats. As if he'd been waiting for this moment, waiting for his lies to catch up with him. Shoulders drooping, Yeager walked away from them, leaving the door open.

Lucy followed, Burroughs on her heels. The detective still had his hand near his service piece, but she didn't think he'd need it. The dangerous part was usually when you confronted the denials, challenged the carefully constructed web of lies, not after they already admitted defeat.

"I'm sorry about the pictures," Yeager said, dropping down into a black leather recliner. The entire room was done in black and chrome, a match to Melissa Yeager's kitchen. As if their entire married life had been devoid of color. "But they have nothing to do with Ashley—well, they do, but not the way you mean."

Lucy slanted a look at Burroughs who merely shrugged. She sat down on the leather sofa, her knee mere inches away from Yeager's. "Why don't you start from the beginning."

"It wasn't my weekend, I wasn't supposed to have her. I mean, I have a right to my own life, you know?"

"The weekend when Ashley ran away and came here? What did she find, Gerald? Something that scared her?"

He leaned forward, elbows on his knees, face buried in his hands, muffling his words. "Yeah. Then she got angry—said I didn't love her, that I never had."

When he didn't look up, she knew Ashley had probably been right. She leaned forward, her elbows on her knees. Her voice low, secretive. A keeper of confidences. "What did Ashley see, Gerald?"

He blew out his breath. Then he looked up, not meeting her gaze but looking past her, out the window, searching for an escape. "A friend of mine. Mark. He's the one in the pictures. I know he looks young, but he's really twenty-three, we're two consenting adults. I swear, I didn't even know Ashley stole the camera until a week later when she called. She threatened to tell her mother about Mark unless I let her come live with me."

"What did you say?"

"I'm not going to let my own kid blackmail me." He sat up straight, looked her in the eye once more. "Should have known, growing up in that house, with that woman, she'd never learn any respect."

"So Ashley told her mother? About you and Mark?"

"Her mother already knows. Why do you think we split up? I told Ashley that, said I didn't care if her mother saw the pictures. After that she stopped talking to me." He sighed as if he were the injured party. "All I did for that kid, and she cut me out of her life, just like that."

Right, it was all her fault. "Mr. Yeager, do you have a computer?"

"Of course I do."

"Good. One of my technicians will need to take a look at it. Is there anything on there that might cause problems?"

He shook his head. "No, just more photos of Mark and me. Go ahead, you can look anywhere you want."

The phone rang and Yeager jumped. He looked to Lucy for permission before answering it. She nodded her assent.

"Hello?" Yeager's face creased into a scowl of anger and worry. Lucy tensed—was it Ashley? A ransom demand? "I'm on my way. Get the others back inside before any harm comes to any specimens."

He slammed the phone down. "Someone stole my specimens. I have to go."

"Mr. Yeager, we need you here. In case Ashley calls."

He blinked. He'd forgotten about Ashley. Lucy exchanged glances with Burroughs.

"But—"

Burroughs gave it a try. "Surely your assistants can care for your—ah—specimens?"

Yeager slumped back in his seat.

"Were they poisonous?" Lucy asked, thinking of the snake handlers. Maybe Pastor Walter's flock had tried to replenish their serpent supply.

"Poisonous? No, of course not. They're harmless. I'm not sure why anyone would want forty-two *Colubridae*. They're not exotic, not worth anything."

"Probably just a prank," Burroughs reassured him. "Kids playing."

A knock rattled the door. Taylor, right on time with the warrants. The technician got busy with the computer while Burroughs and Lucy searched the guest bedroom where Ashley stayed. Nothing except some toiletries and a pair of baggy pajamas.

"Mr. Yeager, now that we've discussed everything, would you mind taking a polygraph?"

Yeager shrugged. "Sure, whatever."

"We'll also have someone stopping by to monitor things. In case Ashley calls," she added.

It seemed best to have someone keep an eye on the father. Now that she'd wrung all his secrets from him, she doubted he had anything to do with Ashley's disappearance, but she'd been wrong before. No sense taking any chances.

Once they were back in the elevator heading down, Burroughs slouched against the wall.

They reached the lobby and headed out to the car.

"Where to now, boss?" Burroughs asked as he turned the ignition on.

"Back to Ashley's house." Lucy plopped down into the passenger seat, feeling discouraged. "Think you can have your precinct guys keep an eye on Yeager?"

"We call them zones here in Pittsburgh."

"Right. And someone needs to talk to Yeager's boyfriend."

"The infamous Mark." The car had warmed up considerably, basking in the eighty-five degree sunshine. He turned on the AC and pulled out onto the street. "I'll do it myself if you don't have something more constructive for me to do."

"I wish I had something more constructive for *me* to do. I hate this part, the waiting part. But until we crack her computer and finish tracking phone calls there's not a whole lot more to do."

He turned a corner and they pulled up to an Eat 'n Park. "Sure there is. We can have lunch, recharge."

She said nothing. Food was the farthest thing from her mind and she doubted she would taste anything she ate. Dammit, there had to be something more she could be doing.

No fourteen-year-old's life could be such a dead end.

Burroughs didn't give her any choice, getting out of the car and waiting for her to join him. He held a small thermos.

"Refilling the coffee?"

"I wish. My testing gear and insulin. I carry it in case my pump fails, but it needs to stay cold."

"Jeezit, Burroughs. You should have said something, we could've stopped sooner."

"I'm good. Snuck a protein bar before we left the house." He shrugged. "Got it down to a science. Go ahead and grab us a booth and I'll be back in a jiff."

The restaurant was busy, but a wave of her credentials got Lucy the next available table. While she perused the menu and waited for Burroughs, she called Taylor and got an update.

"Got the LUDs from mom's phone. The call that woke her this morning came from Ashley's cell phone."

Lucy dropped the menu she was holding. Damn, maybe Burroughs was right. Ashley *was* playing a game—tormenting her mother for starters. "You're kidding. Got a location?"

"Not yet. Since the call already happened…"

"It will take time." She was all too familiar with the routine. "Anything on dad's computer?"

"Some guy on guy stuff, nothing illegal. No suspicious web browsing. I'll comb through his emails later, but I want to get back to Ashley's unit."

"Why? Think you have something?"

"I don't know what it means, but I was right. Her hard drive was scrubbed."

"English, Taylor."

"A program was used to overwrite all the sectors multiple times. It's the same thing the government does to clean hard drives before disposing of them."

"You mean a fourteen-year-old kid somehow got access to a government program?" Boy, that opened up a whole huge can of worms.

"That's the problem. These programs have been around for years—they're used by every level of government and also available on the web. Anyone could have sent it to her or she could have Googled it for herself."

"Well hell, that doesn't help." Lucy squeezed a lemon into her water. It felt so good to wring the life out of something right now. A stray seed caught in her wedding ring. She flicked it clear.

"It might if I can trace it back to its source. Anyway, I'm working a reconstruction program. It compares each sector on the hard drive then—"

"How long?"

"Maybe as early as tomorrow. If we're lucky."

"I need it sooner. And don't let up on her ISP. We need her emails and instant messages."

"They promised them this afternoon."

"Hey, is Fletcher still around?"

"The ICE guy? Haven't seen him. But you know, some people actually take weekends off. Besides, I've got things covered here." Taylor was territorial with sharing "his" cases with other agencies.

"He worked a bust with me this morning."

"How come I wasn't in on it?"

"Because it wasn't your case." It was like running a nursery school, reassuring the boys they'd all have their chance to play. "Anyway, do me a favor and call him, let him know I'll need him tomorrow morning. We're going to bring in the Canadians—it's some kind of bank holiday up north this weekend and they're taking advantage of the long weekend."

His snort of disapproval carried through the phone. "Yeah, some holiday, taking a tour to meet a little kid for sex."

"Call me when you find anything." She hung up just as Burroughs slid into the seat across from her.

"So, how's your kid?" he asked, nodding to her phone.

Guilt flushed her. She needed to call home. "It was Taylor. Nothing new."

"Uh-huh." He looked at her over top of his menu. "Taylor. He has a thing for you, you know."

She waved his comment aside. Last thing she needed was water cooler gossip. "He's just excited. First big case."

"I can't get over how well orchestrated this was," were his first words after ordering a bacon cheeseburger and onion rings. "Scripted."

Lucy shook her head without even realizing it. Stopped herself and masked her emotions. Best not to get too involved—baring that, at least not to reveal her involvement. But Ashley's artwork had tipped the scales for her. Such raw pain, gnawing despair. "Not by Ashley."

"Of course by Ashley. Who else?"

"No. I don't think she's in control."

"So you think she was coerced? That she's a victim?" He tilted his head, thinking, then frowned. "No. I don't buy it. She's been planning this a long time—maybe all summer if what the mom said is right. She had a definite objective, knew exactly what she was doing, we just need to figure out where she's headed."

"We can't write her off as a routine runaway," Lucy protested. She didn't care if the evidence so far indicated otherwise, she had to go with her gut.

"Oh, I don't think there's anything routine about it. I think Ashley's leading us on a wild goose chase—she is in control. And we're just puppets."

"She's only fourteen for chrissakes."

"A fourteen-year-old who is smart, knows what she wants, and had the resources and freedom to put her plan in action. Trust me, she's playing us."

Even though she disagreed with him, it was too early in the case to ignore any possibility. "Okay, walk me through it."

"Right. She leaves from school, why? To buy time."

"Plus mobility," Lucy put in. "No bus stop near her house and she doesn't drive."

"So she must have wiped her computer before she left for school. Something like that has to take several hours at least."

"Not to mention taking the camera card and setting up her alibi with her mom last week."

"What fourteen-year-old thinks that far ahead? When I was her age, I couldn't remember to make sure I had clean underwear for the next day." Burroughs tapped his fork handle against the tabletop as he thought. "Told you. Scripted."

Their food arrived and both of them dug in. Lucy had ordered a breakfast platter, tons of protein, it should keep her going until she stopped to eat again. Lord only knew when that might be.

"What about money?" he asked, wiping ketchup from his chin.

Lucy shrugged. "No bank account or credit cards that she could access. Mom gave her twenty a week in allowance, who knows how much she had on hand in cash."

"Twenty a week? Sheesh, don't tell my kids. They get five and that's only if they do all their chores."

They finished eating and returned to the Impala. Lucy stood with her car door open for a few minutes while Burroughs cranked the AC's blower. She remembered warm Indian summers when she was a kid in Latrobe, the air heavy with the smell of yeast and hops from the Rolling Rock brewery, but never this hot.

While she waited, she leafed through Ashley's binder again. Raw images of screaming mouths, tortuous geometric shapes resembling mazes with no escapes, and few images of hope.

On the last page, set apart by several blank pages, was a portrait. A young man slaying a demon. Standing beside him, hidden by shadows, was a feminine figure with a sword drawn. It was hard to tell if she was poised to stab the man in the back or come to his aid.

Which was Ashley? The victim cowering in shadows... or the assassin, ready to strike?

Chapter 11

"Let's get back to the house." Lucy climbed into the broiling car.

"You think the mom is hiding something from us?"

"No. But I need to get a better feeling for Ashley. What kind of kid she was, what kind of person she would turn to for help. There has to be something in the house."

Lucy's phone rang when they were about three miles away from the Yeager's house. It was Walden. "We may have something. A body."

"Where?" she asked, grabbing a pen and her notebook.

"Tastee Treet on Route twenty-two just past Murrysville. A young woman. While working the scene, they found Ashley's ID."

"Is it Ashley?" Her voice remained neutral but her molars clamped down with a pulverizing force that spiraled pain into her jaw.

"Don't know for sure."

"We're about ten minutes away. Stay with the mom. I don't want her hearing anything about this until we know what's going on."

"No problem."

She hung up and repeated what he'd said to Burroughs. The slightest frown was Burroughs' only response as he steered the Impala through the traffic. Minutes later, she spotted the crime scene: fire truck, ambulance, a smattering of police cars from several jurisdictions all crowded a tiny dirt parking lot. Men in uniform milled around the outside of the ramshackle shack that housed the Tastee Treet.

Burroughs slid the Impala between an Allegheny County Sheriff's vehicle and the Murrysville volunteer fire rescue squad. Two kids in their late teens, wearing firefighter turnout pants, sat on the rear bumper of the squad. They looked up at Burroughs and Lucy but didn't meet their eyes, instead their gaze slid away, back down to the hard-packed dirt. Lucy spotted a puddle of vomit nearby and guessed it belonged to one of them.

The building itself was small, maybe 700 square feet. It listed to one side. Lucy had the urge to tell the group of cops and firemen leaning against the far wall, laughing and smoking, to move around to the opposite side of the building, push the other way and try to re-balance things. White paint was peeling from around fogged windows, the roof was missing several shingles and the cardboard signs with the daily specials had rotted in place within their Plexiglas holders.

She pushed open the front door, setting off a much too cheerful jangling from a brass bell. A half dozen police officers were gathered at the counter, laughing.

"Jeezit, it's not a carnival," she muttered.

"They heard the FBI was coming, didn't want to miss their chance at the big time," Burroughs said.

"Help me clear them out." She plastered a smile on her face and addressed the crowd. "Gentlemen, I'm Supervisory Special Agent Guardino from the FBI. Who is in charge here?"

An Allegheny County deputy turned from where he'd been chatting with the other men at the counter. "Well now, Special Agent from the FBI, we've just been trying to figure out why you'd be interested in our little case." He shifted his duty belt, adjusting the weight, and glanced at his audience. "This sure as hell ain't no case of domestic terrorism."

"Unless the French did it," a Murrysville officer put in. "Get it? French fries?"

The few chuckles and nods he received in response gave Lucy some idea of what she might be dealing with. And why the two boys out front had lost their lunches.

"I called the FBI," Chief Deputy Dunmar said as he entered from the door behind the counter. "Get your butt off that counter, Lassiter, and clear these people out of here." The deputy jumped to his feet. "Now!"

Lucy gave Burroughs a nod. "See, that's how it's done." She beamed at Dunmar and for once it wasn't fake. "Thank you, Chief Deputy. Mind running over things for myself and Detective Burroughs?"

"No problem at all," he replied, his shirt buttons threatening to spring off as he puffed up with importance. "If you follow me."

He led them behind the counter, past the soft serve machines and deep fryers. One of the fryers was covered with clear plastic, a smattering of black fingerprint powder visible beneath it.

A small room was chiseled out of the back corner of the building. In it there was a card table and two folding chairs. A young woman with blond hair pulled back into a hair net and wearing a polyester, robin-egg blue uniform, sat at the table, her face buried in her hands, crying. A uniformed police officer stood beside her, looking miserable.

"This our reporting witness?" Burroughs asked in a low voice that barely carried over the sound of the girl's weeping.

Dunmar nodded. "But everything you want to see is out here."

He pushed open an emergency exit door in the rear of the establishment. Here there was a green metal dumpster and several large airtight liquid waste containers. One of them had the lid off and a foul stench emanating from it.

Burroughs hid his retch with a cough. Dunmar didn't bother to hide anything. Instead, he freshened the wad of chaw in his mouth and stood at the door, not going any closer.

The smell wasn't the usual odor of decomp. Instead, it blended odors of burnt flesh, fried doughnuts, and French fries into a sweet and greasy melody of death.

Lucy breathed through her mouth, leaving Burroughs fumbling for his notebook as she approached the vat. If not for the burnt flesh part, the smell might have been at a home at any McDonalds or Krispy Kreme.

"Actually not too bad once you get used to it," the guy from the medical examiner's said. He squatted on the far side of the container, taking photos.

"I think that's what bothers me the most." Lucy stayed clear as he positioned a ruler beside a wet footprint and shot another picture. "Okay if I take a look?"

"Yeah, the crime scene guys finished a while ago. I was just keeping busy until you got here. I'm ready to roll anytime you are."

"Roll?"

He nodded to a hand truck parked beside his van. "Thought it'd be best to take the whole vat in. Empty her in the lab, save all the trace."

"Good idea." She looked over her shoulder. Burroughs was now engaged in earnest conversation with Dunmar, comparing notes on the Steelers' home opener. Lucy crept closer to the barrel. It stood chest high, she had to bounce up on her tiptoes to get a good peek inside.

Maybe Burroughs was the smart one. Avoiding this. A woman had been folded into the vat of oil.

Her hair was brown, long like Ashley's, swirling around in a mass of overcooked French fries and other debris congealed into a waxy yellow substance that caked the top of the liquid.

"Rigor's come and gone," the assistant Medical Examiner said. "She's been dead since sometime Friday. Can't say for sure until we get her back for the PM. Want to see more?"

"Yes, please." Lucy forced a polite smile, even though every instinct in her body absolutely, positively did *not* want to see more of the mutilated corpse.

He drew on a thick, black rubber glove that covered him up to his armpit and reached in, snagging the corpse's hair and pulling her head up. Golden brown oil ran off the curves and planes of the woman's face and neck. What it left in its wake was something Lucy was certain she wouldn't be able to banish from her dreams for months.

There was no face. The eyes were gone, faint rims of the orbital bones gleaming white around a red, swollen mass of blisters. The nose looked like some creature had bitten it off, leaving behind a chalky white mass of irregular tissue. And the mouth—no lips, no tongue, a few teeth gaping from a large hole gnawed from grey-white-red swollen flesh.

"Did the same with her hands," the ME said. "I figure he maxed out the fryer to about four -hundred degrees then plunged her face into it, held her there a good long time."

He released the jaw and the head fell forward, splashing in the oil, disturbing the layer of wax-coated debris.

"We found more teeth inside in the fryer pan. It'll take a few days but we can probably get a decent dental reconstruction. That and DNA are gonna be your only hope of ID'ing her."

"It's not Ashley." The knowledge eased the stranglehold locking her jaw muscles. She stepped away from the container and took a deep breath.

"You sure?" Dunmar asked. "They found her wallet in the trashcan inside the employee break room."

"I'm sure. Ashley only had one piercing in her ears. This woman has four earrings on this side plus a cartilage piercing."

The ME let the woman slip back down beneath the oil. "You looking for someone named Ashley?"

"Missing kid from Plum," Burroughs said, coming closer but not looking into the container.

The ME frowned. "Might have something that helps." He closed the lid on the dead woman and trudged over to his evidence case. "One of her hands was shoved up against the lid of the container. The flesh was gone, as you can imagine, but I found these intertwined with the bones and soft tissue that remained. Photographed and bagged them before any more damage could occur."

He handed Lucy two plastic evidence bags. One contained an oily hank of long, dark hair, torn out by the roots. The other the remnants of a Piaget watch. The band had been mostly destroyed,

97

the crystal was shattered, but the engraving on the back was clear: *To Ashley, love Dad.*

Lucy wordlessly handed them to Burroughs who took one glance and reached for his cell.

"I figured our victim grabbed them as her attacker held her down in the fryer."

A vision of Ashley holding another woman down in the vat of boiling oil filled Lucy's mind. The stench of frying flesh filled her throat, gagging her. Could Ashley have done this?

Could Lucy have been wrong about everything?

Chapter 12

Burroughs hung up his phone. "Dad confirmed it—he gave Ashley the watch for her birthday last year. Said she never took it off."

Lucy nodded, still trying to absorb the new information. "Call me when you have any results," she told the ME and turned to Burroughs and Delmar. "I'm going to talk with our witness. You know her name?"

"Doris. Doris Sykes."

She left the men outside and returned to the break room, relieving the uniformed officer. Scooting the second chair beside Doris's, she sat down and took the girl's hand in hers. Doris's shoulder shook with silent sobs, but after a few moments she looked up.

"Doris, my name is Lucy Guardino. I'm with the FBI. Can you tell me what happened today?"

Tears still streaming down her face, Doris nodded silently. Her eye makeup was clumped into pockets of baby blue and black, threatening to topple from over-mascaraed lashes with each blink. She sniffed and took the tissue Lucy handed her, blowing her nose.

"How old are you, Doris?" Lucy began when the girl didn't speak.

"Eighteen."

"Eighteen. Good." Doris kept nodding, so Lucy bobbed her head as well. "How long have you been working here?"

"Almost two years. Well, two summers. But I graduated in June, so nows I'm full time here." She straightened, dabbing at her eyes and succeeding in smearing her makeup further. "Got promoted to Assistant Manager after I graduated."

"Assistant Manager. Wow, that's great. So you have keys to lock up?"

"Yes ma'am. I work three to closing Wednesday through Friday. All day on weekends—I'm in charge then."

"That's a lot of responsibility. Who's the manager?"

"Mr. Tillsbury. Well, he's the owner. Opens weekday mornings at eleven, gets things started for lunch."

"He works alone until you get here at three?"

She shook her head in scorn. "Mr. T? Nah, he just makes sure the bank deposit adds up and does the ordering. He's usually out of here by one at the latest. And he never comes in on Saturday or Sunday."

"So today you opened. Who else was here?"

"Ronny Clarkson, he only works weekends. He's a lazy sumthin-sumthin. That's why I was the one emptying out the trash in here, that's how come I was the one—" Her hand covered her mouth even as she kept on talking, trying to shove the terrible words and images that accompanied them back down inside. "I was the one who went out there, found that—her—the body." Fresh tears started up. "Is it," she gulped and tried again, "is it Noreen?"

"Who's Noreen?"

Doris shot a quick glance over her shoulder and leaned forward until they were shoulder to shoulder. "Don't tell Mr. T, promise? I don't want to get her in no trouble."

"Noreen works here?" She nodded. "What's her full name?"

"Noreen Crenshaw. She only works part time, has a baby to watch out for. Usually works eleven to four on weekdays."

The woman had been dead more than twenty-four hours, the ME had said. Yesterday. Right around the same time Ashley was last seen. "Was Noreen here yesterday?"

Another nod. "Most of the time. Said she had to leave, so I came in early. Place was empty."

"You mean she left it unlocked? No one was here?"

"She locked the register. Not like there's much else to steal except hotdogs. And who'd take the bother to cook them themselves? This time of year the place is always empty. Mr. T only keeps it going 'cause if he sells it, his wife would make them move to Florida and he don't want to go."

Lucy tried to steer Doris back on track. "You spoke with Noreen? Was anyone here with her? Any customers?"

"Doubt it. She must have been real bored 'cause the place was as clean and spotless as I've ever seen it. Everything scrubbed down and shiny."

"What exactly did she say? When did she call you?"

Doris slipped a cell phone from her pocket and flipped it open. "We didn't talk. She texted me."

Damn technology. Didn't people actually talk anymore?

Doris tapped a blue enameled nail on the phone keys then turned the screen around. GOTTA GO, SORRY, CANT HELP IT, N

"I just figured it was something to do with her baby."

Lucy looked at the time stamp. 2:11 pm yesterday. She pulled out the picture of Ashley. "Have you ever seen this girl before?"

"Not in person. But her picture was on the bus pass I found in the trash with that wallet the police took."

"She's never been in here?"

She sucked in her lower lip as she concentrated. "No ma'am."

"Do you have any pictures of Noreen?"

Doris pushed back her chair and reached behind Lucy to the bulletin board. "Here's one of her and me right after graduation."

Lucy took the photo. Two smiling faces beamed out at her. Noreen's brown hair was pulled back far enough to reveal a sparkling array of earrings dangling from her ears. Five from the left and four from the right.

"I need to take this. Did Noreen have a car?"

Doris frowned. "Yeah. But it's not here."

"What kind of car is it?"

"Toyota Corolla, blue, hatchback. Real old and pretty rusty."

Lucy didn't think she could get anything else helpful from the manager. "Thanks, Doris, you've been a great help." She started out the door, then couldn't help herself, and turned back. "You said Noreen had a baby?"

Doris nodded, tears seeping from her eyes again. "Jared. He's four months old. Looks just like his mommy."

Lucy forced herself not to think of the motherless baby, instead imagined Noreen's last moments, begging for her life, for her baby's future, fighting her attacker.

Could Ashley have done that to another girl? Did she have the strength? Not just physical strength, but the psychological will it took to dehumanize and kill.

She turned to her resident expert and called Nick. She told him what they'd learned so far. "I've heard of teenagers who kill in groups or go on sprees, but what about carefully planned murder? A murder whose only purpose was to cover your tracks?"

"If it is her, the fact that she chose a target who looked like her but overlooked details like the earrings is definitely indicative of juvenile thinking," he said. "As is wiping the place clean, destroying the face and fingerprints but not thinking of DNA and dental records."

"Yeah, what's with that?" Lucy asked, tapping her wedding ring against the phone, wishing she could see his face as he spoke—a lot of times Nick would lay out persuasive arguments both for and against a position, seeing both sides clearly, but she could always tell by his face where his heart really lay. "These days with *CSI* catching criminals in thirty seconds flat, you'd think a kid would think of that. It's as if our killer can't really focus for long—he comes up with big ideas but can't implement them fully."

"Like a kid with ADHD," Nick suggested.

"Or an adult. I don't think it's her," she said flatly.

"Okay." His neutral tone. The therapist's tone. Which meant he disagreed with her.

"I'm going with my gut here."

Silence. "You usually do. You gonna make it home for dinner?"

"No." Even if she could take the time, she wouldn't—working a case this messy, she felt like she was contaminated. It made her queasy to think of bringing it home with her. "Megan doing okay?"

"No more fever—just moping about maybe missing soccer on Monday."

"Give her a kiss and hug for me." Megan still let her father touch her, even if she rebuked Lucy's shows of affection. She hesitated. Best to face the music. "My meet tomorrow with the Canadians got moved to the morning. I won't make it to Mass with you guys."

The fact that he didn't even bother to sigh was a bad sign. As if he knew all along she wouldn't be there with her family. "I'll tell her."

Guilt stabbed through her. Not only at missing time with her family but at making Nick play the bearer of bad news. Again. She stroked the phone, wishing it was his face—or Megan's. What else could she do? "Love ya."

She hung up and returned outside where Burroughs, Dunmar, and several other law enforcement officers were overseeing the ME's removal of the container. From a distance, of course.

"This is your victim." She handed Noreen's photo to Dunmar and told him about the missing car. "She worked here and went missing between two and three pm yesterday."

Dunmar arched an eyebrow at her as if she were a particularly bright pupil who had surprised him. "That so? Damn shame there's no security cameras or any other way we could track the vehicle from here. But I'll get my boys and the Staties working on any traffic cams, see if we can get a bearing on which way it went."

It was a long shot, but worth a try. She looked out past the Tastee Treet at the traffic zooming by, bumper-to-bumper on Route 22. A very long shot.

"I think we should try to cover any possible dumping grounds within a five to ten minute radius. He wouldn't have wanted to leave his vehicle here for long while he dumped Noreen's."

Burroughs cleared his throat at that. "*He?* Who's to say Ashley didn't kill that girl and steal her vehicle?"

"We need to cover every angle," Lucy argued. "If Ashley was taken from here, then it's a whole new ballgame. We should see if we can find anyone who was here yesterday, maybe saw Ashley or anyone else."

"*If* there was anyone else."

Lucy hated to admit it, but she was starting to wonder herself. This whole case was screwier than the snake handlers she'd dealt with this morning—and she'd thought they rang the bell on the whacky-meter.

She looked back at the forlorn Tastee Treet. *Ashley, what the hell have you gotten yourself into?*

–

Ashley couldn't tell if she'd been there for hours or days. The complete absence of light and outside sound made her too anxious to venture away from her pole. She clung to her pole, at the bottom of a dark pit, close to the molten lava that formed the earth's core—hot and dark and empty, like the sixth level of Hell in Shadow World. That'd been the hardest level to beat. It was where she'd lost Draco. Her friend, her ally, her love.

Just like she'd lost Bobby. Or had Bobby lost her? Was he dead already or sitting in his own Hell worried about her?

At first she called for help. Until her voice died. Then she tried to think of ways to escape—hard to consider when engulfed in all-consuming blackness.

Eventually, she found herself treating her leash as a crutch, like a rope a blind woman would use, keeping her from falling—or worse.

She gave up on walking. Even after drinking, she was too dizzy when she stood. Better to keep her body pressed against the solid ground—anchored, secure. One hand wrapped around her pole for security.

When she grew thirsty again, she tried to ignore it. But the heat sucked the moisture from her. The more she ignored her thirst, the way her tongue felt swollen, her teeth aching from being so dry, the worse it got. The thought of venturing back out into the darkness made her stomach rise up in rebellion, she would have puked if she had any spit to swallow.

She needed water. Or she would die.

Reluctantly, she let loose of her pole and crawled in the direction where the bucket and commode sat on her left.

It was gone.

Panicked, she flailed out, lying flat on her belly, kicking and moving her arms as if swimming over the vinyl floor, inching along, guided by her tether. Her thirst escalated with her terror. Without water, she would die.

She found herself gulping, swallowing air, her tongue so parched it filled her mouth like a dead dish rag. As dead as she'd be if she didn't find the water. Dead, bloated, rotting, stinking, dead. Dead. Dead.

Terror blinded her more than the lack of light. She tried to scream, to wail, to cry for help, but couldn't force any sound other than a weak whelp. Her entire body rattled with pain and fear.

Had someone moved the water? Taken it away? Was someone there with her, watching her? Invisible, silent?

After what felt like hours of searching, thrashing, crawling, her body pressed against the floor the only thing telling her which direction was up, she surrendered.

Sprawled on the floor like a drunk in the gutter, her fingers and toes and face numb, heartbeat thundering in her head, eyes blinking, unseeing but still able to squeeze out a few tears.

"Move, dammit, move." The sound of her voice was better than the sound of her frantic sobbing.

She lay frozen except for her chest heaving, breathing so hard and fast, she was dizzy as if falling and there was no bottom. Nothing except another level of Hell, she thought with an absurd giggle.

This wasn't Shadow World. This was no game. "I can't. I can't do this. I'm going to die."

She knew she should be thinking of all the good times, of her parents, of her friends... but her mind was a total blank. What good times? She had a faint memory of a little girl being pushed on a swing, but it didn't feel like it had happened to her, it felt like something she'd seen once in a movie. Or a Hallmark commercial.

And her parents? They probably hadn't noticed she was gone. Maybe they were even happy, relieved they wouldn't have to bother with her anymore. Friends? There was only Bobby...

That thought brought fresh tears. What if the man had caught Bobby, killed Bobby—because of her?

He didn't deserve that; he'd only been trying to help her. God, if he was dead, it was all her fault... and the worst thing was, she'd never even had the chance to finally meet him in person, to tell him how she felt about him.

The pattern from the linoleum imprinted itself on her face as she lay there, weeping tears so thick with salt they scratched her eyes and refused to fall.

She wasn't stupid, she knew what the man was going to do to her, she'd heard the stories, seen the movies. Raped and tortured and beaten and killed. That's how they all ended.

There were never any happy endings. Never.

Ashley squeezed her eyes so tight it made her head hurt. No, she wasn't going to think about that. She was going to get control and get the hell out of here.

Focus. She started with simple things: breathing. Slow, deep, steady.

She sat there for several minutes, concentrating on her breathing, her mind still reeling from her panic attack. No more. She was in control. Just like Vixen, her character in Shadow World.

That thought brought a laugh. Shadow World, a land of darkness where characters fought overwhelming odds to survive. She'd won, beaten everyone—well, not her, but her character, Vixen had.

Vixen was at home in darkness. Darkness was her friend. Too bad Vixen wasn't here instead of Ashley.

Her heart still fluttered with fear, but the pounding in her head vanished. Soon she could feel her hands and feet again. *Good. Now keep moving, find the water. You need the water to survive.* This time it wasn't her voice, but Vixen's giving her direction. Giving her strength.

She started crawling once more, slower, her hands searching the floor before her. The darkness was so complete that it felt as if her hands weren't part of her. Disconnected. How well she knew that feeling, it had gotten her through a lot of hard times.

Harder times yet to come, the voice behind her eyes whispered. She froze. Lay there on the dirty floor, sweltering in the stench of death, divided between the here and the gone. It would be so very easy to let go. Go away. Maybe forever this time?

No. Not until she found the water. She wasn't going to give the bastard the satisfaction of surrendering so quickly. She had to stay alive. She would—

Her hand flailed out, searching for the bucket. Hit it too hard, too fast, sent it rolling over onto its side.

Warm water spread out along the floor, her palms slip-sliding through it as she yanked the bucket, tilted it upright. Had she saved enough?

She lowered her hand into the depths of the five-gallon bucket. Found a scant inch remaining at the bottom.

Splashed the water as if that could magically multiply it. Brought her hand, dripping, out of the bucket, and squeezed the water and sweat into her mouth. Her shirt was soaking wet, clammy with the heat, stinking of sweat and fear. She took it off, desperately wrung it out over the bucket.

Lowered her hand again, measured the water with her finger. Just shy of her first knuckle.

Shit. She swallowed. Her mouth was dry. The air was too heavy to breathe; she was going to drown in it even as she died from dehydration. Heat stroke. It drove people crazy, she'd seen a video in health class on it.

Things had just gotten a hell of a lot worse.

She rolled over on her back. The view was the same as when she was on her belly, unremitting blackness swallowing her whole.

Lay her head back, kept her eyes open—looking for what, she didn't know.

Bottom line, she was going to die. Not even Vixen could save her this time.

Chapter 13

When they arrived back at the Yeager house, Lucy wasn't surprised to see that Walden had anticipated her needs. She and Burroughs found him sitting at the dining room table, an art deco glass and chrome monstrosity that could seat twelve, leafing through the family photo albums.

"Got anything?" she asked, taking the chair beside him and reaching for a stack of prints.

She flipped through them: all of Melissa in her modeling days, gaunt and hungry looking, her body almost as flat as a boy's. These weren't professional shots, they were candid pictures, presumably taken by Gerald.

"Plenty more like that," Walden said, indicating the numerous shots of Melissa. "Not so many of the kid."

"Not too surprised," Burroughs said. "Turns out dad's into boys these days."

Walden raised an eyebrow.

"Legal boys," Lucy clarified. "Barely. Where's the mom?"

"Convinced her to take a shower, change clothes. She's been real quiet since you left. The Sheriff sent two deputies to camp out for the duration. They're handling all communications through their command center. And we've got mom's sister from Philly coming to stay with her—she wasn't real happy about that, though."

"The body in Murrysville wasn't hers," Burroughs told Walden. "But Ashley's wallet was found nearby. And someone definitely didn't want this body to be identified quickly."

"Think they were trying to pull a switch? Make us think Ashley was dead?"

Lucy looked up at that. "Not unless they think we're blind. The girls were the same general build and coloring but what kind of idiot wouldn't notice the piercings?"

"An adolescent idiot," Burroughs said, apparently channeling Nick. "Someone nervous, exhilarated with getting away with murder, not thinking clearly."

"You think the kid is working with the Unsub?" Walden asked. His face was its usual impassive blank slate, but his eyes had narrowed ever so slightly. "Or she *is* the Unsub?"

"I'm just saying, don't assume anything," Burroughs replied.

They all nodded to that. It was Cop 101. Trust no one, assume nothing.

Still, it wasn't a leap in logic Lucy was ready to make. She glanced through the windows to where the butt-ugly command center still sat. "Any problems?"

"Nope. They're doing a pretty good job of coordinating everything. As long as Dunmar has the press's ear, he's happy."

"Fine with me. Did you eat?"

He seemed surprised by the question. "Yeah, had some pizza."

"Good." She shivered in the cold house and didn't think it was from the air-conditioning. "Gather up this stuff and write out a receipt. I'll go tell mom we're leaving." She turned to Burroughs. "You want to tag along? We can always use an extra pair of eyes."

"You're gonna let little old me in that big, fancy federal building of yours?" He said with wide-eyed innocence, batting his lashes. "I thought you feds never asked for help from us local yokels."

Lucy smiled at his use of the term. "This one does. But only if you don't have anything better to do."

"Got some dirty socks that need washing, guess they can wait."

-

Walden left, hauling the photo albums with him. Burroughs stood by as Lucy searched for her car. She clicked the remote but no chirp answered her. The cul-de-sac was empty of cop cars except for Burroughs' Impala, the dreaded Mobile Command Center, Dunmar's Expedition, and a Plum Borough squad. The other official vehicles had been replaced by news vans, cameramen at the ready.

"Where did you leave it?" he asked, barely hiding his amusement.

"I left it with a local yokel—an officer from Plum Borough PD," she told him. Shadows were lengthening, transforming the tall, boxy houses into grim gothic strongholds.

She jogged down to the end of the street where the initial police barricade had been. The Subaru sat a block away, parked at the curb in front of a fire hydrant.

Burroughs laughed. "Two to one he left you a ticket."

She ignored him, still uncertain of what to make of the detective's constant hovering. He'd been helpful, but also attentive above and beyond inter-agency cooperation. Lucy's cell phone rang. "Guardino here."

"LT, I got something from the cell records," Taylor's voice loud, buzzed with excitement. "Dozens of messages from some guy, screen name of Draco. They end about a month ago, but I traced the guy and he's in Pittsburgh. Real name is Fegley, Robert Fegley."

"Give me the address." She repeated it to Burroughs who scribbled it in his notebook. He grabbed his cell phone as she spoke with Taylor. "Background?"

"Nada. Clean slate. Kid's only seventeen, though. There could be something in a sealed juvie record."

She glanced at Burroughs who was working his own phone. "Nothing from us. Guys at Zone Five don't show any history with the address either."

"What about her computer?" she asked Taylor.

"Still working on it. Oh yeah, that ICE guy Fletcher's pissed he has to work tomorrow. Even tried to con me into going instead, said he'd come in and work Ashley's computer for us."

Just what she needed, cyber nerds in a turf war. "You saying you need help?"

"Nah, I'm good. Collared some of the High Tech taskforce guys to help with the minor stuff. We've got pizza coming—"

"This isn't a party, Taylor." The High Tech Computer Crimes Taskforce was where Taylor had worked before he left to attend Quantico and become a full agent. "Do you need Fletcher or not? I can get ICE to sign off if you think he'd be helpful."

"The guy isn't even an agent or a computer forensic specialist, he's just a glorified desk jockey—"

Taylor still suffered from FNG Syndrome. On top of an already overly healthy ego. "So were you until this year," she reminded him. "If you need him, call him. Either way, he still has to work the UC op tomorrow."

"No, seriously boss, I'm in the zone here. I can handle it, honest."

"A girl's life may depend on it," she reminded him as she reached the Subaru. She was relieved when he took a minute to digest that before replying.

"I'll think about it. Don't worry, we'll bring her home, LT."

She opened her car door and suppressed an oath. Nowicki had left her car unlocked. Taylor's voice still prattled in her ear, something about sectors and frags. Lucy reached below the driver's seat, checked her back up Glock 27 that was hidden there. Magazine was intact, one round still chambered.

The seat was moved back, probably to accommodate the six-something uniformed officer when he parked the car. She re-adjusted it to fit her five-five frame but then paused. Sonofabitch.

She didn't realize she'd said it out loud until Taylor went silent. "What's wrong, LT?"

"Hang on a sec, Taylor." The passenger seat was moved back as well. Just far enough for someone to get comfortable while they rifled through her glove box. Lucy didn't keep anything personal in there—kept her registration and insurance papers with her driver's license in her wallet.

An image of Megan sitting in that seat this morning, a slip of paper in her fingers... Shit. She reached over to the compartment on the passenger door. Found the doctor's bill from this morning.

With Megan's name, their address and phone number printed oh-so-neatly on it.

Folded into it was a business card. Belonging to Cindy Ames. On the back was drawn a smiley face with hearts for eyes.

Lucy scrunched the card into a wad of sharp edges, squeezing it into her fist.

Burroughs had pulled his car up beside hers, waiting. He rolled down his window. "What's up?"

"That reporter, Ames. You said she put your family on the news? She'd really sink that far, endanger a couple of kids that way?"

A vertical crease formed between his eyebrows as he frowned. "Yeah, she really would."

"I'm going to have to play hardball with her. My car's been searched by her."

"You can't know that."

"She left her calling card." She tossed the balled up business card through the window at him and raised her phone once more. "Taylor, I need you to track down the station manager for—" She looked to Burroughs.

"WDDE, Channel two," he supplied.

"Track them down and act real formal. Tell them you have a situation. That I was witness to a public," more than two people being public, "and on the record conversation where one of their reporters Cindy Ames committed libel—"

"You mean slander," Taylor said. "Libel's in writing."

"What are you, a lawyer?" She asked, then remembered he was. Had his JD although he'd never practiced law or taken the bar exam. And his PhD and a MBA. Damn whiz kid.

"So I'm like going undercover?" he bubbled.

A thirty-four year-old whiz kid-puppy.

"No," she said in a tone that usually made Megan jump. "You are *not* going undercover. You *are* representing the Bureau in an extremely delicate situation. Tell the manager that while I would prefer not to testify, unless he removes this particular reporter from the story, I may be forced to go public. Make sure he knows we have

Ashley's safety foremost in mind and appreciate his cooperation, all that jazz."

"Oh, cool. A con job. Should I say I'm the SAC? No, no, Assistant Special Agent in Charge would be more believable, wouldn't it? Or I could—"

"Taylor." He kept rambling. "Taylor."

"Yeah?"

"Burroughs and I are headed over to Fegley's. I want you to take however much caffeine you drink and cut it in half, all right?"

"Yeah, sure, but—"

"But what?" She started the Subaru and waved Burroughs into the lead.

"I don't drink caffeine, LT. It's bad for—" She hung up and followed Burroughs.

--

What would Vixen do? became Ashley's new mantra as she tried to gain control of the situation. Vixen would never surrender, for starts. Okay, then neither would she. After all, she *was* Vixen.

That was just a game, playing, a contrarian voice echoed through her mind. Ashley shook it off. Her fingers curled with the desire to cut, slice—just once, please—but she denied herself the pleasure. Vixen didn't cut—she killed.

First, know your enemy. Call him Mr. Skankypants. He'd thought this out, prepared, planned ahead. But what about Bobby? Had Mr. Skankypants prepared for Bobby?

Bobby's either dead or out there thinking you stood him up. Either way, forget about him, he's no good to you. The voice was Vixen's, all calm, cool, collected. The killing machine skulking in the shadows, hunting.

But Ashley couldn't let go of Bobby's face, pulled it up in her mind. He wouldn't give up, that just wasn't in him.

So then he's dead. Just like those girls who came before you, Vixen continued in her merciless drone. *What else did you think that stench was? Skankypants has killed before, he's planning to kill you next unless you move your ass and find a way out of here.*

Ashley had blocked out the odor that engulfed the room, but suddenly it was back, smothering her, dirt thrown on a grave.

A shallow grave, Vixen taunted.

Ashley rocked back and forth, gnawing on her fingernails. Not the thumb, the sharp one, that one she saved. But the others were fair game, all bitten down to the quick, ragged and torn. It wasn't as good as cutting.

She pulled her fingers from her mouth. Wolves and coyotes gnawed their legs off when caught in a trap, so did foxes…

A focused calm seized her. She stroked the inside of her left wrist, feathering old scars and the fresh welt that still ached with satisfying memory.

Bending her leg, she inched her sock off, tugging against the tight restraint that held it in place. The wire cable sat right above the bones jutting out from either side of her ankle, resting against her bare flesh. She couldn't get a regular finger between it and her skin, but her pinky finger she could jam in. Not much room, but she would make it work.

Poking, prodding, taking mental measurements, she decided it wouldn't be necessary to cut off the entire foot. First, she'd try lubrication, see if she could move the cable below the ankle joint. Then she might need to trim a little of the padding around her heel, that was all.

The picture in her mind didn't scare her or gross her out, instead it intrigued her. No way she could do all that with one fingernail. How long would it take to chew it off?

Could a person even do that?

Last resort, she promised herself. First the simple things. She slashed her nail along the skin above the cable, the searing pain a release, bringing her body and mind together in a sharply focused instant.

She was alive, she was in control, and she was going to stay that way. No matter what it took.

Chapter 14

Seventeen-year-old guy with a fourteen-year-old girl. Creepy, but not an uncommon situation. Lucy sighed, remembering her first serious boyfriend—seventeen to her fifteen.

Here in Pennsylvania, it could still technically be rape, since there were more than two years difference in age. As long as Ashley wasn't coerced. Then it was definitely rape.

If any sexual activity occurred. If Ashley was with Fegley. If she was alive.

Still, it was the best lead they had. Even if it did mean Burroughs was right and she'd been wrong about Ashley. Better wrong than to have a dead kid on her hands.

But how did Ashley's watch end up with Noreen's corpse? Could she and Fegley have killed together? Thrill seeking, loving the planning, the anticipation, never seeing Noreen as real, as a person, just an object to satisfy their needs.

Lucy scissored her jaw, breaking the tension, popping the ligaments until they crackled. Had she built up such a fantasy about Ashley being the pitiful, unloved teen that she'd blinded herself to the facts?

If so, maybe she should listen to her boss and stick to her office and desk, get off the streets.

She took advantage of the privacy to call home. Megan and Nick were watching football, assuring her that other than Pitt being down by twelve, everything was fine. She wanted to ask Nick for advice but didn't have the heart to interrupt their daughter-father bonding. Although she felt a little jealous that he was the one doing the bonding instead of her. Okay, maybe more than a little jealous.

Mostly she wanted her little girl back. The perfume of No More Tears. The singing together in the car, heads rocking, palms drumming. The pride that filled Megan's eyes every time she introduced her mother, the FBI agent.

Those times were long gone, maybe forever.

Next, she dialed her mom. She used the speakerphone, hating the hands-free ear thingy that looked like something out of *Star Trek*.

"Lucy, I thought you were working. Did you find that little girl?" Coletta Guardino answered.

"Not yet, but I've got a lead. Nick said you were going out tonight?" Silence. Lucy squirmed, adjusted her rearview mirror. More silence. "Mom, I'm not prying."

"Your father has been gone for twenty-five years. Don't I have the right to make friends? Find some happiness?"

Guilt settled down on Lucy's shoulders like a worn out shawl. Make that a hand-crocheted, labor of love, fingers bleeding from being pricked and worked to the bone, worn out shawl.

"Mom, you are the happiest person I know. You're so happy you wear people out. Between bridge and bingo and St. Vincent's and helping at the shelter and the library and your book club..."

"I know, I know." An exasperated sigh vibrated through the cell phone. "But this is different. This is someone who's interested in me. Just me. As a person."

"Tell me about him. What's he do? How'd you meet?" Lucy tried to keep her tone casual. Was her mother really dumb enough to meet a guy on the internet? Knowing what Lucy did for a living, the kind of predators she hunted?

"He's the sweetest man. Charlie, that's his name. He's sixty-one and he lost his wife to cancer three years ago."

"Go on. Charlie, does he have a last name?"

"He does."

"Mom." Lucy drew the syllable out, very aware she sounded just like Megan, but not caring.

"Once I told Charlie what you do for a living, he said you'd want to run a background check or something. He even gave me all the information you'd need to do it. Said people these days couldn't be too careful."

"Great. Give me the info and I'll take care of everything for you."

"No. I trust him. That's good enough for me."

"Not for me. Come on, Mom. You're smarter than this."

"I didn't need any background check on your father when I met him. I used my own good judgment, followed my heart."

"This," she almost said "creep" but hastily bit the word back, "man isn't Dad. And times have changed. A woman in your position can't risk—"

"A woman in my position can't risk wasting any time. I'll see you tomorrow. Love you."

The dial tone echoed through the car. Lucy stabbed the End button and cranked up the radio. Metallica, *King Nothing*. Perfect.

She drummed her wedding band against the steering wheel, wishing she could bang her head instead and wondering how many sixty-one-year-old white males, first name Charles, lived in south-western PA, and what the odds were that she could track down the right one before tonight.

-

Jimmy's heart staggered as he watched Ashley slice into her own flesh. He jumped up, toppling his chair, ready to run to her, save her.

No. Follow the plan. She has to see that she's powerless; she must surrender.

He righted the chair, sat back in front of the computer, hypno-tized. Ashley was mixing her blood with water, smearing it below the leash. He heard her grunts of frustration as she tugged and yanked on the metal cable, trying to force it over her ankle joint.

After a good half hour, she finally collapsed, hugging the support beam as if it were a lost lover.

She didn't cry like she had earlier. Instead she was talking to an unseen presence in the darkness. "Please. Please, help me."

She was calling to him. For him. Jimmy stroked his fingers across the image of her face as she pleaded.

"Yes, Ashley. I'll save you."

Step three, almost complete. Next came step four: offer a new reality.

Chapter 15

Burroughs led Lucy to an address off Fifth Avenue in Point Breeze. The Pittsburgh Center for the Arts was situated on a lush spread of grass a block away, adding a touch of class to the blue-collar neighborhood. She pulled up behind the detective's Impala and waited for him on the sidewalk. Her little blue Subaru looked distinctly unimpressive parked beside the oh-so-obvious unmarked cop car.

"Willie Stargell lived here." Burroughs swept a hand at the brick ranch house before them. They started up the drive. There was a long porch with a handicapped ramp.

"In this house?" she asked, noting the curled shingles on the roof and the stained, sagging gutters.

"Well, no. I don't think. This block—or maybe the next one over."

So much for Burroughs' treasure trove of baseball trivia. Lucy pushed the doorbell. The front door was open, only a screen door laced in white wrought iron curls barred their entry. She looked inside. A long, narrow hallway with oak hard wood floors led into a darkened space in the rear of the house.

A man appeared, flipping on a light switch, and she saw that the space was the kitchen. He stomped down the hallway as if he were climbing steps, his beer belly sloshing to and fro beneath his Steelers T-shirt. He wore Bermuda shorts—the kind that men of a certain age and physique really, really shouldn't ever wear—and had white socks on with dirty flip-flops.

"Yeah?" he asked by way of greeting.

"Detective Burroughs," Burroughs flipped his shield. "Is Robert Fegley here?"

"Where else would he be? What'cha want with Bobby?"

"We need to speak with him." Burroughs opened the screen door, not waiting for an invite.

The man, who appeared in his mid-forties, twisted his mouth as if he'd swallowed some stale beer and stayed where he was, blocking their way. "And you are?"

"His father. William Fegley. He ain't done nothing."

Lucy ignored the two men, more interested in the shadows playing against the wall of the kitchen beyond them. A motor whirred. The shadow of a man's head and torso, grotesquely deformed by the angle of the light became visible. It appeared much too low on the wall, slowly inching up as it grew larger, reminding her of the monster the boy and girl in Ashley's drawing fought. A bizarre half-man, half-machine demon.

The whirring stopped. A man's voice called from beyond the kitchen. "Who is it, Pops?"

"The cops. They want—"

"Have you found Ashley?" The unseen voice broke with excitement, now sounding boyish. The whirring resumed, higher pitched as if a motor were being pushed to burn out. Lucy edged past Fegley in time to see the shadow collapse.

A motorized wheelchair spun around the corner, filling the narrow corridor. "Where's Ashley? Is she okay?"

The boy-man in the wheelchair was tall but rail-thin. Spindly legs Velcroed into white plastic splints stuck out from a pair of gym shorts. His arms were equally wasted, one hand fastened to the wheel chair controls by another swath of Velcro. His face was the only thing animated, alive—the rest of his body was rigid, supported by belts and buckles, but his face... His face was the face of an angel.

Ashley's angel. From her artwork. Blonde hair, wavy, past his collarbones, skin unmarred by either the shadow of a beard or too much sun, crystalline blue eyes that tugged at Lucy as if she alone held the answers he needed.

"Ashley?" he said again, slumping back into the chair, his face falling into the shadows.

His father made a strangled noise but remained frozen as Lucy stepped past him and approached Bobby Fegley. When she drew near, she saw his tears. Twin tracks of anguish more heart-felt than any of the wailing she'd witnessed from the Yeagers.

"Bobby, I'm Lucy Guardino. I work with the FBI and I'm the one in charge of finding Ashley. Is there some place we can talk? I need your help."

He nodded, torqueing his face far enough to one side to wipe it against the roll of terry cloth that covered his neck support. Using two fingers, he maneuvered the chair's controls, spinning it ninety degrees and propelling it through the kitchen. His father's clomping footfalls sounded behind her and she turned.

"He's a minor, I should be there, watch over him." He strung the three sentences together into one exhalation, his expression a mixture of anguish and confusion.

"No, Pop. This is private," Bobby said without pausing or turning around. He crossed over a wide threshold into another room.

Instead of following Bobby, Fegley stopped at the kitchen table and turned to them, hands held palms up. "Someone's gotta work, ya know? And he's so damn independent, he don't need me—"

She caught Burroughs' eye and inclined her head. He engaged Fegley's attention while she sidled to the side, out of his line of vision, listening. Fegley sank into a chair and Burroughs took the seat opposite him.

"Bobby's seventeen?" Burroughs started. Fegley nodded. "Technically he doesn't need a parent present unless he requests it. And he hasn't done anything wrong, right?"

"Of course not! How could he? Look at the kid why don't cha?"

"What happened?"

Fegley blew his breath out, his face dampening to neutral. "His mom and him, in the car. He was twelve, so she lets him sit in the front seat, special treat, ya know? Anyway, they never saw it coming—eighteen-wheeler lost his brakes on the hill coming into Murrysville. Her airbag didn't help her none. His worked too damn good, snapped his neck."

Burroughs nodded in unison with Fegley's bobbing head, his body language mirroring the other man. Lucy left them and crossed into the next room. Originally a dining room, it had been converted to a bedroom suitable for a wheelchair bound boy. A hospital bed with an electric lift took up most of the space. But the center of attention was a large flat screen computer monitor rivaling anything they had at the Federal Building.

"My tech guys would love this," she told Bobby, watching as he stretched his thumb and first two fingers to manipulate a mouse. The screen came to life and with it Bobby's expression.

"Yeah, I use it for school, so my dad lets me dip into the settlement money for upgrades."

"You don't go to regular school?"

"I tried. At first. But," his voice caught, "it just didn't work out. So I do cyber school."

"Isn't that lonely?"

His right shoulder twitched, she guessed it was the closest he could come to a shrug. "Frank and Andy are here most of the time. And there's Dad."

"Frank and Andy?"

"My personal care assistants. They help me, ah," he glanced in the direction of a doorway leading into a large bathroom, obviously not part of the original house design, "get around and stuff."

She noticed the clear tubing running from beneath the leg of his shorts and down into a plastic collection bag. Kid had it rough, but he seemed to handle it all right. Better than his dad, five years later. She reminded herself to call Megan again as soon as they were done here.

"How did you meet Ashley?" She drew up a wheeled desk chair and sat beside him as he fiddled with the computer controls again. The screen filled with a graphic: Shadow World.

123

"Here. It's a MPRPG," he added.

"You lost me already."

"A multi-player role-playing game. The DM—domain master—creates a world and the rules and anyone, anywhere in the world with a computer can create a character and join in. Except Shadow World is special—the DM has it limited to players from western PA."

"Both you and Ashley played this game?"

"I play lots of these. This was the only one Ashley played—she was kind of obsessed. Ran five different characters."

"It was a way to be anyone she wanted?" Lucy hazarded a guess.

"Right. To tell the truth," his cheeks colored with a blush, "that's why I like SW best. Maestro, the DM, he's set it up so girls really get into it. It's not about killing monsters as much as being smart, working together, that kind of thing. Shadow World has more female players than any of the others, except for Sims of course."

"Of course," she agreed, having no idea what Sims were or why girls were drawn to them. "Can I see Ashley's characters?"

"I can show you the data sheets and avatars, but wouldn't you rather see the way she drew them? They're so life-like, it's amazing."

"You have copies of Ashley's artwork?"

The chair whirred as he toggled a switch to elevate him and extend his arm far enough to snag a handle. A large, shallow drawer popped open between them, revealing a stack of sketches inked with vibrant colors.

"She mailed them to me a few weeks ago. That was the last I heard from her. I figured it was her way of saying goodbye. After she found out the truth." His gaze dropped down to the disappointment his body had become. "I understand. I mean, what girl…"

"You and Ashley met in person?"

"No. We've talked online for almost a year, also on the phone and texted each other. Then she said she wanted to meet, that she needed my help. I sent her my address, told her I had a disability and couldn't leave the house easily. That's when the pictures came in the mail. I figured she must have come by, seen me, and freaked. I never heard from her again. She wouldn't answer her cell, my emails bounced, nothing."

"This was when?"

"Six weeks ago."

The week before Ashley ran away to her father's house.

"How did she act before then?"

"All summer she's been kind of weird. Making up new characters, then dropping them. She was doing great in the game—on track to win it all real soon. But somehow that freaked her out, like she thought she'd lose me or something. I told her we'd still be friends. But there were others hassling her. See, Shadow World is different than any other game out there. Maestro has his domain set up so that when someone wins the Crown of Symyria the game stops and all the other characters die in a cataclysmic battle."

"But this is all make-believe, so why were they so upset?"

His eyes widened as he shook his head at her ignorance. "You don't understand. Some of these guys have been playing SW since it started. To have a girl, just a kid, come along and win it? Not to mention losing characters that they've created and built—some of these characters were selling on eBay for like hundreds of dollars. But as soon as Vixen won the crown, they'd all be dead. Worthless."

"Vixen?"

"Ashley's main character. That top one."

Lucy slid the first sheet of sketch paper from the drawer and held it up. A muscular young woman, brown hair and brown eyes like Ashley's stared back at her. There the resemblance ended.

Vixen's eyes were slanted, exotic looking, blending into swept-back hair and high arched cheekbones, making her look like she was part fox. Her costume continued in the fox motif: fur pelts as bra and skirt, long talon-like nails, a bandolier weapons belt held a snaggle-toothed barbed sword over one shoulder, a curved dagger hung at her hip and she was barefoot. Her expression was one of haughty confidence, bold, daring—a lot like Melissa Yeager's runway photos.

Very different from the self-conscious, eyes averted, Ashley captured in the few family photos Lucy had seen. "Tell me about Vixen."

He rocked his neck from side to side until it cracked. "She was Ashley's favorite SW character, but not mine. You know the stories about boys raised by wolves? Think girl raised by foxes. A loner, cunning, no loyalty. She won by hiding in shadows, deception, taking advantage when others were chivalrous, swooping in for the kill if others hesitated. She stole, broke all the rules of civilized behavior—"

"Did she follow the rules of the game? Or was she cheating?" Lucy could well see the Ashley she was growing to know compelled to win at all costs, but she didn't think the girl would cross the boundaries and break the rules of the domain master.

"Oh no. She never broke any of Maestro's rules. But there are unwritten rules, you know? Lately, she didn't even seem to care about her allies. Only about winning. At any cost." His voice dropped.

"What was the cost, Bobby?"

"After she created Vixen, about five months ago, she killed off her other characters like they were cannon fodder. Good characters— people I considered friends. Then she led Draco to the slaughter."

From the tone of his voice, this fantasy world was more real than the world he found himself imprisoned in. Lucy shuffled the pages of artwork. She held up another sketch, this one of a woman in leggings and a heavy cloak, holding fire in the palm of her hand. "Who's this one?"

"That's Enchantra. She was the last to go. She was a powerful mage, could transform any element into its opposite: water to fire, earth to air, that kind of thing. She used her power to save people from the demons of Ocre. Destroying the demon king was one of the final challenges in the quest for the crown. Draco and Enchantra faced him together, side-by-side. Together they mortally wounded him. But as he lay dying, Vixen rushed in and beheaded him, dealing him the killing blow. All his power transferred to her."

Lucy remembered the drawing in the back of Ashley's notebook. The one that seemed so powerful yet so sad at the same time. "That's when she betrayed you? You're Draco, right?"

He nodded, his lips curled down as if trying to swallow a bitter pill. "I was Draco. Enchantra was wounded. We could have escaped together. But Vixen killed the king and unleashed his hordes of demons, trapping Enchantra. I tried to save her, but we both were killed."

His voice grew heavy as if he spoke of real people. Lucy looked away while he composed himself and turned to the next drawings. More prototypes of warriors similar to Vixen, but the final one intrigued her. It was a lovely, almost Raphelesque sketch of a woman with wings. "Who's this character?"

"Angel. No weapons except for her mind. She protected the innocent and avenged them by forcing villains to relive their crimes over and over every time they slept. My favorite of all Ashley's characters. I tried to encourage her to develop her, but she dropped her without even trying her in the game. Said she was too lame, too weak. That dreams never solved anything."

Lucy glanced at the date at the bottom. May. The same time Ashley created Vixen and embraced her dark side. The same time Melissa Yeager noticed problems with Ashley. "May. End of the school year, everyone's feeling the pressure. Did you notice any changes in Ashley? Did she confide in you at all?"

His finger twitched the toggle switch, sending the chair back and forth in a rocking motion. Bobby's version of pacing.

"Ashley had it rough last year. She transferred to Gateway from Plum, so she was the new kid. And she kind of had a crush on this older guy. She must have been obvious, 'cause some of the other kids were teasing her. Then the guy's girlfriend and her friends jumped Ashley in the girl's room one day."

"Was she hurt?" Lucy well remembered how vicious junior high girls could be.

"Not physically. Emotionally she was trashed. Then the bullying continued—there were web pages dedicated to outing Ashley as a lesbian, a whole cyber-smear campaign."

"Do you know who was behind it?"

"Ashley had some ideas but she didn't know what to do about it. But I did." His eyes lit up with the gleam of a true champion. "I spend all day with computers, so I'm pretty good with them. I set a trap—set up a voice mailbox and email addy using Ashley's info. When they started spamming it with hate mail, I traced it back. Two girls."

"Think they're involved in Ashley's disappearance?"

A smile quirked at his lips. "I doubt it. They've moved on to high school this year. And I zinged them good. Stole their address books and spammed the hell out of everyone in it—with all the evidence leading back to the girls. They got cyber-slammed by their friends but good."

"So that made Ashley feel better?"

He lowered his gaze, long, blonde eyelashes caressing his cheeks. "I wish. She felt kind of embarrassed by all the attention. I don't think she ever even told her parents about it all. But that's when we started getting more serious—I mean, don't get any ideas, nothing creepy, how could there be?" His gaze swept the length of his motionless body. "Ashley, she's so special, how could a guy not like talking with her? She's bright and funny and talented. If only she weren't so down on herself all the time."

"Did she ever email you any photos?"

"Photos? No. We talked about setting up a webcam but I didn't want her to see—you know. Frank helped me send her a photo of me, only my face. So she wouldn't know the truth. She used it to come up with Draco's look. Mainly we just chatted. Until she sent me her drawings."

As he spoke, he flicked the computer mouse and a tall, handsome boy with blond hair and piercing blue eyes appeared. His hair was long, tangled around his head in spikes ending in flames. His torso was naked except for a sash made of red and gold dragon scales that held a long-sword. His breeches were also made of dragon scales and his dagger was a dragon's claw.

"Nice. She put a lot of time into this."

He blushed again. "Yeah. Told you she had talent. I don't know why she wasted it on Vixen."

"Think maybe that was her way of standing up for herself? Battling the bullies?"

"Maybe. But seems like creeping around in shadows and going off on your own isn't the best way to do things."

"So, did she win? The Shadow World crown?"

His shoulder twitched in that heart-breaking almost-shrug. "Dunno. After Draco was killed, I was locked out of the game. Maestro wouldn't let me back into the site. A few days later was the last I heard from her. That's when we talked about meeting in person, when she said she needed my help. But she never said with what."

Lucy considered this. "If I put you in touch with my tech guys, would you let them access your email exchanges with Ashley?"

"Sure, anything to help." He rolled the chair back from the desk, met her gaze with a sorrowful expression. "Guess I let her down. I should have been a better friend, should have been there for her."

This boy had done more than either of Ashley's parents, that was for certain. Lucy laid her hand over his. "I think you were her best friend, Bobby. Her champion."

His hand jerked below hers, sending the chair rumbling backwards. "Fat lot of good I was. Please find her, help her. You can do that, can't you?"

"I'm trying my best."

Chapter 16

The Pittsburgh Federal building was a concrete and glass stump of a cube located just east of the Steelers training facilities on Carson Street. Burroughs had never been inside before, feds usually kept to themselves.

One more thing that set Guardino apart, he thought as she chauffeured him through security and got him a visitor's pass. He had to leave his weapon in a lockbox, but that was to be expected.

They took the elevator up to the second floor. Bleached oak doors, all closed, lined the hallway. Most of the doors were labeled: JOINT COUNTER-TERRORISM TASK FORCE. There were no names of the individuals who worked behind the blank doors, as if they were interchangeable cogs in Homeland Security's vast machine.

Guardino led him to the far end of the floor to a closed door that read: Sexual Assault Felony Enforcement, High Technology Computer Crimes Task Force, Innocent Images National Initiative, and Operation Predator.

"What are you guys, the redheaded step kids?" he asked as she swiped a key card to unlock it.

She shrugged. "They like the press we generate and give me the people I need to get the job done, so I can't complain."

They stepped into an antechamber with a secretary's desk, vacant given that it was Saturday. Behind the desk was a list of all the agencies working the multi-jurisdictional task forces under Guardino's command. Talk about your overachieving. There were at least two dozen. No wonder Guardino was so good at marshaling the troops and multi-tasking.

She opened another secure door and they entered a short hallway. Hand-lettered signs pointed in one direction for Innocent Images Initiative, another for Operation Predator. The door before them also had a handmade sign but this one was cross-stitched and framed. In delicate, old-fashioned style letters it proclaimed:

ABANDON HOPE ALL YE MOFUCKING PERVERTS.

Below the statement was an embroidered cheerful yellow smiley face.

"One of my guys is Army Reserves. He brought that back from Iraq, said cross-stitching made the downtime go faster."

Burroughs chuckled at the dark humor. To the side of the door, someone had stolen a caution sign and plastered across it: WARNING, ILLEGAL ACTIVITIES IN PROGRESS. ENTER AT YOUR OWN RISK.

Burroughs arched an eyebrow at her. "Take it this place isn't included in the nickel tour."

She laughed, a low, rumbling throaty sound that shook her entire body like she really meant it. God, did she have any idea how sexy it was to find a woman who knew how to really laugh instead of merely twitter or giggle as if laughing were against the law?

"No one except us comes back here. Not if they can help it." She unlocked the door and they entered a large open room that took up the rear corner of the building. Tinted windows lined two sides, a glass-walled office sat in one corner, and the rest of the area was filled with workstations and more computers than he'd ever seen outside of the time he and Kim had taken the boys to Florida and they'd toured Cape Canaveral's Mission Control.

"Wow. You could run the country from here."

"Not quite. Most of these machines aren't hooked into any government network. We only use them for dirty work—going online."

"Playing games with the bad guys. How many active cases do you have going at a time?"

131

They stepped into the glass-walled office. It wasn't large, but it felt spacious. Probably because she had her desk jammed back in the corner, leaving room to move freely around a small conference table and chairs.

"SAFE has one hundred-twenty-seven, I'm developing several dozen more with Innocent Images—when we're ready to issue warrants, the SAFE squad will handle those as well as any from Operation Predator that turn federal. We've a few multi-jurisdictional task forces running, including some international ones."

"Shit, how do you keep all that in your head?"

"I don't. Told you, I have good people working for me. I just set them loose and try to stay out of their way. Hardest part is we have almost two hundred cases pending trial—I'm dreading juggling the schedule once we get court dates."

"Two hundred? But you've only been here three months."

She leaned against her desk, which matched the rest of the decor: bleached wood, very modern. Except for the small tropical jungle she had growing along the sunny side. Not your grandmother's shriveled African violets, Guardino had cascading vines with delicate white and purple flowers that smelled better than any perfume, several orchids, and a few desert-like plants with weird-shaped flowers.

"Blame Taylor," she said. "His first case, he infiltrated a big web-ring, was able to nail one hundred thirty-one targets. Of course, word has spread, so we're not likely to get that lucky again anytime soon."

He looked around. The obligatory flag and portraits of the president and the FBI director lined one corner, other than that there was no vanity wall—unless you counted the photo of Guardino with a man and a girl, white-water rafting through rapids. That photo along with one of the three of them, smiling and dressed up for a Christmas card, were the only personal items on her desk.

"You got lucky reeling in those three Canadians," he reminded her. "Are a lot of your suspects international?" It'd be nice to think that all the perverts had been chased north across the border and far away from his kids, but he knew that was a pipe dream.

"You'd be surprised. Last year, while I was still in DC, we closed down a major sex trade/drug operation that was centered here in Pittsburgh."

That brought him up short. "You're kidding. Human trafficking here? C'mon, this is Pittsburgh."

"We worked with DEA, ICE, and Interpol, tracing Ecstasy from the Netherlands to Marseilles, where some of it was used to purchase women from Belarus and the Ukraine. Then the drugs and women were shipped to the port of Savannah, the drugs distributed all over the eastern seaboard, while the women were sent here."

He sat on the corner of her desk, taking care not to upset the plants. "How come I didn't ever hear anything about this?"

"The women were kept in a production studio two blocks away from Pittsburgh Police Bureau Headquarters on the North Side. They were being used for Internet porn—the highest bidder could script whatever he wanted done to them and view it on his computer." She opened up a filing cabinet and handed him a folder filled with photos. "That's just a taste of what some of them suffered at the request of the site's patrons."

Burroughs flipped the file open and almost gagged on the bacon cheeseburger he'd eaten earlier. He swallowed hard and slapped the file back on her desk.

She took it, held it gently as if it were something precious. "Off-duty officers were guarding the production studio and the women, and we found several prominent police administrators involved. So we went in quietly, grabbed everything and made our arrests. A few people we turned, and we're using them to work our way back to the guys running the show."

Burroughs digested that. There had been several surprise retirements last year, but scuttlebutt had attributed them to pressure from the union and a change in the political climate. "Why didn't you guys make this public? It would have been a major media event."

"I prefer to work behind the scenes. John Greally, my SAC, agrees. And with the involvement of the police department, it didn't seem in the public's best interest to undermine their confidence. DEA has some guys undercover, infiltrating the Netherlands drug ring, so they didn't want to draw any attention either. The ICE guys wanted to grab the headlines, but since they screwed up, they kept quiet."

"Customs screwed up? How?"

"We had eleven girls in that facility. My agents secured it, began evidence recovery and handed the girls over to Customs. By the time they made it to the detention facility, there were only ten girls. One of them, Vera Tzasiris, was missing."

"So they lost one. After what they'd been through, can you blame her for not trusting the authorities, taking off if she had a chance? What happened to the other girls?"

"After they testify, they'll be offered asylum here. Until then, they remain in detention."

He shook his head. "Seems kind of unfair. Locking them up, I mean."

"Better than what they could expect if we hadn't gotten them out of there." She removed one small photograph before returning the file to its locked drawer. "Still, I feel bad about the missing girl, Vera. I took her statement myself before we turned her over to ICE. I promised her that she was out of danger; the worst was over. It'd be nice to find her someday. Make sure she was all right."

She didn't meet his gaze, but he got her meaning when she slid him the three-by-five photo. It was a headshot, the kind you see on dating sites or used by actresses. The girl in it was in her early twenties, dark hair, a wide, toothy smile that reminded him of Julia Roberts.

He admired Guardino's pragmatism and the fact that it didn't totally crowd out her humanity. And it felt good that she trusted him not to betray her confidence. He had a feeling her attitude of putting victims first didn't always go over so well here in federal country, where the name of the game was cover your ass. "I'll keep my eye out. See what I can do. Unofficially."

She nodded her thanks. "I've done all I can through our channels, but no one at HQ wants her brought in, too many mistakes might be made public." She glanced out the glass walls of her office. Several men and women were clustered around a desk brimming over with computer equipment. "Well hell, what's going on now?"

Lucy stepped out of her office just in time to prevent a civil war.

Or more precisely a public lynching. The bullpen—a large open room filled with moveable desks and workstations—was currently configured into a horseshoe centering around Taylor's desk, brimming with computer equipment. Standing beside Taylor was Fletcher, the ICE surveillance tech. Surrounding him was the rest of the High Tech Computer Crimes Task Force.

"You can't disconnect from the write-blocker while you're running EnCase," Taylor was saying.

"Besides," another H-Tech member lectured Fletcher, "we only work from images, clones, not the original. What were you thinking?"

The rest of the cyber-warriors voiced similar sentiments. Fletcher was turning red, holding his hands up against the hordes attacking him.

Lucy stepped into the fray. "What's the problem, gentlemen?"

The H-Tech team backed off, leaving her facing Taylor and Fletcher. Taylor slanted a look and a scowl at Fletcher, then shook his head. "Nothing, LT. I've got everything under control."

She had her doubts about that, but let it slide.

"I appreciate you trying to help," she told Fletcher, leading him away from the nest of wires and electronics that had overrun Taylor's desk.

He looked back over his shoulder with a tight-lipped frown. "I was setting up for tomorrow and they said you needed help with the

Ashley Yeager case." His voice was taut and she wondered what she'd missed prior to her arrival.

Lucy nodded to Burroughs. "I'll be back in a minute."

She led Fletcher to his workstation. She and her team were the lead on Operation Honeypot but since ICE would be involved in the post-arrest negotiations with the Canadian authorities, the ICE Special Agent in Charge, Grimwald, had wanted his people involved throughout.

So far, Fletcher had been an asset, even if he was a bit eager. *Agent-wannabee*, she'd pegged him, because of the way he hovered and volunteered for any little assignment during their briefings. Just like Taylor had been before he made it into Quantico.

"It was nice of you to give up your weekend. Especially after working so hard this morning."

He shrugged and inclined his head in a self-deprecating bounce. "I felt bad about the girl. Just wanted to help. I didn't realize you guys follow a different protocol than we do."

"Hey, no problem. Listen, we need to get started early tomorrow on Operation Honeypot. Why don't you head home, spend some time with your family?"

"I'll finish setting up the equipment first. My family knows how important my job is. Sometimes there's a price to pay."

Lucy bit back a sigh as a sudden image of Megan, her face flushed with fever, dashed through her mind. "Yeah, there's always a price. I'll see you tomorrow."

Taylor came up behind them. "Hey, LT," he said. "Fletcher said you forgot these on your op this morning."

She turned as he released a cascade of rubber snakes from a pressurized can. She yelped and batted the things away, realizing too late that the rest of the squad had gathered around.

Everyone laughed except Burroughs, who looked puzzled. Lucy joined in on the laughter as well. "Okay, you guys. You got me good."

Walden came in, just in time to see the aftermath of the joke. "Can I have your autograph?"

He handed her a printout of a still shot of Indiana Jones caught in the snake pit with a torch--only Lucy's photo replaced Harrison Ford's face beneath his fedora.

"I'm not going to live this down, am I?" Lucy asked, thumb-tacking the photo to the nearest corkboard. It was good to see Walden had a sense of humor, she'd been beginning to doubt that his expression ever shifted out of dour deadpan.

"I take it you had a run-in with a snake?" Burroughs asked as she ushered him, Taylor, and Walden into her office.

"Told you, you should have taken me this morning," Taylor said, plopping onto one of the chairs at the conference table. "I'm not afraid of snakes."

"Neither am I—at least I wasn't until this morning."

As Walden drew a timeline on the white board and began to add all the points documenting Ashley's recent behavior, Taylor gleefully told Burroughs about the op at the snake handlers' church. His version sounded much more exciting than the real thing had—and far less messy. Burroughs straddled a chair behind the conference table and pivoted to grin at Lucy.

"Gee, the glamorous life you feds lead. So were the twins molested? Or were the creeps really trying to save their souls?"

Walden paused in his writing. "Staties said they still aren't sure. The first forensic interview didn't get much from them except they missed their parents."

"It's out of our hands," Lucy said, bringing their focus back to Ashley. She remained standing, behind them, pacing the area between the table and her desk.

"She planned this," Taylor said, eagerly as if it was an original thought.

"With help," Burroughs added. "No way a girl her size could have gotten the waitress's body into that bin by herself."

"So there must be two," Walden said. "Either Ashley working with someone, or someone else coercing Ashley."

"Either way there had to be communication." Burroughs took the handoff. "What did you get from her cell phone?"

"Just the Fegley kid. And nothing from him in over a month. Only other calls were from her mother."

"So who *has* been talking with Ashley this past month?" Lucy asked. She still didn't agree with their assessment, but she wanted to hear their thoughts without influencing them with her own opinions.

They looked at each other. "She has another cell," Walden suggested. "Bought herself a prepaid."

Trying on theories was like trying on new shoes—and so far they all pinched Lucy's toes. Until now. Walden's suggestion felt right. "Untraceable."

She narrowed her eyes at the board. She didn't like committing to one line of investigation or one theory of the crime too early, but Ashley had been missing twenty-nine hours already. Statistics said if she were taken by a stranger or coerced by a predator, she'd be dead in less than forty-eight—actually, most were dead within three hours of an abduction, but Lucy refused to think that way.

How could they be this far into things and nothing still made sense?

"What about Tardiff?" she asked.

"Not in any registry, never charged with a crime," Walden supplied. Lucy leaned forward, hearing an implied "but" in his tone. "However, he has had several civil actions brought against him for improper supervision of a minor. All settled out of court, all sealed."

"Well hell." They all knew what "sealed and settled" was code for: guilty. She moved to the front of the room and a clear space at the board. Wrote Tardiff's name up high. "So we have one freaky-deaky involved—"

"But as far as we know he hasn't even been in town lately and hasn't had contact with Ashley," Taylor said.

"Then it's your job to track him down, verify his whereabouts. I don't want to wait for the New York office to get back to us."

Taylor nodded eagerly, his puppy-dog grin returning now that he had a new bone to play with. "I can cross-check his calls with mom's, see if he's using an alternative cell, maybe we can track him that way."

"Just do it. I'm tired of hearing about this guy and not having any facts." She turned back to the board, wrote Ashley's name. Below it she added: *Victim? Willing accomplice? Coerced? Acting solo?*

"I still say she couldn't do the Tastee Treet girl by herself," Walden said as she wrote the last.

"The chick was pretty skinny," Burroughs put in, obviously still liking the idea of Ashley as a do-er.

"So was Ashley," Walden argued.

Lucy tried to be objective. "Consider the force needed to hold someone face down into a vat of four hundred degree boiling oil. They'll be fighting with everything they have and you have to hold them there for what—a minute or two?" She shook her head and crossed the solo item off the list. "I don't think so." Burroughs opened his mouth to protest and she pointed the marker at him. "Not unless your ME says otherwise. Why don't you follow up on that as well as check in with Monroeville, see if anything else popped during their canvass. Oh, and while you're at it, you can phone in your report to the mayor."

His mouth snapped shut. Did he really think she'd believe he was hovering so close to her because he liked how she filled out her sweater? She may be new to Pittsburgh, but she wasn't born yesterday.

He flashed her a sheepish grin. "Sorry about that. It's an election year."

"Not really interested in politics right now. I'm interested in facts. And we're pitifully short on them. Which brings us back to her computer."

All heads swiveled to stare at Taylor. He held up his hands, palms out, fingers splayed. "You guys need to understand, these things take time."

"Just tell me what you have so far." Before he could open his mouth, she added, "In English."

The light in Taylor's eyes dampened. He opened his mouth, closed it again. "Nothing."

"Nothing?" Lucy placed her weight on the table, leaning forward. "You and your geniuses have been at it all day."

"We have a lot of possibilities—we're analyzing every fragment we can isolate, I have a team working on tracking the scrubber program back to its source code, another one tracing her email and online activity. But there's nothing concrete, no solid leads." He hung his head. "I'm sorry, we need more time."

Lucy straightened, wrapping her arms around her chest, holding back from telling Taylor what they all knew—Ashley Yeager didn't have more time to spare.

—

Ashley was motionless. Jimmy would have thought she was asleep, except that her eyes were open. Staring into space, staring straight into his heart.

Pressure built behind his eyes. One finger stroked an eyebrow as he grew clammy with sweat. Was it time?

He crouched before the video monitor as if by getting closer to the screen he could get closer to Ashley. Only one chance to do this right. He glanced over at the large aquarium that sat on the floor beside the monitor.

Dozens of snakes coiled, slithering over top of each other, confined to an impossibly small space. Several raised their heads and stared at him with cold, reptilian eyes. Jimmy didn't like snakes. It had taken every ounce of courage and willpower for him to collect them.

Ashley was even more terrified of them than he was. She'd told him about what her father had done to her, forcing her to handle anacondas and other snakes in front of crowds of visitors to the zoo when she was young. How he'd chided her for her fears, tried to "cure" her of them by making her handle the snakes until she'd broken down in terror during one of the shows and wet her pants.

Jimmy wished there was another way. He tapped the wall of the aquarium and the mass of snakes writhed as if it were a single creature. None were poisonous, of course. But their effect on Ashley would be devastating.

The whole point. She had to break with her old life in order to join him in their new life together.

Only one chance. Was she ready?

The lilting sounds of his Piano Man ringtone jolted him. He checked the number. Alicia.

Ashley and step four would have to wait.

Family first.

Chapter 17

Melissa's footsteps echoed in the empty house. She was exhausted but couldn't sit still long enough to fall asleep. Her sister had arrived from Philadelphia, cooked a huge meal for themselves and the sheriff's deputies, picked a fight about Melissa not eating, and then retired to the guest room while Melissa prowled the house, trying hard not to think. Finally Melissa ended up in Ashley's room.

Blissfully alone. It felt good after a long day where strangers had dogged her every movement, where she had to play a role for the cameras and reporters, and her emotions repeatedly swamped her, dragging her down until she had nothing left.

She didn't turn the lights on. The bed sprawled, a ghostly white square in the middle of the room. Naked. The police had taken the sheets and covers. For what, Melissa did not want to dwell on.

They had left Ashley's pillows. Melissa climbed onto the barren bed. The air conditioner cycled on, startling her with its chilly breath. She curled up into a fetal position.

She had no one else to hug, so she hugged herself, burrowing into the pillows, trying to escape.

The faint sound of a phone ringing propelled her from unconsciousness.

It was all a dream, was her first thought as her hand shot out, searching through empty air for the phone.

It wasn't there. She rolled over, eyes open now, realizing where she was. In Ashley's room. On Ashley's bed. Alone.

It wasn't a dream.

The phone rang again and her heart slammed into her throat as she leapt from the bed. How many times had it rung already? She ran down the hall to her room, her bare feet drumming against the hard wood in a frantic, primal rhythm.

"Don't hang up," she called out even though she knew the sheriff's people wouldn't let that happen. She lunged across her bed, snatching the receiver. "Hello?"

At first there was only silence. Melissa's chest heaved with adrenalin, her heart pounding so hard she couldn't swallow.

"Hello? Ashley? Is that you?" Her voice was sandpapery with unshed tears. "Speak to me. Ashley, where are you?"

More silence. Melissa's hand clenched the phone so tightly her fingers went numb. So did her lips and toes. During those few seconds her entire body became one impenetrable block of ice.

"We know your secret." A taunting, sing-song voice that wasn't Ashley's jolted through the air.

She leaned forward, elbows between her knees, fighting nausea. "Where's my daughter?" She couldn't feel her tears against the frozen tundra of her face, but she saw them as they splashed her robe, small, irregular dark splotches on the shiny silver fabric. "Please let me talk with her, I beg you. Please."

Laughter was her only answer.

–

"Allegheny County is relaying a call. It's coming from the kid's phone." Burroughs poked his head in from the bullpen as Lucy was talking to Ashley's English teacher.

"I'll have to get back to you, Mrs. Forrester." Lucy hung up and rushed out to where everyone gathered around Taylor's station.

"Where's my daughter?" Melissa Yeager's voice shrieked through the speakers.

"We know your secret," came a man's whisper. Followed by the sound of laughter. Then the click of a receiver being hung up.

"Too short to trace, but if they don't turn the phone off, we can get GPS," Taylor announced to everyone. He touched his Bluetooth ear set. "I got it, thanks." His fingers tapped methodically on his keyboard for a moment before he swiveled to face the H-Tech team. "Okay guys, we've got the file. I want the voice analysis and background noise dissected like yesterday."

The computer guys broke up into smaller groups, chattering eagerly. A chance to get in on a real-life real-time possible kidnapping was more exciting than playing with internet porn.

"Play it back for me," Lucy asked Taylor. "Burroughs, you get on the horn with Verizon and you don't hang up until they have coordinates for us. Walden, reach out to the mom, tell her we're working it, we'll let her know as soon—you know the drill."

Before she could say more, Melissa's voice filled the air once more, sounding tissue thin, shredded. A computer screen filled with jagged waves as she spoke. The entire conversation lasted only thirty-eight seconds.

"Sounds like a man," Taylor said.

"Play the laugh again," she directed. They both listened to the final seconds of the call. "That was more than one person. At least two, and one of them sounds like a woman."

"She's right, Taylor," one of the H-Tech volunteers called out from a nearby desk, one ear covered with a headphone. "Two people: a man and a woman. Stress analysis indicates possible intoxication."

Taylor grinned up at Lucy. "Wouldn't that be great? She's out getting high with her boyfriend, no worries? As soon as we nail down the GPS, we'll have her home safe and sound."

Except for the fact of the dead waitress lying on a slab in the ME's morgue. But Lucy didn't dampen his enthusiasm.

"Room the call originated from is approximately sixteen by twenty-two feet, wood floors, twelve foot high ceilings, several large windows along one wall," another tech called out. Lucy didn't ask how they figured that out, at this point, she didn't really care if it was science or magic.

Burroughs nodded to her from where he stood on the side of the room, away from the loudest of the chaos. He was writing something down, then hung up his phone. "Got it. The cells narrowed it to either 5514 or 5516 Broad Street, that's in Garfield."

"Garfield? Whose jurisdiction?" Lucy asked.

Taylor popped a map of Pittsburgh on the large monitor in the front of the room, a flashing red square marking their quarry.

"Mine," Burroughs said with a satisfied grin.

"Call for a warrant," she told Walden as he rejoined them. "Burroughs, contact your SWAT team, tell them I might need them within the hour. Taylor, I want to know everything about every person at those addresses. Names, criminal records, what they ate for breakfast. Call me with the results. Let's move."

"LT, I can do that in the car," Taylor protested, reminding Lucy of Megan. "Can't I come? You might need me."

When he turned those puppy-dog brown eyes on her, it was hard to remember Taylor was only three years younger than she was. But he had a point, he wasn't tech support anymore, he was a full-fledged agent. "All right, ride with Walden."

Walden followed her into her office where she donned her Kevlar. "Got the warrant."

He closed the door and leaned against it. She still hadn't figured out why the door was solid wood when the walls around it were glass, but decided it was a good thing if you were going to have 200 plus pound guys like Walden leaning against it.

"What's the problem?" she asked, adjusting the Velcro straps and shifting her shoulders under the weight of the bulletproof vest.

"Aren't you moving kind of fast on this? Let the locals set up surveillance, lock down the block. We wait until morning, we can have it narrowed down to an exact location, get reconnaissance, maybe even get a helo up... More planning time, more back up, better chance of everyone getting home in one piece."

Lucy smiled. It was the most polite insubordination she'd ever experienced. He was right; it was by-the-book, the way things were meant to be done at the Bureau.

"Burroughs told me a joke while we were riding together today," she said. "How many Feebies does it take to change a light bulb?"

Walden came close to glaring at her, then played along. "How many?"

"All of them. Ten thousand to study the problem, twenty-six hundred to fill out forms in triplicate and wait for approval, seventeen to monitor from a safe distance, and one agent to go undercover and bribe a confidential informant to climb the ladder and do the dirty work."

He shrugged, palms up, hands empty. "Your point being?"

"You've been working this case all day. You think that was Ashley and her boyfriend getting high, calling mommy dearest to gloat?"

His face went blank but behind his eyes a battle was being waged. "We don't have any evidence she's in immediate danger. Standard procedure—"

Lucy leaned forward, hands slapping her desk. Technically Walden was her second-in-command. It was his job to point out any potential flaws in her thinking. But she also needed to know where he stood, how he was thinking. Not just what the rulebook said he should be telling her.

"If it was your case, your call. What would you do?" she asked, keeping her face nonjudgmental, meeting his gaze head on.

There was a long pause. Longer than it would take either of them to recite the appropriate sections of the FBI's op-manual.

Finally Walden came the closest to a genuine smile she'd yet to see from the man. His lips parted wide enough that she could actually see his top teeth. For a second, maybe even two.

"I'd go in hard and fast, ready for anything. I wouldn't wait."

She cleared her Glock, checked the magazine and reloaded it after chambering a round. "My feelings exactly. Any problems riding with the kid?"

He gave a small shake of his head. "Nah. He just likes to talk a lot is all. Unless you want to keep an eye on him. It is his first real deployment."

She'd thought of that. Taylor was wound tighter than a meth tweaker, but that seemed to be his nature. "He'll do fine."

He nodded and stepped toward the door, then turned back. "You sure? It'd give Burroughs a chance to feast his eyes on a fine piece of big, black man's ass."

She snapped her head up at that. "What are you implying, Special Agent Walden?"

All evidence of his smile vanished at her tone. She strode around the desk to stand beside him. "Surely you don't mean that your ass is better looking than mine?"

A rumbly chuckle escaped him as she craned her head to look over her shoulder at first her rear, then his.

"No ma'am. Never."

"All right then." She leaned against the conference table and looked out the glass walls to where Burroughs was talking on the phone, lounging in Walden's chair as if he owned the place. "I appreciate the offer, but it's not a problem I choose to address. At least not at this time."

He mimicked her position, also staring at Burroughs, his face falling back into its usual expressionless mask. "Can I ask why?"

"First of all, for guys like Burroughs, nothing I say or do will change them. It's in their DNA. Second of all, it's not my job to try to change him. It's my job to find Ashley. So I let Burroughs look all he wants. Who cares? As long as I get what I want."

The half-hidden smile crept back. "You're using him."

"Well, duh. You heard Burroughs. It's his turf. If I stick next to him, I can maybe keep things from escalating if he takes it in mind to grandstand. And," she holstered her weapon, "if things do get hot and heavy, I can use him to direct the SWAT guys. I'm sure they wouldn't cotton to taking orders directly from a Feebie."

"I like how you think, boss." The almost-smile became a real-life actual smile. Walden gave her a mock salute and left to gather his own tactical gear.

Lucy grinned as she grabbed her windbreaker. Nicest thing anyone had said to her all day.

Even nicer was the prospect that maybe she was wrong about all this, maybe Ashley had left just to spite mamma bear and papa bear and was waiting for them in Garfield, toked up and full of life.

Her gut told her otherwise, but it never hurt to hope.

Chapter 18

Guardino drove. She was a good driver, no complaints there. Burroughs appreciated the way she steered the big SUV through the Southside's Saturday night uncaring and unyielding traffic. She wasn't impatient, merely focused, looking ahead and anticipating openings in the flow, slip-streaming into them. At one point she turned on the red and blue wigwags concealed behind the grill, then shut them off again once the snarl of congestion was passed.

No fuss, no muss, just getting the job done. He decided that was what attracted him most. Of course there was also the physical thing. Most women donning Kevlar looked squat, bulky, as if the layers of protection turned them into squared off blobs. Not Guardino. Even beneath the bulletproof vest, she gave off a vibe that was all woman. Maybe it was the spread of her hips or the glint of Amazon warrior-steel her eyes took on when the body armor came out.

Whatever it was, it was making it hard to keep riding with her. Not without thinking the kind of thoughts a cop shouldn't be thinking about another cop, much less a Feebie.

Needing distraction, he flipped open his phone. Found a text that didn't help matters any. Damn *her*. He'd told her he never wanted to see her again, but she was one of those women who didn't have the word "no" in her vocabulary.

I WANT TO C U TONITE, she had texted him. I WANT U TO F ME TIL I SCREAM.

He tapped out a reply: NO, CAN'T.

She wrote back: YES U CAN. STUCKUP BITCH WON'T GIVE U WHAT U NEED. NOT LIKE I CAN.

He tried again: NO.

Her reply: YES. I KNOW WHAT U WANT, I CAN MAKE IT HAPPEN. TONITE.

He flipped the phone shut, saw Guardino glance at him. "Donkey Kong," he lied. "It relaxes me. I could download it to your phone if you'd like to play."

She waited a little too long before replying. He had the feeling she knew he was offering more than a retro vid-game. Had the feeling she knew exactly what kind of fantasies had been tantalizing him ever since he first saw her striding up the road at the vic's house, plowing through the uniformed cops faster than a bum through a baloney sandwich.

That's how it always was for him—same as with Kim and all the women before and after her. Lust at first sight. There was just a type of woman who crawled under his skin and set up shop there, teasing his nerve endings, tugging at his attention until he couldn't think of anything else.

Lucy Guardino was one of those women.

"I don't play games," she replied in a neutral but firm tone.

He shifted in his seat, putting his cell phone away. He got her message, loud and clear.

Jeezit, it was gonna be a long night.

--

"I got him!"

Lucy jumped as Taylor's excited voice shrieked through the radio.

"I used the GIS program to eliminate—"

"The name, Taylor." A yawn forced its way past her clenched teeth and she didn't bother to cover it.

"Oh, yeah. Sorry. The apartment they're in is leased to Delroy Littles. It's on the second floor of the fifty-five fourteen building, apartment two-D."

"Littles? I know that name," Burroughs said, even as he was dialing his phone. "Friend of mine in narcotics has been looking for him."

"Makes sense. He's had several arrests, only two convictions—both for possession with intent to sell. First one for marijuana, second for methamphetamine." Taylor paused. "Never found with a weapon, does have one TRO from a girlfriend alleging abuse, though. Still on parole from the last conviction. Nothing outstanding."

Burroughs snapped his phone shut. "Narcotics thinks Delroy might be working with a big fish in the meth trade. They've been hoping to pop Delroy on a parole violation and turn him."

They were still several blocks away from Broad Street, if Lucy remembered the map correctly. Which meant she needed a plan, fast. "We send Pittsburgh SWAT in hot and heavy, scare the crap out of Delroy and the girl in there with him. If the girl is Ashley, then we're good to go. If not, the extra firepower should help convince Delroy this is no ordinary parole violation, enough so maybe he'll talk to us about Ashley and give the narcotics guys what they need." She paused. "Anyone got any better ideas?"

"Sounds good to me," Burroughs said. "The SWAT guys love any chance to make a noise."

"If it isn't Ashley," Walden's thoughtful voice sounded over the speaker, "we could take Delroy back to the Federal Building—might add to the intimidation factor."

Burroughs chuckled. "Hell yeah. If Delroy thinks this is a federal beef, he'll shit his pants."

"And be oh-so-very grateful when we kick him loose to your narcotic squad instead." Lucy nodded. "I like it."

Twelve minutes later she, Burroughs, and the Pittsburgh SWAT Team leader, a guy by the name of Erikson, were huddled over a layout of the apartment building.

"Go in loud, but we need to minimize property damage and for God's sake, no shooting unless necessary," Lucy said, a little nervous that she wasn't dealing with the elite FBI Hostage Rescue Team. But

Erikson seemed to understand the situation and was willing to play by her rules.

"My men know there's a civilian on the premises," he told her. "We'll neutralize all threats with minimal necessary force."

The stabbing in her left ear returned, her jaw clamping tight as she watched Erikson lead his men inside the building. She was grinding her teeth again. She forced herself to yawn, feeling the pop in her jaw and ear. Damn, she hated watching, waiting.

A few moments later the apartment's windows were lit up by an explosion of light and sound. A flash-bang grenade used to stun the occupants. Even from street level, Lucy could hear pounding footsteps and men yelling, "Police, down, down, down!"

She ran across the street and started up the steps. Burroughs followed close on her heels. By the time she reached the top, the radio was broadcasting the all clear. She entered the room, still filled with hazy smoke, to find the black clad, helmeted and masked SWAT officers straddling two civilians who lay face down, coughing.

Lucy crouched down beside the woman as Erikson restrained her arms with a Flex-cuff and another cop patted her down. It wasn't Ashley, she saw right away.

"Gun!" the cop frisking the woman called out, drawing everyone's attention.

"Hell, that's not mine!" Delroy shouted. "I don't know nothing about no gun. Honest!"

The cop pulled a .38 Smith and Wesson from the woman's boot and handed it off. A few minutes later, after finding no more weapons, they hauled the man and the woman to their feet.

"Find the cell phone?" Lucy asked.

"Sitting on the table. Still on."

"We'll need to bag and tag it." Taylor and Walden appeared in the doorway and she nodded to them to take care of the documentation. "See if there's any evidence Ashley's been here."

"You got it, LT," Taylor sang out, his eyes lit up brighter than the flash bang. Walden trailed after the younger agent, shaking his head, looking a tad embarrassed by Taylor's exuberance.

Lucy turned her attention to Delroy and his lady friend.

"I've heard a lot about you, Mr. Littles," she started, scrutinizing him like he was an item displayed on E-Bay and the auction was heating up.

"Look," he craned his head forward, so anxious that spittle accompanied his words, "I don't know nothing about that gun, you can't hang me on that, I've been clean ever since I got out, you ain't gonna find nothing—"

"One call to your PO and I'll find something on a drug test," Lucy continued, stepping closer, violating his space and pitching her voice to a most intimate level. "Won't I, Mr. Littles?" It wasn't a bluff. He reeked of garlic and ammonia, that weird stench meth addicts exuded. He wasn't totally high, but he'd used recently.

"Please lady, you can't do that, don't call Havelock, the guy's got a hard on for me, he'll send me back so fast, and I ain't done nothing wrong. Please, can't we work this out?"

She smiled sweetly and stepped back. "Maybe. Depends how cooperative you and your friend are." She nodded to Burroughs. "Go ahead, take him in. I'll meet you at the Federal Building."

Delroy gagged as he tried to find the right words. "Federal? I ain't done nothing federal, hey, can't we talk this out, I'm clean I tell you, you can't do this, I got rights you know—"

Lucy smiled as two SWAT officers started to drag him out. Stopping them just as they reached the remnants of the front door, she said, "Go ahead and let him wait here." She gestured for them to place Delroy onto one of the kitchen chairs. "If you're straight with me, Mr. Littles, maybe we can avoid the trip down to Carson Street."

"I told you, I ain't done nothing wrong." He gave the last word a twang, drawing it out to two syllables. "So of course I'll cooperate."

Lucy stood in front of him, forcing him to stretch his head back to make eye contact. "Since you're in custody, I need to explain your rights to you, Mr. Littles." She gave him the Miranda warning. "Do you want a lawyer? If you do, please tell him that you're being charged with first degree murder, attempted murder, kidnapping, felony sexual assault, gross sexual imposition, sexual assault of a minor, assault and battery, and terroristic threats."

His eyes bugged out at her litany of charges. He opened his mouth, licked his lips, debating his options, then closed it again. Lucy let the silence lengthen.

"If you are convicted of any of those charges, given your record, you're facing life in prison," she added salt to the wound. "If you are convicted of homicide, you're facing a death sentence." She leaned forward, her face a few inches away from his, close enough to smell the fear oozing from his pores. "So tell me, Delroy. Would you like your lawyer?"

"I-I ain't done none of those things. Just tell me what you want lady, I'll play it straight."

"I want to know where you got this cell phone." She dangled the evidence bag containing Ashley's phone before him.

"I found it."

Lucy raised a skeptical eyebrow.

"No, no really, I did. Someone left it at the bus stop on Liberty Avenue. I found it yesterday."

"Did you make any calls from it?"

"Yeah, yeah, but only two. See I didn't have no charger and the battery was low, so I took a look and found these nasty pictures of a girl. Figured maybe the owner was a married guy or something so I could shake him loose a few bucks. A finder's fee, you know?"

"Go on."

"So I called the last dialed number, figured that'd be his home. Only this lady answers. Freaked me out and I hung up. Then tonight me and Hildy we were just goofing around and we called the lady back, just to mess with her, ya know? Didn't mean nothing by it."

Lucy straightened, crossing her arms over her chest. Delroy squirmed, his gaze locked onto hers as he pleaded. "Honest, we was just fooling. Ask Hildy, she'll tell you. Look, there's nothing federal about it. You got the wrong man."

"No, Delroy. You got the wrong phone. This phone belongs to a little girl who was kidnapped."

His face fell. "Aw shit. You're kidding me."

"Wish I was. Now, I'm going to check out your story and do my best to keep you out of a federal penitentiary. But the only way you can strengthen your case is to give the Pittsburgh Police your full cooperation. Can I count on you for that?"

"Oh yes ma'am, whatever you say, I'll do it, I will." The words gushed out as his eyes widened with fervor.

"I'm going to let these fine gentlemen take you into custody. But if I hear you haven't cooperated with them..." She scowled, letting her threat sink in before gesturing to the SWAT guys to haul him away. Delroy went eagerly, already jabbering to his escorts.

Lucy picked her way through the detritus that covered the floor and went into the bedroom where Taylor and Walden were finishing their search. "Anything?"

"Some drug paraphernalia, a few pieces of women's clothing but nothing that matches what Ashley was wearing," Walden answered. "No signs of anyone being held against their will."

"No computers," Taylor said with a disappointed frown. "Nothing but Ashley's phone and a trac-phone that was in the woman's purse."

Burroughs returned. "What about the woman?" He nodded to the other room where two more SWAT guys were watching Delroy's lady friend spout off tirades of highly explicit and imaginative expletives. "You want her?"

Lucy considered. With Delroy's being a parolee, she had a little legal standing. Tenuous, but it was there. She didn't have any standing with Delroy's friend. "We have an ID on her?"

"Yeah. Hildy Figeruaro. Age twenty-two, no wants, no warrants. From the looks of her, she's been popping heroin and meth. She's pretty strung out now, it's hard to get anything coherent out of her."

"Why don't you have PBP take her in on the weapons charge, give her time to sober up? Then if I need her, we'll know where to find her."

"Sure. She won't get bail until Monday, so there's time." He went to make arrangements. Lucy strolled around the room, admiring the architecture with its high ceilings and ornate woodwork. Trying her best to ignore the urge to scream. Wasting time, that's all they'd accomplished.

Wasting Ashley's time. For the first time since this morning, Lucy allowed herself to add: *if* Ashley was still alive.

She yawned, stretching her jaw until her ear popped, relieving the stabbing pain that spiked down her neck. Rocked back and forth on her feet as she looked out the naked window from her position beside the sex-soaked unmade bed, her shoe kicking a meth pipe aside. Her wedding ring caught the light from the lone bare bedside lamp and flared in a rich red gold, the only pure thing in this place.

"You want anything else here, boss?" Walden asked.

Lucy shook off her reverie, turned her back on the darkness beyond the window and rolled her shoulders, shrugging the Kevlar's weight into a less uncomfortable position. "No. Let's go."

—

Ever since she could remember, Ashley had fought hard to avoid straying too far. Her parents would accuse her of being "flighty" or daydreaming and would chide her for "going away."

Going away, that's what it was, a helium balloon taking flight, drifting into the heavens, finding new places, new people, a new life.

When she was younger, a mere word would snap her back to the here and now. Then she learned to do it herself—a pinch on the back of her arm would suffice. But soon that wasn't enough to reconnect her and instead she'd scratch herself. That evolved into writing—she'd scrape hidden words into her skin, words she wasn't even supposed to know, words she wasn't certain described her or others. Fuck, shit, slut, asshole, bitch.

When that stopped working, she learned the power of blood. First a needle, a mere pinprick on the tip of a finger. As she concentrated on the crimson drop of blood, the sting of pain, she'd be able to convince herself that she *could* feel, that she wasn't totally empty inside, that she belonged here in this world.

She saw a girl in her class slice herself with her thumbnail and Ashley soon followed in her footsteps, experimenting with many sharp objects and techniques. If she cut too deep, there was too much blood, it would stream out, make an unsavory mess and draw attention.

Too shallow and there wasn't any blood—and at this point in her addiction she needed blood. Blood and pain were her bridges back to reality.

Until now. Now she lay curled around a metal pole, sweltering in air so heavy she had to gulp it down in quick bites, the stench of terror and death smothering her, her legs dead except for the occasional pins and needles, darkness all around her, seeping into her veins, seizing her heart.

She had begun this journey eager, ready to escape. To a new life, to new hope.

Hope. It was an obscenity in this new world she found herself in. Far better to simply leave, let herself go, than to waste energy on hope.

She stared into darkness so complete she couldn't tell if her eyes were open or closed. She didn't blink to try to find out. She was already gone...

Chapter 19

Burroughs couldn't help himself. He couldn't face the prospect of going home to the empty apartment he rented in Shadyside. Empty. That was the operative word.

When the boys weren't there, the damn high ceilings and hard wood floors made his every movement echo, rattling his teeth like a lone bullet forgotten in an ammo box.

Other than a few bottles of Yuengling and some moldy pizza, the fridge was empty. Except for two shiny new frames from Target surrounding the boys' school photos, the walls were barren.

He ought to get a rug, ought to get some dishes instead of eating off paper plates, ought to get a real table and chairs instead of the card table his folks had lent him. Ought to get a life.

Correction. He had a life—he'd just thrown it away.

Of course, he'd had a little help.

He drove down Carson, away from the federal building and wondered at the smiling couples loitering outside of Blue Lou's and Mario's. Three a.m. and people were still out having a good time, finding things to talk about, to laugh about.

Stopped at a red light, he watched as a man reached out to tuck a strand of hair behind his date's ear. A casual gesture, the woman didn't even seem to notice except that she interlaced her fingers between the guy's as they continued strolling. The scene was so familiar, yet so foreign. Burroughs felt blind-sided.

He headed downtown instead of east to his apartment. Downtown was where the devil lived, ensconced in a ritzy condo on Fourth Avenue.

He had a thousand opportunities to change his mind—as he did every time he made this drive.

Thought about Guardino. Lucia Theresa Guardino, what a name to be saddled with. But somehow it suited her. He liked the way she was strong as steel but not hard, no sharp edges, just determination that would not be bent or broken.

He appreciated the way she refused to give up on Ashley, rallying the rest of the cynical group of cops to fight for the kid as well. Hell, even he had fallen for it, starting to think the kid might still be alive.

Guardino combined good people instinct with charisma, making her a born leader. Not strident or overbearing like most women in position of power, especially in law enforcement.

Not one of the guys, though. She stood apart. He had the feeling that had cost her, a lot.

He remembered how her voice changed when she spoke with her kid on the phone; the way her eyes widened, her breath quickened and she flushed when she joked with her husband—hell, after spending the day with her, he could about tell every time she even thought about her husband. Her pupils dilated, a faint blush crept up her throat. And she thought about him a lot.

Kim never looked at him that way, not even when they were newlyweds. Or maybe he'd just never noticed.

He pulled into the underground parking lot at the Carlyle. Licked his lips, hands still clenched tight on the steering wheel. This was the last place he should be tonight. Especially working this case.

But it was the only place left for him to go.

He called upstairs. She was waiting at her doorway when he arrived a few minutes later.

The door was open only a few inches, just far enough to silhouette her in the glow of the light behind her. She'd staged it to perfection: hair rumpled as if she'd just woken, skin glistening and smelling of jasmine, a hint of eye liner and lipstick, mouth parted in a welcoming pout, and gold silk robe unbelted, slit open wide enough to confirm that she wore nothing beneath it.

The devil herself, offering everything he needed and nothing he wanted.

"I knew you'd come tonight," she purred, grabbing his shirt and tugging him to her when he hesitated. "After seeing the way you looked at her today, I knew you'd be in my bed tonight."

"What are you talking about?" He pulled back, one foot still in the hallway, freedom only a short sprint away.

She pulled him inside and shut the door behind him. Too late. He was trapped.

"You're such a sap, Burroughs. Always falling in love at first sight. But you have your damn code of honor. Worse, you actually believe in honor." She tossed her head, strands of hair flitting across his neck, sparking against his sweat-sheened skin. "You think that makes you special, but really it makes you a fool."

She combed her fingers through his hair, then forced his head down so that he looked her in the eyes. He felt a flutter start in his stomach—anger and fear and disgust and lust all kicking at his guts, fighting to see which would win.

"As soon as I saw her wedding band, I knew I would have you tonight," she continued.

She was wrong. His being here had nothing to do with Guardino. It had everything to do with him. He couldn't face being alone in that empty apartment. He didn't like to think that he needed anything, but he needed her. Someone. Anyone.

Her mouth met his. Before he could respond, she bit his lower lip. Laughed when he jerked his head away, raised a hand to wipe the blood.

"Go to hell, Cindy."

"Only if you come along for the ride." She shrugged free from the robe, its fabric caressing her curves as it cascaded to the floor. He reached for her and she didn't resist. Instead, she melted beneath his greedy touch as he grabbed on and refused to let go.

Lucy left the Subaru in the driveway. No sense risking waking someone with the sound of the garage door, especially when she'd soon be leaving again. She walked in through the front door—the door usually only strangers and guests used—and made her way to the kitchen in the dark. The light over the stove was on, providing a warm welcome.

In movements so practiced she didn't stop to think about them, she safed her Glock, putting the ammo on top of the refrigerator and leaving the empty weapon in its special pocket in her bag. Then she kicked off her shoes and opened the fridge.

She wasn't hungry until she saw the neon post-it note on a plate of chicken salad. *Eat me,* it ordered. Beside it sat a large tumbler of milk labeled with the command: *Drink me.*

Shaking her head, she removed both and sat down at the table where a place waited for her. Images of Ashley raced through her mind as she started to eat. Terrified? Or laughing at them?

They were quickly replaced with thoughts of Megan: did she have another fever tonight? Was her throat still sore? Or had Lucy overreacted, taking her into the doctor this morning?

Yesterday morning, she corrected herself, glancing at the clock. The second hand beat then twitched, beat then twitched.

As if each second ticked away left it breathless and palsied. Yet, it wouldn't stop.

Lucy swallowed the rest of her food and set the dishes in the sink. She tried to be quiet, but hadn't discovered a way to climb the staircase without producing a symphony of creaky groans. She stopped at Megan's room.

Megan lay asleep, seemed comfortable. A full glass of water sat at her bedside. Lucy crept in, knelt beside her, felt her face with her palm. Maybe a little warm, but it was a hot and humid night. Her breathing was raspy, not quite as bad as her father's snoring, a bit congested.

Maybe it was just a cold after all. Or allergies. Lucy kissed her on the cheek, arranged her covers and stood watching her.

Megan's room was a mess—as it always was, now that it was her responsibility. Her kingdom. The deal was, as long as she kept up with her laundry, had clean clothes for school, and didn't leave any food or dirty plates up here, she could do what she wanted with the room.

It was so very different from Ashley's room. Here, the fabrics and colors were bright and clashing. Beads hung in the open closet door, photos were taped all over the mirror, the wall without windows was a crazy collage of pages torn out of magazines and newspapers—things that "spoke" to her, Megan said. Books and magazines and dirty laundry all piled together on the floor. The only sacrosanct area was the top shelf of the bookcase where framed photos of family and friends and Megan's soccer and Karate trophies stood.

This was how a girl's room should look. Full of life. Hopeful.

Lucy blew her daughter another kiss and left.

Nick was asleep in their bedroom at the end of the hallway. She crept past him into their bathroom, closing the door before turning on the light.

Her thoughts still buzzed and, despite how tired she was, she knew she'd have a hard time sleeping. She took a quick shower, hoping to strip away some of the stress of the day, and slid into her side of the bed.

Nick rolled over, curled an arm around her shoulders, pulling her into his chest. And held her. Not asking anything, not demanding anything, just there for her.

It never ceased to amaze her, after so many years, how much she needed him. Needed this. These silent moments where she could pretend the outside world didn't exist.

His fingers danced through her wet hair as she listened to the strong, steady rhythm of his heartbeat. Finally her body relaxed, easing into his familiar contours.

"How was your day?" she asked. "Megan feeling better?"

"Said she was achy, but no more fever. I gave her some Advil before bed."

"She seemed fine when I just checked her."

"Maybe it was a twenty-four hour bug. With school starting, the kids share everything."

"Yeah, that's what the doctor said. You had a new client today, didn't you? How'd that go?"

The Pittsburgh VA didn't have an opening for someone with Nick's expertise, so he had started his own practice. Because he was the new kid in a city brimming over with world-renown psychologists, he was offering weekend and evening hours as an enticement. Which played hell with their home schedule, not to mention the added expense of setting up an office, but he was really enjoying the work, so Lucy didn't mind.

"Good. Guy's a vet from the first Gulf war; Holtzman referred him after he got fed up with the clinic. I think I can really help him."

"Of course you can." She shifted her body so their heads were side by side on the pillows. Her palm smoothed over his sparse chest hair. He settled his hand over hers, his fingers weaving between hers.

"I heard about your case on the news. Sounded like a tough one."

Her sigh was swallowed by the night. "Yeah. This kid—fourteen, in a house full of everything money can buy, two parents who say they love her—yet she's so alone. I get the feeling she's been that way for a long, long time."

"You think she ran away? To something better?"

"I think she ran away. To something worse." Her gaze flicked to the numbers on the bedside clock. 3:42—thirty-eight hours since Ashley had been last seen.

"If anyone can find her, it's you." He pulled her close again.

"Wish I could be so certain." Her eyelids drooped as her breathing synchronized with his.

"I am."

Blackness engulfed her as she fell into sleep.

Before she could finish the journey, panic jolted her awake and upright. "Did my mom get back from her date okay?"

Nick was too far gone. "Dunno," he mumbled. Then he was asleep again.

Lucy envied him. She grabbed her cell from the bedside table. Double-checked it for messages. Nothing. Her finger quivered over the buttons, poised to call her mom. Almost four in the morning. She couldn't call, not for anything less than an emergency.

She set the phone back down, this time right on the edge of the table, trimming a millisecond or two off her response time. If it rang.

Laying back on the pillow, she edged into sleep. Visions of Megan, her mother, Nick, Ashley chased through her mind… and snakes. Hissing, biting, coiled, striking snakes, fangs dripping blood and venom.

–

Jimmy's butt was asleep. But he couldn't stop watching. It had been hours and she hadn't moved—not an inch. If it wasn't for the microphone picking up the sound of her breathing, he'd swear she was dead.

She looked so lost, so alone. He wanted desperately to go to her, comfort her, let her know that he was here for her.

But he didn't. He stuck with the plan.

Although he had double-checked his references. The one from Vietnam had been most helpful: *Catatonia. A result of internal conflict when the subject cannot incorporate conditions of new reality in terms of old values. Last stage prior to old values being discarded and new reality becoming acceptable, frequently associated with delusions and hallucinations.*

Tomorrow, he thought, stretching his fingers to touch her face on the screen. Tomorrow he would take her to the next stage, introduce her to her new world.

Tomorrow he would save her from the ghosts of her past.

Chapter 20

Sometime before dawn, Lucy woke feeling restless, irritated and needy. Nick was happy to oblige when she reached for him; morning was his favorite time to make love.

Lucy straddled him, needing to feel in control, and they made love quietly, still uncertain of how sound traveled in this creaky new house of theirs with Megan only two doors down at the end of the hall. His hands feathered over her, coaxing, guiding, never demanding—not until the end when his hips thrust up, meeting hers, and the bed rocked and groaned as they both climaxed.

She remained on top, curled up, her arms and legs clutching either side of his chest as if fearful someone might steal him away. Nick fell back asleep but she couldn't, her mind chasing young girls and dark demons and slick talking monsters.

Finally she clawed her way out from under the covers and got ready to go to work. She filled her thermos with coffee, making sure there'd be enough left for Nick, and defrosted two sticky buns for him and Megan. Special Sunday treat.

Before she left, she found herself in Megan's room. It was barely seven o'clock. She wasn't going to wake Megan. She just wanted to look at her, make sure she was all right.

Megan stirred as Lucy sat on the edge of the mattress, twisting her wedding ring, watching her daughter. Megan's breathing was still congested, her color pale in the sunlight filtering through yellow gauze curtains. Lucy brushed her hand across Megan's cheeks. They felt cool and dry. She bent over, kissed Megan's forehead. Also cool.

She traced her fingers along Megan's neck. The glands there still felt big, the size of walnuts. Their old doctor had once said that they'd normally be around the size of a peanut. He'd also said the same thing as the new doctor. That swollen glands were usually a healthy sign of the immune system fighting off disease.

Unable to restrain herself, she bundled Megan into her arms. "Hey sleeping beauty," she murmured when Megan squirmed awake. "Just wanted you to know that I love you."

Megan pulled away from her mother's embrace, one hand rubbing at her eyes. "Mom." She smothered a yawn. "Why do you *always* have to do this? I'm fine."

"I know you are." Lucy gave her another kiss, this one on the cheek.

Megan wrinkled her nose. "Yuck. You smell like coffee."

"Love you too." Lucy relented and stood to leave. "I'll probably be gone all day again."

"Whatever." Megan shielded her eyes from the morning sun and burrowed into her pillow.

Lucy took a step toward the door, stopped. Megan was already falling back to sleep. She hesitated. "Hey. You know that if you or your friends ever needed anything or wanted to talk or whatever… You know your dad and I are here for you, right?"

"Mom, just go find that girl everyone's talking about so you can stop bugging me already." Megan pried open one eye. "Okay?" She drew the word out to three long-suffering syllables.

Lucy stood rooted, unable to tear her eyes away from her daughter's rumpled dark hair standing on end, the ancient soccer jersey she wore as a nightshirt, or the tattered teddy bear standing guard over her from the other side of the bed.

"I love you, Mom," Megan sighed, a grand concession. Didn't bother opening her eyes as she said the words Lucy had been aching to hear.

"Love you too, Kalamazoo."

Megan groaned at the childhood frivolity and rolled over, her back to Lucy once more.

Cindy woke kneeling face down on her bedroom floor, one wrist handcuffed to the bed frame. Burroughs rarely allowed her to sleep in the bed with him—not unless she appeased him more than she had last night. And she made him earn everything she gave him. Those were her rules.

Before moving or opening her eyes, she listened. Hard. No sounds of life, the apartment was empty. Burroughs was gone. Sometimes he liked to stick around, watch her struggle to free herself, taunt her. Sometimes he caught a second wind in the morning and he'd take her on the floor, any way he wanted—any way she let him. Not today.

She smiled and stretched her arm out, reaching for the handcuff key she'd taped to the bottom of the nightstand. After last night, she doubted Burroughs would have a second wind for a long, long time. Hard to believe an old guy—he was forty-one to her twenty-seven—could keep it up like he had last night. She'd never seen him so… needy. They'd done it twice before even reaching the bedroom, their usual tug of war, both fighting for control until she decided when to surrender.

Her body was sore and bruised. She was certain he'd left hand-prints on her butt and arms. Not to mention various scratches and bite marks. She rolled over onto her back, enjoying the way the plush chenille rug caressed her naked skin. Burroughs had been chasing demons last night, and she'd been happy to torture his soul and reap the benefits.

Unlike her other three lovers—the news director, station manager, and a city councilman—Burroughs always satisfied Cindy's physical needs. Multiple times. Once she submitted, she was able to experience orgasms with the merest stroke of his hand, graze of his tongue. No other man had ever—*ever*—been able to coax her to climax like Burroughs could.

The others were business. Burroughs had started out that way as well. A reporter could never have too many friends in the police department. She and Burroughs had quickly crossed the line, taken things further. It wasn't a relationship but rather a mutual addiction.

Her fingers trailed over her bare stomach, following the path his teeth had taken last night. She wasn't quite certain who needed whom most and that made her a little nervous.

During sex she was always in control. Always. But the way she kept thinking about him in between times—that was a bit frightening. Especially as she was certain he never thought of her. Not that way.

She sat up, shaking her hair free of its tangles. As long as this thing with Burroughs was good for business, she wouldn't worry about it. Two mutually consenting adults having good—make that great—sex, what was there to worry about?

Her phone rang. She grabbed it and hopped onto the unmade bed.

"Cindy, it's Felix. We're at that address you gave us. The blue Subaru is gone, though."

"That's all right. Film some establishing shots—be sure to get the house number in the frame." She slid her palm over her red satin sheets—Burroughs' favorites—inhaled the musky scent of sex, and found herself wishing he had stayed. Probably was with Guardino right now. The bitch. Because of her, Cindy was off the Yeager story. Temporarily.

"There's a man and a kid coming out, dressed for church," Felix said. "Looks like they're walking."

"Film them, call me from the church or wherever they end up. I'll meet you there." She hung up, staring at the depression Burroughs had left behind in her pillows. Imagining his reaction when she turned the tables on Guardino. He'd stay all night after that. Most definitely.

Cindy rolled over onto her stomach, burying her face in the pillow, kicking her legs with wild abandon. Laughter rippled through her.

Guardino was going to be her ticket to a lead story—maybe even a primetime special.

And Burroughs was going to help.

She loved it when a plan came together.

Chapter 21

"You've got the camera in the necklace," Fletcher, the Customs guy, said as he draped the heavy, enameled choker around Lucy's neck and cinched it tight. "Microphone in your belt buckle." He started to thread the belt through Lucy's jeans but stopped at her glare. Instead he backed away and held it out to her. "Um, I guess, you can—"

Lucy took the belt and quickly secured it. The back of the monitoring SUV was stifling and she was drenched with sweat. Maybe she was coming down with whatever Megan had.

"Testing, testing," she said in a low voice.

Fletcher watched the monitor and nodded. "Good to go."

"Cover team in place?" Lucy asked.

"Parking lot and adjacent room. No movement reported since the subjects returned from the restaurant."

Of course not. The three Canadians were saving their energy for their special Sunday morning treat. "Got my purse?"

Fletcher handed her Ruby's denim bag. "Wallet with license and credit cards in the name of Ruby Miles, photos of Katie, gum, Kleenex, house keys…"

Lucy rummaged through the frayed bag, verifying that her cover details rang true even though they hadn't changed since yesterday. Part of her ritual, part of the waiting. "Move in as soon as I leave the room. Crisis intervention if I mention a play date. Everyone clear?"

He stopped short of rolling his eyes. "Like we didn't just do this yesterday?"

"I didn't ask about yesterday, I asked about today. Everyone clear on the alarm signal?"

Fletcher tapped his earpiece and relayed her inquiry. "Everyone's on board."

She stifled a yawn. Shook her hands, flicking away her anxiety, and glanced at the clock. Fatigue and heat swaddled her and her eyes drooped.

"Lucy, it's time."

She jerked awake, sending a searching glance Fletcher's way. He had his back to her, didn't seem to realize she'd drifted off. She slid her wedding band free and completed her final ritual. A quick kiss for luck before carefully sealing the ring in the change section of her real wallet inside her real bag.

They were parked at the Monroeville Mall, a few miles from the meeting place. Lucy had offered the men a few options, and they had chosen a small motel off Route 22. She would take the van there, make the final arrangements, verifying and documenting that all three men were there to meet with four-year-old Katie, and then leave. Her back up team would do the take down. No fuss, no muss. Not today.

She drove the van there, to where the three Canadians waited for their chance to meet with four-year-old Katie. She parked in the space in front of the room beside the subjects'. Checked that the van didn't block any sight lines to the target door or window.

She yawned, popped her ear, left the van running, got out and locked the door behind her.

The motel door opened before she could knock. Eager.

A man with sparse blond hair, wearing a dress shirt and navy slacks stood on the other side. "Ruby?"

Lucy ran a finger over her collarbone, adjusting her choker as she got a good view into the room. "Are you Earl?"

He nodded, his Adam's apple bobbing in time with his head. She stepped past him into the room.

An overweight man with brown hair and glasses approached her, his arm outstretched to shake her hand. "I'm Johnny."

The schoolteacher. She clasped his hand and turned to look at the third man in the room. He stood by the window, hands out of view as he peered through the drapes. "Where's Katie?"

Ivan, the lawyer. He sounded like a lawyer, all questions that really weren't questions but demands, his tone half whining and half pouting, expecting to have things done his way, right away.

Lucy spun around, surveying the room for any unexpected surprises, then perched on one of the two beds. Both were still made, there were no suitcases to be seen—they must have stayed somewhere else last night. The only personal items in the room were two large cameras and a digital video recorder set up on a tripod.

"I can't believe how hot it is," she said, fanning herself with one hand. "Bet it's a lot cooler up where yunz are from."

"Yeah, about twenty-seven Celsius," Earl, the podiatrist, said.

"I didn't come here for chit chat. Where's the girl?" Ivan snapped.

"She fell asleep, so I left her in the van while we discussed our arrangements. Don't worry, I locked the door, she's fine." She smiled at the other two. "Sleeping like a little angel. She's so excited about having her picture taken, just loves the camera." She rummaged through her bag and handed them several snapshots of Katie. Maternal pride stretched her smile wider. "She could be a real star someday if I can afford enough money to build her a real portfolio, you know?"

"She's darling," Earl said, running one finger along his lips as he stared at the photo. Johnny was too engrossed to say anything, his upper lip now shiny with sweat and anticipation.

"Well, gentlemen, your money made it into my account, so I guess if we're clear on the ground rules, we're all set to go." Lucy nonchalantly crossed her legs, leaning back on the bed. "I get to stay the entire time, photos only, no touching."

"But kissing," Earl put in, his gaze still fixed on the snapshot in his hand, "you said kissing was all right."

"If that's what you want. Is there anything else you want?"

"I want, er, I'd like to give her a bubble bath," Johnny said, his gaze darting up to meet hers then sliding away again. "I'd pay extra."

"How much?"

"Five hundred."

"US, not Canadian?"

"Yes."

"And you, what do you want?" She addressed the lawyer, still staring out the window.

Ivan jerked the drapes closed and whirled on her, a pistol in his hand. A Taurus 9 millimeter—a serious weapon, no frills, just deadly.

He was taller, younger, and in better shape than the other two. Unlike them, he wasn't dressed for the occasion, instead wore black jeans and a black polo shirt. A twisted scowl cemented itself on his face but the gleam in his eye was pure desire.

She'd seen that same gleam in junkies and psychopaths. She had the feeling Ivan might be both. Lucy jumped up, her gaze fixed on Ivan's hands.

"Look, if you guys are cops, I haven't done anything wrong," she said, edging toward the door. Ivan stepped in her path, aiming the gun at her face. She caught a glimpse of the other men's faces. They appeared shocked.

"What do I want?" Ivan said with a sneer. "I want your car keys and then I want you to kneel on the ground and start praying."

Chapter 22

Lucy froze. Ivan was too far away for her to jump him and way, way too calm for her liking.

He'd fantasized about this a lot, a whole helluva lot. He wasn't like the other two, she realized now. Ivan targeted little girls not because he was a dedicated pedophile, but because they were easy to control and terrorize.

Damn. How could she have been so wrong? Her breath collided with the knot of fear tightening her throat. She gulped them both down hard.

"I don't have the keys," she said, keeping her voice low and her gaze on his hands, avoiding any challenging eye contact.

"Don't mess with me, bitch!"

She saw his backhanded slap coming, and rolled with it, dropping to her knees. He lunged forward, grabbing her hair, twisting it in his free fist before she could reach her weapon. Which would have been a suicide move anyway. Just as calling in her team would be. Until she calmed him down and got the gun farther away from her.

Instead, she reached for her hair, trying to ease the pressure ripping across her scalp. Ivan planted the Taurus' barrel in the center of her forehead, pressing so hard it gouged her flesh. Adrenalin roared through her brain, so loud she had to strain to hear his words.

"Earl, search her bag. Get the keys," he ordered. "Johnny, find something to tie her up with."

"Where'd you get the gun?" the schoolteacher asked, standing frozen on the edge of Lucy's peripheral vision. He'd gone pale, couldn't seem to stop licking his lips.

"Never mind that. Just do what I say. Tie her up." Ivan's words came fast, as if he had rehearsed them. Lucy bet he had—late at night, alone in the dark, one hand wrapped around his penis, the other stroking his gun as he fantasized this moment. He sounded excited, thrilled with anticipation… triumphant.

Show the fish what they want, but don't let them have it.

A quick flash of her family filled her vision. She blinked it away. She had to focus, stay in control. If she was going to get out of here alive.

The dentist dumped her bag out on the bed. "No car keys here."

"Where is it, bitch?" Ivan yanked her head back so hard fire raced across her scalp, bringing genuine tears to her eyes.

"I told you. I left the van running, it's too hot to leave a kid out there," she blurted in a gush, letting the tears flow. "Please don't hurt Katie, she's just a little girl, please don't—"

"Earl, go see if what she says is true. If it is, bring the girl and the keys back."

Earl left. *One down, two to go.*

"What do you want?" Lucy asked, stalling for time. Johnny didn't seem much of a threat. It was Ivan she needed to worry about. As long as she wasn't restrained, she could get out of this. Alive.

"I'll tell you." Ivan's gun remained centered on her forehead but his gaze grew unfocused as he relived his fantasy.

She'd bet this was the closest he'd ever come to fulfilling it. For all his mental rehearsing, he was still a virgin.

"First of all, I'm going to give you want you wanted. You get to watch. Earl and Johnny will take their photos, finish with the girl. Then we're going to take a drive out to the woods. And then," his mouth parted in anticipation, sweat gleaming from his upper lip, "it's my turn."

Uh huh. Couldn't any of these whack jobs get creative? Always the same old sadistic fantasies, it was almost comical. Except for the nine-millimeter aimed at her brain.

"I can't find any rope," Johnny said, his voice petulant now that he'd gotten used to the idea that their innocent little hijinks had suddenly morphed into premeditated murder.

"Rip the cord from the lamp."

"I tried, I can't."

"Then use the phone cord. Damn it, do I have to think of everything?"

He rocked back, his gaze shifting from Lucy to Johnny. Just the opening she was waiting for.

"Play date!" she shouted.

She grabbed Ivan's gun hand, twisting it away from her. His grip on her hair tightened, ripping a hunk out. Momentum was on her side as she used the movement to propel her. She launched up in a ferocious head butt, catching him under his chin. The impact rocketed through her skull. She followed through, propelling him down to the ground, twisting his gun hand so hard bones popped as they separated, landing with her knee on his windpipe.

Blood covered his mouth and jaw. His scream ricocheted through the air. The door slammed against the wall. The room filled with shouts of, "FBI, drop the gun, drop the gun, hands, hands, hands!"

The gun was long since dropped. Ivan's scream sputtered into a gurgle. Johnny cried, blubbering as her team slammed him to his knees and cuffed him.

"We've got him, Lucy." Fletcher pulled her up and off Ivan.

Lucy had to force her hands open, releasing Ivan's mangled wrist. Her head hurt, her scalp burned, her hand throbbed, and nausea knocked her jaws together.

Black spots dancing before her eyes reminded her to breathe. She stumbled back as two agents hoisted Ivan to his feet and dragged him out the door that now had a serious dent in its center and hung crookedly on one hinge.

"Okay, people, this is a crime scene, let's get to work," she said, tugging her jacket off, it was too tight, too hot, too heavy.

Cameras flashed, notebooks came out. She backed out the door, letting the evidence collection proceed.

"You okay?" Fletcher asked. "The medics said Ivan's wrist is broken and he about bit his tongue in half. Good thing we got him on tape while he could still talk."

He trailed after her as Lucy walked to his SUV. Her hands trembled so much it was a strain to open the rear door. She slumped onto the running board, just in time before her legs gave out.

Twice in two days—what the hell had gone wrong? There'd been no hint that either Pastor Walter or the Canadians were violent, yet she'd almost gotten her team killed twice in two days. Greally was going to flay her alive for this.

"You got everything, then?" The words were thick, her mouth dry.

"Crystal clear." He leaned against the bumper, arms crossed, chest puffed as if he'd been in there with her instead of just listening and watching through the camera implanted in her choker.

"Good." With trembling hands she retrieved her wedding ring, brushed it against her lips and slid it back where it belonged. She reached for her bag, grabbed a water bottle and drank half of it, almost choking in her urgent need.

"Your cell phone has been going nuts. Again." His voice dripped with disapproval.

God. Megan. Or her mother. Her throat tightened again and she spewed a mouthful of water onto the pavement. "Give me it."

He rummaged in the back of the SUV and handed her the phone. She punched the buttons for voicemail.

"Now, don't worry," Nick's message started, and she had a terrible, gut-whirling feeling of *deja vu*. "Everything's fine. Megan fainted while we were at Mass and the ambulance brought us here to Three Rivers. The ER doctor is with her now. Everything's all right."

Ambulance? Fainted? Megan had never, ever fainted before. Everything was most certainly not all right.

Her jaw muscles clamped down hard, grinding her molars together. Lucy hit the speed dial for Nick's phone but there was no answer. She started to leave a message but instead hung up. She had no message, she had no answers—only questions.

Fletcher was still there, making no excuses for eavesdropping. Lucy really didn't care. "I need to get back to the office anyway, I'll drop you at Three Rivers."

Lucy snatched the keys from him. "I'm driving."

–

Lucy had long ago grown used to the feeling that someone was jabbing ice picks in her ears. Anytime there was a tough case, the constant pain lancing through her head and neck was the price she paid.

Nick had tried hypnosis, her dentist had tried a bite guard (which she had promptly lost), and she had tried popping Advils like they were M&M's, all without relief.

Now her anonymous tormentor had taken a sledgehammer to those ice picks and was pounding the hell out of them, creating a roar of tympani echoing through her brain.

On top of it all, Fletcher was talking. Hoping to distract herself from the shifting images of Megan slumped on the floor, strapped to an ambulance, crying for her mother as strangers poked and prodded her, Lucy stretched her mouth into a yawn, popping her jaw joints, and allowing Fletcher's voice to cut through the white noise of pain.

"My mom was in a hospital for a while," he was saying. "Don't worry, she's doing fine now, but the doctors and nurses, they're really good. I'm sure they'll take really good care of your daughter. What's her name?"

"Megan." Megan with her smile like sunshine and her sudden flashes of scarily sophisticated humor and her freckles that looked just like her father's. "She's been sick. I never should have left her." Lucy's grip on the steering wheel tightened and she clamped her jaws shut.

"You had work to do," he said self-righteously as if repeating a mantra. "Important work. I mean, what if those perverts had gotten their hands on a real kid? Four years old? I just can't understand anyone interested in sex with a baby like that."

"Our job isn't to understand them." She changed lanes, cutting off a little old lady hunched over the wheel of a Buick and cursed the fact that the surveillance vehicle had no lights or siren.

"But you do. Understand them, I mean."

She shot a glare at Fletcher. He ignored it, pivoting his body to face her from the passenger seat, fumbling with a small netbook computer plugged into the cigarette lighter. He carried the damn thing with him everywhere, but she'd just now noticed that it was a personal computer, not one of the ICE ones. Way he clutched it, Lucy wondered if he spent his downtime surfing for porn. Hoped it was legit—she was in no mood to arrest someone on her own team.

She almost laughed at the thought. Nick would have told her she was trying to deflect her anxiety or accuse her of carrying her cop-paranoia too far. Both would be true.

"You know how they think, what they want, what they're going to do next," Fletcher continued. "How do you do that?"

Then why had she been caught by surprise twice in two days? Dammit, how had she fucked up so badly?

"Believe me, that's not the same as understanding them." Lucy spotted an opening in traffic and swerved into it. "I don't give a shit why they do what they do, all I want to know is what patterns they'll follow so I can stop them before they hurt someone."

His head was genuflecting as if she had quoted scripture. "But they follow patterns for a reason, don't they? I mean, I can understand why a full-grown man would feel attracted to a younger woman, happens all the time. But why a little girl or boy?"

In her mind she was ticking off things she'd have to delegate if Megan was seriously ill. Hated herself even for thinking that way, for assuming the worst. Wasn't that like asking for it to happen? But she was the boss, she couldn't just drop everything. Lives depended on her team working at peak efficiency. Lives like Ashley Yeager's.

Walden or Taylor would call her if anything broke. Right now all they could do was keep working the street and the cyber angle.

Which left her with a fifteen-minute drive and too many worst-case scenarios to dwell on. So instead, she answered Fletcher's question.

"It doesn't matter if you call it an illness or a perversion or a compulsion," she told the eager specialist. "You have to think in terms of the victims."

"But those guys, back in the hotel, they weren't like serial killers or crazy people you see in the movies. I mean the ones without the gun. They didn't think of the little girl as a victim. They weren't trying to hurt her."

"They didn't think of her at all—other than as an object to gratify their needs. If they did hurt her, they wouldn't feel guilt or shame. But they would feel remorse."

"Remorse? Why?"

"They'd be upset because their object wouldn't be available to them anymore. They'd be forced to rely on the second best thing— their memories and fantasies. That's the real trick to catching the worst of these guys. They're all driven to experience the real thing."

He hummed a fragment of an old Coke jingle. *Ain't nothing like the real thing, baby*. "So to catch them you give them what they want."

"Exactly." She steered the van onto the Squirrel Hill exit and cursed at the backup at the red light. While they waited, she flipped her phone open, called Nick. Still no answer. Then she tried Walden. "Hey, anything shaking loose on Ashley Yeager?"

"No and no. Lots of calls to the hotline overnight. The Staties and Sheriffs haven't found anything worth our following up. We found the first bus driver but he didn't remember her at all, no surprise. Haven't found any other drivers or evidence that she took another bus."

"She had a plan. No way East Liberty was her final destination before she just happened to end up at the Tastee Treet."

"I know," he sounded as exasperated as she was. "She could have walked to another bus stop, caught a ride with someone, who knows."

"It's not important. We know she ended up at the Tastee Treet. Any luck with Noreen's car?"

"No joy."

"What about Tardiff?" She didn't like the idea of the photographer floating in the breeze, an unknown quantity.

"Well now, there's an interesting story there. He called the missus this morning."

"And?"

"And he's actually here in Pittsburgh. They didn't talk much, Melissa shushed him and got him off the line quick, but Taylor tracked him. He's been staying in a Shadyside executive rental for the past week."

"You bring him in?"

"Wasn't there. I have Burroughs' guys working on it."

"Don't let him drop through the cracks."

She inched forward in traffic, coming alongside a girl who looked like Megan riding in the back seat of an Explorer. The tympani returned, threatening to jar her brain loose. Dammit, she needed a break. Ashley needed a break. And so did Megan. *Please Lord…*

"I'm not sure how long I might be held up. Megan fainted at church and she's at the hospital."

There was a pause as if Walden started to say something then changed his mind. "She gonna be all right?"

"I don't know yet. But call me if you guys hear anything. Just because I'm out of the office doesn't mean I'm out of the game."

"Relax, boss. We've got everything covered. Burroughs is coming in and the H-Tech guys have been working all night. Taylor thinks they might be close to something."

Traffic surged forward. "Call me. I mean it, Walden. Call me if anything breaks."

She hung up and concentrated on driving. Sunday morning deli-connoisseurs snarled traffic on Murray Avenue before she made it to Wilkins and could cut over to Negley.

"Want me to go help them with Ashley's computer?" Fletcher asked. "These transcriptions can wait until tomorrow."

"No," she said sharply, remembering his goof yesterday. "Thanks, but I don't want to risk any hotshot lawyer giving me grief about chain of custody or evidence tampering. You drop me off and head back to the office, get everything documented and secured."

"Sure, you're the boss," he said, but his tone reminded her of Megan's favorite pouty whine. When she stole a glance at him, he was settled back in his seat, staring out the passenger window, his face a blank.

Whatever. She stopped herself from rolling her eyes and chan-neling Megan. Having a pre-teen in the house must be contagious. But she didn't have time to worry about bruised egos. She had a helluva lot bigger things to worry about.

The brightly colored sign for Three Rivers Medical Center appeared and she turned into the main driveway. She threw the SUV into Park and grabbed her purse, her grip tight and sweaty. She didn't even bother to say goodbye to Fletcher as she sprinted into the building, its cheerful colors greeting her as if she'd entered another world. No amount of paint or chirpy Disney music could disguise the hospital from what it really was. As soon as she took her first breath inside the lobby, she could smell the truth.

This was a place of death.

—

Ashley's legs jerked as if to stop her from falling. Her stomach kept tumbling in free-fall as her pounding heart followed. She flailed her hands out, hit something metal and grabbed onto it.

She was so dizzy she could barely raise her head. Slowly, memo-ries began to reconnect. She'd been running away, following Bobby's plan, they were going to escape together.

But Bobby wasn't here. It was just her and the rotting corpses of whomever or whatever stinking up the air.

She licked her lips; they were rough as caked sand. The rest of her also felt gritty, dried sweat chafing with every movement. Water, where was her water? She inched her hands through the darkness, the knowledge that the bucket might be gone raising a wave of acid up her throat.

She laughed. A frail and hollow noise that echoed through the space. Guess she wasn't ready to die after all. Her fingers brushed the bucket at her side. She raised it to drink, careful not to waste any.

Nothing came.

She rubbed her hand down the side. Dry. A little moisture remained at the bottom, not enough to do more than coat her finger.

Gone. It was all gone.

Every muscle in her body felt braided with pain, stretched beyond endurance. Her left ankle worse of all, now swollen, it pulsed beneath the cable that restrained her—since she was blind here, she had gouged it without her usual precision and expertise.

All for nothing. Gingerly she stretched, listening to joints crack and groan like an old woman's. How long? How long had she been here? How long before he returned?

How long before he started?

Because if her silent yet stinky companions were any gauge, the worst was yet to come.

Her eyes burned with tears but none came. When she wiped them only small grains of salty residue rubbed against her finger. Despite her thirst, she still had to pee. She resigned herself to the arduous task of searching for the commode.

Better now than wetting herself when he got started. Maybe she was going to die, but she'd be damned if she'd humiliate herself for his pleasure.

If things got too bad, she'd just float away again. Go to her quiet place.

If she was lucky, she'd never return.

Chapter 23

There was a line at the information desk, so Lucy didn't wait. She jogged down the hallway, following the signs labeled PEDIATRIC EMERGENCY DEPARTMENT only to find another desk and another line.

More people waited here, clustered in small groups punctuated by crying babies, snuffling toddlers and coughing adolescents. An open doorway beckoned from behind a nurse sitting at the desk, beyond it light gleamed from white tiled walls as men and women in scrubs and lab coats hustled between rooms.

Lucy strode past the busy receptionist and nurse, not realizing until her momentum carried her over the threshold that the doorway was equipped with a metal detector. Alarms blared, babies screamed, and two lumbering guards came running down the hall to intercept her.

"Step against the wall, ma'am," one guard said, blocking her passage as the other approached her warily from her side.

Lucy reacted with a cop's instinct, pivoting to shield her weapon and keep her gun hand free. Her jacket fell back, exposing the thirty-two she'd holstered on her hip after the take down earlier.

"Gun!" the second guard screeched, his voice so high pitched that it, coupled with his bulk and pock-marked face, made Lucy think: *steroid abuser*. He fumbled at his holster, actually drawing his gun and pointing it at her.

"Calm down," she shouted over the claxons and the sound of footsteps and screams as the waiting room emptied, women and children fleeing. "I'm on the job. If someone would turn off the damn alarm."

Neither guard seemed to hear her, now both had their guns drawn and pointed at her, their stances wide-based, their faces creased with worry and sweat. The second one's hand was shaking so badly and he was blinking so fast Lucy thought he might burst into tears.

She wanted to tell the rent-a-cops that they were both too close and standing face on, offering her big-time easy targets if she was someone looking to do harm.

Instead, she raised her hands in surrender, one hand on the top of her head, the other pulling her jacket open by her lapel. "Go ahead and take it, but for God's sake be careful. There's one in the chamber."

They hesitated and exchanged looks, neither wanting to approach the oh-so terrifying 5'5", 130 pound menace to society. The alarms died and they stood at an impasse in the empty hallway.

"I'm FBI," Lucy said in a calm voice she hoped would overcome her appearance. She'd forgotten that she still wore the tight jeans and trailer trash makeup. "My daughter was brought here by ambulance and they called me off a case. My credentials are in my purse along with my service weapon."

She shrugged, allowing her purse to fall to the floor. Both guards jumped at the noise.

For an instant Lucy thought they would shoot her. Her pulse stuttered and sweat dripped between her breasts. A young doctor poked his head out from an exam room, pulled it back in again even faster.

Lucy kicked the bag to the first guard. "Please, I just want to see my daughter. Her name is Megan Callahan. I'm Supervisory Special Agent Lucy Guardino. My husband is Nick Callahan. She was brought here by ambulance—"

As she spoke the guard warily crouched and rummaged through her bag, first bringing out her Glock and then her credentials. He flipped them open and finally nodded.

"She's telling the truth," he said, holstering his gun. Lucy let her breath out as the second guard, the twitchy one, followed suit.

"Sorry about that," she said, trying her best to keep her anger from her voice. The first guard handed back her credentials and purse. "I've never been here before, I was just so worried about Megan."

"Yeah, well, next time you should follow the rules, lady," the second guard said, his voice still in the soprano range. "Just 'cause you're FBI doesn't make you special."

"We'll need to lock all weapons in the vault while you're here," the first one said, extending a hand and gesturing to the thirty-two. Lucy removed it and handed it over. She felt naked, couldn't remember the last time outside of her home that she'd walked around unarmed. "If you come with me, I'll find out where your daughter is and get you a receipt."

Lucy meekly followed, irritated by the additional delay. From the hostile stares greeting her from the exam rooms as well as from the staff and patients trickling back into the waiting room, she decided it wouldn't do any good to protest.

Luckily the guard actually seemed to know what he was doing when it came to paperwork. He locked both guns in a small safe behind the security desk in the main office, printed her a visitor's badge and found Megan in the computer. "She's been admitted," he told her. "Fourth floor, room four oh' two."

"Thanks," she told him as she clipped the badge on. "I'm sorry about earlier."

"Most excitement we've had around here in months. Hope your daughter is all right."

–

Lucy rode alone in the elevator, a steel box that moved haltingly as if afraid to startle anyone with excessive speed. She slumped against the rear corner, swamped by the adrenalin rush of being held at gunpoint twice today, combined with fear for Megan and guilt that she hadn't been with her. A cold sweat slicked her skin, making her healthy tan appear sallow in the overhead fluorescent light and her headache had locked her jaws tight.

Breathe, that's what Nick was always telling her. Just breathe. Easy to say but not so easy to do when your lungs felt wrapped tight in duct tape and your heart was pounding so hard it gagged your throat.

Being in a hospital wasn't helping. Too many memories of when she was Megan's age—she'd practically lived in her father's room while her mother was at work that summer. The nurses turned a blind eye as she'd roamed the halls, fetching newspapers and magazines for her father and other patients who made quick use of her mobility. And of course there were the countless trips to the market across the street. Their little secret, her father had said, a twinkle in his eye that made Lucy feel grown up and reckless and brave.

Her stomach lurched as the elevator halted and the doors opened. "Fourth floor, pediatrics," a disembodied voice told her.

She stumbled out, planted one hand against the wall and straightened. Breathed in, breathed out, pressing her palm flat against her stomach to force the air out, trying in vain to exhale her fears with it. Megan needed her. No time for memories or weakness.

When she found room 402 the bed was empty. Nick sat in a recliner beside the window, idly thumbing the remote for the overhead TV. Lucy paused in the doorway, watching, gauging. Nick was always calm, so it was no surprise to see him sitting instead of pacing like Lucy would be. But he was definitely worried—hence the mindless channel surfing.

"I got here as fast as I could," she said. He looked up, dropped the remote so that it dangled by the cord connecting it to the big hospital bed. "Where's Megan? What did the doctors say? Is she going to be all right?"

"CAT scan. They wouldn't let me go with her." He stood.

"CAT scan? Why? What's wrong with her?"

"The doctors said it was just a fainting spell. But she had a fever again when we got here—"

"A fever? Didn't you check her before you went out?" She hated the anger that bled into her voice but was powerless to stop it. She had to lash out at someone and Nick was her only target.

"Of course I did. She was fine." His voice was irritatingly calm. "They need to do more tests before they know for sure what's going on."

"Tests? You mean they don't know what's wrong with her?" Panic wove into the anger.

Nick approached her. Wrapped his arms around her. Held her tight, too tight. Despite his level voice, she felt the waves of tension cascading from his body. "They said," his voice cracked, "they said one of the things they're checking for is cancer."

"Cancer? Jesus, Nick! Why didn't you call me? No, it can't be—" The word struck her harder than a slap, suddenly there were tears in her eyes, the room spinning out of control, collapsing around her.

"They're not sure, said they just want to rule it out. Be on the safe side. I did try to call you but my phone died and by the time—" He stopped, a puzzled look on his face as he pushed her bangs away from her forehead. "Is that blood? Christ, were you hurt?"

She feathered a hand through her sticky, plasticized hair. There was a goose-egg forming where she'd head butted Ivan but she didn't feel any bleeding. "I'm fine. How long before they bring Megan back? I want to talk to the doctors—"

He kept a hand on her waist, steering her away from the bed and into the bathroom. "They've been very good about updating me as soon as they know anything. Your charging in isn't going to help."

She squinted in the bright lights; there were flecks of dried blood on her face and forehead. Wordlessly, as if she were a child, Nick ran a washcloth under water and began to wipe her face clean of blood and layers of sweat-caked makeup. She released herself to his attentions, too shaky and agitated to do a good job of it herself.

"What happened?"

"A subject got a little frisky so I broke his nose." She edged her hips onto the countertop, avoiding his gaze, but couldn't block out the sound of his sigh as his fingers found the swelling on her scalp. "With my head."

"I thought the whole idea behind this move and your promotion was that you'd be supervising, out of danger."

"Nick—" They'd had this conversation too many times in the last three months. She was in no mood to return to it now.

"Lulu, I can't be worried about both you and Megan." His voice dropped to a low rumble, his Virginia accent stronger. It was the closest to upset Nick ever came.

She intertwined both her hands around his, ignoring the wet washcloth pressed between their palms.

"Hey," she said, tilting her head to face him dead on. "I promise. You don't ever have to worry about me. Everything I do is so I can come home to you and Megan."

A small furrow of doubt creased his brow, making his boyish features appear suddenly older and wiser than his thirty-nine years. She kissed his forehead, her lips following the trail of freckles down the bridge of his nose, finally coming to rest on his mouth. The washcloth fell to the sink with a splash as his arms wrapped around her.

This was why she did what she did, why men like Burroughs were distant shadows compared to Nick. Their bodies pressed together, a silent communication of need and sharing, two hearts racing, vibrating in concert, draining her fear away.

Her jaw released its death grip, her head stopped its throbbing, her shoulders relaxed their hunched posture. Nick was her touchstone, her anchor. When she was with him, she could face anything—they could face anything.

Fourteen years and it hadn't changed. Their very first kiss had sparked this same passion, a passion that if anything had grown over the years.

When they parted a few moments later, she felt more in control than she had since getting his message. She clung to him, cherishing his strength as she assessed the situation. "Does Megan know?"

Nick made a sound that was halfway between a chuckle and a sob. "She's the one who asked the doctors," he said, his chin resting on her head, his fingers pressing into her shoulders. "They took her blood but then came back talking about more tests—I was blind, all I could think about was that they wanted to stick her again and I got angry that they had to do it again. But Megan, she looks up at them and says, 'if I have cancer can I shave my head before my hair falls out?' Just like that."

"Sometimes I think she's smarter than both of us," Lucy confessed, wiping her tears on his shirt. It was his favorite white broadcloth, butter-soft from being washed so many times. And now it was stained by tears and cheap mascara.

"Well, the good news is the doctors said that there are a lot of other things it could be besides cancer. Said that was near the bottom of their list, but they need to be certain, so they're checking everything."

"Megan was okay with that?" Lucy asked, because she sure as hell wasn't.

"Yeah. After the doctor explained that the CAT scan didn't involve any more needles, all she was worried about was soccer."

Typical one track mind. Sometimes Lucy worried Megan took after her a little too much. She slid from the countertop, her butt wet from the splashing water. Another few breaths and she could trust her voice. "Megan will want her PJ's and clothes, maybe her iPod—"

"Your mom's at the house now, packing bags for all of us." He followed her back into the main room.

Oh Lord. Her mother poking through all their things? Not that she had anything to hide from her mother, but still—a pang of long-instilled childhood guilt chimed through her as she tried to remember if she'd picked up her dirty clothes from last night. Almost laughed at the automatic thoughts, the least of her worries. She slumped onto the edge of the bed. "So there's nothing to do except wait."

That coaxed a smile from Nick who was all too used to her essential lack of patience. He sat beside her, wrapping an arm around her shoulders and nuzzling the still wet skin behind her ear. "We could always neck some more."

He wasn't serious, but the mere fact that he could try to joke made her feel more confident that Megan truly would be all right. Before she could respond, a wheelchair pulled up to the door.

"Mom," Megan called out as the attendant pushed her into the room. An IV was attached to her left hand, clear plastic tubing connected to a machine on a pole with wheels. Her color was a little pale, but other than that she looked fine. Better than Lucy, in fact. "What on earth are you wearing? You look like Ashlee Simpson."

From Megan's look of consternation and her shrill tone of disapproval, Lucy concluded that this was not a compliment.

"How are you doing, kiddo?" she asked, rushing to help but feeling hopelessly inept as the attendant efficiently transferred IV tubing and plugged a wire into the monitor. He lowered the bed to a suitable level and smiled at Megan.

"All right now, you ready to hop out of that chair?"

Megan's nose wrinkled as she grinned. "Come on, just one more lap around the block. I'll race you."

"Sorry, no can do," the attendant replied, bending down and wrapping the arm without the IV around his neck as he leveraged Megan to her feet and in one smooth motion pivoted her onto the bed. "You take care now, Miss Megan."

"Thanks for the ride." Megan slumped back and began playing with the bed controls. Lucy rushed after the attendant.

"Thank you," she told him as he handed a binder with Megan's name on it to a clerk at the nursing station. "Did the doctors say how soon it would be before they had the results? Did they say anything about how the scan looked?"

He gave her a kind smile, shaking his head. "Sorry, ma'am. I'm sure they'll let you know as soon as they have any information. Take care now."

He wheeled the empty chair down the hall to the elevator bank. Lucy pitched her head back as an exasperated sigh escaped her. Neon smiley faces grinned down at her from the ceiling tiles. She thought about the need to decorate the ceiling, visualized kids trapped in beds, trapped in their bodies like Bobby Fegley.

She straightened, reminding herself that no news was good news.

"Hi, I'm Megan Callahan's mom," she introduced herself to the ward clerk, an older woman who was juggling a phone and several charts. "When you have a moment, I'd really appreciate it if you could page Megan's doctor. I need—I'd like an update on her test results."

The clerk smiled and nodded. Lucy returned to the room. Megan was perched on a throne of pillows, had commandeered the TV remote and was bossing her father as she directed him in moving the TV to the perfect angle. Nick was smiling, his hand never far from touching Megan's arm. Lucy joined them, sliding onto the bed beside Megan.

"So, you've had quite an adventure," she said, burying her face in Megan's hair and hugging her hard. An alarm began to beep, its shrill soprano pitch making Lucy reach for her weapon. Nick calmly punched a button on the monitor, silencing it.

"Did I do that?" she asked.

"Got to watch out for the pulse ox," Megan said, waving her finger with an air of authority. Attached to it was a piece of tape with a glowing red spot. "It sends waves of light through my skin and can measure the amount of oxygen in my blood. See," she gestured to the monitor, "it says one hundred now, that's the best you can get."

"So your oxygen is the best ever. How's the rest of you?"

Megan pursed her lips, considering. "The IV kind of hurt and then I had to get more blood work, but I was really brave, wasn't I, Dad?"

"You sure were, princess." Nick leaned down to plant a kiss on her forehead.

"And my tummy was upset, but that feels better now too. So can I go home now?"

"Not until they find out what's wrong with you."

"But soccer's tomorrow—"

"Megan," Lucy snapped, then immediately regretted allowing her frustration to leak into her voice.

Megan didn't flinch, instead that sly smile returned and Lucy knew she was being played. By a twelve-year-old. Again.

"No soccer until the doctors say it's all right."

"Hmm," Megan said, fluffing her pillows, "well, if I'm stuck in bed, guess I'm going to need some video games to play. Or a laptop computer, one with a DVD player, no an iPad—"

"Megan Constance Callahan, where did you get the idea that being sick meant you got presents?" Lucy asked.

Nick blushed and looked away and she had her answer.

"If you're here longer than overnight," might as well hope for the best until she knew otherwise, "I'll stop and pick up the new Evan Bedard book you wanted."

"I don't have to wait for it to come out in paperback? Very cool," Megan said, rubbing her hands together. Mission accomplished.

A knock on the door came and an aide appeared, wheeling a large cart with a TV bolted to the top. "I'm Melody from Child Life services," she chirped. "Your nurse told me you might like to play some video games." She parked the cart at the foot of the bed and handed Megan a futuristic looking remote control/toggle switch/keyboard that rivaled anything NASA had. "Do you need help working it?"

Megan shook her head, bouncing up and down on the bed with delight as she clicked the unit on and found a game she liked. Music began blaring from loudspeakers.

Lucy followed the aide back out to the nurses' station. "Any word from my daughter's doctors?"

"Sorry, Mrs. Callahan," the clerk said. "Dr. Scott is tied up in the ICU but he did say that he was still waiting for Megan's test results and that he'd be up to speak with you just as soon as he could."

Lucy's smile strained her facial muscles as she forced herself not to take out her frustration on the clerk. The ice picks and sledgehammers played chopsticks on the nerves around her face, pain shooting through her jaw and down her neck. She leaned against the counter, fingers shoved in both ears, trying to relieve the pressure. She glanced back up at the bright yellow smiley faces and reminded herself that her daughter was the one shrieking with delight in the room across the hall, not lying in an ICU.

The thought didn't help, because suddenly she was filled with a vision of Megan in the ICU, fighting for her life, sallow and wasted, her hair gone, her eyes sagging shut as she struggled for every breath.

The vision wasn't conjured from imagination. It was exactly how her father had appeared when he died.

Panic seized her heart, holding her breath hostage, as fear gagged her. She stumbled down the hall to the public restroom, nausea blurring her vision, falling to the floor in front of the toilet, cradling her head between her knees. With the door shut, it was dark except for a nightlight illuminating a nurse's call button. Acrid hospital smells assaulted her: bleach and tile cleaner and soap and fake vanilla deodorizer. But they couldn't mask the odor of tobacco smoke—someone had obviously snuck in here for a cigarette.

The stench was the final straw. Cigarette smoke had made Lucy violently ill ever since she was a child and realized what she had done to her father. All those secret missions to the market, buying him and his fellow patients cigarettes, never realizing that a man missing most of his right lung and all of his left one due to lung cancer was using his addiction and his daughter to hasten his death sentence.

Overwhelmed by her fear and the memories and the smells, Lucy leaned forward and vomited. When she was done, her body shook uncontrollably as she curled up on the cool tile floor, not caring what kind of microbes might have taken up residence there.

She remembered her father laughing as the other two men in his hospital room blew smoke rings through their tracheotomies. She'd been fascinated by them and their mechanical voice boxes, they sounded like the *Wizard of Oz*.

Her father had sent her out for his special "treats" everyday—right up to the very last day when he had collapsed while they had been watching Gilligan's Island. One minute he'd been laughing at Mr. and Mrs. Howell and the next he'd been coughing up bright red blood all over her and the starched white sheets. She'd been so scared, so very scared.

She helped him lie back, not realizing that in his weakened state that position left him drowning in his own blood and fluids, while she'd run to get help. The nurses raced back with her, only to find her father lying perfectly still, eyes slit half shut, arms stretched out as if reaching for her. Dead.

One minute laughing, the next dead.

Chapter 24

Burroughs found himself humming as he waited in the lobby of the federal building. Someone, hopefully Guardino, was on their way down to escort him. Visitor pass and fellow law enforcement officer or not, the government didn't let just anyone wander alone through their sacred hallways.

He snuck a still warm Krispy Kreme from the box he'd picked up on the way over. Usually after a night with Cindy he'd be beat, spend the next day recuperating. Not today. Today he was jazzed, bouncing on his feet, couldn't wait to get a jump on the Ashley Yeager case.

Was it the case or Guardino? He had his answer when the elevator doors slid open and found Walden waiting for him. Well shit. He slumped against the elevator wall, barely nodding a greeting to the Special Agent.

"Brought you guys some donuts," he said as if Walden couldn't detect that from the green and white box he carried or the tantalizing odor emanating from it.

Walden merely arched an eyebrow and made a "hmpf" type of noise. "Lucy isn't here."

"Did I ask?" Burroughs straightened, not liking the proprietary tone in the other man's voice. He and Walden were the same height, but he had a good ten pounds and five or six years on Walden. He could definitely take him.

Walden didn't seem to agree. He squared off, staring Burroughs in the eye. "You didn't have to. That's the point."

"Come on. Don't try to pretend like you never thought of it yourself. Working all day with perverts, being forced to watch all that porn—I'll bet she keeps you up at night."

Walden stood motionless except for the veins bulging at his neck. "I'd highly suggest that you keep your eyes, your hands, and your imagination focused elsewhere."

"Hey, I don't need this shit. You all invited me here to help out, remember?"

The doors slid open before Walden could reply. The agent stalked away, opening the first of the locked doors, forcing Burroughs to put an extra bounce in his step in order to catch up before it slammed in his face.

Jeezit, you'd think he was one of the bad guys or something. Oh well, more donuts for him.

Burroughs made himself at home at an empty workspace. Most of the techies looked like they'd spent the night, slept in their clothes if they'd gotten any sleep at all. Taylor, the ADD poster boy, was hyped about something, bouncing back and forth between two workstations. Walden took his seat and began working the phones.

Burroughs grabbed his own phone and checked in with the Zone Five guys to see if there'd been any sign of the elusive Mr. Tardiff. No joy. He began following up on calls that had been tagged by the folks manning the hotline.

One woman in Murrysville reported seeing a girl wearing a blonde wig and fishnet stockings driving in a white Escalade with a "big, fat, black man" adding that they were "obviously up to no good" and that the girl had given her the finger.

Another reported seeing suspicious lights dancing in her back yard—she lived a block away from the Yeagers, so Plum had sent a car over, but found nothing.

Those were the most promising of the bunch. He sighed and reached for another donut. Between the sugar, the Viagra he'd been popping all last night, and the exercise Cindy had provided, his blood sugar would be haywire, but hell, you only lived once.

As he chewed, he remembered everything he and Cindy had done last night. But somehow, other women's faces kept superimposing themselves on top of Cindy's. Kim. Guardino. Kim.

"Hey, Burroughs," Taylor called right when Burroughs was getting to the good part of his morning fantasy. "You were with LT when she cleared that Fegley kid, right?"

Burroughs spun around in his chair, pulling it in closer to the desk. "Yeah, why?"

"I've been thinking."

"Always a dangerous thing," one of the H-tech guys chimed in from the peanut gallery.

Taylor ignored him. "If Ashley got a new phone a few weeks ago, she probably got a new email as well, you know something anonymous like Hotmail."

"Okay."

"So, why would she do all that unless someone told her to?"

Burroughs blinked then nodded. "Sonofabitch. Do you have her old emails?"

"The AOL account hasn't been used in over three weeks," Taylor said eagerly, wheeling his chair over to plop down a stack of printouts in front of Burroughs. "Here are her emails for the last two months."

"It will stand out. He'll only use it the once," Burroughs said, already skimming back through the pages.

"And it will probably be from an untraceable source like a cyber café," Taylor added, taking half the stack.

"But with a name she'd recognize and trust." Both men were silent for a moment as their pens scratched over the transcripts of emails.

Jeezit, kids talked a lot about nothing, Burroughs thought, going cross-eyed at the lines of inane messages about music and weather and characters from Shadow World.

"I got it." Taylor stabbed his pen through the page, impaling it upright.

"Who is it?"

"Draco-five-nine-eight. From an Internet café. He says, call me and lists a number." Taylor was already reaching past Burroughs to use the computer terminal, his fingers dancing over the keys. He shook his head, clearly unhappy by what he was seeing. "No go. The phone's untraceable, prepaid cell. Bought with cash."

"Draco was the name Fegley used in the online game he played with Ashley."

"You sure he's not our guy?"

"Trust me, this guy isn't capable of swatting a fly. But..." He trailed off, remembering what Guardino had told him about Shadow World, the online fantasy game Ashley had lost herself in. "It had to be someone else from that game, someone who knew Ashley had a thing for Fegley—"

"You mean Draco."

"Whatever. Can you check out the names—the real names, like on this planet—of the Shadow World players?"

"Already started." Taylor beamed, his exhaustion faded. Burroughs couldn't help but smile at the younger man's enthusiasm. Christ, he didn't think he'd ever been that young or naively optimistic.

"Hey, Taylor." Taylor jerked his head, his eyes not leaving the screen, his fingers never pausing in their rhythmic labor. Burroughs slid the donuts over to him. "You did good, kid."

In her dreams, Ashley had been underwater. It was still dark, but cool, so much better than the stifling stench of her waking here and now. The water had been her friend, she could move anyway she wanted, free of pain or fear.

Then something hit her body. Slapping her awake.

Before she could respond or wonder, another object thudded against her, then another and another. She screamed, flailing her arms, trying to kick the writhing, coiling, spitting creatures away from her. She'd come awake trapped inside her greatest nightmare.

Snakes. Raining down from above. No matter how far she moved, they kept on coming, sometimes just one or two, other times a whole group. As if the heavens above had opened up and released the wrath of God.

She cried and pled with the unseen puppet master who delighted in torturing her. "Stop it! Please, please." Her voice was worn down to a shadow of a whisper. "Please, I'll do anything."

Her answer was a coiled mass of reptilian flesh hurled at her face.

Snakes surrounded her, biting her flailing limbs, whipping their bodies against hers. Anytime she moved, another sank its teeth into her flesh.

Curled up in a ball, arms wrapped over her face, she no longer dodged the reptilian missiles, merely flinched and shrugged as they pummeled her.

An awful thought occurred to her. At first she banished it, it was too awful to imagine. But she couldn't ignore it, not as snakes curled around her swollen ankle, crawled up under her pant legs and shimmied down her neck.

"Daddy?" She dared to peer into the darkness above. "Daddy? Is that you? I'm sorry. I'm so sorry. Please. Daddy?"

A torrent of a dozen serpents was her only answer.

"What do you want?" she tried one last desperate gamble. "I'll do anything. I'll strip naked, I'll suck your cock, I'll—" She paused, trying to imagine what a pervert would want from her. "I'll let you fuck me. I'll do anything, just make it stop!"

Thunk, thump, thwack. More snakes hit their target, hissing in anger. She moaned and rolled on the ground, trying to dislodge them, only to land in another coiled mass. The chain jerked, halting her movement.

"Please."

Her pleas went unacknowledged. Her invisible God continued to hurl snakes down on her, she couldn't say how long it lasted— minutes, hours, days? Time had lost all meaning.

Finally she curled into a tight ball, no longer flinching while the snakes explored her warm body. She didn't even feel it when they bit her. Didn't care as they slithered beneath her clothing, their cold, dry skin pressing against hers, their tongues tasting her sweat.

She drifted away for the longest time, not feeling a thing… not a thing.

She became nothing.

Chapter 25

Megan's laughter carried from her room two doors down as Lucy emerged from the restroom, still shaky. It was the sweetest sound Lucy had ever heard. She closed her eyes, listening hard, imprinting the sound on her memory. A gift to be unwrapped later.

A sudden image of Melissa Yeager, so beautiful and helpless to do anything for her daughter, flit through Lucy's mind. She choked on a sob before swallowing it down. Megan wouldn't have to worry about going through this alone. Nick and Lucy would never abandon her. Not like Ashley's parents had.

Ashley. She couldn't forget Ashley—not while Lucy was her only chance.

The desk clerk waved at her. "Mrs. Callahan? I have Dr. Scott on the line for you."

Finally, a chance to get some answers. "Hello?"

"Mrs. Callahan, I'm so sorry that I haven't had a chance to get up there and meet you in person, but I wanted to call and fill you in on Megan's condition."

"You found out what's going on? Why she's sick?"

"No, I'm afraid it's one of those good news/bad news situations. Her CT confirmed an enlarged spleen and liver, but it didn't reveal any other abnormalities other than several axillary lymph nodes."

Axillary—that meant armpit. Wasn't that where Hodgkins' Disease started? Lucy hugged her free arm around her chest. "Are you telling me she has cancer?"

"No, no. I'm telling you that there are some worrisome symptoms, but that so far we do not have any confirmation of the cause. It could be as simple as a virus or infection—"

"Or it could be cancer."

He hesitated, obviously not appreciating her blunt style. "Well, yes."

"So what's the plan?"

"I'm going to repeat some of the blood work in the morning. And by then we should have some of our other tests for infectious diseases back. If nothing shows up or if anything looks worrisome, then we'll need to discuss the possibilities of a lymph node biopsy."

Lucy's breath escaped her in a whoosh that made her head rush. She sagged against the counter. "More tests but no answers."

"I'm sorry, but that's the best I can do for now."

"If it is," she swallowed hard, "cancer, can you treat it? Have we caught it soon enough?"

"Depending on the pathology, I'd have to say Megan's prognosis would definitely be favorable. But nothing is for certain until we know exactly what we're dealing with."

Lucy was silent, trying to process the information.

"I'll come up as soon as I'm done here in the ICU and go over everything with your husband and Megan. But in the meantime, I didn't want you to be unnecessarily worried. All in all, the fact that we haven't found anything seriously wrong is an excellent sign."

An excellent sign. But no guarantee. "Thank you, Dr. Scott."

She was surprised to find Nick and Megan engrossed in a video game when she returned. Their household was not big on TV, instead focused most of their free time together on physical activities, reading, cooking, gardening, talking. Hopelessly old fashioned and out of touch with reality, as Megan constantly reminded them. As if spending actual face time with her loving parents was a punishment, unimaginable extreme cruelty.

Yet, here she was, gleefully teaching her father how to zap aliens and strategize as they plotted their way through a labyrinth. Nick was stretched out on the bed beside her, his teeth worrying his lower lip as he concentrated.

Lucy stood beside the bed, watching, wrapping one arm behind Megan. She asked Megan to pause the game while she filled them in on what Dr. Scott had told her.

Megan quirked her mouth, considering the new information. "No needles until tomorrow?"

"Unless something changes."

"Can you be with me when they do the test?"

"We'll ask Dr. Scott to be sure, but I'll do my best."

"Can I have a kitty when we get home? I read that pets boost the immune system so people don't get sick so often."

Nick looked away, one hand covering his grin. It was so typical of Megan to consider all sides of the problem and quickly turn it to her advantage. Lucy rumpled her hair, drawing a look of disapproval.

"No pets," she gave Megan the same answer she had for months. "Not until we get settled and you show that you're responsible enough to take care of it yourself."

"But, Mom..."

Lucy's heart squeezed in agony. God, it was so hard to say no when Megan turned those big, dark eyes on her. Especially when she'd been so brave and when she was so sick. Megan had never had more than the stomach flu before now.

"We'll see."

"All right!" Megan bounced with triumph and grabbed her remote. "Come on Dad, I'm going to kick your butt."

"Not if I blow away all your goblin hordes."

The screen filled with an explosion of light and zapping sound effects as lightning bolts crisscrossed. A few minutes later a tinny version of "Taps" sounded.

"Dead again, Dad," Megan crowed, bouncing in a makeshift victory dance. "Want to come back as a mutant zombie or start the game again and be human?"

"I was trying to get killed. Zombies have way more fun," Nick said. He reached his left hand up, stroking Lucy's arm. "You okay? They brought a lunch tray if you want anything to eat."

She glanced over at the two trays sitting on the windowsill. Megan's was empty except for what looked to be remnants of a chicken finger smothered in ketchup and mustard, the "adult" tray with its roast beef slathered in congealed gravy was barely touched. "Thanks, I'm fine." She squeezed his hand, silently asking him the same question: *are you okay?*

He considered the answer for a moment, their eyes locking behind Megan's back, and slowly nodded. But his smile had vanished.

Megan reset controls on the game. There was some complicated scrolling and clicking until she was satisfied.

"Did you teach yourself how to play this?" Lucy asked.

"Sure. It's easy."

For a twelve-year-old. Lucy thought of Shadow World, the game Ashley had buried herself in. "So the computer generates all the scenarios, makes all the decisions?"

"With just the two of us, yeah," she said, leaning to one side as she piloted some kind of sled pulled by werewolves through an ice field. Rumbles and crashes of falling icicles reverberated from the speakers as she dodged deadly shards and avoided falling into chasms. "But you can also play with a group, have one person set up the universe, control everything."

An evil cackle sounded as an army of vampires attacked. Megan deftly outran them, leaving in her wake a frozen track of holy water that vaporized any who followed. Nick was hunched forward, waiting for the right moment to unleash his mutant zombie.

"How does that work? Does the person in control just set things in motion and everything is decided with a roll of a die? Or could he set things up differently for different players? Customize it?" A glimmer of an idea was forming as she watched Megan and Nick fall under the spell of the game. "Could they maybe even communicate with individual players?"

"A conversation with God," Nick mumbled as his zombie tackled one of the werewolves and began to eviscerate and eat it. Complete with slobbering sound effects. "Sounds like fun."

Both he and Megan were silent for a moment, fighting their way into a dark cavern, scattering hordes of goblins.

"Look out above!" Nick shouted, almost bouncing off the bed. A swooping form of a vampire bat filled the screen, quickly followed by cries of pain and the funeral dirge. "Ah, Megan, eaten by the Queen of the Vampires, what a way to go."

Megan flounced back on her pillows. "Better than being a carrion-eating zombie."

She released the controls while Nick reset the game. "If there's one person in charge," she said, "why wouldn't they try to make it harder for some players, the really good ones, and make the game last longer? Doesn't that make it more fun for everyone?"

Which was exactly the opposite of what the creator of Shadow World had done. Lucy stared at the screen, now filled with character options and world building suggestions, neon colors spinning and flashing as Nick tried various combinations.

Shadow World was designed to attract female players, Bobby Fegley had told her. Yet, in the end, the domain master had eliminated all but one player—Ashley. What had he called himself? The Maestro.

"Megan Constance Callahan, you are a genius!"

Both Nick and Megan looked up in surprise. "Why? What'd I do?"

"I think you may have just helped me crack this case."

"That girl you're looking for? Ashley?"

Lucy hugged Megan hard, making the pulse ox machine sputter and alarm. Nick quieted the monitor. "I have a new idea that might help me find her. Thanks to you." She grabbed her cell phone and dialed. "Taylor? How'd you like to do some field work?"

His adrenalin buzz crackled through the handset. "I'd love it. What'cha need? Should I get my vest, sign out any weapons?"

"Sign out a vehicle, bring your laptop and meet me in front of Three Rivers in ten minutes."

"Will do!"

With the opportunity to take action, to actually accomplish something more than waiting in dread for answers she couldn't control, Lucy felt a little better.

She hugged Megan again, mussing her hair and earning a scowl. "I'm going to leave for a short while, but I promise, I'll be back tonight. Is that okay?"

"You're going to go find that girl? Because of what I said?"

"Yes. I hope so."

Megan's sly grin returned. "Does that mean I can have my own computer? Maybe I can help some more."

"No. It means you may have just helped save a girl's life. How's that make you feel?"

Her face lit up, freckles dancing across the bridge of her nose. "Kind of good. Like Christmas morning. Is this how it always feels?"

"Yes." Lucy's smile mirrored her daughter's. She kissed Megan's head. And for the first time in months, Megan didn't pull away. "Every time."

She slid off the bed and reached for Nick's hand. "You okay with this?"

"You heard the doc, they won't know anything more until morning. Go, you're wearing out the floor with your pacing anyway." His voice was lighthearted but brittle. The wrinkles forming at the edge of his eyes betrayed him.

"Seriously, Nick, if you have a problem with this—"

He stood, blocking Megan's view. "I don't have a problem with you finding that girl, trying to save her." His voice dropped. "I do have a problem with you wearing yourself ragged and coming back with nothing left to give your own daughter."

She understood his words but knew there was more to it. Nick never picked a fight unless he was certain he'd examined all sides of the equation.

"Megan, honey, go ahead and set up a new game. Your father and I are going to be right outside."

Megan looked up at that, a bemused grin on her face. "You can fight here. I don't mind."

"We're not fighting, sweetheart," Nick said in his calmest voice, syrupy with a hint of his Southern accent. The one he only used when they were fighting. "Your mother and I just need a little private discussion. That's all."

"Whatever." Her attention turned back to the computer game. "You'll be back tonight to stay with me, right, Mom? You promised."

"I promise. I'll be here tonight." She kissed Megan on both cheeks and her nose, earning a familiar grimace and eye roll, then walked out into the corridor and kept going until she hit the stairwell. Nick followed her without saying anything until the door slammed shut behind him.

"What was all that about?" She whirled on him, her voice low but powerful enough to bounce from the cement block walls.

"It was about you always needing to find another kid to save, another crusade to fight. If the worse is true, if Megan has—" he faltered. "If she's sick, then we're going to be in for the fight of our lives right here."

"You think I'm using work as an excuse to avoid reality?"

"Yes. You think if you save this girl, you'll gain some protection, somehow be able to keep Megan safe as well. We call it magical thinking."

"I don't need any of your psycho-bullshit right now, thank you very much."

"Say you save this girl, Ashley. What happens when you lose the next one or the one after that? Where does it stop? You can't save them all."

She stared at him, not even realizing her gun hand was resting on her hip where her holster would usually sit. But Nick did. He glanced down pointedly at her hand before enveloping it in both of his, stilling her trembling.

"You can't save the world, Lulu," he said, his voice filled with longing and sorrow. "But you can help your daughter get through this. And me. You can help me. I need you. We need you."

His face was filled with concern and fear. How could she explain to him that without her work she wouldn't have any strength to lend to her family? Being out there, seeing what she saw, doing what little she could to stop predators, it wasn't something she wanted to do, it was something she had to do.

She had no words to offer him, nothing rational that he could analyze without twisting it around and turning it into nonsense. All she could do was shake her head, small little beats of denial, her gaze locked on his, hoping he would understand. Tugging her hand from his, she stepped away.

"I'm late." She jogged down the stairs, her footsteps echoing behind her, knowing that he watched her back every step of the way.

--

"Want me to try to follow them?" Cindy's cameraman, Felix, asked as Guardino ran out of the hospital entrance and hopped into a black Chevy Blazer.

Cindy watched the SUV drive away. "No. Wait here. I'm going to go meet the family."

He outfitted her with a button camera hidden inside a brooch. She grabbed a discarded visitor's pass from the garbage can in front of the entrance. Security was always a joke around hospitals. She smiled, thinking of the scoop she'd been handed—thanks to her instincts.

She headed into the hospital and within minutes was on the fourth floor at Megan Callahan's room.

The door was open. Inside, a young girl lay against several pillows, sleeping. A video game stood at the foot of the bed, whirling colors of a screen saver spinning across it. Beside the girl lay a man, his eyes closed, but his hand moving, patting the girl's arm in a soothing rhythm. He had the lean build of an athlete, wiry without being muscle bound, red-gold hair with an enticing hint of a curl, and appeared to be younger than the thirty-nine years she knew he was.

Cindy had done her homework, had learned everything she could about Nick Callahan and his wife. Always paid to know the enemy.

She unbuttoned her suit jacket, made sure the camera lens was clear of any obstacles, and nudged the door so that it creaked a bit.

Callahan's eyes sprung open and he sat up, untangling his arm from his daughter's. "Yes?"

"I'm sorry, Dr. Callahan, I can come back later if you like," she said in a demur voice even as she stepped into the room. "I ran into your wife downstairs, she didn't mention you were asleep."

He slid from the bed and walked around it. He was only an inch or so taller than her own five-ten, but he seemed taller, the way he moved, so confident and graceful. Could men be graceful? Elegant, that was the word. She had a sudden image of an eighteenth century nobleman and knew instinctively how to proceed. For once, sex wasn't the way to get what she needed from a man.

"I'm afraid I didn't make a very good impression on Mrs. Callahan," she said, conjuring a blush. "She doesn't hold the counseling profession in very high regard."

She edged her glance up to see how he took the implied insult to his own profession. He merely smiled, his eyes gleaming, and she knew he was thinking of his wife and some shared intimate joke. A pang of jealousy hit her. No man ever looked that way when they thought about her.

Burroughs came close, though. When they were together, he'd stare at her with an intensity that made her skin glow like it had been targeted by a laser. She could never tell if his stare was fueled by love or hate—doubted he knew, either.

Callahan's head bobbed with a soundless laugh. "Lucy firmly believes in the benefits of therapy, just doesn't have the patience to sit still long enough to experience it herself."

He led her outside, keeping his voice low. Silently, he closed the door and gestured to two chairs at the end of the hallway. "Are you one of the hospital counselors?"

She strolled with him, enjoying the way his gaze lingered as he examined her. Bingo. Half the battle won.

"It must be quite frustrating for a psychologist of your caliber," she said, crossing her leg so that her ankle almost but not quite brushed his, "giving up a NIMH grant when you left Virginia to come here?"

His lips tightened even as his face retained its bland geniality. Ahh, a sore spot.

"Is that where your wife was going? Back to work?" She injected a hint of concern into her tone. "How does that make you feel? Her leaving you when Megan is so ill."

His stare hardened, he leaned back a bit. She'd pushed too hard.

"You look very familiar, Miss—" The silence lengthened. "I'm sorry, I didn't catch your name. And you don't seem to be wearing an ID badge."

"I'm Cindy." She shoved her hand out fast, before he could think more about the missing ID, and gave him her mother's maiden name. "Cindy Janluski."

He took her hand with a strong grip, surprised her when he stood and gently tugged her back up to her feet as well. "Cindy. So nice to make your acquaintance."

As they began walking back to the nurses' station, he tucked her arm in his like a gentleman caller from the old days.

"I appreciate your interest in my daughter's well-being," he continued in that same melodious lilt perfumed with magnolias and mint. "But, please tell your boss that if I ever see you or another reporter come anywhere near my child again, I will press charges. I believe it's a felony offense to interfere with a federal agent's family."

Before Cindy could pull away, he leaned over the counter and addressed the ward clerk. "Would you please have hospital security come and remove this meddlesome journalist before she has the chance to invade someone else's privacy?"

"Really," Cindy said, yanking her arm away from him with a force that rocked her on her heels. "I can see myself out. Although you may want to explain to your wife that if she wants to get along here in Pittsburgh, she'd do best to cooperate with me."

"You're lucky it was me here to meet you and not my wife," he said as a hulking, acne-pocked security guard arrived. "She'd shoot first and worry about the paperwork later."

He gave her a quirky half smile as if he were imaging just how a confrontation between her and Guardino might end. From the pitying expression he bestowed on her, she had the feeling he had no doubt that Guardino would win.

She couldn't wait to prove them both wrong.

Chapter 26

Jimmy climbed down from the ladder leading from the hayloft to the outside of the barn, sweat dripping from his face. It wasn't just the sweltering temperatures in the barn or the exertion of carrying the buckets filled with squirming reptiles that had hijacked his heart rate and made his breath heave from his chest.

Ashley's cries haunted him. When she'd called out for her father, he had almost broken.

He glanced at his watch. The books said it would take hours, maybe even days to shatter her will. But it had only been six minutes and twenty-seven seconds.

He wiped tears and sweat from his cheeks. Glanced at the closed barn doors behind him. He couldn't take it, couldn't bear the thought of her in pain for any longer.

"I'm coming sweetheart," he sang out as he sprinted for the farmhouse, even though he knew she couldn't hear. "I'm coming."

It only took him a few minutes to finish his preparations. The last thing he did before leaving the house was to take one last look at the monitor. Ashley lay absolutely still, the black forms of the snakes slithering over her body. Her eyes were open, not blinking, her face blank.

"It's all right." She'd been so strong, so brave. She was worthy of his love, had earned it. "It's all over now."

His phone rang. Damn. Work.

He frowned, considering, staring at her image on the screen.

Just a little while longer.

"I promise." Jimmy kissed his fingers, placed them on the screen. He grabbed his car keys and ran.

–

Lucy called Bobby Fegley while they were en route and filled him in on her theory. He seemed excited by the prospect of being able to help. When they arrived at his house, his father met them at the door and led them to Bobby's room where he was feverishly working already.

"Nice set up," Taylor whistled in appreciation as he opened up his laptop and joined Bobby. "Bet I've got some toys you'll like."

They started talking cyber-gibberish, interrupting each other at a fever pitch. Lucy let them go at it a few minutes, watching the large monitor flow from one website to another, trying to track the creator of Shadow World.

"Why is he so hard to find? I thought these guys thrived on attention," she said, standing behind the two. Bobby's neck muscles bulged with tension and she hoped she hadn't made a mistake involving him. But no one knew the game or Ashley as well. "Isn't creating a successful game their idea of fame?"

"For most," Taylor answered her. Bobby remained silent, jaws gritted together, sweat beading his forehead. "But some prefer the idea of becoming cult figures. Like super heroes, they shield themselves in secret identities."

"Is that what this guy has done? This Maestro?"

"No." Bobby scratched out the single, terse syllable. "No. He's hiding."

"Don't worry, Draco," Taylor said, already finding a nickname for Bobby as he did for everyone. Except Walden, Lucy had noticed. Walden was Walden to everyone, even the over-eager Taylor. "He can't hide from me. Not for long."

"Could you tell me if it's Tardiff?" she asked, anxious for some shred of evidence to lead them to Ashley.

"No. It doesn't work that way," Taylor said. He paused, searching for words to explain the realm of cyberspace to a Luddite. She waved him back to work and resumed her pacing, calling Walden as she did.

"Any sign of Tardiff?"

"No. PBP talked their way into his room and it was cleared out. He'd only rented it for the week, so today would have been check out. Maybe he's gone home."

Maybe. Or maybe he'd gone to wherever Ashley was. "Tell the New York office to put some eyes on his place. I'm gonna talk to Melissa, see what's really going on."

She'd rather go in person but she didn't want to leave Taylor and Bobby. It felt like if she was going to catch a break in this case it would be through the same route the Maestro used to catch Ashley. Shadow World.

She called the sheriff's detail, asked them to put her on a private line with Melissa. "I need the truth about Jon Tardiff."

Melissa coughed and Lucy could almost see the former model's hand going to her throat. "I already told—"

"Melissa, I know he's been in town all week."

"It's not what you think. He had nothing to do with Ashley."

"So she never saw him?"

Melissa's sob whined through the phone. "Of course she saw him. He was here to ask me to marry him."

Hell, that could change everything—if Ashley stood in the way of Tardiff getting the woman he'd wanted for years... "What happened?"

"What do you think happened? Ashley threw a fit, said she wasn't leaving Pittsburgh, that she'd go live with her father."

"But she couldn't, could she?"

"No. Gerald refused to have her. Said he has his own life to live." Bitterness flooded her words. "And Jon can't leave his work, move here."

"What did you decide, Melissa? Who did you pick?"

A long pause, the only sound the other woman's breathing. "I told Jon we'd have to wait. Until Ashley was grown and on her own. I chose my daughter."

Shit, shit, shit. "Why the hell didn't you tell me before?"

"I couldn't let you think—Jon didn't have anything to do with this. He couldn't."

"Give me his number. The one you use. The private one."

"How'd you know?"

Because they weren't stupid and Tardiff's registered cell hadn't been used recently. Lucy didn't bother to explain. Instead she took the number Melissa gave her. Then she told the deputy with Melissa to keep Melissa away from the phones until further notice.

She turned to Taylor. "Looks like we might have our man."

He pivoted away from his computer. "No shit? That's great. What 'cha gonna do?"

"First let's see where he is—can you ask the guys to track this cell?" Taylor interfaced with the H-Tech guys better than she could, spoke the same language.

He got on his phone, gibbering away eagerly.

Bobby kept pounding the keys on his computer. His body was shaking, covered with sweat. Lucy crouched down until she was at eye level and laid her hand over his. It fluttered like a firefly trapped in a Mason jar. He wrenched his gaze away from the computer and stared at her.

"Do you need a break? Maybe this wasn't a good idea."

His jaw clenched with determination. "No. I'm fine. Sometimes when I get a strong feeling about something, my body overreacts." He grimaced in embarrassment. "Part of the nerves and reflexes being all tangled up."

"I know how that feels and I don't have any excuses. Can I show you something my husband taught me? He's a psychologist, deals with soldiers and other people with a lot of stress."

"You mean like guys who've been blown up, lost their legs and stuff?"

"Right. Now close your eyes for a second and focus on your breathing." She kept her voice calm and steady, a close approximation to Nick's and led him through a quick deep breathing exercise. Cube breathing Nick called it. It worked when you could take a moment and concentrate on it—only problem was that Lucy seemed never to be able to find the time to do that when she felt most stressed.

Like before she blew up at her husband outside their daughter's hospital room.

As Bobby took deep, soothing breaths, she massaged his hand between both of hers, stroking the pressure points Nick had showed her. She felt her own tension retreat as she guided Bobby. Hmmm, it felt good to drop the weight from her shoulders, to unclamp her jaws.

He opened his eyes, now clear, his face relaxed, the sweat and trembling gone. "Thanks."

"No problem." She rotated her neck, producing some loud cracks, and stood again. "We really appreciate your help finding Ashley. She's very lucky to have you as a friend."

"Got him," Taylor exclaimed, snapping his phone shut. "He's on I-80 headed east. The State Police just pulled him over."

"Is Ashley with him?"

He shook his head. "No. The car was empty except for Tardiff. They're bringing him back here for questioning."

Lucy blew her breath out. The tympani in her ears had returned. "Okay, back to work on tracking her through the game."

"You do know that we may never get a link to a physical location?" he asked. "This is virtual reality."

"Right now it's the only thing I've got." The only thing Ashley had. She closed her eyes as the men turned their backs to her. Had she fucked up again, lost Ashley because she hadn't twigged to Tardiff sooner?

"Hey, Draco," Taylor said, totally lost in cyber-land once more. "Look at this. What if we tracked back from here?" Both men began working their machines as if they were racing for a prize. Lucy had no choice but to wait.

217

Twenty minutes later Taylor's phone rang and he jerked back, shaking his head as if surprised to find himself in the real world. He grabbed it. "Yeah. No shit. Okay, keep working." He hung up and turned to Lucy. "The H-Tech guys discovered the origin of the program that wiped Ashley's computer. It's one of ours."

"Ours as in government?"

"Ours as in Homeland Security. Specifically ATF, FBI, and ICE."

An electrical shock tingled along Lucy's nerve endings. She began to pace the room, her hands bunching into fists then opening again in time with her steps.

"Does Tardiff have any government connections?"

Taylor shook his head. "No. I ran his life under the microscope. No way he could have gotten that program on his own."

"So either he's not our guy or he had an accomplice." She thought hard. "If Tardiff's motive was to marry Melissa, why would he create Shadow World, use it to trap Ashley? Surely there's easier ways to take care of a surly teenager." The easiest involving a shallow grave, but she didn't want to think about that. "The whole thing doesn't make sense."

"How could Tardiff have predicted that Ashley would even want to play Shadow World?" Taylor asked.

"Maybe it's a chicken and egg thing," Bobby chimed in.

Lucy stopped. Considered. Bobby's words tickled her, an itch that couldn't be scratched. He was on the right track, she was certain.

"So our guy isn't Tardiff?" Taylor's disappointment colored his voice, as if he'd been personally insulted by their lack of progress. "We're back to ground zero?"

"No. Not quite. We know a helluva lot more than we did yesterday. Our guy has to be local to have planned out the Tastee Treet meet," she said, thinking out loud. "Computer skills, enough to build Shadow World and cover his tracks. He's a white male, mid-twenties to late thirties, never married, probably no long term relationship except with his mother—might even still live with his mother. He's not a pedophile."

"He's not?" Taylor asked, his gaze never leaving his screen. "I thought these guys were all pedophiles."

"Not this one. He's looking for someone he can control easily, a woman he can mold to his needs. That means a younger woman, emotionally immature. He wants a long-term relationship. He's not driven by a sexual obsession with youth, he's more like Frankenstein, trying to create the perfect mate."

"So the game, Shadow World, was his hunting ground?" Bobby put in.

She hesitated. It was total speculation—farfetched speculation at that. She should call Nick, get his professional opinion, facts rather than fantasy. But she didn't want to distract him from Megan. Guilt stabbed through her at the thought of Megan alone in the hospital. What if Nick was right? She was just transferring her fears about keeping Megan safe onto her job?

If so, she might be condemning Ashley, wasting time chasing a shadow.

No. This felt too right, she felt close to this actor. She knew him. What he wanted. How he thought.

"Bobby's right. He created Shadow World to test his subjects. It's his honey trap," she continued, waiting for the men to contradict her theory. But instead they both nodded, even though their eyes never left the computer screens. "Probably invited them into private discussions, learned as much as he could about them. Then he'd groom them—see how far he could manipulate them, how pliable they were."

"Like seeing if they'd sacrifice their best friend if he asked them to?" Bobby asked.

"Even that. I think you were a real obstacle to him. Ashley thought it was you she was meeting on Friday, not him."

"Me? But we haven't talked in like a month."

"How hard would it be for him to monitor your conversations, learn everything he needed to know about you?"

"The online stuff, that'd be easy. A lot were in the Shadow World chat rooms, at first anyway."

"I'll bet he inserted a Trojan horse into Ashley's computer," Taylor said. "He'd be able to monitor every key stroke she typed."

"He'd know her passwords, everything." Bobby's eyes narrowed in anger. "That sonofabitch. He cut me off from Ashley—probably pretended to be me, told her I had a new phone number or email address, sucked her right in."

"He's been watching her for a long time, would know everything about her," Taylor said.

"Watching her—" Lucy was close, there was something slippery just beyond her grasp. "Monitoring her." She made another circuit of the room. "Can you tell if he accessed the webcam on her computer? Trace the video feed or whatever you call it?"

"No. This guy has his own servers set up—that's why it's so hard for us to trace him through the game, he doesn't use a third party host."

Another dead end. But she was certain this guy would be watching Ashley. From a distance at first—his goal was to create a long-term relationship, he'd chose his partner carefully.

"So we have a white guy, computer savvy, Pittsburgh area, and he has access to Homeland Security computer programs." She shook her head. "That could still be dozens, maybe even a hundred or more men."

"At Quantico they told us some serial killers try to insert them-selves into the investigation. To feel powerful, smarter than we are," Taylor said.

She stopped at the far end of the room, holding her body still as energy surged through it, feeling as if she leaned over the edge of a precipice with precious little to hang on to.

"No. He doesn't care about us. He cares about Ashley. He'll do whatever it takes to protect their relationship. If he gets involved with us it'll be to sabotage the case, throw us off track."

She feathered her fingers over the base of her throat she thought through every person connected with the case. Hated to think it could be someone on her team, right under her nose. Someone she'd trusted.

Then she stopped short. She knew where she was going—it had been right in front of her—but took time to take a deep breath in, let it out again before she condemned a man. After all, she had no proof. Just what Nick would call one of her "niggly" feelings.

"If I gave you a name, could you see if the scrubber program came from him?" she asked Taylor, reluctant to voice her suspicions. But the more she thought about it, the more certain she was.

"No, but I can check to see if he's used or downloaded the same version of the program. He'd have to download it from one of our computers and then transfer it." He squinted at her. "Who do you think it is?"

Lucy blew her breath out as if preparing for a leap off the high dive. "Fletcher."

"No way," Taylor said. "That guy's an idiot."

"It's him. I know it." She grabbed her phone. "You find me proof."

Chapter 27

Lucy called Walden, filled him in on her suspicions. "Not much we can do without proof," he told her.

"I know. Check out his workstation; see if you can find anything we can use to get a warrant. Have the H-Tech guys check out his computer—it's government property so he has no expectation of privacy. But for godsake, don't tip him off."

"Hang on, let me see if he's still around."

Lucy resumed her pacing, filled with an urge to use Taylor's phone and call Three Rivers to check on Megan. If she saved Ashley, Megan would be fine—what had Nick called it? Magical thinking? She didn't care. She believed it to her core. Had to, with two girls' lives at stake.

Walden returned before she could. "Security says he swiped out already. Want me to call him? Try to see where he's at?"

"No. I'll do it. You start checking him out, work on a warrant for his home."

"We don't have probable cause. Unless something shows up here." Walden, always the voice of reason. "And I don't think I should let anyone else in on this."

He had a point. In the federal building, gossip traveled faster than a laser guided missile.

"No sense riling up the brass on a Sunday," she reluctantly agreed, even though she hated the fact that they'd have to proceed slow and careful.

"Especially as we have no evidence. I'll call as soon as I have anything."

If Fletcher did have Ashley, what would he do when exposed? Kill her would be the obvious answer, and if he were a straightforward sociopath like Ivan, it was exactly what she'd expect him to do.

But Fletcher had spent months grooming her, had developed an elaborate ritual around his actions, even created an alternative universe to hunt in. He wasn't going to give up his prize, not easily.

He'd run. Take Ashley with him. Go underground and hide in the shadows just like in the fantasy realm he had invented. Probably had a lair stocked and waiting.

She had to take a chance, lure him back before he ran.

She dialed Fletcher's cell.

"Jim Fletcher," he answered, his voice bright and cheerful.

"It's Lucy," she kept her voice bright. "I was wondering how the surveillance footage from this morning came out. Was the quality okay?"

"Yes, Lucy. The quality was just fine. In fact, I just hung up with the tech who was processing it. Why, is there a problem I don't know about?"

"No. No problem. I was worried that with everything going on things might have gotten garbled."

"Shouldn't you be worried about bigger things than me doing my job? Like your daughter. Is she okay?"

"She will be. Thanks for asking. I was wondering if you could meet me at the office, give us a hand with the Ashley Yeager investigation."

Fletcher's laughter sounded relaxed and carefree, hardly the sound of a killer on the run.

"Sorry, Lucy. Normally I'd be happy to oblige, but you see, the tech guy also told me your team had cracked Ashley's computer. Not to mention the fact that Taylor or one of his klutzes just tried hacking into my server. Hope he didn't have anything sensitive on that hard drive."

She spun around and slapped Taylor's hand from his keyboard.

"So, Lucy, have I finally gotten your attention? Before I go, I just want to let you know how much I enjoyed working with you. Don't worry about Ashley. She won't ever have to worry about anything again. I'll keep her safe."

The line went dead.

"He said something about your hard drive," she told Taylor. "He knew you had reached his server."

Taylor's fingers dashed across his keyboard. "Not me, I wasn't even close."

They both turned to Bobby who had a wide smile on his face. "Got him," he said triumphantly. "I got the sonofabitch."

"Bobby, what did you do?"

"He had an early warning system, but I saw it and made a back door in. Before I triggered his alarms, I sent him a very nasty bit of code."

"Is it something I can use to track him? He has Ashley and he knows we're onto him."

"Maybe. Next time he uses his password, his C drive is going to be copied onto mine."

"He said something about destroying the hard drive of whoever was going after him. Was he bluffing?"

"Nah. That early warning system of his included a nice tape-worm. But the guy thinks pretty linear—it was easy to contain once you knew it was there."

Taylor slapped Bobby on the shoulder and beamed like a proud father. "Wow, kid. You're pretty amazing, you know that? You can come work for me anytime."

It was good to see Bobby actually smile for the first time since she'd told him about Ashley's disappearance. Lucy just wished she had time to enjoy it herself. Instead, she was back on the phone to Walden.

"I was just getting ready to call you. His workstation is clean. No evidence there, unless it's on his computer."

"Never mind. We've enough for a warrant. He admitted to having Ashley. Trace his cell and ask Burroughs to issue a BOLO. I'll meet you at his house."

"We're are on our way," Walden told her. "You might want to call the SAC first—Fletcher's boss is looking for you."

"Of course he is. I'll take care of it, just get me that warrant." She hung up and motioned for Taylor to gather his gear. "I have to go now, Bobby, but I'm going to send one of our tech guys over to monitor your computer. Is that all right?"

"Sure, that'd be great. Let me know as soon as you find Ashley, okay?"

"I will."

She let Taylor drive while she manned the phone. Her first call was to John Greally, the Pittsburgh field office's Special Agent in Charge.

"Lucy, what the hell have you done this time?" came his greeting. "I've got ICE supervisors calling me from DC, wanting to chew your ass, saying you're investigating one of their guys without going through proper channels. What's the deal?"

"James Fletcher, one of their support people on Innocent Images, is the same guy who killed that woman in Murrysville and abducted Ashley Yeager."

"Shit. Are you certain?"

"John, he just admitted it to me on the phone. I'm heading out to his house now. Walden is getting us a warrant as soon as he can find a judge on a Sunday afternoon."

"Just so happens I've one right here with me on the eleventh hole. I'll expedite the warrant. You do your best to document the hell out of everything and keep the press as far out of this as possible."

"You know I can't—"

"Just do your best. Last thing we need is for this to turn into a shark feeding frenzy and spook Fletcher into killing that girl."

"We're on the same wavelength there."

225

"And Lucy, this is going to get hairy, political-wise. You'd damned well better bring home the bacon, cooked and smelling so good no jury can resist."

"Don't worry." But she was worried—with Fletcher's access to federal computers and resources, they might have a tough time finding hard evidence. His unrecorded confession wasn't enough. And he damn well knew it.

"Call me as soon as you finish at Fletcher's."

"Yes sir."

"And Lucy, be careful. Just because this guy isn't a fully trained agent doesn't make him any less dangerous." He paused. "How's Megan?"

"She's fine. We're just waiting for tests and seeing where to go next." The knot at the corner of her jaw began to pulsate, and she gave up pretending that everything was all right. "John, they say it might be cancer."

He made a tiny, aborted choking sound before he spoke again. "I'm sure everything is going to be all right. I'll try to stop by and bring Jackie to visit her." Jackie was John's youngest daughter and was the same age as Megan.

"Thanks John. She'll appreciate having someone other than us to talk to. You know how it is, being cooped up with booooring adults all day," she mimicked Megan's whine.

–

Grimwald, the ICE Special Agent in Charge, pulled up alongside Lucy and her team at Fletcher's modest house in Lawrenceville, not far from Three Rivers Medical Center and Megan, Lucy couldn't help but notice. She decided it was a good omen.

The SAC barged out of the unmarked black Suburban like he was being launched from a cannon. "You can't do this!"

Lucy waved her team inside Fletcher's two-story bungalow. "Taylor, priority is the computer, any electronics and any papers. Look for photos, maps, anything to give us a clue where Ashley may be. Walden, look for any possible hiding places on the premises. I'll join you in a minute."

"No. Stop. You cannot do this. You have no right!" Grimwald shouted.

Taylor and Walden didn't hesitate, which made her smile. She pivoted and blocked Grimwald as he stepped forward. "I have a search warrant which I am legally serving. Detective Burroughs, you're my witness. We are in Pittsburgh city jurisdiction, are we not?"

"Yes ma'am, Supervisory Special Agent Guardino."

"Am I violating any state or city laws as I am lawfully executing this federal warrant?"

"No ma'am, not that I can see."

She darted a glance at Burroughs. A smirk sprinted across his face and he rocked back on his heels, obviously enjoying his stint as straight man.

"And is there any evidence that Immigration and Customs Enforcement would have jurisdiction in this matter?"

"No ma'am."

"To hell with jurisdiction," Grimwald sputtered, his face now a apoplectic shade of red. "There's ways to do things, intra-agency cooperation, you can't just—"

"This is a man who is holding a fourteen-year-old girl, who already killed a woman!" Lucy was shouting, leaning into Grimwald's space until her chest was almost touching his. Grimwald stepped back.

"Fletcher is my responsibility. Let me handle things my way. You're hysterical, jumping the gun. What if the media hears about this? About the way you launched a one woman witch hunt?"

"If you'd like to discuss this with the media, be my guest. Detective Burroughs, if you would remain with Special Agent in Charge Grimwald and ensure that he doesn't interfere, I'll join my team."

She could swear she heard Burroughs snicker as she turned her back on the men and started towards the house.

"This isn't over, Guardino! I'll have your job!"

Lucy ignored him. Her phone rang and she grabbed it just as she stepped onto Fletcher's porch. "Guardino here."

"Hi Lucy, it's Jimmy Fletcher. Boy, Agent Grimwald sure does look angry. What did you say to him?"

She froze and pivoted, turning in a complete circle. Ahh, up in the eaves overhanging the porch was a small camera. Clever boy with his gadgets. She stood under the camera and waved. "How's it going, Jimmy? Want to come on in and talk about it? Maybe tell me where Ashley Yeager is?"

"You know I would never hurt Ashley. You of all people should understand that. I've saved her. We're a lot alike, you and I."

What warped planet was he living on? "Gee, I'm flattered. Listen, let's talk about it. Where do you want to meet? You pick the place, anywhere you feel comfortable."

His laugh was a tinny echo as if machine-made. "I might not be a special agent, but I've read the protocols. Please, don't insult me."

"If you don't want to talk, then why did you call?"

"I thought it only fair to warn you. And your people. I'm not like the scum you're used to dealing with. Like I told you, I don't want anyone to get hurt. You've twenty seconds to evacuate my house. Starting now." He hung up.

Lucy sprinted into the house. "Taylor, Walden, out! Now! There's a bomb, clear out, clear out!"

Walden came pounding from the rear of the house.

"Where's Taylor?" she asked.

"Upstairs." He started towards the steps but she beat him to them.

"Get out. Get fire, police rolling," she called over her shoulder as she dashed up the steps. "Taylor!"

She was counting seconds down in her head as she ran. Three open doors, one closed. Seven, six… Taylor was in the front room, the solid oak door shut behind him. She burst into the room, the door bouncing off the wall with a loud bang that made him jump to his feet. He held an evidence bag in one hand and a laptop in the other. Ruffled edged lace curtains danced around the large open window beside him.

"LT, what's the deal?" he asked.

Four, three.

"Bomb," she cried out. She hurled her weight across the room, propelling them both out the window. They hit the porch roof as the world shattered.

A fireball of heat and glass and wood and flame launched them into space. Lucy grabbed onto Taylor, his eyes registering shock and fear.

Heat seared her back. A loud roar devoured her senses, obscuring everything except the sight of the ground racing up to slam into them.

A shock wave smashed through her. Her ears popped and suddenly she could hear again. Sirens and a car alarm and men yelling and someone screaming. She tried to inhale, tasted dirt and grass. Coughed, gasped and coughed once more.

That wasn't her screaming was it? She rolled over onto her side, regretted it as pain spiked through her back. No. She wasn't screaming, she could barely breathe. It was Taylor who was crying, whimpering in pain.

The peaceful blue sky had been ripped asunder, now filled with swirling debris, smoke and flames. They weren't far from the house, only twenty feet or so. Flames shot out of the old frame structure, greedily reaching out to neighbors on both sides. Then she spotted the propane tank in the neighbor's side yard.

She tried to struggle to her feet, to reach out to Taylor, but strong hands beat her to it. Burroughs and Grimwald dragged Taylor back, away from the inferno while Walden and Lucy did their own bizarre version of the three-legged race.

"Need to evacuate," she managed to grate the words past her tattered vocal cords. "Propane—" She couldn't speak, so she raised a finger in the direction of the tank.

"Already working on it," Walden reassured her. "You okay, boss?"

"Fine." She straightened against the car bumper and immediately regretted it as more pain lanced through her. So much pain that she wasn't even certain where it came from. "Taylor?"

An ambulance screeched to a halt beside them. Burroughs and the medics helped Taylor onto a stretcher. Taylor's left forearm was bent like a Kennywood roller coaster. Medics crowded around him, blocking her view.

Lucy looked around, her gaze swimming. She must have lost a few minutes because firefighters already swarmed over the house, hoses blasting water in every direction, sending rainbows arching over the crowd of cop cars and gawkers.

The grins on their faces told her this was another fun day at the office for them—no fatalities, no collateral damage, they had things under control, this was their kind of fire.

"Make sure they know this is a crime scene. We need as much evidence preserved as possible." Her voice was stronger now. If she didn't move, didn't really breathe, the pain wasn't too bad. "Someone take a look around the yard. Taylor was holding a laptop when we went out the window."

"Got it," Burroughs told her, holding the splintered remains of a laptop keyboard aloft like a prize. "He fell on it." The detective sauntered over. "Think I'm going to think twice about letting you feds step on my turf again."

"Bastard. He was watching us through a wireless camera. Probably more than one."

"I've got guys scouring the neighborhood, but with all the hubbub, he's had plenty of time to get away. If he was ever even here—he could have the cameras rigged so he can watch them from anywhere, through a computer or even a smart phone." He took a step back and stared at her long and hard. "The medics see you yet?"

"I told them to take care of Taylor. I'm fine." Her legs were trembling despite the support of the car trunk she leaned against. "Anyone find my cell phone? Fletcher called me on it, maybe we can do something with the call."

"I really think you need the medics, Lucy," Walden said, his voice sounding funny.

"No, I need that cell phone. Burroughs, would you go look for it?"

Burroughs ignored her, instead whirling away to grab a paramedic and pull him over.

"Why doesn't anyone listen to me?" Lucy was getting angry now, sweat dripping down the back of her shirt, making it stick to her. "Find the damn cell phone!"

"We will, I promise," Walden said. "Just as soon as the medics check you out."

"I told you, I'm fine."

"Lucy," Burroughs reached around her, snagging her by the waist as she sagged against the bumper. "Listen to me. We'll take care of everything but you need to lie down on this stretcher."

He pulled his hand away and raised it before her face. It was covered with blood, so much blood that it slipped off his palm in a steady stream.

Mesmerized, Lucy followed the drips of blood. They swirled in slow motion, tiny red beads of glistening sunlight, dropping, spilling, falling...

Chapter 28

The ambulance ride to Three Rivers passed in a haze of sirens and beeping monitors and men shouting above her. The medics strapped her face down onto the gurney, which wasn't helping her breathing. The lurching and swaying of the ambulance made her feel more queasy than the last time she'd tried to get on a boat.

"I'm going to be sick," she groaned, not sure if anyone could hear her. Gloved hands appeared below her, holding a yellow plastic basin. She threw up, waves of pain slicing through her until her vision went black again.

She woke up, still face down, this time mercifully motionless. She blinked and inhaled the sharp scent of starched hospital linens. Everything was white, except for the black spots dancing in her vision.

"What happened?" she asked, her voice a weak croak. She tried to raise her head but was overcome by vertigo.

"Hold still, Agent Guardino," came a man's voice from behind her. "You're at Three Rivers' ER. Everything's going to be fine."

The man sounded so calm, so superior that he pissed Lucy off immediately. "I didn't ask where I was. I asked what happened."

She tried to roll over to face him but pain screamed through every nerve ending. Her eyelids peeled back as she clamped her jaws against the urge to cry out. Christ, this was worse than childbirth.

"Don't move." Hands held her shoulders down as her shirt was cut away, the cold metal of the trauma shears slick against her wet skin.

Why was she wet? Oh yeah, there was a fire. Lots of water. And blood—there had been blood, too. Where was it coming from?

"Is Taylor all right?"

"Taylor?" the man asked. Idiot.

"The other FBI agent," a woman's voice supplied. "Ortho's with him, has a Colles' fracture."

"He's fine," the man translated. The sticky-slippy feel of gloved hands probed her back.

"Ah-ye!" she cried out against her will as more pain spiraled through her.

Lucy realized that in addition to removing her shirt, her jeans were now gone as well, there were IV's in each of her arms and sticky pads with wires attached to her chest. Disembodied hands poked and prodded, telling her to "hold still" and tell them if "anything hurt."

"Let's get X-ray in here," the man said.

"No." She put all her energy into the one syllable. The room grew silent and she felt the stares of the ER personnel on her.

"Agent Guardino," the man drawled out her name in an exasperated sigh. "I need you to cooperate."

Lucy decided she couldn't be hurt too bad, no one seemed very excited. There was none of the hustle and bustle major traumas created. Instead, everyone seemed rather annoyed by her intrusion into their workday.

Not as annoyed as she was.

"Tough shit. I've had quite enough of being a patient, thank you very much. I have work to do. Like finding a fourteen-year-old girl and the creep who took her before it's too late. Now, tell me exactly what's wrong and exactly how you're going to fix it and exactly who the hell you are."

She felt more than heard the man's intake of breath. A pair of female legs dressed in blue scrub pants walked to the head of the gurney.

"This is Dr. Williams," the woman who had spoken before answered. "He's a trauma surgeon and he's examining your back, trying to decide if he needs to take you to surgery."

"Surgery? For what?"

"Agent Guardino, you do remember the bomb, don't you?" Williams asked in an oh-so-condescending tone.

"Of course I do. Taylor and I jumped through a window, fell from the porch roof. I had my breath knocked out, but I didn't hit my head or anything. Just hurts a bit to breathe, that's all. Probably cracked a rib or something."

"Actually, you have a rather large piece of metal impaled through your rhomboid muscle," Williams told her. "I need X-rays to confirm that it hasn't penetrated the chest cavity before I remove it."

"A piece of metal? Really?" Well hell, you'd think she'd have noticed something like that. No wonder the guys on the scene were looking at her kind of funny. "Guess that's why it hurts so fucking much when I breathe. How big is it?"

A hand clad in a purple latex glove appeared before her eyes, its thumb and forefinger spread a good five inches apart. "That big," the nurse said. "But there's only about a half inch sticking out from the skin, so we need to see how deep it goes."

"Oh." Lucy sighed. So much for taking control of this situation. "Okay. Let's get that X-ray, then."

"Why thank you, Agent Guardino." The surgeon's sarcasm ripped through the room.

"No problem, doc," Lucy said airily. "Hey, since you've got my ass hanging free, could someone either throw a sheet on me or turn the heat up? It's freezing in here. And I need my guys—"

"After the X-ray."

Lucy conceded the point. The flow of people surrounding her shifted as a large machine was wheeled in. "Any chance you could be pregnant? How much do you weigh? Any past medical history?" an anonymous tech droned out the questions in a monotone that made it impossible to tell if they were a she or a he.

She rattled off answers and gave her personal information to a nurse who squatted down giving Lucy one person she could make eye contact with.

More pain while the tech jostled her, sliding witch's-tit-cold film cartridges under her. The nurse asked if she wanted any meds, but Lucy declined. She needed to keep her head clear. Everyone backed away, there was a final beep, and the X-rays were done.

"Would someone please send in my guys? Anyone? I don't care— FBI, Pittsburgh—" Lucy tried to raise her head to see if she'd been abandoned in the room but couldn't look that far over her shoulder. Then she heard the door whoosh open and footsteps approach.

"Lucy?" It was Nick. She stiffened as fresh pain washed through her. Not pain from the piece of metal in her back, this was a deeper pain. Harder to control. "Oh my God—"

"Is Megan okay?" She wanted to twist around far enough to see his face but couldn't. "Did something happen?"

"Yeah, something happened. My wife apparently developed delusions that she was superwoman and could fly." He took the stool in front of her. His face was pale, closed shut with worry. And anger. "Megan's fine. She's asleep."

"You shouldn't have left her alone."

He jerked his chin up at that. "She's with your mother." He left the unsaid words dangling between them, that it was Lucy who had left Megan, not him.

"I'm sorry." Tears blurred her vision. She blinked hard, not wanting him to see. But of course he did.

"For what? Leaving Megan or almost dying?" There was an edge to his voice and she recognized fear. But his fear and anger didn't stop him from taking her hand as she reached out to him.

"I panicked. I felt trapped—powerless. There was nothing I could do. *Nothing*. Not even cheer her up playing that damn video game. I needed to do something. So when the chance came, I panicked and ran. I'm sorry."

He leaned forward so his forehead touched hers. "I know. Megan knows too. She's a smart kid."

"Takes after her dad that way. You were right, kind of, about that mystical thinking. All day long, I can't stop seeing Ashley and Megan together, like if I can save one, I can save them both."

"But that's the problem with magical thinking. What if you can't save Ashley?"

Shit. She didn't have an answer for that one. Nothing except the one thing that had driven her to this job in the first place. "I have to try."

He nodded, his head bobbing against hers. "I know. But that's the problem, isn't it?"

"I can't help it, Nick. It's not just because it's my job—you and Megan are far more important than any job. You know that. But it's a job no one else wants to do, and few people can do, and—"

"And you happen to be very good at it." He sat back, still holding her hand. "I know. John Greally told me that you found the guy who did this. And he told me you saved lives when you ran into that house."

The shrug came automatically, before she remembered the piece of steel in her back. Pain lanced through her, making her gasp. She blew it out, small little breaths like when Megan was born.

"Should I get the nurse?" Nick asked.

"No. I'm fine. How's Megan? Are any of the tests back?"

"Her color looks better. No fever. The doctors haven't been back." He glanced up, over her shoulder and she knew he wanted to be back with Megan. Watching, waiting. Nick was good at that.

Unlike Lucy.

"When they do, I don't care what time it is, you have them call me." Shit, she'd lost her phone in the fire. Damn, damn, damn. Could anything go right this weekend? She needed to be in contact with Megan's doctors, she needed to be with her daughter, she needed to find Ashley, she needed to hunt down Fletcher... and here she was, lying nearly naked on a cot, freezing her ass off. "I lost my cell. But I'll pick up a new one as soon as I'm back in the office."

"You're not going back to work," Nick protested.

"I have to—"

"No. You don't. Think of your daughter, Lucy."

Low blow. Totally unlike him. "Nick—"

"Okay, then, think of your team. That girl. Ashley. How can you focus on them when you're exhausted and worried about Megan? You've said yourself, a distracted agent is a dangerous one."

She blinked hard and fast, lowering her face so he couldn't see her tears. She couldn't handle this. Not now. "Give Megan a kiss. I'll be there tonight. I promise."

"You promised her, not me, Lucy," Nick said, his voice edged with a fury that was foreign to him. "Don't you dare let her down."

"I know. I know. I'll be there." She looked up again. "I love you."

He sighed and squeezed her hand, then dropped it. Heavy footsteps came from behind them.

"Hey, Guardino, didn't no one never teach you when to duck?" Burroughs said.

"I love you." Nick kissed her forehead then stood. "I'd better get back to Megan."

And he left.

"You okay, boss?" Walden added, moving to the head of the bed.

Lucy turned her head to one side, swiping away stray tears on the sheet. "I'm fine. They're just checking an X-ray. Any word on Fletcher?"

"Dust in the wind," Burroughs said. "Be awhile before we can get much out of the house, but the arson guys are working on it."

"Good. He'll have a car, one that's under the radar. And if he wasn't keeping Ashley in his house—" She stopped, icy cold rushing to her head as she realized she'd only assumed that Ashley wasn't in the house.

"No remains in the debris so far," Walden assured her.

"Okay." She swallowed, pushing past the fear that she was already too late to save Ashley. "Right. I need all the background on Fletcher, his complete personnel file. He's been planning this for a long time and we're playing catch up."

"ICE is cooperating, thanks to the SAC. But unfortunately the media is already all over this."

"Shit." She jerked her head up, ignoring the talons of pain raking down her back. Took a second to breathe. "Get me a new phone, programmed to my old number and wired for a trace. Fletcher called me once, he's gonna reach out again."

"Why? He's got Ashley, he's in the clear," Burroughs protested. "Why risk calling you?"

"Because he's the Maestro, the game master. He won his prize but he wants to play some more. With me."

They talked strategy. Lucy's neck ached with the effort of craning her head up all the time, but Walden seemed to instinctively understand. He grabbed a low stool and sat down in front of her, taking notes as she dictated a to-do list.

"What do you want from me?" Burroughs asked as Walden's list lengthened. He was staring at her with that look in his eye again. That "I'm just a horny guy, so sue me" look that he'd had ever since she'd met him.

"First up, you can stop ogling my ass." He jerked upright, eyes front as if he hadn't even been aware of what he'd been staring at. "Second, get me some clothes for when I bust loose from this joint. Third, give me your phone so I can call Bobby Fegley."

"Fegley?" Burroughs asked, his tone dismissive. "The cripple? What's he got to do with this?"

"He knows that game Fletcher invented better than anyone. Which means he has some insight in how Fletcher thinks. I'll talk to him while the doctors are mucking about."

Burroughs looked like he was going to say something but instead just handed her his cell phone. Before she could dial, the gracious and genteel Dr. Williams breezed in, waving an X-ray aloft as if it were the shroud of Turin.

He took the stool Walden vacated and paraded the film before her. Ribs and a white blob that was her heart she could figure out. She wasn't too sure at first about his prattling about pneumothorax and bleeding, but he finished by regretfully declaring that they weren't there, thus negating any necessity for surgery.

The half a foot long jagged length of metal was rather obvious even to her untrained eye. It showed up bright white, sharp and looked utterly out of place anywhere near the soft curves that shadowed the rest of the X-ray.

Burroughs and Walden leaned forward, trying to get a glimpse as well. Williams stood and snapped the films onto an X-ray view box, beaming like a proud father.

"Jeeesuh," Burroughs whistled in appreciation. Walden was silent, but he moved to stand beside Lucy.

"How long is this gonna take?" she asked.

"Since you're not going to surgery, you don't need me. A few layers of sutures will do the trick. I'll get an intern down here—"

"Don't think so, doc," Walden said in a low, flat Dirty Harry tone. Lucy looked up, saw that he and Burroughs had sandwiched the surgeon between them, both of them wearing their best cop-glowers.

"I think you're going to fix her yourself." Burroughs picked up the ball and ran with it. "Right now." He squared off perpendicular to the surgeon, his hand resting on his gun as if ready for a fast draw.

"Really, gentlemen—"

"You have kids, Williams?" Lucy chimed in on the fun. The surgeon darted a glance in her direction as if he'd forgotten she was there.

"Yes. Why?" The word slid up near to the soprano range and he gulped it back down, tried again. "Look here, I'm very busy—"

"I'm busy too," Lucy continued, holding his gaze although it was making her head throb, stretching her neck up like that. "I'm busy trying to save a little girl's life. And I need to get patched up and out of here in order to do that. Think you can help out?"

He scanned the room as if looking for an escape. Given that his beeper hadn't gone off the entire time he'd been with them, Lucy suspected he'd run out of excuses. He turned back to the X-ray, one finger tracing the length of the piece of metal impaling her.

"Probably should take care of this myself," he finally said with a nod as if it were his idea. "Might be tricky."

Burroughs relaxed his posture and clapped Williams on the shoulder. "Thanks, doc. We appreciate it."

"Get to work, you two," Lucy said as Williams shrugged free of his lab coat and began to assemble an assortment of bright, shiny instruments of torture.

"It's going to hurt like a bastard when I take it out, even with the local. And that'll hurt a bit, too, sad to say."

Williams sounded anything but sad. He held up a syringe with a very large, very long needle on it and flicked an air bubble free. Lucy's head went woozy and she rested her forehead against the mattress, closing her eyes.

"I can knock you out if you want." His tone implied she'd be a wimp if she said yes.

Any other circumstances, she would have begged for the pain meds. She could care less what Williams thought of her. Raising her head, she ignored the rushing feeling that had commandeered her stomach. Good thing she'd already barfed in the ambulance. "No. I need to keep my head clear, get back to work as soon as you're done."

"Your call." He sounded almost gleeful.

Payback for their earlier power games. Hell, why couldn't men just grow up and focus on getting the job done?

She flipped Burroughs' phone open and saw a text message displayed. From one "tvgirl" who apparently LUV'D THE WAY U F'D ME ALL NITE LONG, WHEN ARE U CUMING AGAIN?

Lucy swore. It had nothing to do with the needle Williams used to stab her in the back.

Chapter 29

A very long hour later, Lucy was shuffling down the hallway, wearing scrubs with no bra, her own underwear, shoes and socks, and Walden's windbreaker. She'd almost made her escape to freedom when the nurse chased her down, a clipboard and metal tray in her hands.

Walden and Burroughs stood on either side of her, watching as the nurse rattled off Lucy's discharge instructions, made her sign twenty-three different forms in triplicate, handed her a small bottle of Tylenol with codeine and a prescription for antibiotics. Finally, she unveiled the contents of the tray.

"Almost forgot your tetanus booster, Agent Guardino."

The black spots in Lucy's vision returned along with a thundering in her ears. If the guys hadn't been there she would have treated herself to a nice case of the vapors—her usual reaction to needles. Damn it, why couldn't they have done it while she was out cold when they stuck her with the IV's?

"Wouldn't want to forget that," she mumbled. Her face was cold and clammy. From the looks on Burroughs and Walden's faces, they were in total sympathy.

She handed the papers and bottles to Walden, painfully slid one arm free of the windbreaker, swallowed hard and vowed not to faint.

The nurse didn't even move them into a patient space, instead she briskly dabbed some alcohol on Lucy's upper arm and jabbed the needle in before anyone could say "boo." Even smiled while she did it, Lucy saw as her vision swam out of focus for a moment. Both of the men looked away. Scaredy cats.

It was over fast and before she knew it, Lucy was boasting a Bugs Bunny Band-Aid and the nurse had helped her back into the jacket. "There. You're good to go."

"Where's Taylor? I want to see him before we leave."

Walden answered. "Over here."

She followed the men across the hall to the orthopedics room. Her back felt bruised and tight and swollen, like it was being held together by fishing line. Which, the surgeon had explained, was basically the truth of the matter. Nylon on the top of the skin and something called chromic, which he said was like old fashioned cat gut only better, in a few layers of muscle and connective tissue below the surface. One wrong move and his sewing project could pop wide open again.

Her skin felt stretched so tight that she wondered if it might not have been better just to let the metal remain. Weld it closed or something.

Then she saw Taylor and counted herself lucky.

"Hi, LT, did they get you too?" he said, his pupils constricted and dancing as he held a black rubber mask to his face and sucked on it greedily. His arm looked awful, fingers caught tight in a cage-like contraption straight out of a Fu Manchu movie, a weight pulling his elbow down, the "S" shaped curve of his broken arm bones slowly being straightened out by a surgeon covered with flecks of plaster and frayed bits of fiberglass.

"Wow, Taylor," she said, taking his good hand in hers. "You'll do anything for a few days off."

"Can't feel a thing. They numbed my whole arm up and gave me lotsa drugs. Goooood drugs."

"Nitrous oxide," the surgeon corrected as he re-aligned the bones with a grating noise that made Lucy's eyes bug wide in sympathy. "He wouldn't let us give him anything long-acting. Said he needed to get back to work."

"You catch the bastard yet?" Taylor's words were slurred and his eyelids drooped.

"Not yet. We're headed out now. You going to be okay?"

"Oh sure. I'm fine," he sang the last, his eyes now completely shut.

Lucy squeezed his hand and backed away. "He really going to be all right?" she asked the surgeon.

"Yeah, this looks awful, but they usually heal with no problems. He'll have a cast for the next two months. In fact, soon as I'm finished and get a follow-up X-ray, he'll be ready to go."

Satisfied that Taylor was in good hands, she followed Burroughs to where his car was parked in the no-parking zone closest to the ER doors. He'd left his wigwags going, the blue and red lights flashing from behind the Impala's grille, bathing the brick wall in color.

"You sure you don't want me to take you home?" he asked, holding the passenger door open for her. "You should get some rest."

Resentment flared through her. No one would ever question one of the guys returning to work. Why did they assume she was any different? She'd rest when they found Ashley.

"Get me back to the office." She eased her weight down into the seat, wincing as she twisted to pull the seatbelt tight.

Burroughs pulled out of the hospital drive and turned onto Penn. He drove just like yesterday, relaxed, one wrist draped over the wheel, exuding confidence.

"That reporter, Ames. She broke up your marriage, didn't she?"

He slid one hand to fist the wheel at the eleven o'clock position as he slanted his gaze at her. "After that stunt with Danny and Mitch, yeah. She still hassling your daughter? I can handle that if you want."

Right. He'd love nothing more than to handle "tvgirl" again. "No, I meant your affair with her. That's what broke up your marriage, right?"

Now both hands gripped the wheel tight. But his face was expressionless as he stared at her. "You're kidding me. You think I—"

She was too tired to play this game. Flipping his phone open, she waved the text message in front of him. "Answer me one question, Burroughs. How badly have you fucked my case?"

The car swerved slightly. He started to smile, a phony, *hey-this-is-all-a-joke, right?* smile. She merely glared at him, refusing to look away. Then he gave a one-shouldered shrug of surrender and the boyish grin vanished.

"Cindy and I, we hooked up about a year ago, when the Olsen case came along and I was primary. I didn't give her what she wanted, so she pulled that stunt with my kids."

"Answer my question, Burroughs."

"I didn't tell her anything. That's what I'm trying to explain. This thing between us, it's some kind of warped chemistry, I don't know what—but I would never, ever jeopardize a case."

"You'd jeopardize your marriage but not the job?" She didn't try to bother to keep the scorn from her voice.

"Yes—no. Kim and I were having trouble long before I met Cindy. Look, this doesn't have to be a bad thing. We could use it to our advantage, leak a story to Cindy, use it to bait Fletcher."

Lucy was already way ahead of him there. "It might come to that. In the meantime, I'm going to ask one thing from you. If you can't do it, tell me now."

His Adam's apple bobbed as he swallowed. "What is it?"

"You don't talk with Ames, you don't go near her, you don't fuck her again until we have Ashley safe."

Ignoring traffic for a moment, he swiveled his head to meet her eyes with an altar-boy-innocent gaze. He nodded solemnly. "Sure. The kid comes first."

She couldn't help but notice he had stopped using Ashley's name.

–

"Hey, wake up. You're safe now. Everything is going to be all right."

The worlds circled around her consciousness like fluffy summer clouds, thin and wispy and impossible to grasp. It was a man's voice, that much penetrated. He was holding her, rocking her like she was a baby.

"Here, drink this. Slowly now, slowly."

A trickle of fluid ran down her chin. More sloshed down her throat, gagging her. She jerked up, coughing, her eyes springing open. Dark spots danced before her eyes, everything was shadowy.

The man held her in his lap, she couldn't see his face. He held a water bottle back up to her lips and she drank. He started to pull it away and she grabbed it.

"No. Don't drink too fast, you'll get sick."

She didn't fight, instead lowered her hand to her lap. Waited for him to make the next move.

"I need to get some tools from my truck. To cut you loose." He slid her from his lap onto the hard ground. In the distance she saw a mound of snakes, dark, hovering around the periphery of her vision. Terrified, she grabbed his pant leg, not looking up at him, her gaze focused on the snakes.

"Don't worry, they won't hurt you. I'll be right back." She wrapped her arm around his leg, anchoring herself. He crouched low, gently loosening her grip. "It's all right. You're safe now. Trust me."

Then he was gone and she was alone again.

Trust him? The words were meaningless. The only things that had meaning in her universe were the threat of the snakes, the impending horror of being left in the darkness again, the headlong terror she felt with every breath. She drew her knees up, hugging her legs to her, making herself the smallest target possible.

Without moving her head, she glanced around her prison. It was a barn. Overturned buckets hung from hooks in the rafters above her—the source of the snakes, she guessed. But where was the man who had put them there? Who had brought her here?

Snakes slithered around bales of hay stacked to make walls. The only light came from a door open at one end of the small barn. More bales obscured it, all she could see was the bright light framed at the top of the opening. On the other side of the barn the hay bales were stacked to make seats.

Her fingers spread out into claws, fighting terror as she saw her "audience". Three vaguely human forms sat there, snakes crawling over them, making the plastic they were encased in rustle as if they were alive.

They weren't alive.

Panic seized her, her heart speeding into a furious rhythm that threatened to strangle her. She scuttled back as far as the chain would stretch, kept going, not caring about the snakes or anything except getting far away from the three bodies.

She rolled over onto her belly, lunging for the doorway, the promise of freedom. The chain yanked her back, her ankle screaming for mercy. She stretched out, clawing her hands against the linoleum that extended only a few inches past her reach. Where was the man, her savior? He had promised...

As if in answer to her silent prayers, he appeared again, a tall shadow ringed by light.

"Miss me?" he said brightly, brandishing a large pair of bolt cutters. He immediately went to work on the cable restraining her. "This might hurt a bit."

She said nothing, simply lay there, face down, snakes slithering over her limp hands, ignoring the pain as he pried one jaw of the tool beneath the restraint. There was pressure, a lot of pressure, then a snapping sound.

His hands worked at her ankle. She lay still, waiting.

"You're free. Think you can walk?"

She said nothing, puzzling over his words. Waiting to see what happened next. What new torture was coming.

"Maybe I should carry you." With a grunt of effort he rolled her over and scooped her into his arms. He swayed beneath her weight and she saw that he really wasn't all that tall. He carried her through the maze of hay bales and out into the bright sunshine.

The light burned her eyes. She almost cried out, but stopped herself in time. Instead, she closed her eyes tight and buried her face into his shoulder.

"Sorry I didn't get here sooner," he said, balancing her weight as he shut the barn door. "What's your name? I'm Jim."

She burrowed deeper into his shirt, trying to escape the harsh judgment of the sun. What was her name? Good question. The answer seemed meaningless. A name didn't matter, who she was didn't matter—just as long as she didn't have to return to the darkness.

Floating, she was a lazy cloud, floating. Unfettered, untethered, unleashed.

Free to float.

As if looking down from a great height, she saw the figure of a man carrying a dark-haired girl. Both strangers to her, but she felt sympathy for him as he stumbled, almost tripped and caught himself. Watched as the girl tightened her grip around his neck. Safe, she was safe in his arms.

Knowing that, seeing that, was more than enough. She didn't need answers, she only needed to float. Free...

"Vixen," she finally answered. "Call me Vixen."

For some reason, that made the man laugh. Not at her, more as if he'd won some prize. He hugged her tight, his laughter rippling through him, acting as if she were something special, precious.

"All right, then, Vixen," he finally said. "Let's get you someplace safe and sound."

Chapter 30

Her Special Agent in Charge, John Greally, was waiting for Lucy when she limped into her office, now feeling every stitch and bruised muscle in Technicolor waves of pain.

Greally smiled, a lop-sided grimace that crinkled his eyes. Not because he was happy she was injured, but because they both knew how easily things could have turned out differently. If Fletcher had wanted, Greally could right this minute be making death notifications to three families. Including hers.

She met his gaze with a small nod, assuring him she was all right. He left his seat and pulled a chair out from the conference table for her. Even though she usually preferred to stand, she sank down into it, leaning to one side to shield her back. It had been a hard day already and wasn't over, not by a long shot.

Greally perched on the edge of the table, motioning for Burroughs to wait outside. Lucy was glad her back was to the bullpen; it gave her the opportunity to close her eyes for a moment.

"Better or worse than Baltimore?" he asked. She and Greally had worked together on a RICO operation that had gone smoothly except for a five-car pile-up in rush hour traffic on the Beltway. No fault of hers or Greally's, merely the wrong place at the wrong time.

She'd wrenched her neck and back, been stiff for a week, unable to turn her head. "Better," she lied.

"Hmpf. You don't look it."

"Just tired. This thing with Megan..."

"Yeah. I can only imagine. How is she?"

248

"Fine. Playing video games. But the waiting for answers—"

"It will drive you nuts. I'll bet Nick is glad to have you out of there, you were probably driving him crazy as well."

"Not so sure about that."

"We need to talk about the thing with the Canadians this morning."

"Ah hell." She sat up straight, jerking the stitches in her back. "Are we going to lose them 'cause of Fletcher? The guy held a gun to my face—"

He held up a hand, shutting her down. "I talked with the Assistant US attorney. She thinks we're okay—especially as Ivan's partners are already rolling on him."

She slumped back, suddenly aware that the gnawing in her stomach was hunger, not nausea. "Think you could use some of that SAC clout of yours to get my team some food?"

"Now I know you're going to be all right. Back to the little Mother Theresa we all know and love."

"Hey, stop that." She looked around, made sure the door was closed. "Don't start calling me that around here. Besides, any good leader knows an army works better if you feed it to the enemy." She frowned, knowing she messed up the metaphor but not having enough energy to care. "Or something like that."

Greally was already using the phone at her desk arranging for a delivery from the CheeseCake Factory down on Carson Street. Lucy brightened. But then Greally squirmed, pulled a large rubber snake out from the seat of the chair, and dangled it over the desk. Worse, he only almost smiled.

That's when she knew she might be in real trouble.

A knock came on the door and Walden poked his head in. "ICE just sent Fletcher's jacket. Taylor called, he's being released and insists on coming back. I sent Burroughs after him. I've updated Lowery and Dunmar, they know it's now our jurisdiction. They'll call if anything breaks on their end."

"Thanks," Lucy said. Walden was proving himself a definite asset. "Let's try hard to keep them in the loop—I don't want any exclusive interviews proclaiming a federal cover up when word gets out that Fletcher is one of ours." Greally nodded his agreement. Lucy stood, she couldn't think straight sitting still. "Once everyone's here, we'll start cracking this nutcase."

Greally hung up the phone and stared long and hard at Walden. Lucy appreciated the fact that Walden didn't budge, instead crossed his arms over his chest. Nice to know where he stood after her recent fuck-ups. Maybe Nick was right? No, the misjudgment with the snake handlers had come before Megan got sick.

No excuses.

She couldn't let Walden take the fall for her mistakes. "Why don't you start breaking down Fletcher's file?"

He met her gaze, gave her a nod, and left. Greally kept his seat—her seat, really—behind her desk. At least she hoped it still was her desk.

"Want to give me some ideas about how to explain the last few days to HQ?" he asked. "Distraction over a sick child is nothing to be ashamed about."

Lucy stood up straight, refused to let him see the effort it cost her. "Would you ask any of the guys that? Would you allow anyone to ask you that if the positions were reversed?"

"So it's stress? Is the job too much for you?"

"My team has only been on the job for three months and we've built two hundred cases," she protested. "I'd like to think I had some part of that."

He nodded slowly. "Yeah, that's what your team says."

"You've been talking to my team about my performance?" Christ, they'd never trust her again if they thought she had a screw loose.

"Routine ninety-day review. Or so they think." He paused, placing his palms flat on the desktop. "Highest marks I've ever seen— from your team."

"And from administration?"

"About the worst I've seen. Your paperwork is routinely late—"

"But never shoddy. I bring home the bacon, John. No AUSA has ever complained about any of my cases."

"No. But this is a huge organization. We can't function without someone staying on top of the administrative details—which is your job. *Supervisory* special agent. You're no longer a field agent."

"I can do both—"

"Without jeopardizing your team? Or putting innocent civilians in the crossfire?"

She had no answer to that.

"I need you on Fletcher. No one else could have gotten as far as fast as you have. But that's it. After we wrap it, you're confined to this office. Even if I have to chain you to this desk—" He twinkled a smile, the old Greally, the partner who had her back, had returned. "Although you might just enjoy that."

She had no choice but to play along. "Hey, at least there aren't any snakes."

He scrutinized her, knowing her too well to accept her concession so easily, but said nothing.

–

One of the few perks of being the boss was that Lucy's office had its own storage closet, a space she had transformed into a private changing room. Or "boudoir" as Taylor and a few of the guys put it. Usually she used it to change into casual wear for Megan's soccer games or from regular work clothes to a suit for court or meetings with brass.

Today, while Walden and John Greally were finishing lunch and filling the white board with everything they did and didn't know about James Fletcher, she used it to ditch the hospital scrubs and change into the khakis and sleeveless blouse she'd worn to work.

Until she bent over to pull her pants on, she'd never realized exactly how many muscles were involved with the mere process of dressing. Feeling a little dizzy by the time she'd finished, she sat down on a folding chair and used the privacy to call Nick from her new cell phone.

"Hello?" His voice sounded wary as if expecting more bad news.

"How's Megan? Any word from the doctors?"

"Megan is currently the reigning Queen of the Dark Realm and is now proceeding to kick everyone's butt at John Madden's NFL." The background noise grew muffled she heard a door shut. When he returned on the line, there was a hollow echo and she knew he'd retreated into the bathroom. "The doctor just left."

"Why didn't you call me?" Oh God, what couldn't he say in front of Megan?

"Because there was nothing new. He said the tests are all normal so far, but they still need to consider doing the biopsy if they can't find out what's causing her fever and everything. Said he'll know more by tomorrow after he has a specialist review her labs."

"What the hell good are they if they can't tell us anything?" She pushed onto her feet, the chair clattering to the floor.

"Calm down. Megan's fine. She had a little bit of a fever but it didn't even bother her. She's more worried about you."

Lucy sagged against wire shelves crammed with office supplies. "That's not fair."

"Isn't it you who is always talking about life not being fair?"

Typical. Using her own words against her.

"Are you going to make it back tonight?" His voice had an edge—one that she was slowly becoming familiar with. And not liking. Not at all.

"I'm not sure when. But I'll keep my promise." Somehow.

"I can't believe you went back to work—"

"You know why. Ashley is still out there. Somewhere."

He grunted—another new habit. Fourteen years together, did she know him at all? "You know the odds as well as I do. She's dead."

"Don't say that!"

Silence.

"I'm sorry—"

"I shouldn't—"

Their words collided and they both were silent once again.

Damn, this was hard, she wished she could see his face, watch how he was moving. Was he rubbing the back of his ear like he did when he was anxious? Or was he truly angry and was holding his arms stretched out as if pushing her away?

"Things are happening way too fast, yet way too slow around here right now," she tried.

Finally, he answered. Her husband, her friend, her confidante was back. "Hmmm... sounds like the same as here."

"Yeah, well, next time you vote for a move to a desert island where we don't have to worry about the outside world, I'm definitely agreeing." This time she knew exactly the expression on his face. That boyish wistful faraway look. The same one that had made her first fall in love with him.

A sigh escaped her and the spell was broken. "Did you tell Mom about—earlier?"

"She saw it on the news. I told her it wasn't that bad, just a few stitches."

"How was her date?"

Now he had a trace of amusement in his voice. "She said thank you very much for not siccing the cops on her and she had a wonderful time."

"Did you get the guy's name? Are they going out again? Where's he live, what's he do?"

"Your mother is an intelligent, grown woman. Don't you have enough on your hands without worrying about her as well?"

She turned her back to the door, burying the phone in her hands. "I think I might have fucked up. Backed this guy into a corner."

"What happened?" She quickly gave him the highlights about Fletcher. "Hmmm... sounds like a classic malignant narcissist."

"Gee, thanks doc, that helps a lot. I know what a narcissist is, but malignant makes me think of..." They both knew what "malignant" brought to mind. Cancer. Bone marrow biopsies, little girls with no hair, wasting away and dying before their time.

"The point is," Nick threw her a lifeline, pulling her back to Fletcher, "he needs Ashley."

"So he wouldn't kill her?" She was relieved to have her gut feeling validated. "Why?"

"Malignant narcissists have no self-image, no sense of self without someone else providing it. I'd bet your guy lost that someone when he started this—"

"He mentioned his mother being sick."

"Yeah, a dominant opposite-sex parent would definitely fit the bill. He may have first reached out to older women to fill her role but found they weren't malleable enough."

"So he worked his way down to a fourteen-year-old he could brainwash into doing anything. Is that why she's so valuable? Because of all his time, effort? How far can I push him before that's negated?"

"You don't understand. The time and effort make her valuable, yes, but more than that, he needs her. She's his mirror, he is the reflection in the mirror. He doesn't exist without her."

"Okay, now you're drifting into mumbo-jumbo land." There was a polite tapping at the closet door and she opened it.

"Burroughs and Taylor are back," John Greally told her.

"I've got to go." She clung to the phone, reluctant to hang up, fearful that if she did, something bad might happen while she was absent from Megan's bedside. But the bitch of it was, something bad could happen with her right there beside Megan. And she'd be powerless to stop it. At least there was one girl she could save. Maybe. "Kiss Megan for me, tell her I'll be there just as soon as I can."

"Don't forget your promise."

"I won't. I love you."

"Hey, you be careful." His voice dropped, low and imperative. "Please."

"Always." She hung up and reluctantly returned to the outside world.

A smattering of applause coming from the bullpen pulled Lucy and Greally from her office. Taylor stood just inside the door, a sheepish grin on his face, his arm in a cast and sling.

Lucy and Greally added their own applause to the standing ovation. She escorted Taylor to his desk, enjoying the blush that colored his features.

"Ooh-rah!" Burroughs shouted in a fair impression of a Marine as the clapping died down.

"Okay, everyone back to work," Lucy said as Taylor sat down. "Glad you're back, Taylor. You feeling up to helping out around here?"

"Definitely," he said, still beaming.

"Yeah, you look ready to go," Greally put in. "No field assignments until the cast's off, but I'll clear you for desk duty."

"Thank you, sir." Taylor seemed mesmerized by all the attention. "I wasn't expecting this. It's kind of embarrassing, I mean all I did was get thrown out of a window."

Greally laughed and clapped a hand on Taylor's good shoulder. "A rite of passage. Ask Lucy about her first line of duty injury."

Walden and Burroughs looked up at that. "C'mon, Guardino, spill," said Burroughs.

She shot Greally a half-hearted glare. "It was my first assignment after Quantico. We were back up vehicle on a car stop of a suspected mob enforcer. When we pulled up to the curb to make the stop, I caught my foot in a sewer grate, tripped over the stock of the Remington I was carrying and landed flat on my face. Sprained my ankle and broke my nose."

"Did you nail the guy?"

"The lead car had him before I even hit the ground. Which I found out as soon as my partner, Special Agent Greally over there, stopped laughing." Lucy smiled with the memory. It was in the ER before they took X-rays that she'd discovered she was pregnant with Megan.

"Hey," Greally held his hands up, "I was just glad to be alive. If you'd discharged that shotgun, I'd be a dead man today."

Taylor grinned, bobbing his head, obviously fascinated by the war stories. "How about you, Walden?"

"Sorry kid. Other than a paper cut filling out a FD-28, I've never been injured in the line."

"Don't look at me," Burroughs put in. "I can't even remember the last time I had to draw my gun until I started hanging out with you guys. Think I'm going to call my union rep and ask for hazard pay."

"He didn't hurt you any, did he? I mean—touch you?" The man's voice slowly penetrated the haze clouding her mind. They were riding in his SUV. She felt as if she'd just woken from a long winter's nap: exhausted yet energized, hazy yet focused.

Why was she here? What had the man said, he'd take her someplace safe? She rubbed her torn and swollen ankle. Safe and sound—where she could lick her wounds and prepare. For what, she wasn't quite sure, that was too far in the future to think about now.

"I'm sorry I didn't get there sooner. I was trying, as soon as I heard the Amber alert, I knew..."

She said nothing, half unsure that he was even talking about her. If she tried hard enough she was certain she could forget everything, just wake up to a new life, new person, new world.

Her head bounced against the passenger side window, eyes closed to slits, allowing only a small slice of the landscape to whirl past like an old time silent movie.

"I guess you're not ready to talk. That's okay, I understand. Let me tell you my story, there are some things you need to know."

He laid a hand on her thigh and she didn't flinch. There was nothing scary about his touch, nothing soothing either. It was as if her entire body was numb, unable to tell pain from comfort.

"His name is Bobby, Bobby Fegley," the man said.

He paused to clear his throat. Her pulse quickened. She'd known someone named Bobby once upon a time—hadn't she? Had it all been a dream? A lover, a comrade—until he had betrayed her. Or had she betrayed him?

"He pretends to be a kid, plays online games, makes friends with girls." There was a weird noise, like the man was choking back tears or laughter. "One of the bodies in there was my girl. I've been looking for her, for him, for over a year. And when I heard the news about you, saw your picture, I knew he had taken you. You look just like my Vera."

A long pause as she decided he wasn't talking about her but someone else, some other girl. Whatever he was talking about, it had nothing to do with her, she wasn't there.

Had never even been there.

"I wish I could take you back to your folks, but there's a problem. Bobby Fegley is an FBI agent—no one would believe us, we can't go to the cops."

His words bounced off her awareness, registering only the faintest of impact. She frowned, surely there was something wrong with what he was telling her?

Anxiety churned through her but she hugged herself tight, rocking in her seat, the landscape blurring through her slitted vision. The pain faded and she returned to her limbo of numbness.

"It's just you and me, Ashley," he continued, oblivious to the fact that she was barely there, hanging on only because she needed her body to pump blood to her brain. If it wasn't for that, she'd be long gone, vanished. "Unless. Do you want to go back to your parents, to your old life?"

His words hammered at her, breaking the wall of ice she'd surrounded herself with. She jerked upright, eyes fully open but unable to focus, darkness around the edges, only the road stretching out in front of them clear.

"No." The single syllable was all she could manage as panic seized her vocal cords, clamping them shut. She was shivering but she didn't feel cold, didn't feel anything—didn't want to feel anything.

"Well. All right, then. It's just you and me. I promise I won't let anything happen to you, Ashley. I mean, Vixen." The truck slowed as he turned to look at her. "My name's Jim. Jim Fletcher."

She didn't meet his gaze, instead she closed her eyes once more, rocking herself back into welcome oblivion.

Chapter 31

"Are we sure it's Fletcher?" Grimwald, the ICE Special Agent in Charge, was saying. "Look at his record. He's fucking Mr. Clean. Maybe he has a brain tumor or something."

"It's Fletcher," Lucy answered, resuming her pacing in front of the conference table. If she kept moving, the pain stayed steady at a level she could ignore. "What do we have on him?"

Taylor answered. "He's thirty-four, been with ICE for eight years. Started as a GS-oh' five, now a GS-oh' six. Local boy, graduated from Allegheny Institute of Technology with an associate's degree in computer sciences, this is the only office he's ever worked, good fit reps, nothing that stands out. Employment application lists a mother as only living relative. No sibs, father listed as whereabouts unknown."

"How old are the parents?"

"Let's see. Mother would be, seventy-eight, father ninety-two." He looked up at that. "That's pretty old."

"Yeah, mom would have been forty-four when she had him." Burroughs gave a mock shiver. "Would have been in her sixties when he was a teenager, think how gross that would be."

"Only child, born late in life to his mother, father out of the picture," Lucy said. Sounded like the setup Nick had mentioned. She stopped, another thought hitting her. "Burroughs, work on his early medical records, school, social services—anything to let me know what was going on in that house when he was young."

"Who cares if he wet the bed or flunked gym class?" Grimwald said. "You still don't have any proof besides an undocumented phone call. Maybe Fletcher is the victim here."

John Greally leaned forward from his seat at the head of the table. "Shut the fuck up and let her work, why don't cha?"

He went heavy on his Chicago accent, his expression hardened as if he'd grown up on the Southside instead of Round Lake Beach. Grimwald frowned, shot Lucy a glare, but sat back and was silent.

"He talks about his mother constantly," she continued. "What do we know about her?"

"Alicia Moore Fletcher," Taylor supplied. "Resident of the Golden Years nursing home last three years, prior to that resided at the same address as Fletcher."

"The house he blew up?" Walden asked. "That surprises me, that he'd torch his history like that."

Lucy glanced at Walden. "Good point. Did they live somewhere before that? We need a list of all known addresses. Any property in either of their names."

Somewhere Fletcher had a hole he'd run to—and thanks to Taylor and Bobby, he was definitely on the run.

"Here's something," Taylor put in, looking up from his computer monitor. "There's no marriage certificate for Alicia. Nothing I can find puts the father in the picture at all. He's not listed on tax records, work records, census, nothing. Just Fletcher and the mom."

That felt right. She grabbed the rubber snake from her desk, stretching and pulling it, coiling it, using it to keep her hands occupied as she took another lap of the room, thinking, imagining Fletcher and the forces that had created him.

"I'll bet that's been a driving force all his life—father unknown, a mystery. And mother either badgering him to live up to the expectations of a ghost or condemning him for it."

"Now this is weird," Taylor said, eyes focused on his computer while Walden stood and began adding more info to the profile on the whiteboard. "County records list a James Madison Fletcher as deceased on October tenth, nineteen seventy-four, cause of death homicide."

Burroughs looked up at that. "That's *our* James Madison Fletcher Junior's birth date."

Taylor continued, "His body was partially burned, but with evidence of stab wounds and a fractured skull. Along with him were the remains of an approximately twenty-year-old woman that they never ID'd."

"Cause of death?" Lucy asked, twisting the snake into a knot. It immediately bounced free.

"Multiple stab wounds."

"Why didn't we find that during Fletcher's security check?" John asked.

Grimwald flushed. "Not my department. Besides, just because his father was a homicide victim doesn't mean—"

"The father also had a record for numerous misdemeanors," Taylor added, typing furiously. "Tons of arrests, mainly for fraud and petty theft, only one conviction for trespassing. Multiple jurisdictions. Lots of aliases listed."

"Sounds like Fletcher Sr., was a grifter," Burroughs said.

"Did he ever work with an accomplice?" Lucy asked, her back to the men as she stared at the board with its list of apparently random dates and facts. Fletcher the high-strung but genial computer clerk was only a façade. Finding the man behind the mask would mean digging through his past.

"Record goes back decades. Looks like he had a girl working with him back in the late nineteen forties, name of Alice, Alisha or sometimes—"

"Alicia," she filled in for him. "Let me guess. About ten years later there's no mention of Alicia but of other women helping Fletcher instead. All young."

"Yeah, looks that way."

"What are you thinking, Lucy?" John asked.

Lucy held up her hand for a moment, still absorbing the details. "We need to look at the mom before we look at Fletcher. How old was she when she was first mentioned in the record?"

"Hmm... fourteen."

"Look for missing girls around the same time. Last name Moore, first name probably Alice." She began pacing again, energized as the pieces fell into place. "Alicia is fourteen, hooks up with a charismatic grifter who's twice her age. Becomes his accomplice, his common law wife. The grifter, who likes his women young, tires of Alicia and drifts around. But he always returns to her, maybe even brings his girlfriends along for the ride. Uses Alicia as a safe haven when the heat is on, uses her when money's short, basically uses her."

"This is ludicrous speculation," Grimwald protested. "You can't possibly—"

"Hush," John told him, nodding for Lucy to continue. "Okay, fast forward, how does this help us find Fletcher?"

"And Ashley Yeager," Walden added.

Lucy twisted the snake around her left wrist like a bracelet, its fake plastic tongue catching in her wedding ring. She focused on the way the light sparked from the gold. "Places. Fletcher needs to be grounded. Bobby Fegley told me he was a linear thinker, saw only what he wanted to see, ignored any flaws. Said he designed Shadow World the same way—lots of meaningless bells and whistles, but a straightforward story line. He's going to have a big complicated grand design, but it's going to boil down to familiar territory, familiar places."

"Where? Certainly not the house he torched."

"No. Where he grew up. We'll have to search tax records, see where Alicia lived thirty years ago, any family property. I'll bet there were only one or two places his whole life."

"Unlike his father."

"Exactly. Alicia would want to stay put so Fletcher Sr. could find her when he needed her. They fed on each other, a symbiosis." Done with the snake, she coiled it so that it was one perfect circle, eating its own tail, and threw it onto the conference table.

"Searching records going back that far is going to take time," Burroughs warned. "They won't be computerized. Most of them."

"Yeah." She shook her head, pushing unsettling images of a younger Fletcher with his middle-aged mother from her mind. "Let's get people started on that, his phone records, computer, and an in-depth look at his father. I need the complete police records of his father's and Jane Doe's homicides."

"Where are you going?"

"To talk with Alicia. Get to the heart of the matter."

"Why are you wasting time with an old woman?" Grimwald protested. "Probably senile anyway."

"I think mommy dearest taught Fletcher everything he knows. Maybe including how to kill."

Chapter 32

SUNDAY, 4:22 PM

"Mrs. Fletcher, I'm here to talk with you about your son."

"Jimmy? Is he with you? He's such a fine boy, takes good care of his sick, old mother."

Lucy pulled one of the vinyl chairs closer to Alicia's, now they sat knee-to-knee, facing each other even if the old woman couldn't see her. "Mrs. Fletcher, I'm with the FBI. My name is Supervisory Special Agent Guardino. When's the last time your son visited?"

Alicia pursed her lips, wrinkles cascading over her face, a carica-ture of an old woman searching her confused memories. "Jimmy, is he with you?"

"No, Alicia. He's not."

"You're the Lucy he works with, aren't you? He told me about you." Alicia smiled, her dentures slipping then clicking into place. "Said you let your daughter get sick 'cause you were too busy to watch after her. I'd never let anything like that happen to my child. My Jimmy, he was my world. A mother should be willing to give everything for their child." Her voice dropped to a hoarse whisper. "Even their very lives."

Lucy clamped her jaws shut. Despite the blindness and the age and the failing body, Alicia Fletcher was sharp and cunning. She was trying to manipulate Lucy the same way Lucy wanted to manipulate her.

From the surge of anger and guilt the old lady's words had produced, Alicia had the upper hand. Lucy was glad the other woman couldn't see her. "Tell me about Jimmy. When was the last time you spoke?"

"Jimmy? Oh, he's much too busy to bother with his old mother. Not with that big case he's helping you with. Don't you know where he is?"

Cut the crap, Lucy wanted to yell. She restrained herself. "No. I need to find him." She swallowed hard, forcing herself not to gag on her words. "I need his help, Alicia. A young girl's life may depend on it."

"One of Jimmy's girls? He's had a few you know—since I left him, had to come here. Poor boy, he gets so lonely without his mother to take care of him."

"Have you met any of Jimmy's girls? Do you remember their names?"

Alicia leaned forward. Her hand, soft and doughy in consistency but wrapped in flaky, parchment like skin, landed on Lucy's knee and squeezed. "I might. Might could remember. None of them was good enough, not for my Jimmy. He needs a special girl, one just like me. Is this girl you're talking about special?"

Sudden laughter emerged from Alicia's slit-like mouth, rattling through the room, raising the hairs on Lucy's arms.

If she was searching for a monster, she had found the monster's creator.

Lucy laid her own hand over Alicia's and ground the old woman's bones together. Alicia lurched backwards but didn't scream or call out. Instead her smile broadened into a beam of delight. As if Lucy was playing into her expectations. And by doing so, Alicia had won.

"I'll never help you find my son," Alicia said, her dead eyes meeting Lucy's gaze as if they could see.

"Then let's talk about Jimmy's father," Lucy said. She released Alicia's hand, white imprints dug into the doughy flesh like a hand-print etched in plaster. "It must have been difficult, loving a man like that."

"My husband loved me, he was devoted to me. Whatever he did, it was for my own good," Alicia declared, her chin jutting forward into the air.

"Devoted to you? He left you behind every chance he had. He slept with every pretty girl he ever met, right up to the day he died."

"He had an eye for beauty and he indulged it. He always came home to me."

"Not that last time. He wasn't going to come home then, was he? He was going to leave you for good."

It was total guesswork, but Lucy knew she'd hit close to the kill zone. The color drained from Alicia's lips, the last remaining color on her face, leaving her shrouded in shades of white and ash. She stared, eyes not blinking, and if not for the pulse jumping at the side of her neck, she could have been dead.

Lucy continued. "You'd given him everything—your childhood, your life. Thirty years of your life he had stolen and now he was going to leave you."

Alicia's head trembled as if palsied by her need to deny the truth. "No. Never. It was that slut, that girl who conned him into thinking she was carrying his baby. He would never leave me, not for a filthy whore like her."

"Then why did you kill him, Alicia?"

Lucy had spoken softly but from Walden's rigid stance in the doorway, she knew he had heard her. She wasn't so certain about Alicia. The old woman had stiffened like a corpse in full rigor.

Then she laughed again. A big, rip-roaring belly laugh that shook Alicia so hard Lucy almost had Walden get one of the nurses. The laughter poured forth in waves, hurled into the air, crashing against the hushed sounds of the nursing home.

Walden shut the door, blocking the noise, and leaned against it. Barring any chance of escape.

Finally, Alicia composed herself, one hand patting Lucy's thigh as she caught her breath. Her color was back, a florid red suffused her face and neck. "You're good, girl. Do you know you're the first person in thirty-four years that ever thought hard enough to put two and two together? Can't tell you how scared I was those first few months, waiting for the cops to waltz me away in steel bracelets. But no one ever came."

"Why'd you do it, Alicia?"

"I wanted a baby. I deserved a baby. Someone to take care of me when I got older. Jimmy's baby."

Lucy had assumed Alicia had killed her husband and girlfriend in a jealous rage while Alicia had been pregnant with her son. Now she realized that what really happened was far, far worse. She blinked hard, wondering if she'd heard correctly. No, no surely...

"He took her side. Tried to stop me when he found me with her, carving her open. Called me a stupid, fat old cow and told me to rot in hell." Alicia rocked in her chair. Not back and forth, not bouncing, not agitated. Instead she cradled her arms below her shriveled, sagging breasts, a mother comforting her child.

Her voice dropped, weighted down by the bitter memory. "But he forgot one thing." She tilted her head up, her grey-white eyes boring into Lucy's. "He forgot I was the one holding the knife."

"Who was she, Alicia?"

A heave of Alicia's shoulders was her only answer for a moment. "Harlot, jezebel. She doesn't deserve a name. I took from her what was rightfully mine. Jimmy's baby."

Lucy tried hard not to visualize the scene: a bloodbath, Alicia reaching into the dead or dying woman's womb, cutting her son free...

"So then it was just you and little Jimmy. It must have been tough, raising a son all by yourself."

Alicia shook her head, her voice dropping into a singsong. "No. It was a joy. My Jimmy, he's my joy. My life."

"Help me find him, Alicia. I can save him, protect him."

"He's safe at home. No one can hurt him there." She rocked harder, crooning a wordless melody.

"What about the girl? She might hurt him."

"No. She won't. He said he got a good one this time. One just like me." She twisted in her chair, fumbled at her side for one of the photo albums stacked on the table, chose one, and hefted it onto her lap. "Here, you tell me." Her blind fingers traced the embossed words on the cover and then flipped the album open. "That's me when I was fourteen, when my James saved me."

Lucy took the album, stared at the black and white photo with its yellowed edges. Staring back at her was a dark haired, full-figured girl with a shy smile and down-turned gaze. A girl who, if she'd been wearing black jeans and a sweatshirt instead of a gingham dress with ruffles around the hem, could have been Ashley Yeager.

"Jimmy told me he got it right this time. What do you think, Supervisory Special Agent Guardino?"

Lucy slapped the album shut and stood. She wasn't going to learn Fletcher's location, not from this woman. "I think your husband wasn't the only con artist in the family. You've been wasting my time, Mrs. Fletcher."

Alicia snatched at the book, cradled it against her chest like the imaginary child she had rocked earlier. "You'll never find him. Jimmy's a smart boy. Just like his father."

Her laughter followed Lucy and Walden as they escaped from the room.

–

"Are you as creeped out as I am?" Lucy asked as she drove Walden towards Sligo. Taylor had found an address for a Moore family that had reported a daughter missing back in 1944. The property now belonged to an Arthur Moore, Alicia's younger brother, a retired PennDot worker and widower.

It was a long shot, but better than sitting around doing nothing. In the meantime, Burroughs was getting PBP to sit on Alicia in case Fletcher tried to contact her.

Walden shrugged. "No worse than the usual shit we see every day."

"Guess I'm getting old, but our usual child predator isn't this sick and twisted. I mean," she hastened to add when she caught his sharp look, "they are warped, perverted bastards, but they all share basically the same underlying pathology. Once you figure out their individual take on it, it's all the same song and dance. Come on, Walden, you've been working SAFE crimes longer than I have, don't you think that's true?"

"Seems like whenever I start to think that way, the good Lord throws down the gauntlet and stubborn bastard that I am, I just have to pick it up."

"So you've seen something like this before? A woman so warped by thirty years of loving a man who didn't love her back that she kills him and cuts his child from the womb of another woman in order to raise it as her own?"

"Love works in mysterious ways."

She glanced over at him, uncertain if he was making fun of her or not. His face was its usual inscrutable blank slate.

"You married, Walden?"

He shifted in his seat and she knew she'd made him uncomfortable. He wore no wedding ring, but he had the air of a man who'd been happily married. Unlike Burroughs. She waited, not pressing him.

"Yes. To my high school sweetheart. Sheila." His voice held a hint of nostalgia.

"What happened?"

"Four—no, it'll be five years this Thanksgiving—she died."

"I'm sorry."

"You know how they always talk about high blood pressure and strokes killing all us black men? Well, it's the black women who should really be worried. Especially those with high stress jobs like being the wives of federal agents. I was working the Mara Salvatrucha gang that were responsible for over a dozen executions around the DC area."

"I remember. They went on a killing spree when we apprehended one of their leaders. Targeted federal judges, US attorneys, trying to shut down our case."

"Tense couple of months. I got called out on a raid night before Thanksgiving. We got the guys, did the paper work and I went home. The lights were all on, but that wasn't unusual, Sheila always waited up for me. Said she couldn't sleep until I got home." He turned his head to look out the window.

Lucy shifted her weight, her back and shoulder definitely waking up from the numbing medicine the doctor had used. Sitting still seemed to make the pain worse, so she had insisted on driving but now was regretting her decision as she needed both hands on the wheel to steer around the twisting mountain roads.

Walden made a small sound, half regret, half grief, and continued. "Found her in the kitchen, turkey sitting on the counter, a sweet potato pie on the floor beside her. Doctors said it was a massive heart attack; she died instantly. They said.

"I never could figure out how they know that for sure, figured it's the same as when we have to make death notifications. Always tell the family they went fast, peacefully, felt no pain. Never give them a reason to think things might have gone differently, that they could have done anything differently…"

"That's when you transferred to Atlanta, to the SAFE unit down there?"

"Yeah. Fresh faces, fresh start." He fiddled with the AC control. "Didn't do much good. Still live for the work, just like always. Think I'd have learned my lesson, wouldn't you?" He shrugged, more a shifting of his mood than an actual acknowledgment of emotion. "Take a warning from someone who's been there. Don't let it happen to you, Lucy."

She snorted. "You mean like hunting for a sick bastard like Fletcher when my daughter's sick in the hospital?"

"The doctors tell you what's going on yet?"

"No. They're in a wait and see stage—could be nothing more than a virus, or they might have to slice out one of her lymph nodes and do a biopsy."

"They're worried about cancer?"

"Worried about everything it seems. Just no fucking answers." She rolled her shoulders back and tried to ease the tension from her neck and jaw. "Let's focus on Fletcher. At least we can do something good for one kid."

"If she's still alive."

"I think she's alive. Just like Alicia couldn't let go of her James, I think our Jimmy can't let go of Ashley."

"It's weird that she and Alicia were both fourteen when they met the men in their lives."

"Seems like Alicia saw James Fletcher as her savior, her rescuer."

"Might have been an abusive household. Isolated farm, way back then, who knows what went on?"

"Maybe Arthur Moore can tell us."

"Think Jimmy ever knew his maternal relatives? Could this uncle of his be helping him?"

"The way Alicia got out of there, I doubt she ever went back with her son."

She turned onto a weed-choked dirt road. Drove another half mile and saw an old two-story farmhouse with a single steeply-pitched gable in the middle and windows arranged to look like two eyes above and three teeth below.

A small barn sat twenty yards from the house. There were no vehicles, no movement, no signs of anyone living. She exited the vehicle, her hand on her weapon. Walden joined her, his lips tightened into a single straight line—as close to anxious as she'd seen him.

It was cooler out here away from the city, but still unseasonably warm. The sun was low in the sky, filtered through the trees as if through dirty windows. There was no wind, the trees that surrounded the clearing and lined the road stood still, drooping with dust-covered leaves.

And it was quiet. Way too quiet, even to someone who'd grown up in the country like Lucy. As if birds and animals and stray breezes all avoided this place. No movement came from either building.

Lucy bent down, ignoring the fresh wave of pain rippling through her back, and examined the ruts in the dirt lane. "Someone's been here recently. Tire tracks are fresh."

"Maybe he's gone out for Sunday dinner? Think our Mr. Moore is a big bingo player or the like?"

"Nothing says we can't take a look around." They were still standing near the cover of their own vehicle, a good forty feet from either the house or barn. "Which first?" she asked. "House or barn?"

Walden drew his weapon—a sure sign of how wrong this place was. You didn't go calling on tax-paying citizens with your gun drawn, even if they may be relatives of a killer. You also didn't need a locked and loaded forty caliber Glock to go knock on a door of an empty house.

"There may be a vehicle in the barn," he said, removing his sunglasses and letting his eyes adjust to the eerie half-light. "If he's here, he may be waiting for us to go to the house, make a break for it."

Prepare for the worst, hope for the best and everyone goes home in one piece—typical cop philosophy. Lucy grabbed a pair of binoculars from the gear in the rear of the Blazer. They both donned tactical vests, the weight pulled on Lucy's injured shoulder like a slaughterhouse hook hoisting a side of beef.

Together, they avoided the lane and cut across the knee-high weeds to approach the house. They circled it warily, stopping to examine the porch and the front entrance from ten yards away.

"Cameras," she pointed as she squinted through the binoculars. "One on the corner of the porch roof, aimed at the driveway, one on that post aimed at the front steps. I can't see inside, there are curtains over the windows."

"Let's try around back."

They continued to circle the house. All the windows were covered, there was no other entrance apparent until they reached the rear of the house. Now they were draped in shadow. Lucy shivered, wished for a jacket.

"What are those?" Walden asked, pointing to several greyish blobs sitting in the yard.

Lucy glanced away from her scrutiny of the house. "You're such a city boy. Those are salt licks. For the deer." She focused on the back door. "Wait here."

"What are you doing?"

"He wouldn't have any traps outside, not if he's willing to attract wild animals close to the house. I think I can get a look through a slit in the curtains over the door."

"Maybe the uncle put out the salt licks and Fletcher doesn't give a shit about blowing up a bunch of deer."

She kept walking, slowly, scanning every inch she could see. A camera aimed out from above the door, but it was easy to outflank it and ease her way against the building, staying in its blind spot.

She pressed her body against the door, angled her view through the small slit in the curtains. "It's dark inside," she yelled to Walden. "No movement. Some pots and pans left out, a few cans in the trash, can't make out much—"

She stopped, tried to get a better look. A jacket hung on a hook beside the door. She couldn't see all of it, but one sleeve was bunched up, sticking out far enough to be in her field of vision. It was dark inside, but not pitch black, more of a murky grey.

The jacket was black, cheap cotton, but what caught her eye was the silver stitching on the sleeve. With the help of the binoculars' magnification, the pattern jumped out at her: the Statue of Liberty.

"I've seen that jacket before," Lucy told Walden as she edged away from the house, avoiding the camera's sight lines. "Vera Tzasiris was wearing a jacket like that when I interviewed her. Right before she went missing."

She handed him the binoculars and leaned over as if catching her breath, but really to hide her face from Walden for a moment. How blithely she'd assured Vera that the worst was over, that no more harm would come to her—right before she'd handed her into the arms of a killer.

"Vera Tzasiris?"

273

Lucy blinked hard, ignoring the sting of unshed tears and straightened, pain lancing through her shoulder. "Call Taylor, have him pull the files for Operation Triple-play, it was a joint DEA, ICE, FBI op, went down last year. Fletcher was involved.

"We're going to need warrants for the house, the barn and a BOLO for any vehicles registered to Arthur Moore." Lucy paced as she spoke, the long grass whipping at her legs, movement her best defense against her emotions.

"Get the Allegheny County bomb-dogs up here and their EOD team to clear the buildings. And we'll need the ERT." She paused. Once the explosive ordinance disposal guys handled any nasty surprises Fletcher may have left behind, the FBI Evidence Recovery Team could then search the house in safety. The sun was in her eyes, nicking the tree line with a sharp orange blaze. It'd be dark by the time they cleared the buildings.

"We'll need lights," she added, her gaze now on the barn. She jogged towards it, wanting to get a good look before they lost the light.

It wasn't very large, maybe twenty feet by thirty. Traditional frame, whitewashed with peeling paint and a wooden roof. Not quite two stories high. A pair of half doors on one side below the roof eaves, a ladder standing beside them was the only access to the hayloft she could see. She didn't see any cameras on this side, so ventured closer to check the ladder. It was aluminum, looked fairly new. It had been sitting there long enough to leave indentations in the ground. Only one set, so it hadn't been moved.

Finally she approached the front side of the barn. Over the door, fixed to the metal frame of the spotlight was a camera. Just the one. She edged close to the wall, staying out of its field of vision. The barn doors weren't locked, although a heavy clasp and padlock hung from one door. The doors were cracked open, not wide enough to see through but enough to give her a whiff of an unpleasant and all too familiar scent. Decomp.

Damn, damn, damn. She swiped her face with her palm, felt the tension in her jaw go supernova. It couldn't be Ashley.

Which was a lie. Not as hot as it had been lately. She pressed her palm against one door. *I'm so sorry.*

Whoever was in there, it was too late to help them, but maybe they could help her find Fletcher.

A loud thump reverberated through the silence. Lucy jumped, drew her gun without even realizing it.

"Anyone there?" she shouted. "In the barn, anyone there? FBI!"

Another softer sound, more of a rustle than a thump. Lucy's heart went into overdrive. Maybe Ashley was alive, just a few feet away from her.

Walden came running just as she reached for the door. "Stop there," she told him, pointing to the camera. He had his gun out as well. "I heard something. Inside the barn."

He eased his way along the wall to join her, his nose wrinkling in distaste as the smell of decomp hit him. "We should wait for EOD."

He was right. And she knew it. It was exactly what the Operations Manual, the FBI's Big Book, would tell her to do. She clenched her jaw, not even feeling the stabs of pain radiating down her neck. What if Ashley were hurt? What if she waited and they found her dead when they finally got to her?

"Go, wait by the car," she told him in a strained voice. The sun was almost gone, all that remained were a few brave streams of light battered and broken by the trees.

"No. Lucy, you can't go in there. It's exactly what Fletcher wants."

"Special Agent Walden, I know what I'm doing. Go wait by the car." He ignored her, his face stony. "If I'm wrong, one of us has to be able to get help. I can't leave her in there. Not if there's a chance."

"I'll go in."

"I gave you an order, now follow it." She put every ounce of authority she had behind her words. He narrowed his eyes, frowning even as he gave her an infinitesimal nod, and finally obeyed. She waited until he was clear, all the way back at the car before opening the barn door.

The door swung out, so she could only open it a little less than a foot without risking the camera picking up the movement. She clicked on the Surefire light mounted below her gun barrel, poked her head through the opening.

A wall of hay bales stood about five feet in front of her. They rose to the rafters above. Strange way to store hay. The odor of decomp was overwhelming, as if the straw had absorbed it and concentrated it. She searched for signs of any booby traps and after finding none, she stepped inside.

Listening, she heard another rustle. Something moving against the straw. It sounded as if it was coming from the other side of the wall of hay bales. She paused. If it was Fletcher making the noise—no, that made no sense. He could have cut and run while they were out of sight at the house. If he planned an ambush, there were much better ways to arrange it. Logically, it couldn't be Fletcher setting a trap.

Logic wasn't helping the churning in her gut or the adrenalin-frayed nerves sputtering beneath her skin. She forced herself to breathe, choking down the cloying stench, and stepped forward.

She scanned the darkness ahead. One step, then another into the blackness. Soon she was at the end of the wall of hay. There was a small gap, maybe a foot, before the next wall, this one perpendicular to the first and following the outside wall of the barn.

Lucy remembered the corn mazes she used to run through at Halloween. Farmers would mow labyrinths into their fields, leading kids down spooky paths where anything could be hiding in the towering corn stalks beyond. She'd always emerge, shrieking with laughter and terror, clutching the hands of her friends, frightened to their bones and loving every minute of it.

Somehow, this grown up, indoor version wasn't quite as much fun. She stepped between the two perpendicular rows of hay, now entering the interior of the ring of straw bales.

The space opened up. It was total darkness, but with the help of the Surefire she could see a vertical pole eight feet in front of her. Beside it was an overturned bucket. She took another step.

Stumbled as her foot fell on something soft and moving. Gasping, she lurched to one side, hitting the wall of straw. A heavy weight thudded against her shoulders. She leapt back, reached for whatever had hit her from above. Her hand closed on a writhing mass of muscle, cold, scaly and flailing against her back.

Hell. Not again. She whipped the snake away from her body, shuddering in revulsion. More rustling came from the darkness; it seemed to surround her. She stood rigid, trying to still the pounding of her heart.

The pale circle of light carved out glimpses in the darkness. The ground before her was littered with snakes—one slithered over her foot. She kicked it away, hearing the thump as it hit the ground.

Her Glock-22 held seventeen bullets and she had two spare magazines on her vest. She swung the light around. Everywhere she looked, the ground was moving. There were snakes clinging to the bales of hay, snakes dropping onto the ground, snakes in front of her, snakes behind her, snakes everywhere.

More snakes than she had bullets.

Chapter 33

Lucy's pulse hammered a jungle rhythm. She scuffed her shoes along the floor, kicking away any snakes that crossed her path until she reached the metal pole. At its base lay a thick, vinyl-coated cable ending in a padlock.

He kept her here. With all these snakes. She swallowed; it was hard work with her throat closed tight against the stench of decomp. Talk about a living hell.

She squatted, examining the cable and the overturned bucket without touching them. Why would Fletcher torture Ashley like that when he kept saying he wanted to save her?

Stretching her jaw, she popped her ears and thought hard. Was she wrong in her profile of Fletcher? Was he really just another sick sadist like Ivan, the Canadian? Or that other lover of snakes, Pastor Walter?

The padlock was closed, attached to a piece of metal that had once clamped a loop of cable. It was the cable itself that was cut. Fletcher wouldn't need to do that; he'd have the key.

Unless... Someone else had rescued Ashley?

No. They would have triggered Fletcher's traps. It had to be Fletcher playing at being Ashley's knight in shining armor. Subjecting her to torture, then swooping in for the rescue. Just like his father.

If so, then not only was Ashley still alive, she'd be indebted to him, ready to do anything he asked.

Aw hell, she did not like where this was heading. She stood, swept the area with her light and saw the outline of a portable commode to one side and layers of hay bales arranged like steps on the other. Strange shapes reflected the high-powered beam of light, dark yet shiny. Carefully, she approached the large objects.

The smell of decomp was stronger here, strong enough to gag her.

Wrapped in sheets of clear plastic like mummies, sitting side by side on the hay bales as if they were spectators at a Steelers' game, were two women and a man. Their mouths gaped open in death grins, their eyes bulged out, and they had a front row seat to Ashley Yeager's suffering.

Puddles of body fluids covered their feet, but the plastic kept it contained. No flies or insects had penetrated the coverings; the decomposition had come from their own bodies' bacteria, eventually bloating their abdomens with gas until the intestines and skin ruptured.

Thank God they were fully clothed, sparing Lucy that sight. She backed away, retracing her steps until finally she stood outside once more.

Night had fallen quickly; it was now as dark outside as it had been inside the barn. Walden waited at the Blazer, standing at the bumper, jogging forward as soon as she left the barn.

"You okay?"

"Boy are you glad I outrank you," she said, drinking the cool, crisp air as if she'd been holding her breath for too long. Not far from the truth. "How do you feel about snakes?"

He looked at her sharply. "Hate 'em."

"I used to not mind them." She leaned against the car door, trying to hide the sudden wobble in her legs. "Even played with them when I was a kid." She shook her head and glanced back at the barn, now just a pale blob shadowed against the trees beyond. "Not anymore."

"What the hell happened in there?"

-

It didn't take long for the pristine and silent farm to morph into a cacophony of light and noise. The area was taped off, everyone held back while the EOD guys walked their bomb-sniffing dogs around first the barn, then the house. The dogs alerted at both sites.

Which meant more men and equipment and lights and crackling radios, ribald jokes as two bomb squad members squeezed into their bulky suits, followed by several turf battles that Lucy was forced to referee.

ERT wanted to photograph the barn crime scene prior to the EOD squad searching for the bombs—just in case.

EOD wanted to get the hell in and out again before the heat made them pass out while confined to the self-contained suits that weighed eighty-some pounds and reached temperatures of over a hundred degrees when sealed.

The ME wanted no one to touch anything until they got to the bodies—which may or may not be sitting on top of a bomb.

The Staties groused against the inclusion of Allegheny County's bomb squad since apparently the Moore homestead was just over the Butler county line, making it their jurisdiction. They kept insisting that they could have flown their EOD team in from Harrisburg if they'd been given enough advance notice. Like Lucy had begun her day planning to find a few homemade incendiary devices.

Grimwald showed up, trying to spin-doctor the fact that Fletcher was a bad guy and in his direct chain of command.

Local police and fire turned out in force, acting like it was a fall carnival, wandering over the scene, taking photos with their camera-phones.

Then, just when things were starting to get under control, the media flocked to the site like carrion-eaters to road-kill.

Until the Staties finally had them corralled behind the perimeter, they plowed past crime scene tape, stomped through the woods, blinded hard-working cops with their spotlights and interrupted every conversation with inane questions bellowed in self-righteous voices.

"Agent Guardino, did you see Ashley Yeager? Is it true the perpetrator turned her into a mummy?"

"Agent Guardino, is it true a rattle snake bit you when you rushed in to save the girl?"

"Agent Guardino, how does it feel to be a woman working with all these men?"

The last was especially a puzzle seeing as it came from the only female reporter present—not Cindy Ames, thank God—and since there were three other females working the scene in addition to Lucy.

She shielded her face from camera flashes, rustled up reps from ERT, EOD and the ME and shepherded them to the relative peace of the mobile evidence recovery unit, a large black RV parked in the field beside the lane.

"Anyone got an Advil?" she asked, massaging her jaw joints, feeling them crackle and pop. Never mind her shoulder. It was frozen in place, pain using it as its own command center, hurling new waves of agony whenever she dared to forget about it. "Or six or seven?"

The ERT squad leader, a guy named Jiminez, found her a sample pack containing two Aleve. Lucy dry-swallowed them and spread out a rough sketch of the property on the counter. The three men clustered around her, jostling racks of CSI paraphernalia.

"Okay, here's where the dog alerted, right?" She pointed to both doors of the house and the rear of the barn.

"A definite on the house," Donohue, the EOD tech confirmed. He was wearing the bulky pants of his bomb suit, held up by wide suspenders over a plain white T-shirt. "The barn she was a bit vague—definitely explosives there but either they're spread out over a fairly wide area or maybe they were moved several times, leaving residue behind."

"Could the smell of decomp have thrown her off?" Curtis, the ME guy asked.

Donohue shook his head. "No way. Cookie's the best at what she does. The decomp disturbed her a little, but as soon as she focused, she was good to go."

"Here's my problem, gentlemen." Lucy re-directed their attention. "I have no evidence to help me save a young girl's life except what is in this barn and maybe in the house. What's the best way to maximize evidence collection and minimize the danger to our people?"

"I could go in and photograph, video the interior of the barn since we have an entry there," Jiminez volunteered. "Maybe even collect the items in the center of the barn?"

"But she's going to get most of her evidence from the bodies," Curtis argued. "And the bodies are sitting right where the dog said there were explosives."

"That might be why Cookie alerted to such a large area," Donohue said. "If he had the explosives sitting near the bodies, then moved the bodies to booby-trap them and finally returned them to that location."

"So the bodies are probably rigged." Lucy gnawed the inside of her cheek. "Donohue, could you start your guys working on the two IED's at the house while we document and collect evidence from the front of the barn? We won't disturb the bodies, only photograph them in situ."

Donohue frowned, his two shaggy eyebrows meeting in the middle of his forehead. Obviously a by-the-book kind of guy. Which probably explained why he still had all his fingers and toes. By-the-book was not a bad thing when you dealt with unstable explosives on a daily basis.

"If time is that vital, yeah, we could go that route," he finally conceded. "But I want one of my guys with them, make sure they don't touch the wrong thing."

"Sounds like a plan. Let's get to work. I need to see the photos of the bodies ASAP. I might have an ID on one of them." It had been too dark in the barn for her to tell for sure, but she had a sinking feeling that one of the women was Vera Tzasiris.

Which meant Lucy's promise to her that the bad part was over had been a big, fat lie.

On that less than cheerful note, she waved them on their way. The EOD guys had what looked like a miniature cement mixer on wheels—their explosive containment device. They also had a neat looking robot she knew they were just itching to play with once they made sure the windows were safe to breach and they could maneuver it inside the house.

Jiminez and his crew were busy dragging lighting equipment to supplement their camera flashes. Curtis trudged behind them, carrying only two cameras and looking disgruntled that he was going to have to let the EOD guys touch his bodies before he did.

Medical examiners got that way, very territorial. Nobody touched their bodies unless they said so. And usually they didn't. You told them what you needed: an ID from a victim's wallet, the cell phone shoved into their pocket, the locket with the perpetrator's fingerprints on it. They would fastidiously document it, remove it and allow you to examine it. But the bodies were their domain.

Speaking of people guarding their domain, behind her she could hear Grimwald barking at Walden. She turned to intervene but her cell rang.

"Guardino."

"Hey, it's Burroughs. I've got a situation here."

"I kind of have my hands full myself," she replied, wondering what kind of trouble the detective could have gotten himself into. She'd pretty much sidelined him—diplomatically of course. "Where's here?"

"Three Rivers Medical Center."

Lucy's breath caught, a tight knot of fear that seized her chest and wouldn't let go. "Wh-what happened? Is Megan—"

Her voice broke. She turned away from the scattered clusters of law enforcement, hunched her shoulders as she pinched the bridge of her nose, willing back tears.

"No. Shit, I'm sorry. She's fine. Megan's fine," Burroughs' voice finally broke through the vise grip of terror that held her hostage. "No, that's not it. I'm here with Cindy Ames."

Able to fill her lungs again, Lucy straightened, hand clenched around her phone, wringing the life from it and wishing it was Burroughs' neck. Or better yet, a certain TV reporter's. "Surely I misheard you, Detective Burroughs."

"Look, don't get like that. It's not my fault." His voice dropped, became rushed, earnest. "I'm trying to help you out here. Would you at least give me a chance?"

"Go ahead, I'm listening."

"Cindy and her cameraman were at your house this morning. Shot some film of it and your husband and daughter going to Church, the ambulance coming—"

"You've got to be kidding me. That bitch! Endangering an undercover federal agent's identity is a felony. Go ahead, take her into custody. I warned her. Did she think I was playing?"

"All Cindy ever thinks about is the story. And she got one. She also has pictures taken with camera phones of you in the ER this morning. And eye-witness accounts of how you terrorized the hospital."

"I did no such thing."

"All I can say is, it looks bad. Real bad. Anyway, I was thinking we could maybe make a deal with her. Instead of arresting her, maybe we can get her to lose this story in exchange for a bigger one, a better one." He paused. "One that might help us nail Fletcher."

"What did you have in mind?"

"We let her air an interview with Fletcher's mom. One that implies that you're considering arresting the old lady as an accessory or something nasty like that. Something bad enough to draw Fletcher back to town. You said he was obsessed with his mom. We'll give him a chance to play hero."

"Just like his father." She considered it. "It will take some finessing. No way Alicia Fletcher will cooperate."

"Cindy says she won't have to. Her computer guys can digitally edit things so we can make her say almost anything we want. And most of it will be in the way Cindy sells it on air."

"Start working on a script. I'm on my way."

Chapter 34

Of course it wasn't as easy as merely writing a script. By the time she reached the Golden Years nursing home to meet Burroughs and Ames, Lucy had spoken with John Greally, the WDDE station manager, the nursing home administrator, legal affairs—three times—Burroughs' zone commander, the Pittsburgh Police Bureau's media information officer, and the Assistant Chief of Police.

After assuring everyone that they were not setting up a trap at Golden Years, that they'd arrange the leak to draw Fletcher elsewhere to a secure location, that they would in no way endanger Alicia's health or trample over her rights, that the proper releases would be signed by all, that no monetary compensation was changing hands, and that anything Ames reported would be unbiased—a statement that made Lucy gag, but satisfied the TV station's lawyer—and that all standards of Bureau ethical and moral conduct would be met at all times during the encounter; permission was finally, officially, irrevocably, denied.

"What makes you so certain Fletcher would fall for it anyway?" John Greally had argued when he'd called to break the bad news. "He isn't stupid. He'll know it's a trap."

"Didn't I ever teach you the rules of fishing?"

"Find out what they want and don't give it to 'em."

"Exactly. Fletcher wants to be a hero like he imagines his father was. That's why he called to warn us about the bomb at his house—he doesn't want us to think of him like he's a bad guy. He wants to be a knight in shining armor."

"I really, really hate it when they turn out to be loony tunes. Makes it hard to predict—and the outcome if we make it to trial is never guaranteed. Especially as Fletcher has done a good job of erasing his tracks."

"He's already rescued Ashley, so he's going to feel confident that we can't stop him, that he's outwitted us. If we look like we're targeting his dear ole mum, we'll look that much more incompetent and desperate."

"So he's the hero and he needs us to be the bad guys?"

"Exactly."

"Still just a theory. Not enough to jeopardize the integrity of the Bureau or risk any harm coming to civilians. Sorry, Lucy. You'll think of something else."

"Right." It was useless to keep arguing. The suits didn't care about a young girl's life. All they thought about was how it would play on the evening news or in front of a jury. She hung up just as she pulled into the nursing home's parking lot.

Good thing she wasn't a suit. She knew what was priority here and playing by the rules sure as hell wasn't going to save Ashley Yeager.

Lucy was probably tossing her career down the toilet, flushing a cherry bomb in after, but hell, what else was she gonna do with a girl's life at stake?

She climbed out of the car, slamming the door with enough force to rock the SUV. Across the parking lot, haloed by a bright spotlight, Cindy Ames stood in front of her news van, filming with Burroughs.

"Detective Burroughs, explain to me why this seventy-eight year-old woman with severe health problems faces arrest?"

"First of all, Cindy," Burroughs said, turning his wide smile onto the camera, "it's not the Pittsburgh Bureau of Police who have issued a warrant for Ms. Fletcher's arrest. That order came from the FBI, not us."

"Who at the FBI?"

"Supervisory Special Agent Lucia Guardino. She's in charge of the Ashley Yeager case and she feels that Mrs. Fletcher was not forthcoming with vital information regarding her son's whereabouts. In Special Agent Guardino's mind, this information may be the key to finding Ashley Yeager alive."

"But at what cost? Alicia Fletcher is blind, diabetic, in kidney failure. How could she possibly survive an arrest?"

"Agent Guardino has arranged for Mrs. Fletcher to be admitted to the prison hospital ward where she'll be under guard and able to receive any medical care she requires."

Ames wrinkled her pert and perfect nose in distaste. "It seems to me that the federal government is retaliating because their main suspect in the Ashley Yeager disappearance is one of their own employees. Do you agree, Detective Burroughs?"

"I try not to second guess the FBI, but I'm sure that's a consideration."

They exchanged knowing nods as if they both could say more, if only given the chance. A pause, then Ames signaled to her cameraman.

"All right, cut. That's good for now, we can add more depending on how it goes with Alicia." She turned to Burroughs, wrapping her hand around his arm. "You're a natural at this, Burroughs."

Lucy stepped forward. "Are we all set?"

"Ready." Burroughs disengaged himself from Ames. "Cindy says we should just make it for the ten o'clock news. She's arranged for the other stations to pick it up for their later broadcasts."

"Good. Then there's just one more thing." Lucy held out her hand, palm up. "Ms. Ames, all footage of myself and my family."

Cindy's too-white smile looked ghoulish in stark lights. "Certainly. I keep my word." She reached into the van's front seat and slapped a computer disk into Lucy's hand.

"I told you before the consequences of involving me or my family in a news story. They haven't changed. I will have you arrested if you ever come near us again."

"Ahh… but Nicky was so sweet. He told me to come back anytime I wanted."

Lucy gripped the disk so tightly the edge threatened to slice through her skin. "Just make this work. A girl's life depends on it."

"What? No thanks?"

"For what? You're getting an exclusive story, you'll get your ratings. It's not like you care about Ashley or what happens to her—as long as you're the one reporting it."

Ames shrugged, her expression conveying contempt for Lucy's idealism. "Way of the world. If it bleeds, it leads." She crooked a finger at her cameraman. "Come on, Felix. Let's go granny-bashing."

—

Cindy didn't trust Guardino. No way in hell the uptight pols at the Department of Justice approved this charade. This was the real world, not some made for TV movie. In this world upper echelon federal law enforcement officers were political appointees and depended on Congress for their budget and future. The life of one Pittsburgh kid barely registered on their radar.

No skin off her butt, she was going to get a fantastic story no matter what, but it made her wonder what Guardino would stop at to find this kid.

Never get emotionally involved—you'd think an FBI agent would know that.

"No matter what, don't stop filming," she told Felix. He nodded, shifting his handheld as he followed her into Golden Years. No one roamed the halls, the nursing home residents had all been tucked in for the night, sleeping the sleep of the well-medicated and restrained. A nursing type escorted them to Alicia Fletcher's room.

"Alicia dear? Here are the people I told you about. The ones who want to talk about Jimmy, hear his side of things."

The woman seated in a vinyl chair beside the bed stirred with a dry, scratchy noise like rustling autumn leaves. Her hair was long spider silk white strands. Her skin appeared transparent, stretched too thin over her bony face and plumped up and doughy over her hands and lower legs. But it was the eyes that made Cindy take notice. Despite their sightlessness, they homed in on Cindy like an eagle spotting its prey.

Milky blue-grey, white all around the colored parts, the pupils all but invisible, they were the eyes of a ghost.

Then Alicia Fletcher smiled, lips stretching wide, dentures clicking into place, head craned forward eagerly, and Cindy revised her opinion. Not the eyes of a ghost. The eyes of a demon.

"You getting all this?" she nudged Felix who was scanning the room, his own eyes wide and mouth pursed in distaste. She strode forward, her heels clacking on linoleum floor, Alicia following her progress around the bed, her gaze never releasing Cindy from its talon grip. "Mrs. Fletcher? I'm Cindy Ames with WDDE TV. Thank you for agreeing to speak with me."

"You working with the bitch trying to hunt down my boy?" Alicia asked, her voice surprisingly soft, melodic even. "That FBI agent, Guardino is her name. Eye-talian, probably doesn't even belong in this country, slept with someone to get her job. She's trying to make my Jimmy out to be some kind of criminal."

"I've met Agent Guardino," Cindy admitted, seating herself on a vinyl chair opposite Alicia. "She seems very determined. And confident of your son's guilt in the abduction of Ashley Yeager as well as the murders of several other women."

"Pfui," the word was accompanied by a stream of spittle that just missed Cindy. "Only thing Jimmy is guilty of is following his heart. He's got a soft spot for women who need help, like his father that way."

"You realize that if you're withholding information on Jimmy's whereabouts, Agent Guardino can have you arrested?"

Alicia held both palms up, arms trembling, as if waiting to be cuffed. "Let her. She wants an old woman's death on her conscience, fine with me. I have nothing to fear. My boy's done nothing wrong. It's that Guardino woman, she should be out looking for that poor lost girl instead of persecuting me and my family."

She lowered her hands and leaned forward. "If I die today, it will be her fault. She was here earlier and I swear," she slumped back in her chair, one hand fanning her face, "she almost did me in then. Nurses said my blood pressure shot up so high they thought I'd have a stroke."

"I'm sorry to hear that," Cindy said. She couldn't believe her luck. It was like Alicia was reading the script she and Burroughs had prepped. All she had to do was lead her. The old woman seemed smarter than that, this had to be a scam, but as long as Cindy got her story, she wasn't about to argue. "Is there anything you'd like to say to your son if he's watching?"

Alicia smiled again. Cindy hoped it wouldn't scare off too many in the audience; she'd seen friendlier grins from corpses. "Just that I love him no matter what. I know he's trying to live up to his father's memory and there's nothing that would make me prouder."

That was perfect. And basically the end of her script. No reason she couldn't keep rolling though, might come in handy. "Anything you'd like to tell Agent Guardino?"

Alicia's eyes narrowed to two reptilian slits, her head jutting forward. "People like her get theirs sooner or later. She ought to remember that. She ought to remember family always comes first—"

She froze, one hand clawing at her throat as if she was choking. Suddenly her face flushed first red, then purple as she struggled to breathe. The nurse rushed forward, pushing Cindy out of the way. Alicia collapsed in her arms.

"Keep shooting," Cindy whispered to the cameraman as the nurse hit a button. Several more medical types ran into the room followed by Burroughs and Guardino. The nurses slid Alicia onto her bed, took her pulse and blood pressure, put oxygen on her face and sprayed medicine under her tongue.

"What's wrong with her?" Guardino asked, assuming a position near the head of the bed.

"Probably a massive stroke," a nurse taking Alicia's blood pressure muttered. "She's bottoming out. Do you want me to start a line?"

"No need. She's DNR," Alicia's nurse said. "No CPR, no extraordinary measures."

"Then that's all we can do," another replied, stepping back from the bed.

"Lost her pulse."

"Do something," Guardino told them. "You can't let her die."

"There's nothing we can do. The patient's directives—"

"This woman is a material witness. A girl's life may depend on what she knows. That over-rides any advanced directives."

Two of the nurses looked to the third. "I'm sorry, Agent Guardino. There's nothing we can do. She's gone."

Cindy made sure Felix got a good shot of Alicia's crumpled body, her house-dress bunched up, eyes staring without blinking, hands clenched into useless claws. They backed out of the room before they could be kicked out.

"Man, oh man, that sucked," Felix said.

Cindy smirked, shot him a glare, wondering if he had the stomach for this job. "Are you kidding? That footage just bought me network time!"

"You can't use that. It's totally unethical, immoral, it's, it's—"

"It's ratings, baby. Pure, diamond studded ratings."

—

A scream of frustration clawed its way up Lucy's throat, howling to escape, but she clamped it down tight.

"Everyone step away from the body," she ordered. "This is a crime scene."

"You can't do that," the nurse who refused to resuscitate Alicia told her.

"Already done," Lucy replied, pulling out her cell phone. "Detective Burroughs, escort these women to a room where they can be interviewed and secure Ms. Ames and her cameraman along with their footage."

Burroughs didn't give her any flak. Revealing his good instincts for self-preservation, because if he had, she was all too ready to unload on him. "Please come with me, ladies."

He ushered the bemused nurses from the room. Lucy called the Medical Examiner's office. The tech was the same one who had worked Noreen's death at the Tastee Treet earlier.

"Sure, I'll be right out," he assured her. "You going for a hat trick today, Agent Guardino?"

He obviously hadn't heard about the other three bodies Lucy had discovered. She hung up and headed across the hall to where Ames waited, wondering if she might end up adding to the death count. After all, the ME guy was on his way, maybe he could do two for the price of one?

She sent Burroughs to guard the body and turned to face the reporter.

"You can't keep us here," Ames protested. "It's a violation of our civil rights. We have a deadline."

"Show me the footage," Lucy asked the cameraman, ignoring Ames until she could quench the impulse to throttle her. "I want to see everything."

"You don't think we had anything to do with that! You were listening the entire time—"

"Just show me everything."

The camera guy pushed a few buttons and motioned for Lucy to sit beside him so that she could watch the replay on his small LCD screen. The entire interview took less than ten minutes.

"Go back to when you first entered the room," Lucy directed. The cameraman was flustered, took him two tries of hitting the buttons. "Can you slow that?"

She watched the camera bob around the room as Ames first entered. Alicia was sitting in her chair, turned away, her hands out of sight, fumbling with something. "There. Freeze it." Alicia was reaching as if she'd dropped something in her chair. "Wait here."

Lucy returned to Alicia's room. They couldn't touch the body until the ME released it and she should probably get a warrant just to cover her ass before searching the premises but she didn't have time.

"What are you looking for?" Burroughs asked when she brushed past him and turned on all the lights in the room. Lucy ignored him, searching between the chair cushions.

"Bingo." She grabbed a pair of gloves and picked up the cell phone from where it sat, tucked into the cushions of Alicia's chair. "She set us up. Had Fletcher listening in the entire time."

Lucy carefully hit Redial. She held it between them so that Burroughs could hear. Fletcher answered. "Is that you, Lucy?"

"Who else would it be?"

"You'll pay for what you did to my mother."

"I didn't do anything to her, Fletcher. She orchestrated this all on her own. Was she always such a drama queen?" Lucy hoped she could focus his anger on her, away from Ashley. "No wonder you locked her away in this dump."

"How dare you! I did the best I could—" There was a pause, followed by the sound of laughter. "It's not going to work, Lucy. I'm not stupid, you know. The next sound you hear will be the sound of this untraceable, pre-paid cell phone being flushed down a toilet."

"Figured you for a coward. Running away, not even trying to make things right for his own mother. She knew you would run, Fletcher. Knew you couldn't be half the man your father was."

Burroughs grabbed Lucy's arm, shook his head at her. "Tone it down," he mouthed.

"Just—just you shut your mouth, bitch!"

"Make me. Come and get me, Fletcher. Or can't you handle a real woman? Have to make do with scared, half-starved illegals and little girls like Ashley."

"So you found the others. Maybe you're smarter than I thought." Another long pause. "Maybe I'm smarter than you think as well. Your career means everything to you, doesn't it Lucy? Your daughter is sick, in the hospital, and you abandoned her for the sake of your job. You know nothing about being a mother."

"Don't you dare talk about my daughter—" Lucy's grip threatened to crush the small plastic phone.

"Afraid to face the truth? Now who's the coward?" He hung up.

Burroughs frowned, listened to his own cell phone then pocketed it. "He was right, Taylor couldn't get a trace on it. Why'd you push him so hard?"

Lucy deposited Alicia's phone into an evidence bag. Maybe Taylor could find something useful in it. Or better yet…

"You need to talk to your TV girl. Get her to let us monitor her phones. And put a tail on her."

"Cindy? Why?"

"If Fletcher is too smart to deal with me in person, he'll use her to get to me. Just like his mother did."

"What are you talking about? We set up the interview, not Alicia."

Lucy bent down to point to a crumpled paper medicine cup lying beneath Alicia's chair. Several pills, different sizes and shapes, had spilled out onto the floor.

"Wrong. Alicia played us, just like she spent a lifetime playing Fletcher."

"Son of a bitch. The old witch killed herself." Burroughs gave a low whistle. "Man, this family is nuts."

"You can say that again." Lucy left the medicine cup where it was and rocked back on her heels.

"What are you going to do now?"

"We'll let the ME document everything." She pushed herself back onto her feet. "The next move is up to Fletcher. But I'm betting he'll reach out to Ames, want to go public, blaming me for Alicia's death."

Burroughs' frowned.

"Can you keep Ames in line? If she learns we're using her, we're screwed."

He hesitated. She scrutinized his face, leveling her best "don't you dare disappoint me" glare on him, and he finally nodded.

"Yeah. I'll take care of everything. She won't be a problem."

"Ashley Yeager's life might depend on it."

He looked away, staring at the wretched corpse on the bed. "I know."

Chapter 35

Cindy fluffed her hair and squared her shoulders so that the first camera shot would catch her at her best three-quarters profile before panning to capture her full face. This was what she lived for, what made everything else worthwhile, time on air.

Here she was in control of millions of people, of what they thought, of what they felt. Hell, what they ate for breakfast.

Best of all, they invited her into their homes. They wanted *her*.

She pursed her lips, relaxed her neck muscles, waiting for the weekend anchor to finish his lead in. Thanks to the FBI, her canned footage was being run on every local station, but here at WDDE she got an additional three minutes of air time with a live intro and wrap up of the story.

After tonight she'd be famous. The story was perfect. Sexy and scary and sordid—with the federal agent gone bad angle, it was sure to be picked up for national broadcast. Probably a primetime half-hour special if the kid was found dead.

The red light on camera one glowed and Cindy began. As she spoke, using her voice and eyes to sell it, she felt heat fire her belly. She pressed her thighs together below the news desk. God, this was better than sex.

And then it was done. The cameras were back on the weekend anchor, the lights off her, techs scrambling to relieve her of the microphone and send her off set so they could prep their next shot. She picked her way over the cables taped to the floor and joined the news director in the control room.

"How was it?" she asked, knowing she had been brilliant.

"Fantastic," he gushed. "When can I get follow up? Maybe footage of the old lady locked up?"

Guardino had made her go with a fake ending instead of revealing Alicia's real fate. It was either that or the bitch would pull the plug on everything. No matter. Once the girl was found—dead or alive, but preferably dead for the ratings—Cindy would use Guardino's own heavy-handed tactics to destroy her.

When Cindy was done with her, Guardino wouldn't be able to get a job as a crossing-guard.

"Don't think that's going to happen," she said. "But I could get you more inside stuff from Burroughs, the Pittsburgh detective."

The news director frowned. "He's okay, but feds are more glamorous. Get me the lady fed, what's her name, Guardino. You do that and I'll slot you for primetime tomorrow."

"Any word from the network?"

"Let me worry about the network. You get me the story." He glanced about, made sure no one was within listening range and slid one hand around to grope her ass—his idea of seduction. "I'll see you later, after we wrap up?"

Cindy weighed her options. She'd hoped to see Burroughs again, milk him for info on the case, but he would probably be working the entire night. "Bring champagne and an offer from the network and I'll get you an exclusive from Guardino."

She spun on her four-inch heels, pausing to look at him over her shoulder, giving him her best vamp, noting with satisfaction that his gaze never left her ass. Walking away, she felt the weight of his stare, felt that everyone in the control room had stopped to look at her, like she was a supernova lighting up the dark room.

Retiring to her small office-slash-dressing room, Cindy wondered how long it would be before she got the call to come to DC or New York. No more pandering to station managers and news directors, no more talk of the town features, finally, she would be doing hard news. In the spotlight, front and center. Where she belonged.

Her door opened as she dreamed of her bright future. She looked in her makeup mirror, saw Burroughs enter, close the door behind him, leaning against it, silent.

"What do you want?" she asked, irritated that he'd backed Guardino and insisted she keep Alicia Fletcher's death a secret. "I played along."

He nodded, his gaze fixed on the reflection of her cleavage. She leaned forward, pretending to adjust her eyeliner, giving him a good look. It was as close as he was going to get unless he got her another exclusive.

"That's you, Cindy," he drawled, crossing his arms over his chest. "Always playing."

His shoulders threatened to burst free of his sports jacket and his stare turned smoldering. She inhaled, enjoying the scent of testosterone that filled the room. They could have a little fun here, she decided. There was time.

"You've never minded our games," she reminded him, smoothing gloss over her lips, enjoying the way his gaze followed her movements. "Face it, Burroughs, you have so much more fun with me than you ever would with Guardino. Besides, after tonight, she's finished."

He gave a little shake of his head as if warning her away from danger.

Cindy ignored it, confident she had the upper hand. "She owes me. Big time. Sacrificing my journalistic integrity to help save her ass. I want the inside scoop on the investigation." She spun in her chair, now facing him. "And you're going to get it for me. An exclusive."

Her desk phone rang before he could answer. She reached for the receiver, was surprised when he strode across the room to join her.

"Cindy Ames," she answered. Burroughs stabbed the speaker button just as a man's voice came through.

"Ms. Ames, I'm James Fletcher, Jr. You lied about my mother in your story tonight. I'd like to give you a chance to correct your error."

Cindy scowled at Burroughs as he grabbed her hand, restraining her from silencing the speaker. He jerked his head at the phone, indicating that she should answer Fletcher.

"I'm—uh—I'm very sorry about your mother, Mr. Fletcher," Cindy said, steadying her voice and trying to mask her fury at Burroughs. "I had no choice. I was forced to report the story the way it aired."

"Forced by Agent Guardino?"

"Yes sir."

"I understand." There was a pause. Cindy opened her mouth, ready to jump in with an offer of an exclusive interview but Burroughs held her back. A rustling noise sounded in the background and then Fletcher's voice returned.

"Agent Guardino has a lot to answer for. If I gave you evidence against her, would you be able to promise me that it would air without her interference?"

"I think I could convince my boss of that. If we did the interview on camera and the evidence was compelling."

"And you'll include Agent Guardino's responsibility for my mother's death?"

"Certainly. I was there, I saw what happened."

"I know. That's why I came to you. After the way Agent Guardino treated you, I thought you would agree that it is in our mutual interests to keep the FBI and police out of this."

Cindy wondered at that. How the hell had the guy seen her at the nursing home and still managed to escape? Guardino was incompetent. "How would you like to arrange our meeting?"

Another pause. "There's a playing field. In Frick Park. The one at the end of Nicholson Street. Be there in one hour."

There was a click and he was gone. The buzz of the dial tone echoed from the speaker as Cindy whirled on Burroughs. "You son of a bitch. You set me up!"

"Relax, Cindy." He was already dialing his cell phone. "You'll still get your story."

Anger seethed through her as she listened to him tell Guardino the details of her conversation with Fletcher. She used her own phone to call Felix and arrange for a van.

Burroughs hung up on Guardino just as she finished her conversation. "You're not going to be anywhere near that park tonight."

"It's a free country," she said, standing and grabbing her bag. "You can't stop me."

"Like hell I can't." He blocked her path, both hands coming to rest on her shoulders. His face reddened and she wasn't sure if he wanted to push her away or pull her close. "It's too dangerous."

"It's my job. Besides, you and the FBI will be there. Fletcher won't show without me. No way in hell am I missing this story."

–

Jimmy hung up the payphone at the Sheetz and returned to his Blazer. Ashley hadn't moved, still sat curled up in the passenger seat, looking as deflated as a parade balloon the day after Thanksgiving. Other than the single word and her new name, she hadn't spoken to him, not at all. Hadn't looked at him or made eye contact either.

But still, she had done everything he had asked her. No need to be worried. He'd followed the protocols properly; he'd done it right this time.

He slammed the door on purpose to see if she'd jump. Nothing. It was like she was in a coma—here, but not here.

All part of the process. He had to just keep drawing her in.

"Remember I told you we couldn't trust the cops?" he asked, not expecting her to answer. "Well, I think I figured out a way to get Bobby, to keep him from hurting anyone else ever again." He paused, glanced over at her, hoping she'd at least show some sign that she heard, that she was interested in what he had to say.

He hadn't gone through all this work just to end up with a zombie by his side. He honked the horn at nothing. She didn't flinch. Didn't even blink.

"Bobby has a woman helping him find girls—girls just like you. She's a wicked, evil person." Ashley didn't even shrug in her indifference, just stared straight ahead, her eyes not quite shut. "We're going to go meet her. And then we're going to kill her."

Chapter 36

Lucy groaned as soon as she heard Fletcher's choice of a meeting place. The man might be psychonuts, but he wasn't stupid.

She'd been to those playing fields with Megan's soccer team. There were two soccer fields stretched out side-by-side, wide open, no way to set up an ambush. Worse, it was surrounded by forest, trees zigzagged with jogging trails—no way to cover them all, not in the time allotted.

So she was pretty much screwed. Unless she could come up with something brilliant on the fly. She had to assume Fletcher knew they'd be there, no way he'd trust Ames not to call them. And Fletcher knew law enforcement tactics.

Maybe it was time to drop the rules and borrow a play from the bad guys' book. No such thing as fair in love and war. And since she'd be out of a job by morning, this was definitely war.

She finished making her phone calls, calling in favors and setting in motion a logistical nightmare. Then she called Burroughs back. Technically, Pittsburgh would be running the op—she wouldn't even really be there, on paper that was.

"The only parking is at the Nicholson Street entrance," she told him. "Bring Ames in that way. Make sure her cameraman and the van are stopped at least a block away, one civilian is more than enough to worry about."

"Won't Fletcher be watching the park entrance?"

"Of course. Which is why we're using it. If we take it over, he can't use that entrance or more importantly exit. We limit his options."

"He might not show."

"Trust me. He'll be there. We're playing his game, he's the Maestro, remember?"

"Did the ME find anything at the nursing home?" Burroughs continued.

"Apparently Alicia wasn't as weak and fragile as she made out. She stole both the cell phone and the meds she overdosed on from her next door neighbor."

"I'm three minutes out. What's the plan?" Burroughs asked. "You have a double for Cindy? Going to make a switch here in my car?"

Hah. A double? Only if Lucy could gain six inches and undergo some serious plastic surgery in the next ten minutes. Burroughs obviously had no idea how far off the reservation she'd strayed. She was already ducking calls from John Greally, Grimwald, and the PBP's public information officer.

Thank God, the SWAT leader wasn't in the loop or he'd know that as soon as she answered the summons from on high, she was as good as suspended, maybe even terminated.

But she'd deal with all that tomorrow. And most likely for many days to follow. Didn't matter if she got Ashley home alive.

"Just bring her to the parking lot and we'll go over everything," she told Burroughs.

There was a very uncharacteristic hesitation from Burroughs. "You're not planning to let Cindy meet him herself?"

"Not if she doesn't want to."

"Of course she wants to. She's a freaking reporter; she'd sell her soul for a story this hot. That's besides the point—"

"Legally I can't stop her. If she wants to walk onto that playing field, she's allowed. It's still a free country."

His disappointment vibrated through the airwaves. "You played me, Guardino. I never expected that, not from you."

He hung up before she could attempt to defend herself. But of course, there was no defense. She was about to allow a civilian to put her life on the line all in the hopes that she could save one girl.

Lucy twirled her wedding ring. It slid loose on her finger as if she'd lost weight in the past two days. She'd lost something, that was sure as hell for sure.

It was worth it. It had to be.

—

Jimmy watched Lucy through his binoculars. He'd taken the precaution of stealing the vehicle GPS tracking codes before he left the Federal Building. All the better to know your opponent's movements. And Lucy had been a busy girl.

Not for long.

He'd read enough field reports to know she'd have her people deployed around the possible escape routes, spread too thin to see him in the last place they'd look.

Black Blazer with a full complement of antennas, tinted windows and pilfered FBI plates—he was a ghost in their midst, parked a dozen spots away from Lucy, half hidden by the shadow of the SWAT team's van, and no one was the wiser.

He reached across Ashley and opened the glove compartment. He handed her a snub-nosed revolver. "You ever shoot a gun before?"

She hefted the gun, said nothing as she raised it and aimed out the window at a trashcan.

"It's real easy. Just point it like you are now and pull the trigger. But be careful. There's a bullet ready to go already." He eased the revolver away from her. "Do you think you can do it? Shoot someone?"

Her face was hidden in shadows but her breathing became faster, raspy. "Vixen can."

"Bobby is too dangerous for you to go after," he continued, not letting her know how much it creeped him out to hear her talk about herself in the third person like that. Like she wasn't even there. "I

304

know you'd like to, after everything he did to you. Don't worry. I'll take care of him. What I need you to do is to distract him for me. See that woman there?"

The TV reporter, Cindy Ames, was climbing out of a car, assisted by Burroughs, the Pittsburgh detective. They seemed to be arguing about something.

"You see her? The lady in the red suit?" Jimmy asked even though Ashley was looking right at Cindy. "I need you to follow her into that field, aim the gun and fire at her. It doesn't matter if you hit her or not, I just need a diversion so I can get to the real target. Can you do that?"

There was a long moment of silence before she nodded.

"Say it."

"Yes. I can do it."

"Then you need to run back here to the car as fast as you can. They'll be chasing you, so you have to run fast. If they catch you, they'll send you back to your parents, to your old life. To a life where Bobby can get to you anytime he wants. You don't want that to happen, do you?"

She wrapped her arms around her chest as if warding off evil spirits. "No."

"All right then." He handed her the revolver. "Be careful."

She nodded and slid from the car, hiding in the shadows before vanishing into the trees. Jimmy pursed his lips, hoping it was worth the chance of losing her. But as always, Alicia was right—Ashley had to prove herself. If she passed this test, then he'd know she was truly his, worthy of his love.

As soon as he took care of Lucy, he'd have the rest of their lives to devote to her.

-

Lucy had done the best she could. The Pittsburgh SWAT guys had the streets surrounding the woods covered, Ames was playing along—although disappointed she couldn't take her cameraman into the field of fire with her—Burroughs was still steaming, but since he wasn't in her chain of command, he was as protected as possible.

All she could do now was wait for Fletcher to make the next move. She couldn't sit still, so she'd set up her command post on the hood of her Blazer in the now deserted parking lot. A map of the field spread out before her, marking where all her men were, radio communications up and running, night vision binoculars tracking Ames' progress as she tripped her way across the field—idiot had insisted on wearing heels.

She was tempted to call Nick, get his advice, but there was no time. What she'd done was totally against regs, she'd be lucky if she only lost her job and didn't face charges, but it was the best way to save Ashley and stop Fletcher.

A malignant narcissist, Nick had called Fletcher. What happened when he realized Ashley didn't mirror his twisted view of the world? One false move and she'd be just another inconvenient body to dispose of—like the three corpses in the barn or Noreen.

The image of the Tastee Treet clerk's mutilated face flashed through Lucy's mind. Her shoulders hunched. It ended here, she vowed.

"I'm almost to the center of the field," Ames' voice sounded shrill in Lucy's ear. "There's no one here. I'm going to stroll over by the goal box."

"Just stay out in the open where we can cover you," Burroughs said before Lucy could say anything.

"No problem." Ames made slow progress across the field. "There's someone moving over there, in the trees. Is that one of you guys?"

"Where?" she asked, irritated by the reporter's vagueness. She trained the binoculars on the trees behind the soccer goal. Nothing there.

"To my right. Wait. There's a girl. Ashley!" The reporter's cry cut through the night. Lucy watched in dismay as Ames waved to the dark figure hidden by the trees. The reporter actually ran, as fast as possible in heels, towards the trees, ignoring Burroughs' order to stop.

The figure separated itself from the shadows. It *was* Ashley. She was ghostly green in the night vision glasses, but she appeared unharmed. She stepped out of the tree line just as Ames reached her.

Lucy's heart galloped. "This isn't right," she said into her microphone. "Scan the area, Fletcher would never let Ashley go alone. It's a trap of some sort."

The cold touch of a gun's muzzle kissed the back of her neck.

"Good call, Lucy," Fletcher said as he reached around to take her weapon and pocket it.

Chapter 37

She crouched down among the fallen leaves, cowering like a rabbit run to ground by a pack of wolves. No. Not wolves. Foxes.

Tonight she was the one doing the hunting.

She caressed the gun. It was lighter than she thought, no heft to it at all. Cradling it in her hands, she squinted along the top of the barrel like she'd seen men do in movies. Centered her sights on the woman in red picking her way across the soccer field.

Had she lied? Maybe she couldn't kill.

Vixen can, a voice echoed through her mind.

Was she Vixen? Was that who she was?

Better that than returning to her old life—or to the person she was in the black place, back in the barn. That person was weak, had given up, surrendered. She deserved to die, be left behind, abandoned in the dark.

Wind rustled the tree branches above her. She looked around, deciding upon the best route. The woods were dark but they weren't frightening, not like the other place, the place where there'd been no hope of light. Something scurried near her foot. Snakes?

She aimed the gun and surprised herself when she didn't pull the trigger. No need. She wasn't afraid, not of snakes, not of the blackness, not of killing.

She wasn't that girl anymore.

-

Burroughs watched Cindy through a pair of NVG's scrounged from one of the SWAT guys. His one and only job on this op was keeping Cindy safe.

His hand clenched the grip of his Glock. He couldn't believe the way Guardino had played him—she was so far off the grid on this one, NASA would have a hard time finding her using the goddamn Hubble.

Cindy began running toward the woods. "Ashley!"

"Stop! Cindy, stop. Stay where you are!" Burroughs' shout went unheeded. He left his position in the trees on the near side of the field. It left him exposed but he was the closest to Cindy's position.

He watched in horror as Ashley Yeager smiled at Cindy. Then she raised a gun and shot the reporter.

"Shots fired, shots fired!" Voices collided over the comm channel. Armed men began to swarm the area. Cindy stretched a hand out to Ashley, as if begging for help, then fell face first onto the ground.

Burroughs ran so hard his breathing drowned out the chatter on the comm. Ashley had vanished back into the woods. He skidded on the grass, stopping beside Cindy's body, placing himself between her and Ashley's last position.

Carefully, he rolled the reporter over. Her face was pale and her hand clutched her chest where a dark mark smeared her silk blouse.

"Cindy, are you all right?" he asked, tugging her blouse open to examine the Kevlar vest she wore beneath it. No sign of any injury.

"That girl tried to kill me," she finally said, her eyes fluttering open. "The bitch." She sat up, brushing mud and grass from her blouse. "She's going to pay for this."

"What happened?" Burroughs asked, still finding no gunshot wounds. No wounds at all.

"Are you deaf? She shot me." She gestured at him to help her up. "Well, at me. I tripped. Oh damn, would you look at that? Broke my heel clean off. These shoes cost me twelve hundred dollars."

Burroughs hoisted her back onto her feet. He wasn't sure if he was laughing at her adrenalin-inspired prattling or the fact that she was still alive.

"Hey. This is nothing to laugh about. Those were Manolo Blahniks."

—

Lucy's jaws ground together, sending a shockwave of frustration down her neck. She kept her hands out, posing no threat as she slowly turned to face Fletcher.

He wore an FBI blazer and cap. And carried a Glock-22, the same gun that FBI and ICE agents used. Forty caliber and capable of putting a very large hole into a person's body. Especially at point blank range.

"Hey there, Jimmy," she drawled, hoping someone in the tangle of voices on the comm link was listening.

"You should have left my mother alone, Lucy. That wasn't very nice of you."

"Your mother killed herself. I didn't have anything to do with it." She still held her binoculars. They were heavy but Fletcher didn't seem to see them or her as a threat. The sounds of men calling for an ambulance and searching the woods for Ashley carried through her earbud.

"She told me everything before she died," Fletcher said. "Told me it was your fault."

"Like I forced her to steal medications from her neighbor and take them just in time so she could die on camera? Yeah, Jimmy. That's my fault."

"You drove her to it!"

"She was using me. Just like she used you all your life. She never loved you, Jimmy."

"You don't know what you're talking about. You don't know anything about the love between a mother and child. Look at the way you abandoned yours."

An image of Megan and Nick, their faces crushed by sorrow, filled her vision. She blinked it back, focusing on Fletcher and his gun. "She wasn't even your mother, Jimmy."

"Shut up!"

"Did she ever tell you the truth about your father?" As she spoke, Lucy spotted movement from the woods. Ashley. Instead of stepping out into the open, the girl crept along the shadows' edge, behind Fletcher's back and invisible to anyone except Lucy.

"A hundred times. My father saved my mother's life. They were soul mates."

"Wrong, Jimmy. Your father was a con artist and so was your mother. And when she got too old for him, he picked up other women—girls really. Dozens of them. Did your mother ever tell you how he died?"

"He's dead? Are you sure?" His voice dropped, a wistful boy who'd spent a lifetime in search of his father. Unfortunately, the muzzle never wavered.

"He died the day you were born. Alicia killed him. And your mother." Lucy met his eyes, kept his attention cemented on her. "I saw the autopsy reports. Alicia killed your father because he was defending your mother, your real mother. And then Alicia sliced you from your mother's belly, left her to bleed to death and took you for her own. That was the kind of woman Alicia was, Jimmy."

His eyes were wide with fear or anger or surprise, she wasn't sure what. But he was listening, and thinking, thinking hard.

She held her free hand out, keeping the binoculars in her other hand down by her side, out of his center of attention. "It's over, Jimmy. Give me the gun."

The movement in the woods stopped. Ashley took a step forward, a gun in her hand, aimed at Lucy and Fletcher.

"You deserved better than her, Jimmy," Lucy continued, trying to coax him from Alicia's tendrils. "Give me the gun and I'll introduce you to your real mother. The one who gave her life for you."

A single tear escaped from his eye. Lucy thought she had him. Then Ashley spoke up.

"I did it. I did what you said. Where's Bobby?"

Fletcher glanced over at Ashley. Lucy swung the binoculars, smashing his gun hand into the side of the Blazer. His Glock skidded across the SUV's roof, landing somewhere in the darkness beyond.

She followed up with another swing aimed at his head. Fletcher blocked it, using the binocular straps to pull her off balance, kicking her legs out from under her. Lucy thudded against the gravel, pain stealing her breath as the impact thundered through her left shoulder.

"I knew you could do it." He turned to Ashley. "You and me, we belong together."

Lucy looked up just as Ashley raised the gun and aimed it at her. Ashley's finger tightened on the trigger.

Adrenalin crashed over Lucy, leaving no room for fear. She rolled beneath the SUV, seeking cover, knowing she couldn't move faster than a bullet.

Nothing happened.

Fletcher laughed. "I only gave you one bullet. It was a test and you passed. You did great, Ashley. Now come with me."

Ashley looked down at the useless gun in her hand, her face scrunching with confusion. An ambulance's siren and lights pierced the night, gravel flying as it sped towards them. Fletcher yanked at Ashley's arm, trying to pull her with him. She took a step in his direction.

"No," Lucy called, rolling out from beneath the Blazer and rushing forward.

Fletcher whirled, fumbling to draw her service weapon from his jacket pocket. Lucy changed trajectories and tackled Ashley, covering her with her body.

The ambulance screeched to a halt, a few feet away from her, its headlights blinding Lucy. When she looked around, Fletcher had vanished.

Chapter 38

SUNDAY, 11:58 PM

"Well, you did it," Burroughs said as the medics forced Lucy away from Ashley. "Against all odds, you saved her."

At what cost? Lucy couldn't help but wonder, watching a paramedic jab a wickedly large needle into Ashley's arm, starting an IV. Ashley didn't flinch, her expression wooden, staring up at nothing.

"We found Fletcher's Glock. You said he took yours. You got back up?"

Her Baby Glock was in her car, back at the Federal Building. She hefted her purse, felt the weight of the thirty-two. "I'm good."

"The ambulance driver said she was shooting at you when they pulled in. Said Fletcher didn't even have a gun."

"They're mistaken."

"And you're a piss poor liar, Guardino."

Lucy heard the undercurrent of anger, knew he was still mad at her for using Ames as bait. Tough. She wasn't about to feel sorry for the reporter who'd come out of all this with an exclusive ratings-grabber of a story. "Ames really going to try to press charges?"

He shrugged one shoulder, his gaze darting past the ambulance to where Ames and her cameraman were eagerly interviewing one of the SWAT team members. "Not unless it gets her a bigger story. She will expect reimbursement for damages."

"Damages? What the hell? You guys found the bullet in the dirt. Ashley wasn't even aiming for her."

"Silk blouse, Donna Karan suit, and one pair Manolo Blahniks. She thinks six grand should cover it."

"Six thousand? Dollars? For shoes—if she thinks for one second—" Lucy stopped, started laughing instead. "Let her try. What do I care? I'm probably out of a job anyway."

"No way, you're the hero, you saved Ashley."

She shook her head, followed the medics carrying Ashley on their stretcher across the lot to the ambulance. "Not me, Burroughs. You. As far as the world knows, I wasn't even here tonight." She jerked her head at Ames. "Go, be a hero. I hear it's a great way to get laid."

She climbed into the ambulance with Ashley. He stood watching, and she was surprised to see that instead of the wolfish grin she'd come to expect from him, he was frowning and scratching at his head. As if he was actually thinking twice about his involvement with Ames.

"Maybe there's hope after all," she muttered as the medic slammed the door.

She reached for Ashley's hand, the one without the IV and absently stroked it. Ashley's fingernails were broken and torn, her hands grimy with sweat, fingers cold. Tiny bite marks, some just red, others breaking her skin, zigzagged across every inch of exposed flesh.

"Christ almighty." The medics looked away at the sight of the snakebites and breathed out. Lucy wasn't sure if it was a prayer or a curse.

She raised Ashley's hand in both of hers and blew on it, rubbing it warm again, just like when Megan came in from playing soccer in the rain. "You're going to be all right, Ashley."

Ashley didn't move, except maybe, just maybe, her breathing smoothed out a bit. And her fingers might have curled a bit in Lucy's grasp. Lucy kept hold of Ashley's hand in one of hers and used the other to smooth out her matted hair. To her surprise, tears seeped from Ashley's eyes. No sobs or sounds, just tears streaming as if a dam had broken.

"Please," Ashley whispered, still not making eye contact with Lucy. "I'm not Ashley. I'm not the girl you're looking for. Please let me go. Don't take me back."

"Back where, Ashley?"

"Back to the black place."

Lucy thought about the barn with its stench of death and living reptilian implements of terror. "Back to the barn? Don't worry, you're not going back there. Never again."

Ashley was shaking her head, pulling away in terror. "I can't, I can't go—he promised I'd be safe with him. Take me to Jimmy, take me back to Jimmy!"

She pitched forward, almost tearing her IV out before Lucy and the medic could restrain her. She thrashed and fought, gnashing her teeth at them like an animal, snarling and spitting. The medic gave her something in her IV and then she was quiet, her eyes drifting shut.

"You okay?" he asked, handing Lucy a gauze pad to blot spittle away. "She didn't bite you, did she?"

"No. I'm fine."

"Poor kid's nuts. That whack job did a real number on her. After everything she's been through, she'll never be the same again."

Lucy kept hold of Ashley's hand, had to look away and blink back tears of her own. Maybe she'd been too late, maybe she hadn't saved anyone after all.

–

Burroughs wrapped up the little details—documentation, securing Guardino's vehicle, coordinating resources, evidence recovery—not that there was much except a bullet, the revolver, and Fletcher's Glock—as well as making nice to the brass and SWAT guys. All the glamorous jobs of police work that Hollywood always conveniently ignored.

He was about ready to take off, see if Guardino had been able to get anything from Ashley that would help them locate Fletcher, when Cindy sidled up to him, sans cameraman. She'd gone for a spritely fem-jep look for her story—popped most the buttons off her blouse, pulled it half-way out from her skirt, revealing the Kevlar vest she wore beneath.

Of course her makeup and hair looked camera-ready perfect—one could only sacrifice so much for one's art, he supposed.

"I wanted to return your vest," she said, eyes lowered in an uncharacteristically demur expression as she slipped free of her suit jacket. "And thank you for rushing to save my life."

"You weren't in danger. Not really," he said, folding his hands into determined fists to keep them from helping her out of her clothing. "No way she could have missed from that distance if she was really aiming at you."

She looked up demurely, bit her lower lip as if holding back tears, and waited a beat, expecting more from him. "Still, you couldn't know that. Thanks, Burroughs."

Teasing her blouse the rest of the way from her skirt, she finished unbuttoning it and slid free from its silky embrace, handing it to Burroughs. "Help me with these straps?"

Her scent assaulted him, trapping him despite his best intentions. He felt his body respond to her, just as it always did. Traitor.

He ripped the Velcro swaths open with more force than he needed, tugging her closer to him.

She squirmed out of the Kevlar, left him holding the bulletproof vest in one hand, her blouse in the other. And she stood between them, her breasts barely contained by her lacy demi-bra, pressing her body up against his. "How can I thank you properly?"

Her pelvis ground into his, heat shooting straight to his groin. He wasn't sure who he hated more, him or her. "What do you want, Cindy?"

She traced her fingers over his shirt, eyes downcast as if she had no ulterior motives and had to seriously consider his question. The last SWAT van pulled away, leaving just the two of them alone in the darkness.

"My entire future has changed tonight—thanks to you. My manager says by morning, I'll be on the fast track to a permanent network assignment. Either New York or DC."

"So maybe you should go home and pack your bags." His voice was breathy as if all the blood had abandoned his lungs—and fled south.

Her face twisted into a pout. "You don't mean that. You'll miss me, won't you, Burroughs?"

Her hands dropped below his belt, squeezed. He choked back a groan. He wasn't giving in, wasn't going to be used. Not again.

"We're alone now. I could do you right here—in the place where I almost died and you saved me." She undid his belt, reached for his fly. "You'd like that, wouldn't you Burroughs? My hero."

He blinked hard, trying not to give in to desire. She sweetened the pot, sinking to her knees as she unzipped him.

"It's your wildest fantasy come true, isn't it? Me kneeling in the dirt, letting you do anything you want to me."

Her fingers teased him—Christ! He dropped the vest and her shirt, took her hands in his, twisting them away from his growing erection.

"You want me to use my mouth instead?" She asked, looking up at him, shaking her hair back from her face, grinning wide.

It took him two breaths to clear his mind. "What do you want, Cindy?"

"My manager says if I can get an exclusive of Fletcher's capture or an interview with him, it would double my signing bonus with the network. We're talking seven figures here, Burroughs. You'd do that for me, wouldn't you?"

She licked her lips then leaned her head forward, mouth wide open.

"No." He stepped back, as far away from her as he could, releasing her hands to fumble his fly closed again. Fool, the primitive part of his brain screamed. The part that drove him back to her bed time and again.

317

Arching her head up, her breasts not quite popping free of their restraints, she knelt on her hands and knees. "You sure? Last chance—you know how much you'll love it. I need to be punished for driving your kids away from you, for poisoning your marriage." Her pout was marred by the greedy gleam in her eyes. "Don't you want to punish me, Burroughs? Give me what I deserve? Treat me like the whore in the dirt that I am. Don't you want to feel like a hero, like a real man?"

"Just go away. Leave me alone." She was the one on her knees, but he was the one begging.

He found his car keys in his pocket, unlocked the Impala and dropped into the drivers' seat before he could change his mind. As he spun out of the parking lot, he could see her in his rearview mirror, still kneeling on the ground, laughing.

Chapter 39

"She's my baby, you can't keep me from her!" Melissa Yeager's shout turned the heads of everyone in the fourth floor hallway.

"Ma'am, please, this is the pediatric floor," the doctor, who looked young enough to be a patient himself, cautioned her. "I'm sorry, but she doesn't want to see you or her father. It would be best for Ashley if—"

"I know what's best for my daughter. You can't keep me from her." Melissa shoved past him, glared at the hospital security guard until he stepped away from the door, and barged into Ashley's hospital room.

Footsteps announced the arrival of the doctor following on her heels. "She's suffering from dehydration, some abrasions that we debrided, and shock."

His words bounced off Melissa. She stood frozen, staring down at her daughter.

Ashley, dressed in a hospital gown, lay curled up in a ball, shivering despite a mountain of blankets and the room's oppressive heat. Her eyes were closed so tight they pulled her face into a mass of wrinkles.

At first Melissa felt concern. "My God, what did that monster do to you?"

"Our preliminary examination didn't reveal any other injuries," the doctor told her.

She could see that was true. Sure, Ashley's hair was matted, her color a bit pale, but she was fine. Seemed fine. Just like always.

"Ashley, dear. It's your mother. Open your eyes. C'mon, Ashley, don't you want to go home?"

Ashley pulled away with an animal-like snarl when Melissa touched her exposed wrist. She pulled her body farther under the covers and squeezed her eyes tighter.

Melissa's fear shifted into anger. She knew this posture, knew it all too well—Ashley's way of getting her own way, tormenting her mother into giving in to whatever her current demands were.

For two days Melissa had suffered through hell, been half driven mad with fear that her daughter was dead or worse, and now Ashley was back and she was fine. Just fine. Except she still insisted on making Melissa out to be the bad guy.

"Ashley. I know you're awake. Open your eyes and look at me. Now." Steel lanced through Melissa's voice. She wasn't going to take this crap—not after what Ashley had done. "Do you have any idea what you put me through? Running away like that? I was worried sick."

The earnest pediatrician laid a hand on her arm. "Please, Mrs. Yeager. Let's talk outside, let Ashley rest."

"There's no need to patronize me, young man. I know what's best for my daughter. And it's to go home with me."

"We need—"

"I need you to make whatever arrangements necessary for me to take my daughter home. She's suffered enough, I certainly don't intend to allow her to remain here in the care of strangers."

"No." The single syllable ripped through the room like a predator shredding its victim.

Startled, Melissa looked down at her daughter. Ashley's eyes were open—wide open, the whites showing all around, making her look like a madwoman.

"Ashley, dear. You're coming home. With me."

"No."

"Don't argue with me, young lady—"

"I'll kill you."

The words struck Melissa like a hard slap. "What did you say? You don't talk to me like that—"

"I'll kill you! Kill, kill, kill!" Ashley sat bolt upright, throwing her blankets aside. The veins and muscles in her neck were tight, popping out like a wild animal's. Her teeth were bared, seeking blood.

Melissa stepped back. "Maybe a night here would be best..."

"You're not my mother. I have no mother, no father," Ashley continued in a voice that made Melissa hug herself. A voice hovering on the primordial edge of audible, humming with danger. "If you touch me again, you're dead. I'm dead. Everyone is dead. Everyone is dead. Dead, dead, dead..."

Ashley collapsed, falling out of bed, her body limp, not breaking her fall, eyes wide open but unseeing. The doctor quickly rescued her, gently returning her to bed, replacing her covers. Ashley didn't seem to notice. It was like she was in a trance.

"Has she ever done anything like this before?" the pediatrician asked as he guided Melissa back out to the hallway. "Experienced delusions or catatonia?"

Melissa nodded, unable to speak for a moment. "When she was young, she used to have staring spells. Daydreams. The doctors tested her, said nothing was wrong, that she was just a sensitive child and it was her way to block out excessive stimulus. She's always been high-strung."

She stared beyond him to Ashley who stared directly into the overhead light without blinking, drool escaping from the corner of her mouth.

"I think this is more than daydreams," the doctor said, shutting the door on Ashley—or the girl who used to be Ashley.

Melissa felt something twist and break inside her. She covered her mouth with her palm, but that didn't stop the tears from gurgling out. She never cried, hated crying, it meant you were weak, a failure. But still the tears came—like never before.

"It's all my fault," she whispered. "All my fault."

"You made it," Megan said, bouncing, waking up Nick from where he lay snoring beside her in the hospital bed.

Lucy threw her purse under a chair and wrapped her arms around her daughter, practically smothering her. The damn oxygen monitor screeched in alarm.

She ignored the beeping and buried her face in Megan's hair, kissing her, clutching her, needing her touch.

"Mom, Mom, I can't breathe," Megan finally said, forcing Lucy to reluctantly release her. "You okay, Mom? You look like you've been crying."

"I've been better," Lucy confessed. "How are you doing?"

"Well—" Megan slanted Lucy a "I think I might seriously be in trouble here" look. "Maybe Dad should tell you."

Nick eased his weight from the bed and crossed around it to join Lucy. She felt the weight of his gaze as he took inventory. He said nothing, didn't have to, merely wrapped an arm around her waist and snugged her to his side.

"Tell me what?" Lucy said. "Did the doctors find something?"

"Not exactly," Nick said. "More like they're finally on the right track." To Lucy's surprise he arched an eyebrow and gave Megan his sternest look. "Go on, tell her."

"Well…" Megan tilted her chin down and looked up, batting her eyelashes shamelessly. "I kind of saved someone too. Just like you do, Mom. Only, I guess I should have told you guys."

Lucy frowned, glancing from one to the other. Neither appeared too concerned. She shook her head, in no mood to play mind games and too tired to puzzle it out. "I've had a really, really bad day, Megan. Why don't you just tell me and we'll deal with the consequences later."

"Okay. Remember how you said maybe I could have a cat? I kinda already do." Megan sat up straight, spurting words as if a dam had burst. "He's real cute, orange and fuzzy all over, and he's an orphan, so someone had to save him. He lives under the back porch.

322

I've been feeding him and taking care of him and now he comes when I call him, like he knows his name."

"Megan—" Lucy started. Nick squeezed her waist and she stopped, letting her daughter wind down.

"I feed him, give him fresh water and make sure he's warm enough and now he's getting fat and he's so cute and friendly, and I've been the one responsible for him." Megan beamed up at Lucy. "You said I could have a pet once I proved I could be responsible. So I did."

"The important thing," Nick interjected before Lucy's blood pressure spiked into brain-bursting-stroke-range as she tried to follow her daughter's demented logic, "is that Megan's been playing with a kitten. The doctors are thinking her fever and swollen glands and everything are caused by Bartonella."

"Who's that?"

"Mom." Megan rolled her eyes. "You're funny. Bartonella isn't a who, it's a what. Dr. Scott said it's a tiny bacteria that got into my blood and it's what's been making me sick."

"Cat scratch fever," Nick translated.

All she could think of was the inane song by that name. Lucy felt herself wavering, steadied herself against Nick's sublimely solid body. "Cat scratch—that can be serious."

"It can be if they don't catch it in time," Nick admitted. "But the doctors said if the tests confirm it, all Megan will need is a few days of antibiotics. To be on the safe side, they've already started them."

Lucy glanced at the new bags of fluid dangling from the IV pole. "So, everything's going to be all right?"

"If it is cat scratch, yes." Nick intertwined his fingers with hers, squeezing tight. Lucy squeezed back, turned to look him in the eyes, making sure he wasn't hiding anything. Nope. Crystal clear, he was telling the truth.

"What about the cat?"

"Boots," Megan chimed in. "His name is Boots."

"Do we have to—" She couldn't bring herself to say it, not with Megan staring at her like that. "Is it contagious?"

Nick shook his head, smiling. "Nope. Boots will be fine. Although the doctor said we should get him checked out by a vet and started on his shots and flea medicine."

"So I get to keep him, right? Dad said it was up to you, but he always says that when he wants to say yes but thinks you'll say no, but you don't want to say no, not when I did what you said and proved myself responsible and saved him just like you save kids and—"

Lucy did the only thing possible to stop Megan's rambling. She gathered her not-so-little girl into her arms and squeezed the oxygen from her lungs. Nick joined her, making a loud, squealing tangle of arms and legs on the hospital bed, bouncing in time with the beeping of the oxygen alarm.

Finally they separated, Megan's cheeks red from giggling, Nick smiling his sloe-gin lazy grin of contentment, and Lucy afraid to exhale for fear it might break the magic moment.

–

Jimmy slid into the seat at the hospital cafeteria table, his stomach growling at the smell of Chilimac, French fries, and apple pie. The couple at the table beside him didn't even look up, they were so embroiled in their argument. Jimmy shamelessly eavesdropped as he ate—after all, that was why he was here.

"Why won't you even go up to see your own daughter?" the wife demanded. She was a skinny, high-strung, high-pressure type, all angles and planes and sharp edges.

Jimmy started with pie. Never know when you might die, so start with the good stuff, Alicia always said. It was good—especially for hospital food.

Gerald Yeager pushed the remnants of his own pie around with his fork. "You heard what the doctors said. She's in shock, traumatized. We shouldn't push her."

"Coward. You just don't want to face what you drove her to!" Melissa's voice screeched past Jimmy, raising the hairs on the back of his neck. "You should have seen her, she looked awful. And the things she said to me—she'd rather be with that, that, pervert than come home."

Jimmy hid his smile with a sip of milk. He licked his milk mustache away, restraining his impulse to simply shoot the man and woman and put them out of Ashley's misery. She was such a good kid, didn't deserve such lousy parents.

Good thing she had him now.

He'd only half finished his fries—they weren't as good as the ones at the Tastee Treet—and Chilimac when Melissa stood.

"Where are you going?" Gerald asked.

"Back up to Ashley. Maybe she's calmed down by now."

Gerald blew his breath out in a long-suffering sigh. "Melissa, they have her under sedation, they're sending her to Western Psych tomorrow, they're not going to let you disturb her."

"Disturb her? I'm her mother." She spun on her heel and stalked away. Gerald didn't even watch her leave, simply shook his head and returned to his food.

Jimmy bused his table and followed Melissa onto the elevator. She got off on the fourth floor. He kept riding up to the top of the tower. Fourth floor, that was interesting—Lucy's daughter was on the fourth floor as well.

The elevator stopped at the top then started back down. This time Jimmy stabbed the button for the fourth floor.

He stepped out, looking up and down the two hallways leading from the elevator bank. No signs of any guards loitering outside a patient's door. The clerk at the nursing station looked up. "Can I help you?"

"I'm trying to find Ashley Yeager," Jimmy said, flashing his ICE credentials too fast for the clerk to read.

She didn't even glance at them. "I'm sorry, sir. We don't have any patients by that name. Maybe if you check at the security desk downstairs?"

"Thanks, I'll do that." Jimmy got on the elevator before the clerk could question him or call for assistance. Lucy must have already given the staff instructions, trying to avoid reporters, no doubt.

He whistled soundlessly as the floors whizzed past. Too bad she'd forgotten that he already knew where he could find one special little girl.

All he needed was to pick up a few supplies from his storage locker, make a few phone calls, and he'd have everything he needed to get Ashley back where she belonged.

With him. Safe and sound.

Chapter 40

MONDAY, 1:32 AM

Content that she'd be able to keep Boots, Megan had fallen asleep, sprawled across the hospital bed in blissful abandonment. Nick had sweet-talked the nurses into giving him some bandages and they were now in Megan's bathroom where he was changing Lucy's dressings.

He was none too happy when he saw the surgeon's handiwork. Even less so when Burroughs called. She'd asked him to take over guarding Ashley inside her room, two doors down the hallway. She trusted Burroughs a lot more than any hospital rent-a-cop, knew he'd get her if Ashley woke up and seemed ready to be interviewed.

Learning that Ashley was only two doors away hadn't made Nick any happier. He relented once she told him about the barn and the conditions of Ashley's captivity.

"Sounds like pretty classic brainwashing," he said, smoothing antibiotic ointment between her stitches as she leaned over the sink.

"You always say there's no such thing as brainwashing."

"I say you can't depend on information obtained by torture. Brainwashing is a different matter. The Vietnamese and Russians had some very effective, scientific approaches that were reproducible."

She jerked her head up at that. "You mean scientists studied it?"

"Decades ago, yeah. Under the right circumstances you can make a person forget or believe or do almost anything—if they're already inclined to forget, believe, or do it."

"So Fletcher forced Ashley to live out her greatest fears, got her totally disoriented, and then he convinced her that only he has the power to save her?" She frowned, remembering the barn and the way a short ten minutes in the place had impacted her. "But Ashley's smart, she'd see right through that, wouldn't she?"

Behind her, Nick shrugged as he taped a length of gauze over her stitches. "Not if she didn't want to see. You said she loved this Shadow World, that she drew pictures of a girl in distress and a hero who helped save her..."

"All girls dream of that, it's conditioned into us with every fairy tale we're told."

"Ashley felt her real life was so bad that she'd take any possible escape. I wouldn't be surprised if she'd considered suicide in the past." He helped her back into her blouse and turned her around to face him. "She was damaged goods before Fletcher ever got his hands on her, don't be surprised if she never totally recovers from this."

Lucy wrinkled her nose at him. "Is this more of your 'you can't save the world' philosophy? What happened to the handsome, young idealist I fell in love with?"

"He's still here. Just now he has a wife and child who are his world. As long as they're safe, that's all that matters." He bent down to kiss her, his hands feathering down to her waist, pulling her close. "I'm sorry we fought earlier. I really needed—wanted—you to stay."

"I couldn't. I just—" Lucy glanced through the crack in the door to where Megan lay sleeping, surrounded by hospital paraphernalia. "I couldn't."

"Because of your father, what happened when you were a child."

"No. Because my world is a world of possibilities. That's how I need to think so that I don't leave any stone unturned, I have to imagine every possibility no matter how remote. Or how awful. The one fact I'm constantly dealing with is that the worst possible thing any parent can imagine has happened to their child. If I sit here and open the door, even the tiniest slit, to the possibility of that happening to my child..."

"Lucy, nothing is going to happen to Megan. She'll be fine.

"You can't know that. Not even the doctors can know that."

"All I can do is hope for the best. And keep her thinking that way as well. I've seen too many patients who fall into despair, imagining the worst, and they never climb out."

"See, that's exactly why you don't want me here. I can't look at Megan—here, sick, helpless—without imagining the worst and it tears me up inside."

His lips brushed the top of her head and his hands tightened on her hips. The smell of him filled the room: comfort, warmth, strength.

"Shhh… everything is going to be okay. I know it is. You did the impossible, you found Ashley, saved her."

They both knew Ashley was far from saved. "Now who's believing in fairy tales?"

"Thank you for keeping your promise to Megan."

She rubbed her nose against his. "You are so very welcome."

They kissed again and Lucy was ready to take it farther, much, much farther, injured back and small confines notwithstanding, when her cell buzzed again. "Damn."

Nick backed away, leaning against the shower stall as she yanked the infernal machine from her belt. It was Walden.

"Hey, boss," he said when she answered. "Finally made it to the morgue in one piece. Got a few things for you."

"Go ahead."

"Found ID's on all three victims. The uncle, the ME thinks he's been dead the longest—several years. Which means someone's been collecting his pension for him. Probably how Fletcher and his mom paid for her hospital bills and nursing home and everything. No signs of trauma, he could have died of natural causes or even been poisoned. It's gonna take a while to tell, the ME says he's been mummified."

Lucy cringed at the image that sent through her mind, was glad Walden had pulled the morgue detail instead of her. "And the women?"

"You were right. One was Tzisaris. ME says she shows signs of being beaten and strangled. Dead for months but decomp was slowed—all the bodies were probably kept someplace cool and dry and free of insects for a while before they were moved into the barn. We're still working on that."

The distinctive buzzing sound of a Stryker bone saw interrupted him. A moment later he continued. "The third is a visiting nurse named Connie Thackman. She was reported missing three years ago."

Right around the time Alicia went to the nursing home. "She ever assigned to care for Alicia Fletcher?"

"Bingo. I'll finish up here, but they're going slow—with the partial mummification and all, the ME's taking his time."

"Call me when you know anything more." Then she reconsidered—she might be fired by morning. "Actually, Walden. Stay there as long as you can, but be prepared to take over things tomorrow morning."

"Is it your daughter? Is she worse?"

"No, she's doing all right. But there's going to be some fall out for what happened after I left you." She filled him in on the debacle at the nursing home, Alicia's suicide, and Fletcher's escape.

"Hey, you saved the kid," he said encouragingly. "Don't sweat the rest. It will work out."

Walden was the last person she'd have pegged as an optimist. She hung up. "Go figure."

"What?" Nick asked.

"Walden just told me not to worry, that everything's going to be all right."

Nick wrapped his arms around her, his lips whispering against her hair. "Smart man. Let's say we try to get some sleep. You want the fold-out hard-as-a-rock-bed-thing or the chair by the window?"

"I'll take the chair." It was closer to Megan. If she thought she could get away with crawling into the bed without setting off the damn alarm again, she'd do that.

Nick kissed her once more before opening the door. Finally, they felt back in synch, as if Lucy's world had regained its balance. Megan was snoring softly, one foot hanging out from under the sheets, the oxygen monitor's green light bouncing in time with her breathing. One hundred percent, Lucy noted. Best you could get.

–

Burroughs wondered if Guardino had given him the easy duty because she was pissed at him about Cindy and wanted to sideline him, or because she saw that he'd been pushing himself too hard. His sugar was way out of whack—378 at his last reading despite ramping up his insulin dose.

It always happened when he was under too much stress and didn't get enough sleep. Or exercise. Or eat properly. Which was about every day on this job.

Hard to complain when he was sitting on his ass watching a kid sleep and everyone else was out chasing down leads on Fletcher. He sighed and concentrated on drinking more water, washing out all the ketones before they made him vomit.

The door pushed open and he sprang to attention, one hand on his weapon. Then he relaxed, it was just Mrs. Yeager again. He'd told her she could say goodnight to Ashley—as long as Ashley was asleep and didn't know she was there.

Last thing he needed was a hysterical kid on his hands, especially when Guardino was right down the hall with her own kid.

"It's okay," he whispered. "She's asleep."

Melissa took two steps into the room and stopped as if frightened of her own daughter. "The nurse said the medicine they gave her might help her to forget—" A shudder shook her thin body. "Forget what happened to her."

"I'm sorry, ma'am. I don't know. She's been sleeping ever since I got here."

"They said on the news—something about a barn, where she was kept? Were you there? Did you see it?"

She was still a good eight feet away from her kid, expecting Burroughs to have all the answers, make everything right again in her perfect little world.

Half of him wanted to shake her, slap her silly, and make her wake up to the fact that there was a damn good reason her kid had tried so hard to escape that perfect world.

The other half felt sorry for her, saw that she was slowly starting to figure that out on her own.

Suddenly she started crying. Not bawling her head off, not making any noise to wake the kid, just standing there, shoulders slumped, tears streaming down her cheeks like Niagara Fucking Falls.

"He killed her. He killed my baby. I'll never get her back."

Shit. He ran into the bathroom, grabbed the box of tissues there and handed them to her at arm's length. She had the look of a woman who needed to be held. She'd better look to someone other than him—he'd had his full share of women for the day, thank you very much.

Instead, he took her elbow, she was a bony thing, and led her to the door. "Let's get you someplace private, Mrs. Yeager."

He darted a look over his shoulder. Ashley hadn't moved, was dead to the world. He'd only be a minute. He escorted Mrs. Yeager down the hallway and past the nurses' station to the other wing where the family lounge was located.

She was still weeping, eyes puffy and red, tear tracks like silvery icicles marring her blush and makeup. He tried his best not to look at her, it was embarrassing to see her reserve break so completely, and pushed open the lounge door.

Waiting on the other side was Cindy Ames.

"Mrs. Yeager," she said brightly, ignoring the wad of tissues in Yeager's hand to pull her into the room. "It's so nice to see you. I figured you might end up here."

Burroughs stood at the doorway, his palm resting on his weapon, half-tempted to simply shoot the reporter before she could do more harm. Cindy flashed him a triumphant smirk and he came danger-ously close to easing his Glock from its holster.

She'd taken time to change into a navy pantsuit and new blouse, this one gold with fabric draped at the neckline. New shoes as well, he noticed. She wasn't walking like a drunken sailor with her broken heel any longer.

"I'd love to hear your side of Ashley's story," Cindy said, drawing Yeager down to sit beside her on the loveseat. "Tell the world about your experiences so that hopefully no other family ever has to go through this again."

Melissa nodded uncertainly, dabbing her face with the tissue and glancing at Burroughs as if he were the one in charge of what she said and did. Good. Because last thing they needed was Cindy fucking things up more than they already were—or worse, getting the mom to agree to an exclusive with Ashley. He shuddered to think of what the rapacious reporter would do to the kid's fragile and damaged psyche.

"Cindy, I don't think this is a good idea. Why don't we give Mrs. Yeager some privacy?"

"Detective Burroughs, I don't really believe it's up to you, now is it?" She focused on Yeager with a greedy gleam in her eye. "I have my cameraman downstairs, you wouldn't even have to leave the building. I'm sure you want everyone to remember you as Ashley's advocate, someone concerned with her recovery."

Melissa jerked her head up at that. "Of course I'm concerned, who said I wasn't? I'm her mother."

Cindy patted Melissa's hand. "Exactly my point. I'm so happy you agree." She inclined her head at Burroughs. "You can leave now, Detective. I can handle everything from here."

—

Lucy jerked awake. Fear choked her throat; adrenalin revved her heart into overdrive. She blinked, her vision adjusting to the dark hospital room, one hand automatically reaching for her weapon.

The light snapped on. "Don't make a move, Lucy."

Fletcher sat on Megan's bed, one hand holding a forty caliber Glock to her head. Megan's eyes were wide with terror, searching her mother's out. Expecting Lucy to save her.

"She'll be dead before you can reach your gun. Your other gun," Fletcher said with a chuckle. "Or before either of you can finish screaming."

Lucy fought the truth in his words. Her hand clenched with the urge of blowing a fist-sized hole through his face. Anything to get the monster away from her little girl. She found enough saliva to swallow and faced him. "Where's Nick?"

"Called away. Patient emergency. Or so he thought. I think he left you a note on the table."

Nick was alive. Lucy felt the knot in her throat relax a millimeter or two. Enough so she could breathe. "What do you want?"

"Where's Ashley? You took her away from me." He clucked his tongue, shaking his head. "That wasn't very nice of you."

"I doubt Ashley would agree."

"No. She's mine. I saved her." His voice rose, not loud enough to reach the hallway, but loud enough to startle Megan.

She flinched, pulling away from him. He tapped the barrel of the gun against her skull and she clamped her mouth shut, gulping down tears.

"Let her go. I'll do whatever you want. Please, just let her go." Breaking every rule of crisis negotiation, Lucy pled for Megan's life. To hell with the rules. What good were they if they couldn't protect her daughter?

"Will you? Do whatever I want? Without question?"

Lucy latched onto the opening. "Yes. Absolutely. Let her go and I'll help you escape—take you to Mexico, Canada, wherever you want to go."

"You'll take me to Ashley?" His eyes narrowed, considering her offer.

"Yes." She risked standing, arms wide open in surrender. "We need to go now, before the nurses come to check on Megan. Let's go."

He cocked his head and made an old woman clucking noise with his tongue. "You're not telling me what to do, are you?" He jerked hard on Megan's hair, eliciting a gasp from her.

Think, Lucy, think. She willed her stunned brain to process his words. What did he really want, what did Ashley represent to him?

She lowered her gaze so that her eyes didn't meet his. Bowed her head slightly, allowed her shoulders to slump.

"You know what's best." The words almost caught in her throat, harder to utter than any perversion she'd been forced to act out while undercover. "You're in charge here. I'll do anything you want."

He loosened his grip on Megan and stared at Lucy for a long moment. "Prove it."

"What do you want?" Make it all about him, he's the center of the universe.

"Give this to her." He stretched out his free hand. In his palm lay a syringe filled with a clear substance.

Lucy didn't bother to mask the trembling in her fingers as she took it. She uncapped the needle, assessing its potential as a weapon. None. Not while he held Megan like that. She bit her tongue, fighting the urge to ask him what was in it. Must not question his authority.

She slid her fingers along the IV tubing, tracing it down to the medication port she'd seen the nurses use. Megan's breathing grew tight and raspy. Her hands were clenched in white knuckled fists.

Lucy closed her eyes for a long moment. *Please God…*

"Not in the IV," Fletcher commanded just as she was about to risk Megan by launching herself across the bed at him. Better that than an unknown poison that might kill Megan. "It's ketamine. I calculated it for injection in a muscle—not sure if it might be dangerous in the IV."

She risked looking up at him. His smile was awful: wide and excited, his tongue flicking over his lips as he watched her. "You would have done it, wouldn't you?"

No. "Yes," she answered, not meeting Megan's gaze. "I'll do anything you tell me to."

He nodded. "Yes, you will. As long as she's alive and vulnerable." He jerked Megan's body like she was a rag doll. "Go ahead, give it to her."

"Where?"

"In her arm." He twisted, holding Megan, his gun still against her temple. Now Megan's arm was within easy reach.

Lucy leaned over the bed, her daughter only inches away. Could she tackle Megan, grab her, throw her down, out of harm's way? Fletcher shook his head as if reading her thoughts, tightening his grip on Megan. Lucy glanced down at the needle. It wasn't very big. The worse damage it could inflict was to maybe take out an eye.

Not before he killed Megan.

Lucy raised the sleeve of Megan's hospital gown, exposing her flesh. She angled herself so that she blocked Fletcher's view. Megan trembled. Lucy met her daughter's eyes as she held her hand out of sight, beneath the gown. "Don't worry."

Megan's lips were two thin white lines, sweat beaded on her forehead. But she met Lucy's gaze, her eyes full of trust. Lucy jabbed the needle in. Megan yelped in pain, new tears blossoming on her face.

"Very good," Fletcher said, his voice throaty as if he was aroused by the scene. Probably was, the bastard.

Lucy flicked Megan's gown back into place before Fletcher could see the fluid dripping harmlessly down Megan's arm. Swiftly pivoting away from him to further distract him, she dropped the syringe into the sharps box mounted on the wall. She glanced over her shoulder at Megan, saw her slump, her eyes fluttering. *Good girl*.

"Perfect. She'll sleep for hours, not remember a thing when she wakes." Fletcher laid Megan onto her pillows and aimed the gun at Lucy. "Let's go."

"I never wanted to hurt anyone," he said as they left Megan behind. "All I wanted was to save Ashley. Do you have any idea how those people were treating her? What they did to her?"

Nothing compared to what Lucy was going to do to him. "Those people are her parents."

"They were killing her. They didn't care anything about her."

"And you do?" She steered him down the hallway, away from Megan, away from Ashley, and towards the nurses' station.

"Of course. Why do you think I went through all this effort to rescue her? I love her."

He froze for a beat, emphasizing his words. Just what Lucy had been waiting for. She spun, grabbing his weapon hand and forcing it away from her as she slammed her palm up under his chin. He fired, the sound shattering the silence like a thunderclap from the heavens.

She swept his leg out from under him, still trying to get control of the gun. He went down, the back of his head bouncing from the floor, pulling her with him. The Glock went off again. She felt a rush of hot air brush the side of her face, heard the scream of a woman behind her.

Footsteps pounded close by as she grappled with Fletcher. He grabbed her by the hair, slamming her head against the floor, his knee on her chest, constricting her lungs.

She gasped for air just as she heard Burroughs shout, "Drop the gun, Fletcher. Drop it!"

Fletcher's face barely changed expression as he glanced up and shot at Burroughs twice. Melissa Yeager appeared in the edge of Lucy's vision, screaming. "You killed her! You killed my baby!"

Then Fletcher shot her as well. He shifted his weight to aim at a second woman, the reporter, Cindy Ames.

Lucy found her opening, freeing a hand to chop at his voice box, snapping his head back as she flipped him over. She wrenched his wrist as his weight pulled him in the opposite direction.

He gasped, a harsh, raspy sound like her father's cancer buddies had made with their artificial voice boxes. Now on top of him, she twisted his wrist farther until his fingers went limp and he dropped the Glock.

She scrambled to her feet, holding his own weapon on him. Her ears buzzed with the reverberation of the shots but as they cleared she heard people yelling and footsteps behind her.

"It's all right, I'm a federal agent," she called out, her gaze never leaving Fletcher. She couldn't spare a glance to check on Burroughs or Melissa, hoped that some of the running she heard was someone taking care of them. Fletcher's eyes fluttered, then opened fully. "Someone call 911."

"I don't think you want to do that, Lucy," he said, his smile painted with blood from where he'd bit his tongue. He sat up, rubbing the back of his head.

"Stay where you are," she ordered, her voice low and deadly, her finger moving from the trigger guard to the trigger. "Hands where I can see them!"

"You won't shoot me. Not unless you want to kill all these children." He pulled his left hand out from his side, holding a small remote control he'd plucked from his waistband. "Know what this is?"

"What?"

"A dead man's switch. My thumb moves a whisper and you, me, the entire floor and everyone on it goes up." Now he was grinning at her. "All those children and their families dead. All your fault. Only I can save them."

Chapter 41

She was floating. It was so quiet, so peaceful that she wondered why she'd ever fought this. No worries, no fear, no pain…

"Hey, wake up," a girl's voice broke through her blissful solitude. Then something pinched her leg. Hard.

She blocked the pain, floating further away so that the girl's voice was a dim dream, receding fast.

"Wake up, Ashley. Now. I need your help."

It took a few seconds for the words to penetrate. No one had ever needed her help before. Never.

Curiosity niggled at her, returning her back to her body. Now she felt her ankle throbbing, the chill of air-conditioned air stroking her naked arm, cold fluid flowing into her vein. And once again, greedy fingers pinching her, this time twisting her earlobe.

She pulled away, eyes still shut, raising her hands to ward off the persistent intruder.

"He's going to kill her. You've got to help me."

The sound of a gunshot shattered all illusions.

She opened her eyes. The room was dark except for a light from the bathroom and the red call button alarm.

"Who are you? What do you want?" Her voice was raspy as a rusty knife, scraping her throat. "Leave me alone."

"My mom. She saved you. But he came and took her. Please, you have to help." The girl's words were strung together so close that she almost missed their meaning. The girl grabbed her arm.

339

Another shot thundered through the room, it sounded close. Then there were more, too many to count. Ashley covered her ears, wishing for her warm oblivion.

The girl dropped her arm, ran to the door, edged it open a crack.

"Mom got him, she got his gun." She started to open the door but stopped and quickly shut it, leaning against it, her eyes widening with fear. "She's bleeding and he says he has a bomb. Says he'll kill us all."

-

Lucy kept her grip on Fletcher, one foot planted on his wrist as she leaned over to open his jacket and search for confirmation of his threat. He lay there, grinning, mocking her with his nonchalance as his jacket fell open, revealing a vest brimming with C-4 explosive.

"I think you might want to be a little nicer to me, Lucy." He said. "Drop the gun."

Parents, children, and nurses milled around in the periphery of Lucy's vision. She couldn't see Burroughs or Melissa.

"Let me get these people out of here first," she stalled. She saw a woman at the nurses' station hang up the phone, hopefully that meant the cavalry was on the way and the hospital was being evacuated.

"Help me up and give me my gun back. I won't interfere with the evacuation as long as you take me to see Ashley." He narrowed his eyes, his gaze boring into hers. "Now."

Lucy heard hushed voices behind her as the nurses worked on getting people out of the line of fire. It wasn't like she had any choice but to obey. Fletcher could have half a dozen ways to detonate the C-4 and there was nowhere she could contain him that wouldn't expose civilians to harm. "All right."

She removed her weight from his hand and watched him climb to his feet. He kept the dead man's switch clenched between his left thumb and forefinger, shaking the blood back into his other hand and grimacing. "My gun."

She handed it to him. He didn't seem to have any problem handling it. Should've broken his wrist when she had the chance.

"Very good, Lucy. Now. Take me to Ashley."

"I will, but you're not going to like it."

"Why not?" He squinted at her, ignoring the crying children and sobbing parents who were scuttling away from them, trying to make their escape.

A few fathers made eye contact with Lucy, looked like they planned to play heroes, but she shook her head at them and a nurse hustled them away. She saw blood on the floor as she stepped back, wondered for a moment if it belonged to Burroughs or Melissa before she clamped down on those distracting thoughts. Megan was safe—or would be as soon as she got Fletcher out of here.

"Where's Ashley?"

Lucy blew her breath out, her chest and shoulders collapsing with the weight of the day. "You heard her mother. Ashley's dead."

–

Other than the occasional nick while shaving her legs, Cindy had never seen blood before. One of the curses of being perpetually healthy and usually assigned to fluff pieces.

Now, suddenly, she was drowning in it.

Burroughs had gone all *Lethal Weapon* on her when he heard what sounded like a gunshot, drawing his gun and telling her and Melissa to remain in the family room. Yeah, like they were going to stay like sitting ducks waiting for the slaughter. Not to mention the fact that odds were it was Fletcher doing the shooting.

Still, Cindy hadn't followed him outside. She waited, listening, when a second shot sounded. That noise had catapulted Melissa into action.

"He's here. He's killed Ashley," she began crying, pushing Cindy aside and running out into the hallway.

Cindy heard Melissa shouting, Burroughs yelling, the sound of more gunfire, then silence for a long moment. She poked her head out the door, saw no signs of a threat, and stepped outside.

That's when the screaming started. A nurse was on her knees beside Melissa, trying to stop the blood gushing from Melissa's neck.

She yanked Cindy down, pressed Cindy's hands over the massive wound. "Hold pressure."

The nurse scuttled around the corner where Burroughs' legs jutted out, toes down. Not a good sign, a tinny voice echoed through Cindy's mind even as her hands squished blood, trying to force it back into Melissa.

Children were crying, wailing, parents shouting and screaming, people running, slamming doors, but Cindy's entire world was one woman and a whole lot of blood. Surely too much blood?

Melissa's mouth open and closed. Bubbles appeared, gurgling through the blood. Her eyes drifted halfway shut, looked glazed, vacant.

Still Cindy pressed, her entire weight leaning on Melissa's neck. Then she noticed that the blood wasn't gushing any more. Instead it was seeping, pushed out of Melissa's body by the pressure Cindy was so diligently applying. Gingerly, she slid her fingers to where she thought the pulse should be. Nothing.

Burroughs still wasn't moving and the nurse hadn't re-appeared. But she heard everything, heard Fletcher tell Guardino about a bomb. A bomb? She rocked back on her heels, her hands raising from Melissa's skin leaving bloody palm prints behind. Blood splattered the floor, her slacks, trailed down her arms.

It wasn't her job to be making life and death decisions. She was only here to observe, not get involved. She climbed to her feet, staggering towards the elevator, towards escape.

"Out of our way," Fletcher ordered her. He held a gun in one hand and a car alarm remote in the other. His arm was wrapped around Guardino's neck, the gun at her head.

Very theatrical, but it worked for Cindy. Once she saw those clay-colored bricks strapped to his chest, anything he said was fine by her. She backed away, her heels skidding in Melissa's blood, hands held up in surrender.

"Thank you," he said as the elevator doors opened and he and Guardino climbed inside.

Cindy blinked as the doors closed. Blinked again and in a thunderclap realized that all around her people were moving—nurses herding patients and families down the emergency stairs, two more rolling Burroughs onto his back, another talking furiously on the phone.

She watched as Burroughs opened his eyes, one hand slapping against the floor. "Gun," he gasped. "Where's my gun?"

Cindy saw it. It had skidded under the clerk's desk. She knelt and retrieved it, then crawled over to Burroughs.

The nurses were trying to restrain him, pulling his shirt up, checking him for wounds, but he kept batting their hands away. "I'm fine, I'm fine."

"Holy shit," one of the nurses said, raising the small pager-sized device needled into Burroughs' belly. His insulin pump. There was a ugly red area below where the pump had been attached.

"The bullet. It hit your pump." The nurse turned the pump over, the silver of the bullet catching the overhead light and gleaming.

"Tell me about it," Burroughs grunted, still wheezing as if he couldn't catch his breath. "Hurts like a sonofabitch. Give me my gun and help me up."

Cindy handed him his gun. She held onto his waist while the nurse caught him under his arms and together they helped him up. He leaned heavily against the counter, breathing fast and shallow. His color was pale and he was sweating.

"Where'd they go?"

"Down," Cindy answered.

"Ashley. Did he get Ashley?"

"No. It was just Fletcher and Guardino."

He glanced at the elevator then down the hallway. "I have to get to Ashley."

Staggering, he stumbled down the hall, one hand brushing the wall as if he needed a guide. Cindy looked down at her bloody hands, at Melissa's body and decided it was better to be with a man with a gun, even if he was a bit wobbly, than out here on her own. She raced after him, heels click-clacking on the linoleum.

He stopped in front of a door, waving her back as he held his gun at the ready, using both hands to steady it. He kicked the door in and stepped inside. Cindy saw the lights click on and followed him.

The room was empty.

"Ashley," Burroughs groaned, slumping against the wall, his gun dangling uselessly in his hand. "Where is she?"

—

She allowed the girl named Megan to herd her down the stairs. People rushed past them, some parents, some nurses carrying small children, IV tubing and monitor wires hanging from their bodies. The sound of weeping, panicked voices, and pounding footsteps vibrated into her awareness.

But all she really heard was her mother's voice saying that she was dead. She hadn't been able to see her mother—Megan had been yanking her in the other direction, but Megan had been looking that way and the terror in her eyes after the gunshot told everything.

Her mother was dead.

Her mother said Ashley was dead.

Maybe her mother was right. About everything.

Suddenly they were alone in the stairwell, everyone else streaming out the doors to the first floor. Megan stood on the landing below the main floor, hefting her mother's gun.

"The morgue. She's bringing him to the morgue," Megan was saying.

It made perfect sense. If she was dead, then the morgue was the place for her.

Then it dawned on her that the "he" Megan was talking about was Jimmy. He had saved her once—had he returned to save her again? Bring her back from the dead?

"I'm going with you," she told Megan, clamping her hand over the younger girl's wrist.

Megan gave her a hard look, then smiled as if relieved to have company on this quest, even if her companion was a nameless dead girl.

"Okay," she breathed out. "Let's go."

–

"It was your job to keep her safe!" Fletcher shouted once they were alone in the confines of the elevator. He shoved Lucy away from him, throwing her against the wall. "Isn't that what you always say, the children come first? How the hell could you let this happen?"

He waved the Glock in her face as if the threat of blowing the entire hospital to kingdom come wasn't enough to get her attention. Lucy felt laughter bubbling up and swallowed, stomping it down hard.

"When I tackled her, she hit her head," she improvised. Pain lanced through her shoulder, down her jaw, seemed determined to rock her entire body as it stampeded along her nerve endings. Her knees kept threatening to give out on her—worse of all, she was so exhausted, that she was about ready to let them surrender. "The doctors said given her weakened condition—she was severely dehydrated and her electrolytes were out of whack—that she had bleeding in her brain. It was slow, didn't show up for a few hours, until after they gave her enough fluids to bring her blood pressure back up."

Tears were streaming down his face as she spun a tale using everything she'd ever learned watching too many autopsies. "I'm sorry. We tried to save her, but—"

"Didn't try hard enough." His voice was low and deadly and Lucy feared she'd pushed him too far.

The elevator came to a halt and the doors opened. He shoved her out, his weapon pressed against her spine.

"No one cared about her except me," he continued his lament as they followed the signs to the morgue. Their footsteps echoed in the dimly lit, empty corridors. "You should have left us alone. I could have made her happy. Taken care of her."

They turned a corner and came to a halt in front of a wooden door labeled: *Pathology. Authorized Personnel Only.*

Fletcher nudged her and she tried the handle. Locked. No surprise. They wouldn't want just anyone waltzing in to visit the dead.

A frustrated growl emerged from Fletcher's throat as he raised the Glock, the barrel resting alongside Lucy's face. A flick of the wrist and he'd be firing a forty caliber hollow point into her brain.

Torn between closing her eyes and needing to watch every second, she edged her gaze to center on his trigger finger. Braced herself, images of Nick and Megan cascading through her mind as he squeezed it.

The explosion was deafening.

Chapter 42

Burroughs clutched his belly, wanting to hurl but knowing it would hurt too much and waste too much time. He lurched back out into the hallway only to collide with a man.

"Where's my wife? Where's Megan?" the man asked Cindy and Burroughs as they exited Ashley's room. "What happened?"

"Fletcher," Burroughs said, recognizing the man as Guardino's husband. The whitewater rafter. Callahan, that was his name. He slowly moved down the hall, wishing he could run, wishing he could fucking breathe.

"Fletcher has them? Where?" The man didn't get hysterical, instead cut to the essentials. Burroughs liked that in a man, especially when he could barely draw enough air to keep himself upright, much less talk.

"The morgue," Cindy answered for him.

Callahan sprinted to the elevator, jabbing the button. It opened just as Burroughs arrived, crammed full with patients in wheelchairs and their nurses.

"It's no good," Cindy said. "They're evacuating the building because of the bomb."

"Bomb? What bomb?" Callahan asked. He didn't wait for an answer, instead spotted the staircase on the other side of the elevator bank and ran to it.

He was halfway down the first flight by the time Burroughs made it through the door. Burroughs would have shouted at him to stop, after all he was a civilian and unarmed, but it took every ounce of

347

energy he had to stay upright as he hurtled down the stairs, pain ricocheting through his body with every step.

–

Pressure built in Lucy's ear, deafening her and sending a shockwave of pain through her body. Then it released, a gush of fluid seeping down her neck, the sound of Fletcher's breathing abnormally loud in that ear. He sounded like a beached whale making love, huffing and puffing as he holstered his gun and reached through the large hole he'd blown in the door to turn the handle.

She could have trapped him there, taken him, but it wouldn't have done any good—not with the dead man's switch. She had to get him inside, into the most secure place she could think of.

He pushed her through the open door. The labs were dark. She groped along the wall, found the lights and suddenly they were surrounded by stainless steel tables, bright and expensive looking microscopes and a thick steel door marked: AUTOPSY.

Lucy shook her head, trying to quiet the whooshing noises the gunshot had left behind. Her balance was off and she had ruptured an eardrum. Least of her worries.

She led the way to the stainless steel door. It wasn't locked. Opened it. Beyond was a tile walled hallway. To the right was a glass walled room with autopsy tables. To the left was a larger area with several empty stretchers and X-ray equipment.

And straight ahead lay what she'd been looking for, hoping for. The large, wide, thick steel door of a walk-in refrigerator.

"She hates the dark," he said, shoving her forward. "Get her out of there."

"You're the one who put her in the dark," she reminded him. "Who tortured her."

Now that they were here, she needed to stall, give the staff time to evacuate as many patients as possible. She had no earthly idea if her plan would work given the amount of C4 strapped to Fletcher's chest.

"I know," he blubbered. "I need to make things right. That's all I wanted, was to make things right for her, give her a chance at a new life."

"Abusing a fourteen-year-old girl was your way to make things right?" As she spoke, Lucy heard movement behind her. She edged toward the refrigerator door at an angle, trying to catch a glimpse in the reflection from the darkened windows of the autopsy suite.

"I haven't abused anyone!" His voice quavered and more worrisome, so did the finger holding the dead man's switch.

Lucy stopped and turned to meet his gaze, keeping his attention cemented on her. "I saw the barn, Jimmy. Saw where you kept Ashley—you had her tied up like an animal. And you tortured her with snakes. What else did you do to her, Jimmy?"

The movement at the entrance had stopped. Lucy got a look in the dark windows and felt her resolve crumble. Megan took a step forward, gun in her hand, aimed at Fletcher. Beside her stood Ashley. Fletcher had his back to them. Lucy meant to do everything in her power to keep it that way.

"You're sick, Lucy. I never touched her—not the way you think. I saved her. It was all necessary, for her own good."

Lucy could almost reach the door handle, just a step farther. She kept sidling toward the refrigerator, trying to pull Fletcher along with her, praying for Ashley and Megan to leave. Instead, she saw Ashley take the gun from Megan's hand. Her breath caught in her throat as she remembered Ashley firing the revolver at her earlier.

She reached out, yanked the refrigerator door open. Only one weapon left—the truth.

"Torturing a little girl is for her own good? How about the girl you killed at the Tastee Treet, Jimmy? Did you know she had a little baby, only four months old? What about Vera Tzasiris? She was only nineteen, barely spoke English—did you torture her before you killed her?"

His head jerked in a nod as she hammered him with each accusation. "I didn't have a choice. They all had to die—so that I could save Ashley."

"It wasn't Bobby," Ashley's voice sounded raw and harsh as it echoed down the tiled hallway. "It was you. All along, it was you."

Fletcher startled, almost dropping the dead man's switch as he whirled around. Lucy clamped her hand over his, holding the switch down.

"Megan, Ashley, run. Now!"

Chapter 43

Burroughs reached the busted door to the labs just as he heard the gunshot. He gulped in a lungful of air and ran as fast as he could. Callahan was pulling a young girl, not Ashley, out through a steel door leading into the main lab.

"Lucy's still in there," he gasped.

"And Ashley," the girl cried, struggling in her father's arms to return to the hallway.

"Go," Burroughs told him, raising his gun. He stepped into the hallway, surprised to see Lucy and Fletcher standing in front of an open refrigerator, Ashley holding a gun on them.

Fletcher was bleeding from one leg, Guardino holding him up, one hand wrapped around his hand with the dead man's switch. Her other arm had him in a choke hold. His face was dusky purple and he was slumped in her grasp. His gun lay on the floor, beyond Guardino's reach even if she didn't have her hands full.

"Get her out of here," Guardino shouted.

He stepped forward and Ashley whirled, aiming the weapon at him. Her face was blank as if she didn't know what was real and thought this was all just some kind of crazy game.

He froze, lowering his weapon to his side. "Drop the gun, Ashley. I don't want to hurt you."

"No." A frown twisted her features, making her look younger, a baby really. "I don't—I can't."

"Yes," Guardino said in a low, calm voice. A voice only a mother could produce, soothing and commanding simultaneously. "Yes, you can. Ashley, a lot of people have lied to you, have tried to trick you, but I'm telling you the truth. You need to trust me, Ashley. Can you do that? Trust me?"

Ashley slowly turned, locking eyes with Guardino. Guardino nodded slowly and Ashley mirrored the movement. "Good girl. Now Ashley, you need to put down the gun and go with Detective Burroughs."

"But—no. He, what he did…" Her voice died away, but her intent was clear as she aimed the gun at Fletcher.

"I know what he did. I was there, in the barn. I saw the snakes, smelled the stench. I was there, Ashley."

"You were?" The gun didn't waver.

Burroughs shuffled forward, stopping when Guardino gave him a small shake of her head.

"I was. I wish I had gotten there sooner, I would have saved you."

"That's what he said he did. He lied."

"He did. And he's going to pay for that. But you have to trust me, Ashley. Leave it to me. You were a very brave girl, there alone in the dark with those snakes. Very, very brave. I need you to be brave for just a few more minutes. Do you trust me, Ashley?"

Guardino's hypnotic tone could have charmed a cobra into tying itself into a knot. Burroughs felt his own head nod in time with Ashley's.

"I trust you." The words were halting, but finally Ashley's aim wavered.

"Good. Now. Put the gun on the floor and let Detective Burroughs get you out of here. Close the door behind you. On the count of three. Are you ready?"

Guardino's grip was weakening. Fletcher took a breath, color returning to his face. He immediately began to attack the hand that Guardino held over the dead man's switch.

"One, two, three," she shouted in a rush just as Fletcher was about to claw his way free of her grasp.

"No, Ashley," Fletcher screamed. "I love you! Don't go!"

The gun clattered to the ground just as Burroughs grabbed Ashley and hauled her back through the steel door.

—

As soon as Lucy saw Burroughs get Ashley to safety, she stopped fighting. An eerie sense of calm came over her, time moving in slow motion as if the world around her had become a movie and she was predestined to act out her role.

"No!" Fletcher cried when Ashley disappeared behind the lab door. He whirled on Lucy. "You did this! It's all your fault!"

Lucy didn't answer. Instead she launched her free hand up to grab his chin, yanking his head around to face the refrigerator. Pivoting her weight, she propelled him into the opening, releasing the hand with the dead man's switch at the last possible moment.

His momentum carried her inside with him. The door began to swing shut. She gave Fletcher one last shove to send him reeling against the far wall. She escaped out through the heavy door just as it clanked closed.

She started to run, thought she was running, but instead found herself flying through the air, arms and legs flailing as the building rocked with the blast.

She landed in a heap against the far wall. The lights flickered—or her vision did. Then everything was bright and sparkly as dust flit through the air.

Lucy hacked and coughed, threatening to tear her stitches. Finally she got enough strength to look up. The refrigerator door was slightly ajar, hanging crooked, weird reddish-brown smoke wisping through the opening. A few of the overhead fluorescent bulbs had shattered. Tiles had been knocked from the walls, giving them a crazy checkerboard appearance.

The door beside her slammed open and Nick appeared, followed by Ashley and Megan. To her surprise it was Ashley who reached her first, flinging herself at Lucy and clutching her as if she'd never let go.

Then Megan and Nick followed until her vision was blinded by their warm and wonderfully whole bodies.

–

"C'mon, Burroughs," Cindy said, grinding her hip against his after the medics cleared him, "I'll make you a star."

Burroughs looked at her with contempt and limped away. He joined Guardino and her family at the far end of the lab. Ashley had collapsed, refusing to leave Guardino's side, so the docs had sedated her and taken her back upstairs. Guardino looked like the walking wounded left at the end of a war movie—blood smearing her face and shirt, one arm out of commission, leaning heavily against her husband.

"Don't you ever do anything like that again," Callahan was saying, his arms wrapped around both his daughter and wife. "Promise."

In response, Guardino kissed him. It was a fairly tame kiss, no tongue or anything, but it packed enough power to make Burroughs' stomach clench. When they parted, both Callahan's and Guardino's faces were streaked with tears. Neither seemed to care.

Guardino's eyes were wide with the after-effects of adrenalin, her cheeks flushed, giving her a radiant glow. She smiled, her gaze never leaving Callahan's, her body aligned with his as if they were one.

"You don't have to worry about me," she told Callahan, one finger smoothing his tears.

"Yeah, Dad," Megan chimed in. "Mom was totally the coolest, most awesome, kick ass—"

"Megan Constance Callahan," Guardino interrupted, "watch your language."

Megan clapped her hand against her mouth, obviously also jazzed with adrenalin. "I can't wait to tell the kids at school," she said, pride shining in her eyes.

Burroughs had to turn away. His eyes burned, he swiped them with his thumb, telling himself it was the smoke that made them water. But he couldn't help but wonder if maybe the reason he'd fallen so hard for Guardino had nothing to do with lust or hormones or a midlife crisis.

Maybe she had everything he wanted. Everything he needed. The way her husband and kid looked at her...

She finally noticed him standing behind Callahan and aimed a smile in his direction. "Have you two met?" she asked, indicating Callahan. "Nick, this is Don Burroughs, he's a detective with the Major Crimes squad."

"Nice to meet you," Callahan said, extending a hand. They shook with a firm grip.

"Just wanted to make sure you were good to go," Burroughs mumbled, wishing he could hide the flush he felt on his face. "Before I leave."

He walked away, yanking his cell phone out and hitting the speed dial. "Kim? Yeah, sorry, I know it's late. Listen, can I come over, spend some time with the boys later today? I really need to see them."

Chapter 44

Lucy woke feeling seasick, the bed bouncing as if riding over waves. Was she on a boat? She hated boats. Why on earth would she be sleeping on a boat?

The bed jostled more as a girl's gleeful laughter swam through her consciousness. Megan.

Lucy forced her eyes open. The left would only go to a slit and the right she immediately closed again as bright sunlight stabbed through it. But it had been long enough for her to see Megan perched on the edge of the bed, bouncing eagerly as she and Nick fought abominable ice men.

"Hah! Take that." Megan's voice was strong, brimming with enthusiasm and the sound of it brought tears to Lucy's eyes. Good tears. Happy tears. "No way are we going to be zombie meat!"

"Inside voice, please. You're going to wake your mother."

"Nah, she's already awake. She's just resting."

Lucy couldn't stop her smile. She lurched upright, stretching her good arm out in a fair imitation of a mutant zombie and grabbed Megan.

She squeezed Megan, kissed her on the top of the head and released her, slumping back just as Nick elevated the head of the bed to support her. Ouch. Sitting up that fast had unleashed a headache and several wicked aches and pains, but it was worth it to see Megan's bright smile. Such contrast to the scared and worried look she had had last night when they pulled Lucy from the debris.

"Mom, you look like the bride of Frankenstein!"

356

"Guess that makes you Frankenstein's daughter, heheheh." She mussed up Megan's hair, standing it on end.

"Mom," came the familiar two-syllable whine.

Nick cleared his throat. "Why don't you reset the game while I help your mom get cleaned up?"

"I'd love to have a shower."

"You're not allowed," Megan told her in a stern voice. "They said only sponge baths. Until your stitches are out."

Nick lowered the bedrail and helped Lucy maneuver her stiff and aching body out of bed. "That's where I come in," he said with a lecherous grin, wagging one eyebrow. He pulled her to her feet. A wave of dizziness washed over her but Nick held her steady. Before letting her go, he kissed her thoroughly. "Good morning, Lulu."

"It's afternoon, you know," Megan put in.

When Nick ignored her and gave Lucy a loud smooch, Megan giggled. That sound, so innocent and free, one that Lucy hadn't heard in months, was enough to erase all her pain.

Nick pulled away far enough to guide Lucy into the bathroom, one hand on the small of her back.

Lucy propped herself against the counter top while Nick carefully combed no-rinse shampoo through her tangled hair, taking the opportunity to nuzzle her neck. She had some fresh staples in her scalp, thanks to one of the ER docs, a black eye almost swollen shut, a broken collarbone, assorted scrapes and bruises, and a mild concussion to add to her litany of injuries.

Which basically meant she was alive and had no right to complain—not with Melissa Yeager lying dead in the county morgue.

"Any word on Ashley?"

"They stopped the sedation, but she's uncommunicative. Not quite catatonic, but also not responding to much of anything. She tried to cut herself so they had to restrain her."

Lucy sighed. Ashley had been through so much already.

"It's going to take time." Nick finished with her hair and began to help her out of her clothing, handing her a towel so she wouldn't get

357

a chill. She loved the gentle way his touch soothed her pain, hands gliding over her skin as he washed her as if she were a newborn. It felt good to have someone she trusted so implicitly that she could relinquish all control to him.

"What's going to happen to her?"

He paused, holding a dripping washcloth over the sink. "Depends. Right now she's lost. What her parents started, Fletcher finished—they stripped her of her identity."

"Maybe I should call Taylor, tell him to hold off—" Lucy was surprised by how easily she grabbed onto any excuse not to face Ashley. It was as if she couldn't admit that she'd failed the girl, hadn't really saved her after all.

"No. I had a long talk with her doctors and father. They agree that it can't hurt and it might help."

"What did the doctors say about Megan's tests?" The way Megan's color and energy had returned, she figured it was just a formality. The doctors had to be right about the cat scratch.

But Nick frowned. "Said they had to review them, that the specialist would let us know."

She didn't like the sound of that. "Then I'd better wait here. Let Taylor and Walden handle Ashley."

"I'll call you if the doctors come. You're only two doors away. Go, take care of Ashley."

She jerked her chin up at the tone of command in his voice. "You were the one accusing me of neglecting Megan. Said I was in denial, thinking that by saving Ashley I could guarantee Megan's safety."

"You did save Ashley. And you were here for Megan. Now you need to do this for yourself. Finish it. And," he said with a hint of a smile, "I have a feeling your instincts were right on target. It was a good idea, arranging for Bobby Fegley to come here, meet Ashley in person."

"Some instincts. I actually liked Fletcher—well, in an irritating puppy dog kind of way."

"Speaking of puppy dogs—" He guided Lucy's bad arm into the sling.

She stared at him, aghast. "You didn't."

"Megan thought Boots needed company."

"Nick. No. Look at our schedules—" She stopped herself. What was she saying? After the Office of Professional Responsibility finished with her, she'd be lucky getting a job writing parking tickets.

"John Greally came by," he said, reading her mind as always. "Said not to wake you."

She grimaced. "I'll bet he wasn't too happy."

"He was happy—that you're alive. Not so much about the bureaucratic mess. Something about a public commendation and an official reprimand? Sounds like an oxymoron to me. And a warning that you'd better stay under the radar for a good long while."

The concussion must have made her brain fuzzy. "Are you saying I still have a job?"

"Yep. But you have to play nice, dress up for some fancy cere-mony the Mayor is hosting. Giving you and Burroughs the keys to the city or shiny pieces of tin or some such thing."

Lucy started to laugh, cut it short when pain sliced through her back and chest and shoulder. "Leave it to Greally. God help us all if he ever decides to go into politics."

There was a knock on the door. Nick opened it. Megan stood there, connected to her IV pole with its antibiotic hanging in a clear plastic bag. "Mom, there's some people here."

Lucy glanced in the mirror. No sense scaring Bobby and Ashley with her looks. Nick had done a decent job of cleaning her up. The crisp, white T-shirt hid most of the damage and the sling took care of the rest. Except for the shiner. Not much she could do about that. Nick wrapped an arm around her waist and they stepped out together.

Megan surprised her by giving her an impetuous bear hug. "I'm so glad you're all right, Mom." She bounced on her tiptoes and gave Lucy a quick kiss. "Love you, Lucy-Boo."

Lucy squeezed back. "Love you too, Sugar-Lou."

Over Megan's head she saw Taylor and Walden watching them, neither masking the grins on their faces. Beside them was Bobby

Fegley, a man wearing a nursing uniform standing behind his wheelchair.

"Bobby," she said, regretfully parting from Megan, "thanks for doing this. I know how hard it is—"

"Nonsense," the nurse said. "I've been trying to get him out of that house for months. Do him good to get away from his computer and into the real world instead of a virtual one."

Bobby scrunched up his face, making it obvious that he didn't agree with his nurse's view of the world at large. Lucy could understand why. In Bobby's world, he could remain in control, even play God, escaping his physical handicaps.

"I think it will mean a lot to Ashley. Meeting you in person."

"Taylor said that man, the one who took her, he told her he was me? Won't she," he paused, wiping his face against the towel that lined his neck support, "won't she hate me?"

"You helped save her life. I think once she sees that you really were her friend, liked her for who she was, not the characters she pretended to be, it might help her." Lucy glanced at Nick for confirmation. He nodded his agreement. "You're all she has."

Bobby gave that skewed one shouldered shrug of his. "All right, then."

Nick stayed with Megan while Lucy and the others moved down the hall to Ashley's room. Bobby stopped outside the door where her doctor waited for them.

"So this is the young man?" he said, crouching down so that Bobby didn't have to strain to look up at him. "Nice to meet you. Don't be too scared by what you see. We have her in soft restraints to keep her from hurting herself, and even though the sedation has worn off, she hasn't said much, so don't be surprised if she doesn't want to chat."

Bobby nodded. "Lucy, you're coming, too?"

"She did ask for you," the doctor told Lucy as he opened the door.

Lucy let Bobby go first, telling herself it was to give him room to maneuver his wheelchair but knowing in her gut it was cowardice.

Then she took a deep breath and followed. The doctor left the door open and waited with the others in the hall, within hearing distance.

Ashley lay still, her dark hair fanned out on the pillow beneath her. She looked like Sleeping Beauty or Snow White, waiting for the prince's kiss. Except for the fact that her wrists were bound by soft felt restraints, there was an angry row of fresh cuts on the inside of her left forearm, and her eyes stared straight ahead without blinking.

"Ashley?" The wheelchair whirled as Bobby steered it beside her bed, facing her. "I'm Bobby. Draco." No response. He looked to Lucy, his expression as close to tears as you could get without crying. "I'm here, Ashley. And so is Lucy. She saved you, remember?"

Lucy took her cue and approached, standing behind Bobby's chair, in Ashley's line of sight if she ever cared to look. "We saved you. Bobby was a huge help. He's the real Bobby—not the man who took you. That man lied to you."

Silence. What else could she say? How to coax this girl who had been through so much, lost so much, back to a life where she faced more pain?

"I brought you something," Bobby said. He nodded to the bag that hung from the side of his chair. Lucy reached into it and found two of Ashley's drawings: the one of Draco and the one of the ethereal character, Angel. "Your sketches. Of course, now that you see the real me, you'll probably want to re-do the one of Draco. But it sure was nice to think that someone could imagine me that way, a real hero."

As he spoke, Lucy realized Ashley was watching them, her face slack but a look of desperation and longing in her eyes. She stroked her arm against the sheets, her left wrist, the wrist with the parallel scars. Her movements were jerky, as if she couldn't stop herself. Lucy reached her hand out and clasped Ashley's. Ashley went still once more, but this time her unblinking stare was on Lucy.

"My mother's dead." Ashley's voice startled Lucy; somehow she seemed to speak without moving her lips.

The words hung between them. Lucy felt her gut clench. She had no idea if she should confirm or deny Melissa's death. She'd always given Megan the truth, even when it hurt, so she decided to do the same with Ashley. "Yes, she is. I'm sorry."

Ashley showed no signs of tears at Melissa's passing. "She said I was dead too." Ashley's fingers clawed at Lucy's, gripping her tight. "Please, I don't want to be dead. Not anymore. Don't let me be dead."

A choked sob broke loose from Bobby. "You're not. Ashley, you are the most beautiful, courageous person I've ever known. Please don't talk like that. You're not dead."

For the first time Ashley's gaze focused on Bobby. She blinked, blinked again, her features crashing in on themselves as tears rolled down her face. Sobs wracked her body, not the wild-eyed feral hysteria that Lucy had seen last night, but real, honest to goodness grief.

Lucy undid the Velcro restraint and laced Ashley's hand around Bobby's. Both teens were now openly weeping, sharing their sorrow and pain.

Lucy backed away, out of the room, handing the sketches to the doctor. "I don't think she'll be needing these anymore."

He nodded. "Nice job."

"Wasn't me." She turned to Taylor and Walden. "Everything okay back at the office?" Since somehow John Greally had saved her job for her, she thought she should ask.

"We got a lead on a kiddie porn ring based in Erie," Taylor gushed.

Walden clamped his hand on the younger agent's shoulder. "Nothing we can't handle. You get back to your family."

"Thanks. I think I will. Might even call in sick tomorrow, bake some brownies for my daughter's soccer team, plant some mums, and, God help me, go shopping for a puppy."

She opened the door to Megan's room, stood watching for one brief, bliss-filled moment. Nick and Megan huddled together on the bed, talking earnestly about something. Sunlight streamed in through the window, highlighting the red tints in Nick's hair and Megan's freckles.

Suddenly she understood what Nick had been trying to tell her, that by trying to save the world, she'd been trying to save what was in this room waiting for her. It seemed so careless now, wasting a single second away from her family.

"No worries, boss," Walden said, holding the door open for her. "The pervs and creeps will still be there when you get back."

"I know." She stepped through the doorway. "They can wait. Family first."

Also by CJ Lyons